GENTLE ANGEL

GENTLE ANGEL

A KENZIE KIRSCH MEDICAL THRILLER #4

P.D. WORKMAN

ISBN: 9781774681244 (IS Hardcover)

ISBN: 9781774681237 (IS Paperback)

ISBN: 9781774681220 (IS Large Print)

ISBN: 9781774681190 (KDP Paperback)

ISBN: 9781774681206 (Kindle)

ISBN: 9781774681213 (ePub)

pdworkman

ALSO BY P.D. WORKMAN

MYSTERY/SUSPENSE:

Zachary Goldman Mysteries

She Wore Mourning

His Hands Were Quiet

She Was Dying Anyway

He Was Walking Alone

They Thought He was Safe

He Was Not There

Her Work Was Everything

She Told a Lie

He Never Forgot

She Was At Risk

Kenzie Kirsch Medical Thrillers

Unlawful Harvest

Doctored Death

Dosed to Death

Gentle Angel

Parks Pat Mysteries

Out with the Sunset

Long Climb to the Top

Dark Water Under the Bridge

Immersed in the View (Coming Soon)

Skimming Over the Lake (Coming Soon)

Hazard of the Hills (Coming Soon)

High-Tech Crime Solvers Series
Virtually Harmless

Cowritten with D. D. VanDyke
California Corwin P. I. Mystery Series
The Girl in the Morgue

Stand Alone Suspense Novels
Looking Over Your Shoulder
Lion Within
Pursued by the Past
In the Tick of Time
Loose the Dogs

YOUNG ADULT FICTION:

Medical Kidnap Files:
Mito

EDS

Proxy

Toxo

Pain

Breaking the Pattern:
Henry

Sandy

Bobby

AND MORE AT PDWORKMAN.COM

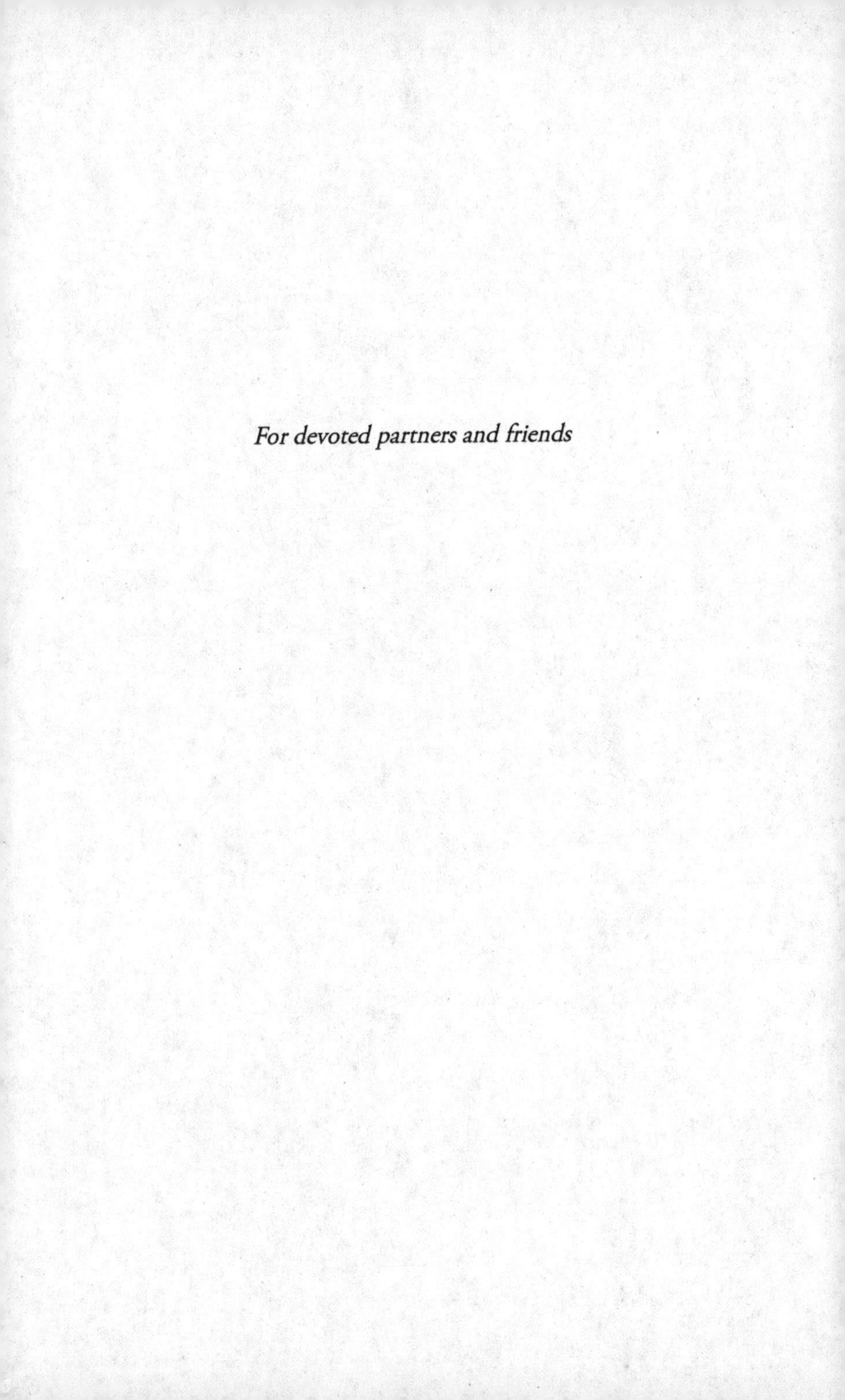

For devoted partners and friends

It felt good to be back in the morgue.

It might sound strange, but after their stressful vacation in a mountain resort, Kenzie and Zachary were both glad to be home and back into the usual daily routines—Zachary running his private investigations business and Kenzie returning to the Medical Examiner's Office where none of the bodies she dealt with were people that she had known personally. Most people considered the work of a medical examiner to be gross and depressing, but Kenzie was fascinated with the work of uncovering what the deceased had died of and found it life-affirming rather than discouraging.

Dr. Wiltshire and the part-time staff had let a number of things slide while she had been gone. She had been prevented from coming to work first due to a virus she had contracted and the antiviral protocol to kill it, and then on a short holiday that was supposed to be a chance for her and Zachary to recover their health and rest before getting back to work. It hadn't exactly turned out that way.

There were a lot of requests and reports to be processed in Kenzie's physical in box as well as in her email queue.

A couple of bodies had been transported from the hospital,

and Kenzie reviewed the intake forms to find out the details and make sure that everything had been filled out correctly. She opened new files for each of them and checked the bodies themselves to make sure that the names and numbers matched the forms that the hospital had sent with them. Always better to catch any clerical errors early. Families tended not to like it when bodies got mixed up.

She was back at her desk printing reports when Dr. Wiltshire got in. The idea of the ME's office being paperless was a joke. They went through reams of paper.

"Morning, Kenzie," Dr. Wiltshire greeted.

"Morning, Doctor. Got a couple of intakes from the hospital today."

He nodded and took a sip of his coffee. "Anything of note?"

"One from a single-vehicle car accident. And one a request from a doctor."

Neither was particularly out of the ordinary. A doctor-attended death did not automatically go to the Medical Examiner's Office, but if the attending physician had any doubts about the cause of death or deemed it suspicious in some way, he could request that the medical examiner perform an autopsy.

"What is the doctor's name?"

Kenzie hadn't made note of it, so she brought the form up on her computer to check. "A Dr. Philemon?"

"Philemon…" Dr. Wiltshire pondered this for a moment. He frowned. "He's in geriatrics, isn't he?"

Kenzie went to the Vermont Health Network website and searched Dr. Philemon in the directory. "Yes, looks like that's his specialty. Does some general practice as well."

Dr. Wiltshire nodded. "Okay. I'll look at them today. How is your workload?"

"Still trying to get caught up. Lots of printing and filing to be done."

"Yeah… we might have let that slide a little."

"A little," Kenzie agreed. She wasn't sure anyone had done any filing during the weeks she had been gone. And since no filing had been done, she couldn't be sure what reports had been printed already. She had to keep going back and forth between the computer and the piles of printouts and the files to try to make sure everything was accounted for and that they could put their hands on what they needed immediately. It wasn't any good if there were lab results floating around that hadn't been reviewed or if they were holding on to bodies that should be moved on to funeral homes because they hadn't been cleared yet.

"Sorry about that. But we didn't want to mess up your system..."

Kenzie laughed and shook her head. "Good excuse!"

He smiled and took another sip of his coffee. "Well, we had to come up with something to explain this mess."

Maybe they could have put some of the time that had gone into thinking up an excuse into actually getting the work done.

"I'll do what I can to get it all whipped into shape... but I'll be ready for a break from the paper this afternoon, if you don't mind me scrubbing in on one of the autopsies."

"Sounds good. I'll be sure to start early enough that you can get through it and still get back to Zachary in good time."

Dr. Wiltshire knew Zachary from a couple of previous cases that he had been involved with. And he knew a little bit about the challenges that Zachary faced.

Only someone who lived with Zachary or was close to him could know the real extent of his difficulties, but Kenzie appreciated Dr. Wiltshire thinking about her and her home situation in setting his schedule for the day. Despite the amount of work she had to do, Kenzie didn't want to be there too late. She would get caught up over time. Being able to spend time with Zachary and keep an eye on his health was important too.

Kenzie was a little disappointed that the autopsy she was able to scrub in on was Dr. Philemon's patient rather than the accident victim. The accident victim would have been more interesting. She suspected that a geriatric patient who had died at the hospital wasn't going to be a particularly intriguing case. Although she couldn't make that judgment. They had recently autopsied a nursing home patient whose death had turned out to be anything but routine.

George had already prepped the remains for them, gathering any forensic evidence and washing the body off. The old man's body lay on the table with a drape over it, awaiting their investigation. Dr. Wiltshire tapped the button on the floor with his foot to start recording, and dictated the patient's name and file number, the date and time, and his and Kenzie's names. He began as usual, making note of the patient's height and weight and his appearance on gross examination. Nothing remarkable. He didn't look any different from any other geriatric patient who had passed away in his sleep.

They checked for any cuts, bruises, or needle marks, as well as making notes of livor mortis. Time of death had been noted by Dr. Philemon, and Kenzie didn't see anything that would indicate that the timing was off.

"Bruising to the chest and ribs," Dr. Wiltshire commented. "Let's get some films and have a look."

He and Kenzie donned the appropriate radiation shields and took several x-rays of the body. The images were processed and ready for their review immediately. Dr. Wiltshire called them up on the screen.

"Some inflammation and fractures," he commented. "What does that look like to you, Dr. Kirsch?"

Kenzie was the student, and Dr. Wiltshire preferred the Socratic model of leading her with questions rather than lecturing. Kenzie had seen the victim's injury pattern in textbooks and didn't have a problem coming up with the answer.

"Looks like CPR was performed."

"Would you perform CPR on an elderly patient like this?"

Kenzie looked at him. "Probably not. He's very frail and what would be gained by reviving him? Even if he could be revived with CPR, chances are he would have brain damage or his quality of life would not be good. Not with broken ribs at his age. I'm surprised there was not a DNR."

"There might have been. If it's not properly recorded and flagged, they might proceed with CPR anyway. Although with a patient of this age," he shook his head, "I'm not sure why."

"I don't remember there being anything on the records we got from the hospital about CPR being performed. They should have noted it."

"Unless this was from a previous incident. If he had a cardiac event earlier, we might not have all the relevant records. We'll need to follow up on whether there was a DNR or a previous incident that required resuscitation."

Kenzie nodded her agreement. She couldn't stop and make a note in the middle of the autopsy, but it would be on the transcript she got back from the recording. She moved the magnifier over the deceased man's arm and examined the IV catheter and tube.

"See something?" Dr. Wiltshire asked.

"No. I just wondered whether I would be able to tell whether anything was injected into the IV."

"Doubtful," Dr. Wiltshire shook his head. "Sometimes there is trace evidence. Crystals, bubbles, things like that. But if it was meant to be injected, adrenaline or some other lifesaving measure, then no. It would just mix with the IV fluid and not leave any visible traces."

Kenzie examined the tubing for another minute, but couldn't see anything unusual.

"Okay. What's next?"

2

I t was a little later than Kenzie would have liked when she got home, but considering how late she had worked other days, it wasn't really bad. She hadn't had to eat a sandwich from the vending machine, but she was more than ready for her supper. She pulled her baby—a cherry red convertible—into her garage and walked in through the kitchen door. Zachary was sitting on the couch with his computer table in front of him, but he looked up when she opened the door, not so focused on his work that he failed to notice her.

"Home, sweet home," Kenzie declared.

Zachary smiled. "How was it today?"

"Still getting caught up. But Dr. Wiltshire understands that I can't get through three weeks of backlog in a couple of days, so I'm not going to kill myself trying."

"That would sort of defeat the purpose. Then you'd never get out of the morgue."

"Well, I would eventually, but it would be on a gurney."

Zachary chuckled. He pushed his table away from him and stretched. "Do you want me to order something?"

"I'm too hungry to wait for delivery." Kenzie put down her bag and opened the freezer door to see what supplies they had.

Even a pizza would take half an hour to heat, and she wasn't in the mood for frozen burritos. She closed the freezer and opened the fridge but, as she had expected, there wasn't much to eat there. Some fruit, a salad that she'd made with perfectly good intentions but then not even touched. Some leftovers from Sunday that she should probably throw out. Kenzie sighed.

"You could have a snack while we wait for delivery," Zachary suggested.

"Well… maybe." Kenzie considered the fruit. She could have an apple with some cheese while she waited for something better to be delivered. That would hold her over and help to keep her calm and relaxed to visit with Zachary but wouldn't take the amount of effort that actually coming up with something and preparing dinner herself would.

Her mother would despair over the lack of culinary and home-making skills her daughter possessed. But then, Lisa Cole Kirsch had employed a cook for most of Kenzie's childhood. Granted, she'd had a sick child to take care of, which was far more impor-tant than making sandwiches. Or mini quiches.

Kenzie removed an apple from the crisper drawer. She decided she didn't have the energy to get out the cheese and cut herself a couple of slices. She sat down on the couch with Zachary.

"Go ahead and order us something."

He nodded and picked up his phone. "What do you want?"

"I don't really care. As long as it isn't something that I have to make." Kenzie bit into her apple. It had been a long time since lunch. While Zachary poked through his phone and decided what to order in, she picked up the remote control and listened to the news headlines as the local news began. As she had come to expect, there wasn't much in the way of good, uplifting news. Negative headlines garnered more attention. When they switched to a story about Brittany "the Bombshell" Blake and her recent close-encounter with a possible killer, Kenzie quickly turned it off.

She turned her attention to Zachary. "So, tell me about your day today." Kenzie mentally reviewed what she remembered of his schedule for the day. "You got in to see Dr. Boyle for therapy today?"

Zachary nodded. He suppressed a smile, looking down at his hands. "It was good. I caught her up on… some of the stuff that happened while we were on vacation."

"I guess you kind of left her hanging before, when we lost cell coverage."

"Yeah. So she's been wondering how everything turned out, but I guess since she didn't get any reports that I'd had a breakdown and was in hospital somewhere, she figured that everything was okay."

"Well, I hope you told her that you did more than just *okay.* For you to be able to deal with the fire at the Lodge was huge." Kenzie smiled at him encouragingly. "I hope you really bragged it up."

His pale face was turning pink. He smiled again, nodding, but not raising his dark eyes to look into hers. It was nice to see him smile, especially as they approached Christmas, the worst time of year for his depression. He ran a hand over his short, stubbly hair.

"She was impressed. She said that she knew I could do it."

"I guess it's pretty amazing what we can do if we have to," Kenzie said. "We think we know what our limits are, but then something comes that pushes us out of our comfort zone… and we don't know until we face it if we can handle it."

"I told her…" Zachary licked dry lips, speaking hesitantly, as if worried how she might react, "that I'm worried… that nothing has changed. That the next time I remember the fire again… the flashbacks will be just as bad. That I won't have progressed at all."

Kenzie wanted to jump in and reassure him that of course he had made huge progress, and he wouldn't fall right back to where he was before. But psychology was not her area and, even if it were, she knew better than to counsel someone so close to her. She was too close to Zachary to have an unbiased opinion. "So… what did Dr. B say about that?"

Zachary picked at a thread in his jeans. "She said that… I'll probably still have some anxiety around it, but now that I know I can get through it, that she doesn't think it will be that bad. She's done exposure therapy with patients before, helping them to get over phobias or anxieties." He shrugged. "I don't know. I guess… we'll find out."

"We could go to a restaurant with candles or a fireplace. See how you feel."

Zachary shook his head immediately. "No way."

"Are you sure? You don't want to take some time to think about it?"

Zachary started to protest again, then looked at her and realized that she was teasing him. He ran his hand through his dark hair again, chuckling. But it was forced. Kenzie might have pushed it a bit far.

"Sorry," she apologized. "I'm a little punchy. Long day."

He laughed again. "No, it's fine. Sometimes… I don't realize when you're joking."

"I shouldn't do that. I'm glad things went well with Dr. B. And if you didn't brag enough about how well you handled the situation out there, I'll tell her at our next couples session too. Because what you did out there was… remarkable. It really was."

"It's not such a big thing for anyone else."

"You were the one who took charge. That would be impressive by itself. Add in the fact that even a candle flame is usually enough to break you down, and that you faced a blazing house fire…?" Kenzie shook her head. "I can see I'm going to have to brag you up more. If that's how you told her about it."

He looked away from her, but not fast enough that she didn't see his smile of pleasure over her insistence that he deserved praise for having faced his biggest fear.

Kenzie had nibbled away most of her apple. She looked down at the core. "How long before dinner is here?"

He checked his phone screen. "Fifteen minutes."

"Okay. I'm going to go get changed. I'm not wearing grown-up clothes for the rest of the day."

She disposed of her apple core and went to her bedroom to change into a pair of comfortable pajamas. It wasn't so much that she hated her work clothes or that they were uncomfortable. She just needed a transition from "work Kenzie" to "home relaxing Kenzie." She would put away any worries from the office and just focus on herself and Zachary for the evening.

She had hoped, with the holiday to the mountains, that she would be able to boost his mood and help him to get to a better place before December. He had already been sliding into depression in October, before the two of them had to endure the antivirus protocol, and his physical decline during the treatment had been much worse than hers. Maybe because she kept herself in good condition, eating and sleeping well, and he had difficulty with both. His viral load had ended up being much higher than hers, even though he had contracted it from Kenzie. And that meant that they had also hit him a lot harder with the drugs they hoped would wipe out the virus before it could affect him as it had the nursing home victims.

The holiday had not gone as expected, but she didn't think he had lost more weight at the Lodge, and he had returned knowing that he had handled one of the things he had feared the most in life. If he could beat his fear of fire, maybe he could beat the depression and some of the other challenges as well. She hoped so.

"Food's here," Zachary called out.

"I'll be right there."

3

Kenzie took her first couple of bites of the Thai curry and relaxed, moaning to express her pleasure.

"This is so good. Great choice, Zach."

He had taken a little of the rice and Thai curry himself, and a piece of naan bread, which he dipped into the curry. "It's pretty good," he agreed. He took a bite or two of the bread. "So how was your day today? You said you didn't get caught up. So does that mean you're stuck with just filing and administrative stuff right now?"

"No. I scrubbed in on one of the autopsies this afternoon."

"Anything interesting?"

"The only interesting thing so far is that it was a doctor-attended death, but the doctor wanted us to look into it."

"Oh. Does that mean he thinks it is a suspicious death?"

"Maybe. He doesn't have to give us his reasons. In fact, it's better if he doesn't bias us in one direction or another. It may just be that he didn't foresee it and wants to be sure of what it was that killed him. So he can be more aware of it next time if there is something they should have caught. Or it might be that he thought there was a problem with the treatment, or even foul play."

"And did you find anything in the autopsy?"

"Not yet. Other than the fact that he was given CPR when it probably wasn't advisable. And wasn't recorded on his chart."

"Why wasn't it advisable? Is there a case where... CPR does more harm than good?"

"In a way, yeah. CPR is an extreme measure, and not often successful, even in a hospital setting where the patient had a cardiac event under supervision. If he does survive resuscitation, then you may be looking at brain damage, broken bones, a lot of pain, and he probably has another heart attack within the week and dies anyway. When you're looking at an elderly patient without a good prognosis... it's better to just let nature take its course. Sometimes."

Zachary nodded seriously as he stirred his soup and then took a bite. He blew on his next spoonful to cool it off. "That makes sense. And that was the only thing you found?"

"So far. We've sent out samples for testing. Asked for some tox screens. If the doctor thinks that there might have been an error made in his treatment, then we need to look for anything that might have caused his death. What was he given? Was it the wrong amount or wrong concentration? Did someone give him the wrong thing? Misread the doctor's instructions? Decide to help him on his way? There are a lot of possibilities. And of course, you only find what you're looking for, and I don't know if we've asked for all the right tests. Hopefully... something will show up, or we'll think of something else that needs to be run before we release the remains."

"Well, I hope something shows up."

"You hope he was poisoned, or that the medical staff made a mistake?" Kenzie asked with a grin.

"Well... I don't know. It isn't as if I have a particular preference. I just hope that you figure it out. Give his family some closure. Reassure his doctor. Whatever else needs to happen."

"Yeah." Kenzie had a drink and some more curry. "So how about you? All I've heard about is your session with Dr. Boyle."

Zachary stared off into space, thinking about it. Kenzie knew how a day could go by and leave her wondering what she had even accomplished, so she assumed he was confronted by the same thing. A full day of work, but what had he actually done?

"I don't know," Zachary said finally. "Worked on a bunch of small files. Getting caught up on the backlog, like you. I talked to Heather and we went over the files that she worked on while I was… unavailable. I'm glad that I had someone to take some of those things off my plate."

Heather was Zachary's older sister, whom he had just been reunited with recently. Prior to meeting with Zachary, she had never held a job. But after helping her with her own case, Zachary had offered to train her on some of the computer work that he did for clients, such as skip tracing and running backgrounds. She was very good on the computer and took to it immediately. She loved having something productive to do and took whatever Zachary threw at her.

"It's pretty amazing how the two of you have just clicked, and she's been able to work on that with you."

Zachary nodded. "Goldman Investigations… I never thought there would be any other Goldman than me. Now there's Heather too."

He looked pensive. Thinking of the two younger siblings that he had not yet been reunited with? Wishing that Tyrrell or Joss were also interested in the private investigations business? Or just thinking about the years that they had all lost together, being separated from each other when Zachary was ten and they were sent to various different foster homes?

"It's pretty cool," Kenzie said. "You can never predict what could happen."

Maybe that would help him to think positively about the future. Good things that could happen in the future, instead of the bad things that he envisioned and dreaded.

"Got anything interesting on your plate?" she asked, when he didn't say anything.

Zachary looked down at his dinner plate blankly for a second, before realizing she was speaking figuratively. "Oh… well, hard to say. I'm still catching up on emails and seeing what people need. And what I'm willing to take on."

That seemed to be the end of their shop talk for the day. There was only so much they could squeeze out of a discussion of their jobs. Especially when they were both just getting back into the swing of things.

"You want to put on a movie tonight?" Kenzie suggested. "Or do something productive like going out shopping?" She looked at the fridge. "We don't have a lot in the house right now."

"We probably should."

But he didn't sound any more enthralled about the idea than Kenzie felt.

4

Kenzie was starting to imagine that she might see the bottom of her in basket soon. Or at least, that it would only be as full as it normally was on a weekday. She didn't want to get too excited, but maybe she was getting caught up.

She looked through the lab reports that she had printed off for Michaels, the hospital patient that she had assisted with the autopsy on. She hole-punched them at the top and slid them onto the brads on the file as she read through the results.

Her heart started to beat fast as she looked at it. She walked with the file to Dr. Wiltshire's office.

He was sitting at his desk, but he was talking on the phone. It didn't seem to be a very animated discussion, but she didn't want to interrupt him in the middle of a call. He looked up, saw her in the doorway, and motioned for her to enter.

Kenzie walked in hesitantly. She couldn't tell him what was going on without interrupting the call. He motioned for the file, maybe thinking that she just needed him to sign off on a report. Kenzie folded the pages up so that the relevant results were showing and slid it across his desk to him.

Dr. Wiltshire looked down at the page and scanned it quickly. He straightened up.

"Larry, I'm going to have to call you back," he told the party on the other end of the phone and, without further discussion, set the phone down in the cradle. He looked up at Kenzie, head cocked to the side slightly.

For a moment, they just looked at each other.

"Kenzie, would you get me Dr. Philemon's phone number, please?"

Kenzie leaned forward to snag the file from him and leafed through the pages pinned to the other side of the folder. "Here it is." She read it out to him; then, after he had dialed the phone, gave the file back to him, open to the lab results. She waited while Dr. Wiltshire waited for an answer. She knew she should probably leave. Dr. Wiltshire didn't need her standing there over him while he informed the doctor of the results. But she wanted to hear the call. At least the beginning of it. At least Dr. Wiltshire's half of the conversation.

She was afraid it was going to go through to voicemail but, eventually, Dr. Wiltshire's call was answered by a real person.

"I'm looking for Dr. Philemon, if he is available," Dr. Wiltshire informed the other doctor's assistant or phone service.

There was a pause. Kenzie couldn't hear the other party's reply.

"It's rather urgent," Dr. Wiltshire advised. "This is the Medical Examiner's Office. If there's any way you could get a message to him…"

They both waited. Eventually, Dr. Wiltshire nodded at Kenzie, indicating that he would be put through to Dr. Philemon. He motioned Kenzie to the guest chair on her side of the desk.

"Have a seat for a moment."

He hit the speaker button on the phone, and they sat listening to cool jazz for a few minutes before the call was picked up.

"Dr. Philemon," the voice on the other end answered brusquely. He sounded younger than Kenzie had pictured him. She had imagined that a geriatric doctor with his own private practice would be elderly, white-haired, able to easily relate to the patients he treated. But he sounded as though he were in his twenties, thirties at the latest.

"Yes, this is Dr. Wiltshire, Medical Examiner. I have my assistant, Dr. Kirsch with me."

"Hello, doctors." A slight hesitation. "Does this mean that you found something of note in your autopsy?"

"In fact, we did," Dr. Wiltshire agreed. "Your patient's potassium levels were off the charts."

"Hyperkalemia." Dr. Philemon considered this for a minute. "So… could it have been kidney failure, or was something administered to him?"

"Given the concentration, I'm afraid that this wasn't a natural death," Dr. Wiltshire advised. "He must have been given potassium chloride in his IV line."

"And I never prescribed it. Harry was in good health. Not perfect, obviously, or he would not have been in the hospital. But I figured he still had some good years left in him."

"He was in the hospital for treatment of kidney stones?"

"Yes, with an attendant infection. We figured the stones would pass on their own. Decided to do a few days of IV antibiotics and see how things went from there."

"So you weren't expecting him to die on you."

"No. Of course, you could lose a geriatric patient at any time. That's the nature of the practice. But I thought… well, I was surprised. Obviously. Or I would not have sent him to you."

"Do you have… suspicions of who might have administered potassium chloride?"

"Well… no. And yes. I mean, there isn't anyone who I would suggest would do something like this… but on the other hand, we know… this kind of thing happens. Someone decides to play God…"

"Yes."

"I'll have to go over the records of the staff… see if I can narrow it down. Who was on the floor when he coded. If anyone has any previous suspicions. I just don't know."

"You're not aware of any other suspicious deaths?"

"We've... lost other patients. But as I say, I specialize in geriatrics, and that's the nature of things. I will... also review any recent unexpected deaths."

"You'll want to look at expected deaths too. Sometimes someone... just wants to hurry things on a little."

"Yes. Of course."

"If there is a pattern, we will need to get the FBI involved."

Dr. Philemon groaned. "I've never been a part of an investigation before. Is that... what's it going to be like? They're not going to suspect me, are they?"

"If you're the one reporting the deaths, then you will at least be lower on the list of suspects. But yes, they're going to want to ask you a lot of questions about where you were when each of the patients died, what medications you prescribed, whether you felt that the staff followed your instructions to the letter... they'll have a lot of questions. As long as you are open and honest, you don't have anything to worry about."

"But are people going to think that I did something even if they determine it was someone else? Or if they can't figure out who it is? Are people always going to think that I had something to do with it and they just couldn't prove it?"

Dr. Wiltshire didn't answer right away. He looked at Kenzie and raised his brows. They both knew what the answer was. Dr. Philemon himself knew the answer, or he wouldn't have voiced it in the first place.

"There will always be people who believe that you were involved and got away with something," Dr. Wiltshire admitted. "But you can't let that keep you from reporting it to the proper authorities. If there is a killer on your staff, then we need to catch him before he can cause any more harm."

"Yes. Of course. I wouldn't hesitate to report it. I'm just... I am just establishing my practice. Something like this… a blot against my name before I'm even established…"

"People have dealt with worse," Dr. Wiltshire assured him. "I can't tell you what's going to happen, but it will be stressful and you'll probably ask yourself why you even became a doctor in the first place. But hang in there. Wait until it has all concluded before you make any decisions about what to do with your practice."

"Yeah. You're right. Just because I have this one patient… that doesn't mean that it's happened to anyone else. It could just be one case. An accident."

"I will not be certifying this as an accidental death."

"No, I didn't mean that, of course. I'm just saying… maybe someone administered the wrong medication. That it was unintentional. Still a case of a poisonous substance being given to him, but… maybe they didn't plan to kill him."

Dr. Wiltshire decided to go on and not to debate the details with him. "We noticed that CPR had been administered."

"CPR. No."

"The patient has inflamed and broken ribs. It looks very much like CPR injuries."

"I didn't. No one attempted CPR while I was there. If they did… I should have been informed. It should have been charted."

"Yes. It should have been."

"I will have to talk to my staff. Make sure that I have the full story."

"I would suggest that you speak with each person independently, without allowing them to talk to each other in the meantime."

"You don't think that they would try to cover for…" Dr. Philemon sighed. "Maybe they would."

"If someone attempted resuscitation by CPR and didn't chart it, then they are already trying to cover something up. Take that together with the patient's potassium levels, and I think you need to be concerned about what's going on in your unit. There needs to be an investigation, even if you can't identify any other suspicious deaths."

Dr. Philemon groaned. Kenzie felt for him. A young doctor, trying to get his practice established, trying to develop his reputation, and suddenly he had to investigate his own staff to see whether one of them were killing patients. It was a doctor's worst nightmare.

"Let me know what you find," Dr. Wiltshire said. "I will be waiting to hear from you. And if you think this goes farther than one patient, then get the FBI involved sooner rather than later."

"Okay. Thank you for your advice, Dr. Wiltshire. I appreciate it."

They disconnected. Dr. Wiltshire shook his head and slid the file across the desk to Kenzie again. "Run a copy of everything in there for the FBI. Or scan it or save copies in an electronic folder, whatever your process is. They're going to want it yesterday."

"The FBI?" Kenzie asked, surprised that he wasn't waiting for Dr. Philemon's findings.

"Yes. I've been here before, and I can tell you that things will move very quickly once Dr. Philemon identifies even one other death that he has questions about. I want to be ready to hand over everything we have within minutes of receiving a call from the FBI."

"You think they'll react that quickly?" Kenzie had always found that law enforcement moved much more slowly than she expected after watching a lifetime of cop shows on TV. Fictional police departments and FBI agents always acted on even the smallest suspicions immediately and, of course, solved the case within an hour. In real life, closing the net on the criminals could take weeks or even years.

"With an established pattern like an Angel of Death killer, they'll react. They'll want to start interviewing suspects and narrowing their focus very quickly. It can take a long time to build a case," he admitted, "but they'll do whatever they can to ensure that he or she cannot keep killing patients."

"Okay. I'll get a copy made right away."

"Of course, if we're lucky, they'll get a confession. Often, that's the only way to get one of these killers. They don't leave a lot of evidence behind, and some of them are very adept at pulling off multiple killings without getting caught. Just think of all the people who die in the hospital or under a doctor's care and never come through this office. People who are sick or dying... make ideal targets."

Kenzie thought back to a case that Zachary had investigated, the death of Robin Salter. Everyone had put it down to either her cancer or the cancer treatment protocol. No one but Bridget and Zachary had thought that it could be anything else. But they had been right. Killing someone who was already dying was much too easy.

5

H ome with Zachary the next night, Kenzie ventured to broach a topic that had been on her mind. Zachary seemed to be in a good place mentally since their return from their holiday and his session with Dr. B, so she hoped that he would be open to discussion. They had finished dinner and were just relaxing together, starting their weekend with some focused couples time. Cuddling on the couch, but with the TV off and other devices put away. He rubbed her shoulder as she leaned against him.

"So, I wanted to talk to you about something..." Kenzie started.

She could feel him stiffen immediately, not even knowing what it was she wanted to talk about. She didn't usually start a conversation that way, so of course he was wary. Maybe he thought it was the beginning of a breakup speech, or the suggestion that he should go back to spending more time at his apartment and not consider her house his home base.

"It's not anything bad," she assured him. "I just know that it's hard for you to talk about."

That didn't help to relax him. "Okay..."

"I want to talk a little bit about Christmas."

She could almost feel the wall go up between them. Zachary may have been forced to confront the specter of the house fire that he'd been trapped in as a child, but his anxieties about Christmas had not gone down with it. The Christmas Eve disaster had had serious, long-term consequences.

"I can't really… talk about that."

"I'm not asking you to do anything, or to plan a Christmas party. I want to talk about what things I can do to celebrate Christmas that we can enjoy together. Things that won't trigger you."

She was quiet while he considered this. They did have some experience in learning how to build their relationship without triggering Zachary's defenses. After his encounter with a sadistic serial killer, Kenzie had barely been able to touch him without his dissociating and withdrawing from any intimacy mentally and emotionally even while still going through the motions physically. But with Dr. Boyle's help, they had been able to gradually build on touches and actions that he could tolerate, until they were almost back to where they had been before the kidnapping.

"What were you thinking?" Zachary asked finally. "I can't do… candles or trees with lights."

Considering that the house fire had started with candles igniting the Christmas tree, that was perfectly understandable, and Kenzie had already taken it into account when thinking about things that they might be able to do.

"Well, I had some thoughts around treats. Cut-out sugar or shortbread cookies, Mandarin oranges, hot chocolate…"

She ventured a look at Zachary's face. She didn't want the conversation to be too intense or confrontational, which was one reason she had waited until they were side-by-side. If Zachary didn't have to look her in the eyes and read her face as they spoke, it would be easier for him.

He looked relieved at the food suggestions. He nodded. "Sure. I like all of those." He breathed out, sighing slightly. "It's not like… we ever had those things at home."

Kenzie didn't know very much about the way his family had celebrated Christmas. She knew that his parents had fought on Christmas Eve over the tree and decorations. A knock-down blow-out fight that had ended with none of it getting done. So ten-year-old Zachary got up in the night to set it all up himself, including lighting the special Christmas candles. Kenzie knew that they had been poor, without money to spend on presents for the children. Or, apparently, any special Christmas treats.

She smiled, pleased that the first item on her list had been approved without any resistance. "Great. I'll have to be careful how many shortbread cookies I eat. Those things are basically just butter and sugar. But they'll be good to boost your calorie intake."

Zachary grinned at that. Kenzie usually tried to make sure that he ate as healthy a diet as possible, which was difficult when she was trying to tempt him to eat more. Since his meds caused nausea in the morning and reduced his appetite overall, concessions had to be made for higher-calorie foods when she could get something into him. He apparently wasn't too disappointed at the prospect of more cookies in his diet.

"How about decorations? I know some things are out of the question." No need to mention candles or trees specifically again. "But there must be some things that wouldn't bother you that would still be festive. Are there decorations some of your foster homes or care centers had that didn't bother you? Or something that Lorne and Pat do?"

"Most of the stuff they did at Bonnie Brown didn't bother me too much," Zachary said slowly. "But it was a concrete building. Not... a wood frame house. So I didn't have to worry so much about... you know."

Fire. And even having faced his fear at the Lodge, he was still concerned about thoughts of fire triggering flashbacks as they always had.

"What kind of decorations did they have that you think would be okay?"

"They had... lights on the walls. High up by the ceiling where kids couldn't reach them. The little twinkle lights. They don't get hot. And they were concrete walls." He gave a little shrug.

"So how would you feel about some little lights here? On the walls?"

Zachary nodded. "Okay."

"You think that would be okay?"

"Yeah."

"And what about the little twinkle lights in jars. The ones that flicker." She didn't call them candles. "Are they okay if you know that they're not real?"

She could feel the tension re-enter his body. They'd been able to go to restaurants that used small twinkle lights or LEDs instead of candles on the tables, but apparently having them at home might be too much.

"I don't know."

"It's okay to say no. I don't have my heart set on it. This is a discussion about what you are comfortable with."

"Then… I guess, no."

Kenzie nodded. "That's okay. I don't want you to have to deal with an environment that makes you feel uncomfortable and on edge. That's why I'm asking."

He still seemed uncomfortable with having told her no. Kenzie considered whether to continue or leave it at that. She had a couple of answers; she could always add more later when he'd had a chance to relax and think about it some more.

"Are there other decorations that wouldn't make you feel anxious? I was thinking about things like a snow globe, some Christmassy fridge magnets, maybe a wreath on the door."

Zachary rubbed his hands on his jeans. Sweaty palms were a sign that she might be overloading him with too much at once.

"A snow globe sounds good," he said. "It's filled with water and it's not a… hazard."

"Yeah. It's kind of the opposite of a fire hazard," Kenzie agreed.

"So that's okay. Fridge magnets?"

"They have them around. Seasonal symbols and shapes. Snow scenes. Ceramic or metal or plastic."

Zachary nodded. "Okay."

He didn't say anything else. Kenzie guessed that was an answer in itself as far as the wreath went. Still too similar to a Christmas tree. No branches that could catch fire, even if there were only the remotest chance that such a thing could happen. She slid one arm behind Zachary and gave him a squeeze.

"Thank you. I know it's not easy for you to discuss. If you have more thoughts, or if we put something up and you change your mind about it, just let me know. It's an experiment, and if it makes you too uncomfortable or depressed, we'll change things."

"Okay." He put his arm around her too and kissed her on the cheek. "That's really nice. When I was with Br—" he cut himself off and turned his face away from her, realizing what he'd been about to say.

"When you were with Bridget," Kenzie finished for him. "What was it like around Christmas? Did she want lots of traditional decorations?"

Bridget was Zachary's ex-wife. Kenzie didn't bar Zachary from bringing her up, but acknowledged to herself that it provoked an emotional reaction whenever he did. When they had first met, Kenzie had been amused by Bridget. Bridget said that she didn't want anything to do with Zachary, to the extent that he wasn't even supposed to go to any of her favorite stores or restaurants where she might bump into him, and yet she didn't seem to be able to let go of him and her emotional reactions to him were dramatically over-the-top. She was clearly still attached to him.

And Zachary was still in love with her, despite the way that she abused him and had kicked him to the curb when she had been diagnosed with cancer. The cancer was now in remission. Bridget's venom toward Zachary had only grown, and Kenzie no longer thought it was funny. Their recent discovery that she was suffering from Huntington's Disease tempered Kenzie's feelings toward her a little, but she hadn't been able to overcome her gut reaction to Zachary's continued obsession with her. It wasn't a choice on Zachary's part. He couldn't help the fact that his obsessive thoughts constantly returned to her. But he knew how Kenzie felt and tried not to bring her up.

Zachary shrugged, looking down. "Yeah. She had a professional decorator and everything. I did my best to… stay out of the rooms that were decorated."

And she probably hadn't appreciated that response.

"She didn't know, in the beginning, how big of a deal it was. She thought I was sulking."

"But she must have figured it out eventually. I mean… I did."

"She always thought it was something I should be able to control."

Kenzie sighed. "Well, this year you don't have to worry about it. We're going to work together. If there's a problem, we're just going to be open in our communication about it, right? Just like we've been doing in couples therapy."

"Right," Zachary agreed.

But his voice wasn't strong. It would take an effort on Kenzie's part to watch for his reactions and ask questions to help him sort out and verbalize his feelings.

6

Even though it was the weekend, Kenzie went into the office for a few hours on Saturday. Zachary said that he had some outside assignments to take care of and she figured she could get caught up on some more of her sorting and filing while he completed them. It would make it that much less stressful returning to the office on Monday.

Sunday, they were both home, spending some couples time together. Kenzie talking to her parents on the phone. Zachary visiting with Lorne Peterson, an old foster father, and Lorne's partner, Patrick Parker, on video conference. Kenzie's parents were divorced, though they were still friendly with each other, so she spoke with them separately. Lisa spoke of her Christmas parties and other functions, and Walter was trying to get a bill pushed through the Legislature before they closed for the Christmas break. Both were focused very much on their own personal projects and, as long as Kenzie was well and safe following her anti-viral protocol and failed holiday, they weren't particularly interested in her work.

"I barely got a chance to meet your Zachary at the masquerade ball," Lisa commented. "We must get together for Christmas so that we can get to know each other."

Kenzie winced. She didn't really want them getting to know each other. She preferred to keep her parents and her boyfriend separate for as long as possible. Lisa and Walter were not Zachary's kind of people. They wouldn't understand him and would just brush off his feelings and challenges as unimportant.

"We won't be able to do anything before Christmas," Kenzie said firmly. "Maybe after. We could do New Year's maybe. Something in January when you're not busy."

Lisa was never *not* busy, and Kenzie hoped that the proposed get-together would be forgotten with her busy social calendar.

"You can't do anything before Christmas? Surely your schedule isn't that crammed."

"Sorry. We can't manage anything before then. You know… Daddy said that you don't really celebrate Christmas anymore. Not the way that you used to when we were young."

"Well…" Lisa's voice was hesitant. "No, of course not. The way you celebrate when your children are young is very different from the way it is when you're an empty-nester. There isn't really any reason for me to decorate like I used to. There's no one to do it *for*."

Kenzie felt the weight of guilt in her stomach. After Amanda's death, it was Kenzie's duty to make her mother feel useful and part of the family, like she wasn't alone. She should have carried that legacy, but she had failed. And no doubt Lisa wanted grandchildren. Maybe if there were, she would decorate the house again, just like in the old days. But Kenzie didn't have children and wasn't convinced that she wanted any. Or that she and Zachary had the time and emotional resources to raise them properly.

Zachary wanted children. He'd helped to raise his brothers and sisters until the family had been broken up, and there had been other children at the various other foster homes where he had lived. Bridget hadn't wanted to have children with him, but was due to have twins with Zachary's replacement, Gordon Drake, sometime soon. It had been a real blow for Zachary to find out that she was pregnant.

"Well… maybe when we come after Christmas, you can have a few decorations up." They wouldn't bother Zachary so much after Christmas. Kenzie remembered all the fairy lights and garlands when she was a little girl. The house had been transformed into a magical world.

"There isn't any reason to have the house decorated *after* Christmas," Lisa pointed out.

"There's no magic about the date. You could decorate and leave them up a few days after Christmas."

Lisa sighed. "Maybe you could find some time in your busy schedule to come before then."

Kenzie rolled her eyes, glad that they were on the phone and not on video, so she could indulge in the small rebellion. "I'll see what we can do," she promised.

But she knew there was no way they would be visiting Lisa before Christmas.

Monday rolled around and Kenzie was ready to get back to work. She enjoyed her time at home with Zachary, but his anxiety and depression did take their toll over time. He was doing well, considering that they were moving into December, but she still needed a break from his dark cloud when she could get it.

When Dr. Wiltshire strolled in with his cup of coffee and his briefcase, Kenzie held out a file for him. "More from Dr. Philemon," she offered.

Dr. Wiltshire put his coffee cup down on the counter of Kenzie's reception desk and took it from her. "What has he found?"

"He's been going back over cases covering the past year, documenting the unexpected deaths and resuscitations. There's a fairly extensive list."

"Did any of them come through this office?"

"No. Mr. Michaels was the first." Kenzie paused. "I expect that some of these others probably registered on his subconscious, until he got to the point where he became suspicious of something, even if he couldn't put his finger on why."

"Is that what he said?"

Kenzie shook her head. "Not in so many words, no. He's been pretty… stingy in what he has offered. Probably thinking about his professional liability insurance."

"Oh, I think I can guarantee that he's thinking of his insurance," Dr. Wiltshire agreed with a grin. He took a slug of coffee from his grande cup. "He'll be very careful of everything he says between now and whenever this is all over."

Kenzie suspected he was right.

"So what happens with this list?" she asked. "Do any of these patients get exhumed? All of them?"

"We won't be rushing into anything. He'll need to start compiling what staff members were involved with each case. Who the assigned doctors and nurses were. Who was on the floor when they died. If there is a pattern in time of day, symptoms, cause of death. See if there is any surveillance footage of the patients or wards. Start installing surveillance cameras in the patient rooms. All of those things. Medical professionals who kill are very hard to catch. They are really good at covering their tracks."

They had been lucky to find Robin Salter's killer. If it had turned out to have been caused by an insulin overdose, they might never have been able to catch the culprit. It was only by luck—or Zachary's careful investigation and out-of-the-box thinking—that had enabled them to catch her. And if the killer hadn't panicked and run, maybe they would never have been able to gather enough evidence to prove it.

"So there's nothing for us to do at this point?" Kenzie asked.

"Just for me to issue my findings. I've already advised our friends upstairs." Dr. Wiltshire rolled his eyes upward to indicate the police department that was housed above them. "They have opened their investigation and are just waiting for my official report. With Dr. Philemon identifying other possible suspicious deaths, they will get the FBI involved. It will be up to them to make the decisions on any exhumation or other follow-up."

7

Kenzie arrived home to an empty house. She called out to Zachary, but knew before she did that he wasn't home. There was just a different quality to the house when he was home. She could sense it as soon as she walked in the door. And it wasn't because he sometimes let the homeless garb he wore for surveillance get a little too ripe. It just didn't feel as much like home if he weren't there.

She checked to see whether he had left her a note on the fridge or sent her a text that she had not noticed. There was nothing to indicate where he had gone.

Kenzie took a deep breath in and let it out slowly. There was no reason to panic just because he wasn't there when she got home. He was a grown man and was allowed to come and go as he pleased without reporting his movements to her. He could be off on a job, running errands, meeting with Heather, or having supper with a friend.

Though he rarely had supper with a friend and always informed her when he wasn't going to be home to eat with her. They had agreed that dinner was couples time, when they would spend the time together catching up with each other, unless there was an emergency that required them to be somewhere else.

Zachary had been doing well since they got home. She wasn't that worried about him. He might have simply gone back to his own apartment to get something he needed or spend some time in his man cave. Everyone needed their own space now and then.

It wasn't necessarily a sign that something was wrong. If he'd been more depressed, she would have noticed it. He wasn't one of those people who was a clown or covered up his pain with fake cheer. When he was suffering, it was obvious. To those closest to him, at least.

Kenzie pulled out her phone and dialed his number. It rang several times, becoming obvious that he wasn't going to pick it up. He was busy with something that couldn't be interrupted. She waited for his voicemail to pick up, trying to compose a message in her head that didn't sound like she was nagging or excessively worried.

Eventually, his businesslike voice answered, announcing that she had reached Goldman Investigations and asking her to leave a message.

"Just me," Kenzie said, keeping her voice light. "Wondering whether you will be home for supper or if I should go ahead without you. Let me know your plans. Okay, talk to you soon."

She hung up and considered the message. Too much? She didn't think so. Once he finished whatever he was working on or the meeting that he was in, he would call her back and let her know where he was or what he was doing.

But of course it wasn't instantaneous. He didn't text her back to say that he was in a meeting and would get back to her. He didn't return the call right away. She changed and put her things away, then went back to the kitchen to consider the situation. She was hungry, so she couldn't wait all night for his reply. Have a snack and hold dinner until he answered? Assume he wasn't coming and go ahead with supper? Make enough for both of them so that he would have something available when he eventually returned?

"Zachary, where are you?" she grumbled.

He had suggested not long ago that she let him put a tracker on her car so that he could be aware of where she was in case anything untoward happened. She hadn't thought about needing to track him in return. There were phone apps, she knew. Maybe they should exchange location tracking on their phones so that she would at least know what part of town he was in.

Of course, being a private investigator, client confidentiality was an issue, and he probably wouldn't want her tracking him any more than she wanted him tracking her. While she had friends who shared locations between spouses, it felt like an invasion of privacy to Kenzie and just reminded her of the fact that Zachary had once before tracked her movements without her permission. It was before they knew each other well and had nearly ended the relationship. She had been furious. Justifiably.

Kenzie took out her phone again and looked at it, just in case she had missed a call or message from him. She knew she hadn't and a glance at her screen confirmed this.

She started pulling ingredients out of the fridge to make herself a sandwich.

———

Kenzie was reading through a news feed on her phone when it started to ring. First she jumped. Then she was glad that Zachary was getting back to her and reached out to swipe the call. But it wasn't Zachary's name and picture on the screen. It was a number unfamiliar to her.

She considered letting it go to voicemail on the assumption that it was a telemarketer. But she didn't know where Zachary was or what he was doing, and it was possible that his phone had run out of juice and he'd borrowed someone else's to call her.

She accepted the call anyway and put the phone up to her ear. "Hello?"

"Is this—uh—Kenzie?" a cultured male voice inquired.

"Yes. Who is calling?"

She waited for the sales patter, even though he didn't sound like any telemarketer she had heard before.

"My name is Gordon. I was wondering… if you happen to know where Zachary is?"

Kenzie frowned? Gordon? She knew that was the name of Bridget's new partner, a man that Zachary had done a couple of jobs with before. But he wouldn't be calling Kenzie if he had something to ask Zachary for. He would be calling Zachary directly. It must be another Gordon.

"He's not here at the moment," she told him crisply. "Can I give him a message for you?"

"This is… awkward. You don't know me, Kenzie. But Zachary has mentioned you before. I thought that I saw him a few minutes ago. But when I called him, he didn't answer."

"He may be busy right now. He hasn't returned my last call either."

But it was a relief if Gordon had seen him. At least that meant that Zachary was alive and well, whatever he was doing.

"The thing is, he shouldn't be here."

Kenzie swore under her breath. It *was* Bridget's Gordon. Zachary wasn't supposed to be there because he wasn't supposed to get anywhere near Bridget's house. There was no protection order outstanding, but Bridget had said more than once that she would take one out if he continued to stalk her.

And for two years, that had not been a problem. Zachary had recommitted himself to therapy, his doctor had changed his prescriptions, and he had been able to stay away from her.

At least, as far as Kenzie knew.

She had suspected recently, before going on their vacation, that he might be following her again. If he were, it was Gordon's own fault for involving Zachary in their problems. Gordon should have known enough to leave Zachary out of it and to hire another private investigator for any investigative work to do with Bridget.

"Where is he?" Kenzie asked finally, closing her eyes.

"If it was him—and I can't swear that it was, but it looked very much like his car and the driver bore a striking resemblance to Zachary—then he's at our home. Bridget's home. He can't be here. He knows that."

"Yes. I know." Kenzie rubbed one hand over her face, trying to keep her rising anger, disappointment, and dread in check as she considered the situation. "What do you want me to do, Gordon?"

"I don't know. I was hoping that if you called him, you could get him to go home. But if he isn't answering your calls... well, I really would rather not involve the police, Kenzie."

"I appreciate that."

She didn't want Zachary to spend the night in a jail cell. For a normal person, a night in a cell might be a deterrent from stalking Bridget. But for Zachary? He couldn't help the obsession. Maybe his meds needed to be adjusted again. One of the unfortunate things about psychoactive drugs was that they could just stop working one day, and then the doctors had to scramble to find something else that would work. She'd noticed a few issues creeping in since their holiday. She had tried to ignore them, to deny what she herself was seeing.

"Gordon... what's your address? I could drive over there, see whether I can see him."

"Certainly." He gave her the address, and Kenzie scribbled it down on a flyer on the kitchen table.

"Thanks. I'll come have a look around. Where did you see the car?"

He described the place where he had seen the car parked. Kenzie jotted down it down as he spoke.

"All right. Be by soon. Is this number your cell phone?"

"Yes...?"

"So I can text you back."

"Yes. Of course."

"Okay. I'll let you know what I find."

He said a polite goodbye and hung up. Kenzie looked down at

the address she had written, shaking her head. "Zachary, what are you up to now?" she demanded aloud.

She looked at her phone again, in case Zachary had texted her while she'd been on with Gordon, but there were still no notifications.

Kenzie drove up and down the streets, looking carefully at the parked cars, and was initially relieved not to find Zachary's car where Gordon had described it. He must have just seen someone else and mistaken them for Zachary. But she kept looking, just in case. Zachary had, after all, not returned her call. He had to be somewhere, and if he were somewhere outside Bridget's house, then it was much better for him if Kenzie found him than Bridget or the police.

It was getting dark. She had almost circled all sides of Bridget's house—which was more of a mansion and would probably have fit six of Kenzie's house inside—when she spotted a white compact of the same make as Zachary's.

"Don't be Zachary," Kenzie said under her breath.

But on the other hand, she hoped that it was, because she didn't want to be left wondering where he was after driving all the way over to look for him. The longer he was away without returning her call, the more she worried something had happened to him. She didn't only have to worry about self-harm. He drove like a demon and could have been in an accident. Some adulterous husband he was tracking might have shot him. A hundred different things.

As she approached the car, she could see that it was Zachary's license plate. She sighed and pulled to the curb a couple of spaces ahead of him. She got out of her car and walked up to his window. He was sitting in the driver's seat, a pair of binoculars to his eyes, which prevented him from noticing her approach. Kenzie rapped on the window with a couple of knuckles.

Zachary jolted and lowered the binoculars abruptly to look at her, face white and frozen.

At first, his face showed relief. She wasn't a cop there to demand what he was doing, or Gordon or Bridget herself. Kenzie was a safe person.

But then she saw him swallow hard as he considered the situation. Kenzie discovering him stalking Bridget was not a good thing. He knew she would be furious about it. And there was the question of how she had known to look for him there.

Kenzie motioned for Zachary to roll down the window, and he did.

"Uh. Kenzie." He licked his lips. "I was just…"

She glared at him, wondering what excuse he was actually going to come up with. But he looked away from her and didn't finish the sentence.

"It's time to go home," Kenzie told him in a calm, even tone. "You've missed dinner."

Zachary touched his phone, mounted on the dashboard, and the screen came on with the time in big, bright letters. "I… didn't know that it was so late."

"It's dark out," Kenzie pointed out.

"Yeah… I guess it is."

He was the private investigator. He was the one who was supposed to notice subtle clues like that.

"I called you."

He could see the missed call list on his screen and nodded. Kenzie could also see Gordon's name on that list. Zachary darted a glance at her and pressed the button on the screen to dismiss the notifications. He reached for the key in the ignition.

"I'm so sorry… let's go home. I didn't mean to be so late."

Kenzie didn't tell him how she had known where to find him or the fact that she knew it was Bridget's house. He had probably guessed that already, but if they started that discussion out on the street, it could get emotional, and she didn't want him to take off instead of going back to the house. She wanted to know that he was home safe.

"Yes. Let's go home."

He turned the key to start his engine. Kenzie walked back to her car. She let him pull out first, and followed him all the way back to the house.

8

She waited on the street until Zachary got out of his car and walked up the sidewalk to the house. Then she drove around to the garage and let herself in that way.

Zachary stood there, his eyes darting around, knowing that he was in trouble and looking for some kind of escape. She could picture him as a little boy or a young teen, having impulsively gotten himself into a fight or another bad situation and knowing that he was going to be punished for it.

"Do you want something to eat?" Kenzie asked, going to the fridge.

"No. I'm not hungry."

His stomach was probably roiling worse than hers. Kenzie opened the freezer and took out a pint of ice cream. She grabbed a spoon from the drawer and pushed it shut. She sat down at the table. "You sure?"

He nodded and sat down in his usual chair. The one that allowed him to see through the front window. He licked his lips nervously, waiting for Kenzie to begin. Kenzie took a bite of her Chocolate Fudge Explosion and let out a long breath.

"I was worried."

"Yeah." Zachary ran his hand over his hair. "Sorry."

"You didn't answer or call me back. You didn't leave me a note or text or anything. I didn't know what to think. Someone could have shot you on a surveillance job."

"They'd have to see me first," Zachary said wryly.

"I saw you before you saw me."

"Well…" He gulped. "Yeah."

"And Gordon saw you."

Zachary scratched his ear and grimaced. "He did. I thought so. I moved after that, but…"

"You should have come home instead of finding another spot to park."

"Yeah."

"How long has this been going on? How long have you been watching her again?"

"This was the first time—"

"No it wasn't. Don't try to sell me that."

Zachary looked down at the table. He sat there thinking about it while Kenzie ate her ice cream. He was licking his lips a lot and Kenzie knew his mouth was dry. Not just because he was in trouble and trying to get out of it, but also because it was one of the side effects of his meds. And he had probably not had anything to drink while on surveillance. She knew he rationed liquids while on surveillance to avoid other inconveniences. She got up and poured a glass of water from the pitcher in the fridge. She sat back down and slid it across the table to him.

Zachary chugged a few swallows. He held one mouthful in his mouth for a few seconds and then swallowed it. He licked his lips again

"You may as well tell the truth," Kenzie said. "I already know you're watching her. It doesn't matter how long or short it has been, we both already know that you need help. So let's get it all out on the table."

"Not a long time."

Kenzie considered that. She thought about what she knew for

sure. The worries that she'd had and how his daily patterns had changed.

"Since before the virus," she offered.

Zachary considered, then nodded. "But not much. Just… a little before that."

"Since your investigation for Gordon?"

He shook his head. "No. Not that long. But… I think… that was a problem."

Of course it was. He'd been able to get his behavior under control. He'd been managing it for almost two years. And then Gordon came to him, asking him to find out whether Bridget had a lover on the side. Zachary was supposed to surveil her for a few days and then just stop again? Gordon had no concept of how hard it had been for him to stop in the first place. Most people had no idea what it was like to fight the kind of compulsions that Zachary had.

"Have you talked to Dr. B. about this?"

He considered for a moment before shaking his head. "No."

"You know that this is the kind of thing that she's there for. When you have a problem that you need help with, that's why she's there."

"I was just… embarrassed. I didn't want to tell her… I thought I could manage it myself."

Kenzie checked the time on her phone. "I think you should call her."

Zachary shifted. "I'll talk to her on Wednesday."

"Wednesday is couples therapy this week. I think you need to talk to her about this individually first. We could change Wednesday to an individual day, but I've already arranged to take time off for it. And maybe there are things we should discuss together, after you've had a chance to talk to her about it alone."

"I don't want to call her at home."

"At least call to see if you can get on her schedule tomorrow, then."

"Her schedule is fully booked with her regular sessions…"

"You don't know that. She might have a cancellation. Or fit you in at the end of the day. Or else talk to her tonight. She said that we could call her at home. You don't want to have to wait two days to bring it up with her. You'll be a wreck."

He still didn't like the idea. Kenzie stood up. She put her bowl in the dishwasher.

"Go use the bedroom. For privacy. Call her. I'll put on the TV and give you some space."

Looking like he'd been given a death sentence, Zachary got up and shuffled to the bedroom. Kenzie heard him shut the door. She turned on the TV and turned up the volume so that she wouldn't be able to overhear any of the conversation.

9

An FBI agent had been assigned to the Michaels case. Dr. Wiltshire was in the office ahead of Kenzie, having received an early call from Agent Josie Menendez. They were already in Dr. Wiltshire's office deep in conversation when Kenzie arrived, but Dr. Wiltshire had left a message for Kenzie to advise her of the developments and to ask her to join them when she arrived.

All thoughts of Zachary and his difficulties were swept from Kenzie's mind as she copied the electronic files she had prepared onto a USB drive, grabbed herself a cup of coffee from the break room, and hurried to Dr. Wiltshire's office. She knocked on the door and entered without waiting for an invitation. He had already asked her to come into the meeting.

"Ah, Dr. Kirsch," Dr. Wiltshire greeted, nodding to acknowledge her. "Thank you for coming. Agent Menendez, this is Dr. Kenzie Kirsch, my assistant, who also scrubbed in on Mr. Michaels's autopsy."

"Josie," Agent Menendez said, standing up and reaching out to shake Kenzie's hand.

"Kenzie." She shook Menendez's hand and then handed her the USB drive. "Our files on the case."

Menendez, a tall slim woman with Hispanic features, smiled broadly and put it into her pocket. "Talk about service. Thank you very much."

"Kenzie is familiar with all the details of the case," Dr. Wiltshire said. "Feel free to ask her any questions if I'm not around. Or even if I am." He smiled. "It's no secret that Kenzie is actually the one running this office."

Kenzie grinned, her face warming. She didn't have the experience or expertise that Dr. Wiltshire did, but she did try to keep things running efficiently for him. It was nice to be recognized, even if it was hyperbole.

"Glad to meet you," Menendez acknowledged with a nod. "I'm sure I'll have plenty of questions for you. I don't have a medical background, but I pick things up pretty quickly. I will be meeting with Dr. Philemon this afternoon. It may take me a few days to get fully up to speed…"

"But these things don't move as quickly as they do on TV," Dr. Wiltshire filled in.

"Unfortunately, no. It can take months to sort out who had access to all the victims. Even figuring out who the victims are may be tricky. We often don't know more than one or two of them for sure. Then we find out when we catch the killer that they have twenty-seven on their list." Menendez rolled her eyes and shook her head. "Unfortunately, this kind of killer can operate for years without any suspicions being raised. And if there are suspicions…" She shrugged expressively. "They just move to another office or another state and start over."

"What about references?" Kenzie asked, sitting down in the other guest chair at Dr. Wiltshire's desk. "How do they get another job if there have been suspicions?"

"Medical staff are in high demand. References can be faked. Or if the staff member is terminated under some kind of agreement, the former employees may be unable to say anything about their suspicions under a nondisclosure clause. Remember that if you don't have proof… well, you don't want to get sued for slander. So the employer agrees to keep it to himself if the employee will leave quietly."

"But... doesn't that just put other patients at risk? Perpetuate the problem?"

"It does. But as long as they are not *your* patients..."

Kenzie shook her head. "Well, luckily my patients are already dead, so I won't ever have to deal with that scenario."

Dr. Wiltshire laughed appreciatively. "We've never had a patient lodge a complaint," he agreed. "All five-star reviews on Yelp."

They all chuckled.

The meeting with Menendez took a lot longer than Kenzie had expected, considering they really didn't have anything to tell her other than what she had already been informed of. And everything was in the files that Kenzie had given her. But of course Menendez hadn't yet read the files, and she didn't have the medical background to interpret everything when she did. She needed it all explained in layman's terms to be sure she had all the facts she needed to pursue the case.

She felt a little sorry for Dr. Philemon, who was bound to have to deal with an even more intense session with Menendez. He would have to go through all the patients he had identified as unexpected or possibly suspicious deaths and to describe what had happened in each. With the number of patients on the list, it might take him several days. Kenzie didn't envy either of them.

Kenzie escorted Menendez out of the suite of offices and sat down at her reception desk. "Just let me know if you need anything from me," she repeated once more. "I'll do whatever I can to help."

"You're just trying to avoid having to do more work," Menendez joked. "By avoiding getting any more patients through here."

"People are dying to get in," Kenzie agreed, repeating their well-worn joke. "But honestly, we're never going to stop the flow. There will always be more work to do here. But I'd rather not have to worry about a serial killer."

"And as far as we know, most of the victims, if any of the people on Dr. Philemon's list are victims of the same killer, didn't even come through this office."

"No. If they were doctor-attended deaths, then we don't get involved unless the doctor believes there's a reason for us to."

Menendez nodded and shook Kenzie's hand once more. "Thanks for your cooperation. I'll be giving you a call."

Kenzie nodded and said another goodbye, then Menendez walked down to the elevator and took it back upstairs.

Kenzie looked over the last few items to arrive in her email inbox, and then decided to give Zachary a call.

He answered on the second ring. Not deeply focused on a job. Maybe trying to make up for having missed her call when he'd been watching Bridget's house.

"Kenzie?"

"Hey, Zachary. I just wanted to check in and see how you were doing. Taking a short break between jobs, here."

"Oh. I'm okay. How is your morning going?"

"Been busy. Interesting. I'll have to tell you about it later." She wouldn't give him any identifying details, but he would be interested to hear of the involvement of the FBI in one of her cases. That was definitely not in the normal course.

"I'm looking forward to it," he said with interest.

"How about your morning? Anything interesting going on over at Goldman Investigations?" Kenzie didn't want to ask him straight out whether he'd stuck to his work or whether he had been over to watch for Bridget again. She wasn't his parent or his therapist. She didn't want to get stuck in the role of supervising his activities or making him report to her. She didn't want to back him into a corner and put him in the position of either having to admit his faults or to lie to cover them up.

"Nothing big. A new insurance file that I'm doing some preliminary work on. Injury claim."

Which meant that he would have legitimate surveillance to do, watching to see if the purported victim were only pretending to be disabled by an injury while continuing other demanding physical activities when he thought that no one was looking.

"Those are always interesting. Think it's legitimate?"

"The accident is. I've looked through the pictures of the vehicles, and it was a serious accident. Whether the victim has long-term disabling injuries... well, that's what they're paying me to find out."

They had been meeting with Agent Menendez in the boardroom and had, Kenzie thought, answered all her questions, until the FBI agent came up with one more request.

"I'm wondering whether we could borrow Kenzie for a day."

"Borrow her? For what?"

"I'd like to get her thoughts on the hospital geriatric unit. As it is before they find out there is an FBI investigation. Another doctor going in there, just checking up on some things, I think that would be a lot more natural than FBI agents showing up and asking questions."

"Well..." Dr. Wiltshire thought about this. "Yes, I can see that. And Kenzie has done some good work investigating in the field before. But it's not really her job. This case has been passed on to the FBI for your investigation. We've done everything we can on our end with the one body that we have."

"I know. It would be a favor, like I said. It could be a follow up to your autopsy. Before you issue your opinion. Then it isn't like we sent her in as our agent."

"Except that you are."

"But not *really*." Menendez grimaced. "I'm not going to give her questions to ask or any specific instructions. You can give her your instructions on anything you would like to know that would help to further your understanding of what happened to Mr. Michaels. I just… would like someone with a medical background to have some familiarity with the unit, the staff, how things work over there…"

"Don't you have any medical personnel employed by your office? No one with a medical background who could look around?"

"Not without revealing that it was part of an FBI investigation. We have strict protocols for dealing with hospitals and situations like this. I can't really send someone in undercover. To act as a patient or a visiting doctor. It's just not feasible. But Kenzie is here. Or you, but…"

"If I went in, I would attract too much attention," Dr. Wiltshire finished. "People would know there was something going on just as much as they would if you sent an agent in. They would immediately want to know why I was investigating a death they thought to be natural."

"They're going to wonder that anyway, but at least with Kenzie, she's younger, less threatening. Less of a…" Menendez looked for the right word.

"I'm just an underling?" Kenzie suggested. "A gofer? Nobody will think that I'm anyone important? I can just do routine follow-up without anyone thinking anything of it?"

"We want someone who is unobtrusive and nonthreatening," Menendez agreed, not using any of Kenzie's words. "From what I've seen of you and your work, I think that you would be able to provide me with a lot of insight, without attracting attention to yourself."

Kenzie thought of the investigating she had done at the Champlain House care center previously. It had been interesting work. She liked pretending to herself that she was a private investigator like Zachary, wondering what he would do in her circumstances, what questions he would ask to elicit the information he needed. What he would see that she wouldn't. She looked at Dr. Wiltshire to see whether he were inclined to grant Menendez's request. He raised an eyebrow at her, a query as to whether it was something she was interested in doing. If it wasn't, he could just shut Menendez down, and Kenzie wouldn't have to find an excuse.

"I don't mind," she told him, "if you can do without me for a day."

"Well, that's not exactly easy, but I suppose if I have to," he grumbled good-naturedly.

"Wednesday is my early day anyway. I could spend some time at the hospital in the morning and do my appointment in the afternoon, and not actually miss a full day's work."

Dr. Wiltshire nodded. "That sounds reasonable," he agreed. "I'll see if I can get Julie in to help with the phones and public inquiries."

"Great." Menendez gave a big smile. "That is very helpful, Kenzie. Thank you."

Kenzie nodded. "Sure. It sounds like an interesting assignment."

"I'll walk out with you," Menendez offered, following Kenzie from Dr. Wiltshire's office. Kenzie walked with her, thinking about the unit at the hospital and what she should look for while she was there.

"What exactly do you want me to find out?"

"You have good instincts. Just follow your nose… see whether there is anything that raises your suspicions. We will be getting as many records as we can for these cases that Dr. Philemon has identified, trying to track which medical staff were present when. But sometimes there are things you see on the ground that you would not know by just reading files and tables. You don't need to worry about interrogating anyone, because we'll still follow up with a tour of the facilities and speaking to the subjects afterward. I'm just looking for… what someone is going to see when people are not on their guard, like they are when they know there is an FBI investigation under way."

That wasn't particularly helpful. But Kenzie didn't want to get too bogged down in the details anyway. She couldn't go in there with crib notes and a series of questions to ask everyone. It was best if she were just free to follow her own instincts, as Menendez suggested.

"Okay, I can do that."

"So, what do you have Wednesday afternoons?" Menendez asked.

Kenzie glanced at her, surprised by the question. It wasn't any of the agent's business what she was doing on Wednesday after she was finished at the hospital.

"I have… a private medical appointment."

"Oh. I see. Anything to worry about? I hope you're okay…?"

"I'm fine," Kenzie said tersely. "Like I said… it's private."

"Of course, of course," Menendez said, and then proceeded to dig some more. "I'm just hoping it isn't chemo or dialysis or something like that. That would really suck."

"Uh-huh."

"I'm guessing it's not just a dentist appointment, or you'd just say that…"

Kenzie shook her head and didn't answer. The woman was persistent, Kenzie would say that for her. Agent Menendez was probably used to getting what she was after.

10

Kenzie took a walk through the geriatric unit. It looked pretty much like any other hospital unit that she had visited or worked in. The patients were all older, of course, but that was true of many hospital units. As people got older, things broke down.

It was quiet. The nurses talked to each other in low tones, and there weren't many loud visitors disrupting the whole unit. There was an occasional yell from a man partway down the left side of the ward. Kenzie wasn't sure whether he were in pain or perhaps had dementia. No one else seemed to be paying much attention to him, so she assumed that it had been going on for some time and everybody was tuning him out for the sake of their own sanity.

After having a look around, she approached the nurse at the nursing station in the middle of the ward.

"Hi. I'm Dr. Kenzie Kirsch. I think Dr. Philemon told you that I would be coming?"

"Yes, he did mention something," the heavyset nurse agreed. Her name tag read Geraldine Pierce.

"I guess… were you on duty the day that Mr. Michaels passed?"

Pierce looked her over with a gaze that matched her name. She raised an eyebrow. "I imagine Dr. Philemon has probably already told you that."

"Well, no. He didn't give me any particulars."

"I don't see why the Medical Examiner has any interest in Mr. Michaels's death. He was an old man. He was sick. There's no reason for the medical examiner's office to involve itself in his death."

So Dr. Philemon had not apprised her of the fact that he was the one who had requested Mr. Michaels's case be reviewed. Did that mean that she was a suspect, or just that Dr. Philemon was playing his cards close to the chest and wasn't giving anyone any information on his suspicions or what the Medical Examiner's Office had turned up so far?

"There are cases that the Medical Examiner's Office has a duty to review," Kenzie said, keeping it as vague as possible. "I take it that as far as you knew, everything was routine with Mr. Michaels's care and his passing?"

"Like I said, he was sick," Pierce repeated, her voice firm.

Kenzie nodded. "He was in for treatment of kidney stones?"

"Well, it was more complex than that," Pierce waffled.

"Oh, yes?"

"Well there are laws," she said. "I can't give you any private details about Mr. Michaels's medical condition or care."

"Actually, since he's dead and it's the Medical Examiner's Office making inquiries, those privacy laws are not in play. We don't need a subpoena for information."

Pierce looked as if she doubted that.

"So, how long was he here?" Kenzie inquired pleasantly, looking away. It was always a good policy to start with easy questions and then work her way to the more complex or controversial ones. It was harder for a person to stop answering once they started. The brain liked to continue down the same path on which it started.

"He had been here for a week or so." Pierce hesitated, then

tapped the query into the computer at her desk and looked at the result. "Six days. He was admitted through emergency."

"He was in quite a bit of pain?"

"Yes. In case you don't know, kidney stones are one of the most painful medical conditions. Similar to childbirth." Pierce's eyes went over Kenzie, assessing her. "But I take it you haven't been through that either."

"No. I haven't." Kenzie's anger flared, but she kept her voice even and pleasant. She didn't appreciate being judged by the nurse, even if she were correct in assessing that Kenzie's hips had not widened during pregnancy and delivery.

Nurse Pierce shrugged as if to say that Kenzie couldn't understand that kind of pain if she hadn't been through it.

"He was on painkillers, then? Narcotic?"

"Of course. It would be medical malpractice not to give the man some kind of painkiller when he was suffering with kidney stones. But he didn't have a reaction to the medication. He just…" She shrugged. "His heart went. It's a lot for an elderly man to go through."

"It is," Kenzie agreed, gritting her teeth as she smiled.

"He wasn't given too much, either," Pierce insisted. "We are very careful here. You can check our records."

"I haven't heard otherwise," Kenzie assured her. "You seem to be under the impression that I'm here to find fault with your nursing. I'm not."

"Why else would you be here?"

"Because it's my job to review the circumstances surrounding the death of one of our patients." Kenzie continued to smile pleasantly, as if she were perfectly comfortable having to face the big, obstinate woman.

"I suppose your boss is too good to come here himself. So he sends a…" Nurse Pierce looked at her and didn't say whatever word she had been considering. "One of his staff instead. How long have you even been with the office? You don't look old enough to be out of medical school."

"I'm flattered. I've been with Dr. Wiltshire for a couple of years now. But I'm sure you've seen a lot of doctors who look younger than me. Some of the doctors graduating now... I swear they don't look a day over eighteen."

Pierce nodded, smiling and showing her teeth. An attempt at looking good-humored even if she weren't really amused by Kenzie's comment.

"Yes, that's true. Some of the baby faces we get through here now! And their training..." She shook her head. "You have to wonder if they are even qualified to take a pulse, let alone to perform surgery or some of the other medical procedures that they are expected to."

Kenzie chuckled, nodding. "I remember when I first had to start treating real patients. I was terrified. I didn't feel like I was competent to do anything. Especially telling the nurses what to do, when half of them had twenty years of experience to my... zero."

"Well, you wouldn't guess it by hearing any of them. They seem to be just fine ordering the nursing staff around as if we were their personal slaves. It's shocking. The *privilege* these young doctors seem to have, right out of the womb. If I had ever talked that way to my elders..."

"It's a different world. Helicopter mothers. Millennials. Phones that can do everything but write prescriptions themselves."

"But all of the technology in the world is no substitute for good old-fashioned know-how. You wouldn't believe some of the young doctors we get through here who make prescriptions based on what they read on their phones." Nurse Pierce shook her head. "No experience, and they're taking their advice from Google."

"You have to keep them in hand. I'll bet you have to do a lot of hand-holding and explaining things to them."

"You'd be right." Nurse Pierce changed direction suddenly. "I don't want you getting the wrong idea about Dr. Philemon, though. He's one of the good ones."

"Not a snot-nosed brat?"

"No. He studies. You can tell. And he's always asking the more experienced staff about their experience and thoughts. Very respectful, recognizes that he doesn't know everything and that some of us might have picked up a few tricks along the way." She nodded approvingly.

"I'm so glad to hear that. I've only spoken to him on the phone so far, but he seemed very… genuine and down to earth. And like he knew what he was talking about. He's not right out of medical school."

"No. Older than you. Although you are…" Pierce hesitated, looking at Kenzie. "You didn't go straight into medicine, am I right?"

"Yes. You're right. I have a few wasted years there where I was trying to figure out what to do with myself. So I'm a bit older than some of the doctors that I came up with."

"And Dr. Phil—that's what we call him, you know. It's a little funny—Dr. Phil is older than you. In his thirties. He's still young compared to those of us with some experience. But he's always respectful. Willing to admit when he is wrong or if he doesn't know the answer to something. A different kind of doctor than a lot of those that we breed now, if you know what I mean."

"He seemed very competent," Kenzie agreed. She shifted her feet, trying to figure out the best way to shift the direction of the interview. "Sorry, I think I got a little sidetracked. Mr. Michaels. He was here for a couple of weeks. In a lot of pain. On antibiotics?"

"Yes. He had an infection and he wasn't doing very well. We had switched to an IV antibiotic and were hoping it would make the difference. But some of the infections that we treat here, it takes a few different antibiotics before we find the one that will work."

"Antibiotic misuse," Kenzie agreed. "It leads to resistant bacteria."

"Doesn't seem like it matters how many times you tell someone that they have to finish their full prescription. They stop once they're feeling better. Then it comes back, stronger, and we have to give them something stronger to even touch it. They say that between that and the antibiotics used in the meat industry, that before long we're going to end up right back where we were a couple of hundred years ago, without any effective antibiotics. Can you imagine? Do you know the number of people who used to die from what we now consider treatable infections? Babies and children. Women in childbirth. And patients like these?" She made a circular motion to include the rooms around them in the geriatric unit. "Older people whose immune systems have taken a beating? Life expectancies were so much shorter. One infection… and that could be the end of grandma and grandpa. Living to be one hundred used to be a big thing, almost no one ever achieved or even thought of being able to achieve such a thing."

"I hope we never see the day when antibiotics are completely ineffective."

"You just watch. We're on our way there now."

Kenzie shook her head grimly. "I hope not. Did Mr. Michaels show any improvement? With his infection? The kidney stones? Were they going to do surgery for the kidney stones?"

"He'd been through one round of ultrasound treatment. You know, trying to break them up in a non-invasive procedure. That didn't work, so they were looking at doing a basket retrieval next."

"Minimally invasive. Were there any concerns about that? Suggestions that it might be too much for him?"

"No. He was in generally good health. Infections and kidney stones are treatable. He didn't have any major problems. Heart or respiratory. Cancer. Nothing like that. He would have handled the treatment just fine."

"If he had survived."

Pierce nodded. "We couldn't have predicted that. Sometimes… there are other conditions that the doctors don't know about. Symptoms that the patient doesn't report or things that he isn't even aware of. I guess… maybe he did have heart problems.

Or maybe it was an embolism or a stroke." She shrugged her big, round shoulders. "I don't know what you found."

And Kenzie wasn't about to tell her. Nurse Pierce, like all the rest of the staff on the unit, was a suspect. If Pierce had been the one to administer potassium chloride, then she already knew Michaels's cause of death. She might have been fishing to see whether the Medical Examiner's Office had found anything yet. Kenzie hoped that she didn't give anything away in her facial expression or body language.

"I would like to talk to some of the rest of the staff while I'm here. I assume that everyone else on duty here was employed when Mr. Michaels passed?"

"Yes," Pierce said slowly, as if looking for some other answer. "We haven't hired anyone new since then. But not everyone who is on now was on at the time that he died."

"No, I understand that. I'm just interested in talking to people, getting a feel for the unit. It seems like a very warm, peaceful place."

Pierce was apparently mollified by the compliment. She nodded vigorously. "Of course, it's never good to have to go to the hospital, but we try to make everyone's stays here just as pleasant as we can. If you can't be home, we want them to be at home here." She gave Kenzie a sugary smile.

"Yes," Kenzie agreed, and turned away so that she didn't have to look at the sickly sweet expression.

11

D espite what she said, Kenzie was not overly impressed by the unit. Like many hospitals, it was a combination of both the antiseptically clean and years of neglect. The floors and walls were stained. Furniture in the family visiting areas looked worn but was not ripped up or obviously mended. The TVs in the visiting rooms were old.

Everything in the rooms looked as Kenzie expected it to. Not too many surfaces to be wiped down. Clean white beds and patients with terrycloth robes wrapped around their thin bodies and hospital johnnies. Quietly murmured conversations beside the beds of sick and dying loved ones.

"Can I help you?" A young nurse asked as she came out of one of the patient rooms, immediately identifying Kenzie as someone who didn't belong. "Are you looking for someone?"

"I'm Dr. Kenzie Kirsch. From the Medical Examiner's Office." Kenzie didn't offer her hand this time. Who knew what procedure the nurse had just finished with and how well she attended to her hygiene afterward. "I've just been talking to Nurse Pierce, and I'm taking a look around and meeting the staff who are on today." Kenzie looked at the nurse's name badge. "Nurse Loudwell."

She nodded. "Mostly they just call me Nurse Cherrie around here. It's nice to meet you. So... you didn't need anything?"

"Just having a walk around. Have you been here long?"

A crease appeared between Nurse Cherrie's brows. "Do you mean today, or how long I've been working in this unit?"

"I meant how long you've been working here."

"Well, I'm not, actually. I fill in some days when they are short. I need the extra hours, and it seems like some units never have enough staff. So I'm on call if they need anyone to fill in here. If someone is sick or has to pick up their kids from school." She shrugged with one shoulder.

"Ah, well that's good of you. So... were you on when Mr. Michaels was here? He was here for a couple of weeks."

"Oh sure, I remember him. Nice old guy. He, uh, passed, didn't he?"

"Yes, he did. He was friendly with you? You enjoyed working with him?"

"Sure. I mean, he was in a lot of pain. The kidney stone patients always are. It can make them kind of crabby, but he was always careful of what he said. Didn't snap back or complain too much. But you could tell... poor guy. What was it, do you know? Sometimes stones can cause internal damage. Blockages or perforations."

"No, I don't think it was the kidney stones."

"Oh. Well, that's good. Not something that they could have prevented, then. I think Dr. Philemon is a pretty good doctor. Young, you know, so some of the oldsters around here don't trust him, but I think he did a good job."

"I don't think it was anything caused by negligence. I think Mr. Michaels received the care that he needed."

"Ah, that's good." Nurse Cherrie nodded. "Glad to hear it." She cocked her head slightly, not sure how to properly disengage from the conversation. "Well... good luck then, on whatever it is you're doing here."

Kenzie didn't offer a more full explanation. Nurse Cherrie

nodded once more, then went her own way, looking back one last time to try to figure out why Kenzie was there.

Kenzie couldn't say exactly what she was looking for herself. Someone like Cherrie would look good for an Angel of Death killing. A nurse who regularly subbed in the unit when she was needed could easily be overlooked when Dr. Philemon or the FBI started making lists of suspects. She might not appear on the staff lists. She might not have even been on duty the day that Michaels had died, but could still have come and gone without attracting any suspicion. People were used to seeing her and wouldn't think anything of it or remember later that she had been there.

She continued her tour of the ward. As she passed one door, she could hear a man moaning within. She stopped and listened for a moment. He didn't call out or talk to anyone else, but kept moaning to himself. Kenzie hesitated for a moment, then entered. The bed nearest the door was empty. The moaning man lay in the second bed.

"Hey, are you okay?" Kenzie asked softly.

His eyes flew open, startled by her presence. He moaned again, his watery blue eyes unfocused. "It hurts," he complained.

Kenzie looked at the pump hooked up to the IV tube in his arm. But it would appear from the screen of the pump that he had already hit his maximum dosage of painkillers.

"Do you want me to get a nurse?"

"They won't come," he said. "Who are you? Aren't you a nurse?"

He continued to moan as Kenzie answered. "I was just walking by and heard you. I can try to get someone for you if you like."

"They just tell me to stop calling them," he explained. He gave a sharp cry as if he'd been hit with a stabbing pain instead of the pain that had been making him moan.

Kenzie couldn't help remembering the nephrology unit Amanda had been in before she had died. The nurses there were all friendly and pleasant. They all knew Amanda and Lisa by name, and some of them learned Kenzie's name too. But they did tend to get irritated with multiple calls over the same issues. They promised to page the doctors, who were never on duty when they were needed. They promised to pass messages along. And they got irritable and reminded them that there was nothing else they could do about Amanda's sickness and pain. They did their best to take care of her but, in the end, there was nothing else that they could do. When Amanda's breathing had gotten too bad, she had been whisked away. And that was the last they had seen of her before the end.

Kenzie realized that she had closed her eyes with the remembered pain of it all. It had been awful, losing her little sister like that. Seeing her mother's acute pain and grief over the loss. Her father's emptiness and anger that the laws had not given them all the tools they needed to save Amanda. He had done everything he could for her, including skirting legal and moral issues and, in the end, that was what had killed her.

She realized that she was holding the patient's hand. It was thin and fragile in her grasp. He gave her a tiny squeeze, staring up into her face, seeming confused and lost, like a little child instead of an old man.

"Is it… kidney failure? Stones?" Kenzie gazed at him, feeling his pain and her own merging together in her chest.

"Cancer," the man said. "It's eating away at my insides. I can feel it, burning holes through everything." He moaned and pressed his other hand to his mouth. "A drink. I need a drink, please."

Kenzie looked at the side table, where there was a small cup of ice chips. She used the plastic spoon to take one out and place it in the man's mouth. He sucked it, making smacking sounds, and closed his eyes again, moaning and sliding into the pain.

Kenzie didn't stick around to find out whether he had known Mr. Michaels. She tiptoed out of the room, doing her best not to disturb the man any further.

There were cheerful voices down the hall. They seemed to

intrude on the ward, like they didn't belong there. Didn't the speakers know that people were sick and dying? They should be quiet, like at a library, not allowing their happy, raised voices to disrupt people's peaceful moments. But despite the feeling that the voices didn't belong, Kenzie found herself walking toward them, curious as to whom they belonged.

She found a couple of volunteers talking to the nursing staff.

Candy stripers, they sometimes called hospital volunteers whose job it was to make things easier for the patients and to bring a little joy and relief into the dreary hospital setting. One of the volunteers had a thin leather satchel or briefcase over her arm. The other had a dog in harness.

Kenzie eyed the dog. She was still leery of dogs around patients after her experience with the virus. She wasn't about to pet the dog or allow it to lick her, that was for sure. She sidled closer to the group of people, to listen in on the conversation without forcing herself into their little circle.

"Blue is excited to be here," the young woman with the dog said. "Where do you think we should start? Who could use a cuddle today?"

"Why don't you try Mr. Damon in room 32," one of the nurses suggested. "He's been feeling lonely lately. No one comes to visit him, and he's an old grouch if you try to engage with him and cheer him up. I'll bet Blue is just what he needs."

The candy striper nodded cheerfully and led Blue toward room 32.

"And..." the nurse looked at the other volunteer. "What are you doing today?"

The woman with the satchel was a little older, but still had that "glow" of a volunteer who knew she was there to make someone's day. She smiled and indicated her bag. "I'm writing letters for people. There are lots of people around here who can't use computers or phones to reach their loved ones, and letters are a great way for them to connect."

The nurse nodded. "And it keeps them busy, gives them something to think about other than how miserable they are feeling."

Kenzie thought about the patient she had just left. She didn't think that dictating a letter would be possible for him. He would need something quite a bit more powerful to get his mind off his pain. Like maybe a higher dose of narcotics. The man was dying of cancer; they could afford to give him a little more relief. If it shortened his life by a day or two, that didn't matter. He would at least have better quality of life for those last few days.

"Try Mrs. Brown in 35. She'll chatter your ear off. It will give her a way to direct her energy."

"Sounds good," the volunteer agreed cheerfully.

Kenzie watched her walk off to visit with the patients. She turned back to Nurse Stevens, a male nurse who had taken Nurse Pierce's place at the nursing station at least temporarily.

"Do you get a lot of volunteers in this unit?"

"A good number," Stevens agreed, looking Kenzie up and down. "Pediatrics probably gets the most, but geriatrics is right up there. People recognize that a lot of them don't have anyone else and could really use the lift."

"That's great. Really nice to see it. How are they vetted?"

Stevens blinked several times. "I'm not involved in that part of the program. You would have to ask someone in administration."

"Are records kept? Of who is here when?"

"Of course. They all check in and out." He leaned on the reception desk. "Why all the questions?"

"I'm with the ME's office. Just looking into a couple of things."

"Why?" His tone was somewhat confrontational.

"Because when we investigate a death, sometimes there are questions that need to be asked outside the morgue. Circumstances surrounding the death. Who might have been around. The events leading up to the death."

"What death? Who are you talking about?"

Kenzie didn't like the confrontational attitude, but there was no point in avoiding his questions. He just had to ask Nurse Pierce or someone else Kenzie had talked to and he would hear the whole story.

"Mr. Michaels."

"Michaels. Our Mr. Michaels? Why would you be investigating that death?"

"That really isn't any of your business. There are certain deaths that we are required to investigate, and Mr. Michaels is one of them. We expect cooperation from the staff."

"Who's not cooperating? I don't like strangers showing up in my ward asking questions. I'm sure you wouldn't be too happy about anyone who showed up at your office and started asking nosy questions about your job either."

"No, I probably wouldn't," Kenzie agreed.

He looked surprised at her response. Whatever barb had been on his tongue to deploy next was checked. He closed his mouth and looked at her.

"But I still need to investigate the case that's been assigned to me," Kenzie said. "Even if you don't like it. Even if I don't like it."

"Why Mr. Michaels?"

"Like I said, it was assigned to me. You take care of the people and duties that you're assigned to, right?"

He nodded his agreement. "Of course. Wouldn't do me much good to avoid it."

"No point in getting fired," Kenzie agreed. "You're here as a nurse, so you nurse the people you are assigned to."

"Yeah."

"Were you on the floor the day Mr. Michaels passed?"

"No. I was off that day."

Kenzie nodded. If he were lying, the records that the hospital passed on to Menendez would tell them so. But she suspected he was telling the truth. And if so, then he was not a suspect in Mr. Michaels's death.

"Do you have the records for the volunteers? Do you know

whether either of those two was on the day that Mr. Michaels passed?"

"Why does that matter? Why would you care if a couple of volunteers were around the day he died?"

Kenzie didn't answer. She just waited for his answer. Stevens glared at her for a few seconds longer, then broke eye contact and went around the desk to the computer.

"It isn't like volunteers are involved in patient treatment," he pointed out. "As you see… they take a service dog in, or write letters, or read books. They are not involved in the actual patient care."

But that didn't mean that one of them could not have injected something into Mr. Michaels's IV. They didn't even have to be able to find a vein to administer poison. Anyone could stick a needle through the IV port and inject potassium chloride, even if they were squeamish.

"Were there any volunteers on the day that he died?"

Stevens tapped a query into the computer and moused around a bit before he was able to find the report or filter that he was looking for. He looked at the data displayed on his screen.

"Roda, the one doing the letter writing, she was around," he said finally. "But I still don't see what that has to do with anything."

"Do you keep records of who she worked with that day?"

"No, just that she was here."

"I'll maybe talk to her, then."

Stevens shook his head. "That's ridiculous."

12

Kenzie followed in the direction that Roda had gone, looking into each room until she saw the young woman sitting at Mrs. Brown's bedside. Kenzie hesitated. She probably shouldn't interrupt the letter-writing process.

Mrs. Brown saw her in the doorway and said something, and Roda turned around to see who was there.

"Hi."

Kenzie walked into the room. "Oh, hello. I'm sorry, I didn't mean to interrupt you."

Looking down at the pen and paper on Roda's lap, Kenzie saw that she hadn't yet started on a letter. Maybe she wouldn't even get that far. It could just be a way to get people to start talking, and the planned letter would never even get written. Like getting someone to talk about herself by offering to write her memoirs.

"Did you need something?" Roda asked, her brows drawing down.

"Well, I was just hoping to talk to you for a few minutes. We can set up a time later, since you're busy right now…"

Roda looked at Mrs. Brown, who seemed unperturbed by the interruption. The old woman smiled at Kenzie, unusually white dentures gleaming from her wizened face. "Oh, that's okay, dear. I don't mind an extra visitor anytime."

Kenzie smiled back at her. "How are you doing, Mrs. Brown? I hope you're not in too much discomfort."

"The worst thing is the boredom. I'm used to being able to get around to visit all my friends. I'm a volunteer, you know, I help to take care of old people."

Kenzie was a little startled by this assertion. Mrs. Brown laughed merrily.

"I know, you think that I'm old, but I get around pretty well. There are a lot of people a lot worse off than I am. I take people meals, sit and visit with them, help to do a few things around the house. Tidying up, washing dishes, making sure their pills are all sorted into containers. I have my whole route…" She sighed. "But here I am, sidelined by a little infection."

"I'm sure you'll be able to get home soon," Roda said. "You're a lot more perky than you were the last time I was by."

"Yes… that nice young doctor said he wants to keep me for another day or two, and then he'll let me go home. In the meantime…" She folded her hands over her chest, giving the appearance of someone trying to appear peaceful and serene. "I try to behave myself and not bother the nurses too much."

Kenzie laughed at her contrite expression. "Well, I'm sorry that you have to stay here so long. I'm glad that you're getting better, though."

"Hospitals are a necessary evil, I suppose," Mrs. Brown said. "Though I would have preferred to just take antibiotics at home."

Roda shook her head at this. "You were far too sick to stay at home. You needed IV antibiotics, and you couldn't take those at home."

"Sometimes you can," Mrs. Brown told her. "They put the IV in and give you a little pump in a belt bag. Gladys had one a few months ago, and she could go wherever she wanted to."

"But you were too sick. You needed to stay in bed, and Dr.

Philemon knows very well that you won't stay in bed if you have any say in it."

Mrs. Brown nodded and laughed.

Kenzie drew over a chair and sat down so that she wouldn't be towering over Mrs. Brown. An intimate discussion group. Maybe having Mrs. Brown there would actually make Kenzie's questions seem less intrusive.

"You like Dr. Philemon?"

"He's a nice young man," Mrs. Brown agreed.

Kenzie looked at Roda to extend the question to her. She shrugged, seeming surprised at the question.

"Yes, he's a good doctor. I don't really work with the doctors, I just interface with the patients…"

"I've only talked to him on the phone," Kenzie offered, "but he seemed like a nice man. And very professional. Like he knows what he's talking about as a doctor. Sometimes you get the feeling that a doctor is just not quite up to speed. But not him."

She waited to see whether they would agree with her or not.

"Oh, yes," Mrs. Brown agreed. "He listens to me. So many doctors, if you're a woman or if you're over sixty, they think you don't know what you're talking about. I've lived in this body for eighty years! I know when something is not right."

"I've always thought he was a good doctor," Roda contributed. "I mean… I'm not a patient, so I can't really say, but he seems like he knows what he's talking about."

"Yeah. One of his patients here was Mr. Michaels…?"

"Harry," the older woman said immediately. "He was a nice man. I was pretty sick when I got here, but I have met him before."

"I saw him." Roda brushed her fingers over the paper mounted on the clipboard in her lap. "He was here for a couple of weeks. But he was too sick for me to do anything with him."

"He was in a lot of pain?"

She nodded. "Yeah. Poor guy."

"Were you here when he died?"

"Such a tragic thing." Mrs. Brown shook her head, her eyes going shiny.

"I was here…" Roda seemed uncomfortable with the question. "Not like I was in the room or anything, but I heard the code, saw the nurses rushing in."

"Dr. Philemon wasn't here when it happened?"

"No. He wasn't around. It was just the nurses, an intern…" Roda trailed off uncertainly. "I don't really know how many people were in there to help him."

"Did they do CPR? Use the defibrillator?"

"I wasn't in the room," Roda repeated. "I don't know what they did. They worked on him for a while. But not at *long* time."

"It never seems much like they show it on TV," Mrs. Brown said. "They like to make it all very dramatic on TV. Bringing the person back from the dead. But in the hospital… well, especially here, where it's just old folks… it isn't like that. There isn't any panic, you know. They do what they can, and then it's over."

Kenzie nodded. "You probably wouldn't want them taking heroic measures." Then she felt awkward saying such a thing to Mrs. Brown. The implication that older people didn't have as much to live for or that their lives were not as valuable made her squirm. Mrs. Brown was full of life. Someone who might live for another twenty years, helping out her less-vigorous friends. "What I mean is, you might not want to be kept alive on a ventilator, or risk having a bunch of ribs broken, that kind of thing."

"Oh, I know dear." Mrs. Brown patted Kenzie's hand. "You have to decide just how much you want them to do. What kind of quality of life you would have afterward. I wouldn't want to be a vegetable. I don't want to be a burden on other people or spend the rest of my life hooked up to a machine. My kids are grown and I've arranged with Shirley that she would take my cats. Everything is in order when it's my time. But it's not my time yet."

Kenzie laughed and smiled at her. "I'm glad it's not. You seem as though you still have a lot to give to the world."

"Thank you! That's a very nice way of putting it."

Kenzie looked back at Roda, trying to figure out how to squeeze any more information out of her. She hadn't been in the room when Michaels had died, so she didn't have much information to give Kenzie. Merely being on the unit didn't make her a suspect. Unless she'd been on the unit when a lot of the other people had died. Kenzie couldn't really see her sneaking into patients' rooms and poisoning them, then sneaking back out again before she was discovered. These Angel of Death killers usually liked to be in on the action, not waiting in another room for the end. But it was possible that Roda still had information she didn't know might be important.

"Which nurses were here when Mr. Michaels died? Which ones were helping him, I mean? That must have been very upsetting for them."

"Well, I guess if they're working here, they have to get used to the fact that some of their patients will die," Roda said slowly. She looked at Mrs. Brown. "I mean… you can't know just by how old someone is, of course, but…"

"We're obviously closer to our expiry dates," Mrs. Brown contributed, making them all laugh awkwardly.

"Yeah, I guess. I think they have to… develop a thick skin. Not let themselves get too close to people."

"Was Nurse Pierce on that day?" Kenzie prompted, hoping to get some names.

Roda thought about it. "Yes, I think she was one of the nurses who responded. And… Nurse Crawford… the new nurse with the blond, curly hair… and I don't know the names of the interns; it seems as if they come and go so quickly."

Kenzie tried to imprint these names on her memory. She didn't want to take out her phone to make note of it immediately. That would probably shut Roda up. "Did he have any family? Mr. Michaels?"

"I don't have any idea," Roda shook her head. "I've never seen anyone visiting him."

"He had a son," Mrs. Brown advised. "He lives out on the

coast. I don't think he made it in for a visit before Logan passed. No one knew… it was unexpected. He didn't have any way of knowing that his father was going to die during this hospital stay. He's been here before. But this time… it was a surprise for everyone, I think."

13

Before leaving the office for the day, Kenzie wrote down notes of her visit to the hospital for Agent Menendez, replaying her memories of her visit on Tuesday and consulting the few notes that she'd jotted down once she had left the unit. It was important to get down her impressions before they started to fade. Not just to give Menendez a clear picture of the people she had spoken with at the hospital, but also in case she ever had to testify in court about any of it. It was much better to be able to refer to notes made at the time than to be trying to recall things over the months or years without any memory aid.

She gave the memo a read-through before emailing it off to Menendez, then checked the time to make sure she wasn't running late for her couples therapy appointment with Dr. B and Zachary.

She wasn't looking forward to it.

Couples therapy wasn't her favorite time. That was one reason they had instituted the ice cream treat after each session. So that they'd be rewarded for going to sessions and it would be easier to go back. And she knew that it would be an even more difficult session than usual, with the revelation that Zachary had again been stalking Bridget.

Dr. Boyle welcomed Zachary and Kenzie into her office and they sat down in their usual places. Zachary was walking slowly and casting sideways glances at Kenzie. Trying to assess her mood and how she would approach their couples session given the latest developments. Kenzie did her best to ignore the looks and to pretend that it was just a regular session, no different from any other.

"So…" Dr. B leaned back in her chair and steepled her fingers together. "How are you both today?"

"Good," Kenzie said, trying not to let it sound clipped or perfunctory. There was no "I'm fine" in Dr. Boyle's office when things were clearly not fine. Hopefully, the "good" would be acceptable and they would move on to Zachary, which was where the focus needed to be.

Dr. B looked at her and didn't say anything. Kenzie looked away, waiting for Zachary's answer.

"You already know how I am," Zachary said finally. "I… screwed up. I don't know what to do."

The therapist nodded her understanding. "How do you feel about it?"

"I know that I'm supposed to stay away from Bridget. And I want to. I just… needed to check on her. With the pregnancy, and the Huntington's, I've been worried. I had to see her to reassure myself that she was okay."

"So you were justified?"

Zachary shifted. He looked at Kenzie, but she didn't have anything to say. "No. I didn't say that. Just saying… what was in my head. I've been really concerned about her."

"But she has a partner taking care of her, doesn't she? She's not alone."

"I know. But Gordon works long hours. It's fine if she can call him if she's in trouble… but what if she can't? What if she can't get to the phone or dial his number? How would he know?"

"Doesn't she have an assistant?" Kenzie asked. "I thought they had someone coming in to help her?"

"Yes. But she's not there all the time that Gordon is gone. She comes in early, and then when she's done everything that Bridget needs help with, she leaves. So... Bridget is alone for the rest of the day."

"If she was in danger, then they would get her more help, don't you think? They have all kinds of money. It isn't like full-time help would be beyond their means. If Bridget wanted someone there full-time, they would have someone there full-time. Or if Gordon thought that's what she needed."

Zachary scratched the back of his neck. He didn't nod or acknowledge her comment. "What's going to happen when the babies are born? Are they going to have a full-time nanny? Bridget can't take care of them by herself."

"From what you said, I thought that Bridget was still in the early stages of Huntington's," Dr. B said. "So what makes you think that she won't be able to take care of them?"

"Bridget doesn't even like children. She never wanted to have kids in the first place. She doesn't have any experience." Zachary shook his head. "Everything... her health, her mental state. She never even wanted to get pregnant."

"She used in vitro. So clearly, she wanted to get pregnant," Dr. Boyle reminded him. "What you mean is, she didn't want to get pregnant when you were with her."

"No. She didn't want my babies," Zachary muttered.

"And that hurt you. Do you think that might be part of why you are obsessed with her pregnancy?"

"Yes. Sure. I haven't been able to get it out of my head ever since I found out."

It was the first time Kenzie had heard him admit that.

"But I was doing good. I was still... staying away from her. Mostly." A glance in Kenzie's direction.

"What does 'mostly' mean?" Kenzie asked, using as neutral a tone as she was able.

"I still… ran into her once or twice. Saw her when she was out shopping or getting gas."

"Unintentionally?"

He nodded and licked his lips.

"Or maybe sometimes intentionally?" Kenzie suggested.

"No. Not on purpose. It wasn't like that."

Kenzie wasn't sure she believed him. She suspected that he had probably driven past her house, even if he hadn't stopped to watch her. Maybe shopped at some of her favorite stores just to see if he happened to see her. The first time they had run into Bridget at a restaurant and Bridget had blown up over it, Kenzie had assumed that it was Bridget's problem. In a town the size of Roxboro, you couldn't expect *never* to run into a person anywhere. And if they both shared similar tastes and had gotten used to dining certain places, then they were bound to run into each other occasionally.

But now, she wasn't so sure that Bridget had been completely wrong. Zachary had been tracking her. Had watched her house. And if he occasionally bumped into her around town, it wasn't beyond belief that he had engineered it that way.

But she let it go. Dr. B could call him out if she believed he was shading the truth. Zachary looked back at the therapist, licking his lips again.

"I was doing good before," he maintained. "I was staying away from her."

"And the pregnancy changed that?"

He shook his head. "Maybe a little," he admitted. "But…" He fiddled with the zipper on his jacket. "It was when Gordon hired me. That's when…" He trailed off and shrugged.

Dr. Boyle frowned. She looked at Kenzie to see whether this made sense to her. Apparently, this had never come up in Zachary's sessions with her previously.

An oversight on Zachary's part? Definitely not.

"Gordon hired Zachary to look into whether Bridget was seeing someone else," Kenzie explained. "And to look into the pregnancy."

"What does 'look into' mean?"

"Put her under surveillance," Zachary said in a low voice. He cleared his throat when his voice cracked. He looked down.

"Her current partner asked the man she accused of stalking her to follow her around?"

"Uh-huh."

"I thought this guy was supposed to be one of our brightest minds?"

Kenzie snorted. She couldn't help it. She tried to quell the impulse to laugh and make a big joke of it. Venting her feelings about Gordon would distract them from the real issues. "In some things, maybe."

Dr. Boyle let out a long sigh. "And surprise, surprise, returning to your addiction sent you tumbling off the wagon."

Zachary raised his eyes to study Dr. B's face, trying to read every detail of her expression.

"No, it doesn't get you off the hook," the therapist said. "Because no matter what triggered this behavior, we still have to deal with it. Don't we?"

Zachary nodded.

"Is this something you *want* to overcome?"

"Yes." Zachary's voice was nearly inaudible. But Kenzie was glad to hear his answer, even if it was quiet. She was afraid that Zachary got too much of a hit from feel-good neurotransmitters when he saw Bridget. That he wouldn't want to stop, even if he knew it could lead to Kenzie breaking up with him.

"Okay." Dr. B gave a brisk nod. "We need to look at the med cocktail, among other things. It was helping before. I wonder whether we need to change anything."

"Can't change anything right now," Zachary said. "I can't afford to… go on a med holiday right now."

"No. We don't want to take you off of anything before Christmas," Dr. Boyle agreed. It was the most dangerous time of the year for Zachary. The time of year when historically he had attempted suicide or self-harmed. "But we might increase dosages or try adding in something new."

"Nothing new," Zachary insisted. "If there are new side effects or if it interferes with something that I'm already on…"

The woman's lips pressed together as she considered this objection. "Are you taking everything as directed?"

Zachary nodded.

Dr. B's gaze shifted to Kenzie. Kenzie held her hands up.

"I don't supervise his meds. That's his responsibility. I know he takes morning and evening meds. I know he gets prescriptions refilled. I don't keep track of when he is taking each pill or when he is supposed to."

Dr. B nodded. "That's perfectly fine. I don't think we need to make it your responsibility. But I know that Zachary has decided to stop taking meds in the past." She looked back at Zachary and raised her brows.

"Yes," Zachary admitted. "It's my body and I know how they affect me. I only take ADHD meds when I need to. I only take anti-anxiety or sleep aids when I really have to. Not every day."

"And the anti-depressants?"

"Every day."

She nodded. "And you believe they are still working?"

"Yes."

"Are they helping with the compulsions or only the depression?"

Zachary was silent for a few moments, considering this. Kenzie wondered whether it was a question that she would have been able to answer if it were her. Was it possible for Zachary to slice and dice his brain activity that way? To see the cause and effect that each med had on each symptom?

"It was easier when I started taking them," he said. "Two years ago. I think they helped me to… put my need to monitor Bridget to the back of my mind. Until… I gave in and started doing it again for Gordon."

"Then maybe with some cognitive therapy, we can help get you back to that point."

He stared down at the carpet and shrugged. Kenzie could feel some resistance to whatever this would entail.

"But that's something that we can discuss in our individual sessions," Dr. B told him. "Now… we should focus on the relationship. I imagine that this has caused some issues between the two of you. Let's get started."

14

Kenzie felt raw leaving the therapist's office. She imagined that Zachary felt the same way, probably more so. While she knew it was probably a good thing for them to talk their feelings out in the controlled environment of the sessions with Dr. Boyle, she couldn't help wondering if it caused more trouble than it healed. She felt a lot more vulnerable and isolated from Zachary than she had going into the session. She had been angry with him over the breach of their trust and his continued obsession over another woman, but she'd been able to keep the extent of those feelings from him. She didn't see how sharing them helped either one of them.

They had come to the session in their own vehicles, so they had to drive home separately. But maybe the quiet of their own vehicles would give them each some time to recover before they tried to go on with the day together.

"Should we stop at the grocery store?" Zachary asked, as they walked out to their cars. "Or at the Fro Zone? We might not have enough ice cream for tonight." He was half joking, half serious.

"I think I definitely need a new flavor," Kenzie decided. Something with chocolate and caramel and marshmallows. Something even more decadent than her usual. "How about you?"

He considered, then nodded. "Maybe something with different flavors in it. A mixture."

Kenzie went for chocolate. Zachary tended to prefer fruit flavors or highly artificial flavors like bubble-gum or cotton candy. He didn't usually like ice creams with mixed flavors, like Neapolitan. But maybe he was stressed enough that he wanted to go wild this time. A rainbow sorbet, maybe. In bright neon colors.

"Fro Zone?" Kenzie concluded. The grocery store had a good range of popular flavors, but it sounded like they were going to need to step it up a notch.

"Fro Zone," Zachary agreed.

"Okay. I'll meet you there."

They each returned to their own cars.

Wouldn't it be ironic if Zachary decided he had to drive by Bridget's on the way to the ice cream shop? After all the talk about her during the session, his obsessive thoughts about her were probably pinging around his head at light speed.

Kenzie decided to leave the parking lot first so that she wouldn't be tempted to follow Zachary, dogging him to make sure that he didn't take any detours.

But when she pulled up to the ice cream shop, he was already there ahead of her.

Kenzie awoke the next morning feeling slightly hung over. She hadn't had anything to drink, so she could only blame it on the ice cream and the emotional wringing-out that she had done during the therapy session. Zachary was, as usual, out of bed ahead of her and already hard at work on his computer in the living room. Only when she looked in on him, Zachary wasn't occupied with typing or reading what was on the screen of his computer, but was watching out the window.

"Hey, stranger," Kenzie greeted.

He turned and saw her watching him. "Oh. Hi. Did you have a good sleep?"

"Yeah. Not bad. I feel as though I could have used another three or four hours, but… work calls."

"Did you wake up a lot?"

"I don't think so. And I don't remember having any dreams. But… I feel like I had too much to drink."

"You didn't have anything," he said with surprise. "Did you?"

"No."

"Maybe you're dehydrated, then. They say that alcohol makes you feel so bad because it dehydrates you."

"You're right." Kenzie headed to the fridge. "Maybe that's it." It wasn't as if she'd made sure to have a properly balanced meal and enough water the evening before. She had been treating herself. Way too much sugar and chocolate and nothing good for her. She filled a tall glass with water from the filtering pitcher in the fridge and forced herself to drink half of it before heading to the shower. She left the rest on the table to drink before her coffee.

"How about you?" she asked Zachary. "I know I don't need to ask whether you slept well, but how are you this morning?"

"Okay." He swallowed. "Kenzie… I'm really sorry. About all of this. You don't need to be dealing with all of my crap, and Bridget and all…"

"You've apologized. I understand that it's… that you can't control what thoughts come into your mind, and that it's difficult not to give in and act on them. I'm trying not to be angry or judgmental about it. We've both got stuff to work on to make this relationship better."

"But it all starts with me. You wouldn't have all of this in a *normal* relationship."

"What's normal? All relationships have problems. They're all made up of two people with different outlooks and problems and ways of communicating. Look at the divorce rate. At the dating apps. I'm glad that we have Dr. Boyle to help us work through it all. That was a good suggestion."

His earlobes got a little bit red. He always did have problems taking a compliment. But this time he didn't push it away or put himself down. He just gave a short nod and looked down at his computer screen as if occupied.

"Okay," Kenzie said. "See you at breakfast."

Following her shower, Kenzie hadn't even sat down at the breakfast table when her phone started ringing. Looking down at the screen, Kenzie saw Menendez's number. She tried to decide whether she needed to answer it, or whether she could return the agent's call once she was at the Medical Examiner's Office.

What if there had been another death?

"Sorry," she told Zachary, walking back out of the kitchen and toward her bedroom where she could shut the door for privacy. "I just have to take this."

She swiped the screen and put the phone to her ear. "Agent Menendez?"

"Josie."

"Josie," Kenzie corrected. "Can I help you with something?"

"I have your memorandum of your conversations at the geriatric unit, and I wondered if we could go over it. Get your impressions and discuss possible directions to go with the investigation."

Kenzie paused in her walk to the bedroom, irritated. She had put all her impressions into the memo. That was the whole point of writing it. To memorialize what she had thought and felt about each of the people she had talked to, and about the unit in general. And Dr. Philemon.

"Yeah, I'm not at the office yet. Can I call you back in a while?"

"Oh, of course. I thought maybe we could get together for coffee or breakfast?"

"I'm just having mine now. Sorry. I'll call you back in an hour."

It would probably be longer than that, since she would want to sort things out when she got into the office, and wouldn't call

Menendez back until everything was ship-shape for Dr. Wiltshire's arrival.

"Oh, okay," Menendez agreed, sounding disappointed. "I guess... we'll talk then."

Kenzie disconnected the call and turned around to rejoin Zachary for breakfast. He looked surprised. "That was a quick call. Usually when you say just a minute, it's a bit longer."

"I thought there might be some urgency, but there's not. I can call her when I get into the office."

"Good."

They worked together to get everything ready, then sat down and ate. Kenzie found it difficult to focus on Zachary, thinking about Menendez and why she had called so early. Was there something in Kenzie's report that had caught her attention? Something important? Or was Josie Menendez just lonely and looking for some company before jumping into her workday?

15

Her call with Menendez had been unremarkable, and the day's tasks routine, which helped Kenzie to relax and feel more like herself.

Kenzie had noticed that Zachary seemed restless and agitated most of that evening, but he said he was okay when she talked to him and didn't offer if there was something in particular that was bothering him. Dr. B had raised the dosage of his antidepressants after some discussion, and Kenzie wondered if it were causing negative side effects.

He went to bed with her as usual, but kept shifting around and couldn't find a comfortable position to cuddle with her. Kenzie was getting irritated that every time she got settled in, he moved again. She needed to get her sleep if she were going to be able to function at the morgue in the morning.

Eventually, he whispered an apology and got out of bed. He would go watch TV for a while and maybe fall asleep on the couch. That's what usually happened on those nights that he couldn't settle in. Though she didn't like it when they had to be separated at night, she was also relieved that he'd decided to get up. She really wanted to be able to get a few solid hours of sleep before she had to get up again. She never did well when she was short on sleep.

She thought that she had drifted off for a while, but when she was next aware and turned over to get comfortable, she thought she could hear something. It niggled away at her, and she couldn't get back to sleep again, despite how tired she was. She finally listened to the little voice in her head that kept telling her she needed to get up and make sure that everything was okay. Sometimes there was a reason for those worrisome little thoughts. A door left unlocked or strange activities at a neighbor's house. Or maybe just a branch scraping on the side of the house in the wind, bothersome but not a worry.

She stepped into the living room and saw that Zachary was pacing up and down the room, into the kitchen and back. His movements seemed stiff and agitated.

"Zachary?"

He didn't look at her, but kept pacing, a fixed expression on his face. Grim. Lost in his troubled thoughts, whatever they were. Kenzie raised her voice.

"Zachary!"

He didn't see her until she stepped into his path as he paced back across the room. He stopped, startled, and stared at her for a minute before appearing to recognize her.

"Kenzie!" He looked around, trying to orient himself in time and space. He looked at the dark window, then back at her. "Are you okay?"

"I am. It looks like you're having trouble, though."

He shifted around, itching to be pacing again. Kenzie took a step back so that she wasn't in his way. He stayed put for the moment, opening and closing his hands.

"Can't sleep," he acknowledged.

"What's going on? Is it your meds? Were you having a flash-back? How can I help?"

"Nothing you can do." He stepped from one foot to the other.

Kenzie looked at him, waiting for an explanation. Normally,

she wouldn't push him to say what was bothering him. But that rule did not apply when he was so agitated during the night that he woke her up, whether it was with a nightmare or with pacing around the house looking like he was going to explode.

"It's just my brain. Won't quiet down. I can't… stop it from spinning."

"Do you think it is because of the dosage increase? Is it making you anxious?"

"No." He started to pace again, unable to keep still. "It's just… things. I can't get them out of my mind."

"What things?" She didn't want to bring up Bridget's name in case it were something else. She didn't want to introduce more restless thoughts if that weren't what he was already focused on.

Zachary cleared his throat a few times as he paced, as if he were trying to begin, but couldn't quite get the words moving. Kenzie was becoming more convinced that it was a problem with his prescriptions. She knew that he'd had reactions in the past. Some severe ones when he had first begun taking medications as a kid. It might be that he just didn't recognize what was going on.

"I'm worried about Bridget," he said finally. "Her and the babies."

Kenzie let out a long sigh. So the increased level of his antidepressants wasn't helping to control the obsessive thoughts. Not yet, but it could take weeks for them to see a change. "I'm sorry you've having problems with that. Is there anything that might help? You could try a meditation technique, or you could watch something on TV to distract yourself."

"She's in the hospital," Zachary said. He pulled out his phone and looked at the screen. "I don't know whether everything is okay."

Kenzie walked into the living room and sat down on the couch. She put her feet up beside her and pulled a blanket around her. She was so tired. But she couldn't go back to sleep while Zachary was in this state. She needed to help him to sort it out.

"How do you know she's in the hospital? Did Gordon tell you

that?"

He slid the phone back into his pocket and shook his head. "No."

Kenzie's stomach clenched. Gordon hadn't told him. She highly doubted that Bridget would have told him. That meant that he knew some other way. By personal observation.

"How do you know, then?"

"She collapsed. She had to go to the hospital in an ambulance. I don't know what that means for her or the babies."

"How do you know she collapsed?" He hadn't remotely tracked her car to the hospital. That really left only one answer.

Zachary ran his hand through his hair, frowning. "I saw her."

"When? Tonight? Were you out just now, after bed?" If he had been taking off after she was asleep, that was new behavior. At least, she believed it was. It could have been going on for some time. How would she know the difference? She could check the security logs on her burglar alarm. See whether he had been deactivating the alarm to leave the house late at night. But she didn't want to be monitoring him. She didn't want to snoop through security alarm logs to see whether he were telling her the truth or not.

"Not tonight. Earlier. This afternoon." He swallowed hard and kept pacing, not looking at her. Probably not wanting to see any judgment in her eyes. "She was out in the garden. By herself. She just… she fell down and didn't get back up again." He chewed on his lip. Kenzie saw a fleck of blood. "I watched for her to get up again, and she didn't."

"So what happened?" Kenzie prompted. She could see him in her mind's eye, rushing into the garden, holding her head in his lap and trying to wake her. Calling 9-1-1.

"I called Gordon. He called for an ambulance." He met her eyes. "I didn't go into the yard. I just told him."

It must have been excruciating for him, but he had tried to follow the rules. Never to go onto her property, even though he knew she was in medical distress.

"So Gordon knows that you were watching her."

"Yes."

"And he didn't hire you again, did he? To keep an eye on things? You just did this on your own?"

He nodded. "I was just checking. Making sure that she was okay. I knew she would be alone."

"But you know you're not supposed to."

"Yes."

He resumed his pacing. Kenzie thought about the timeline. If Bridget had collapsed in her garden in the afternoon, then probably twelve hours had passed since then, with no word back from Gordon as to how she was doing. No wonder Zachary was so anxious.

"I would invite you to come sit and cuddle…" She patted the spot on the couch next to her.

"I can't sit," he said ruefully. She had known that he wouldn't be able to. She couldn't cuddle and comfort him. That wouldn't solve his problem.

"Did you message Gordon? Ask him to let you know how she was?"

"Yes."

And he still hadn't gotten back to Zachary. Gordon was usually considerate and tolerated Zachary's interest in Bridget as if he weren't threatened by it. She didn't think that he would hold back information maliciously, because he was angry with Zachary for spying on Bridget when he knew he wasn't supposed to. If Bridget had suffered a medical emergency, he would be grateful to Zachary for having seen it and for letting him know. He might not give out any details about Bridget's condition, but he would let Zachary know that all was well.

"It's been a long time if it was fainting spell," Kenzie said. "I would expect them to give her fluids and put her in a bed or send her home within a few hours. Maybe run some tests to make sure it wasn't anything serious. But it *isn't* a long timeline if she's gone into labor."

Zachary stopped walking at looked at Kenzie. "It isn't?" he asked hopefully.

"No. Labor and delivery can last for hours. Eighteen, twenty-four, thirty-six... It isn't as if she just skinned her knee and they put a bandage on it and send her on her way. If Gordon hasn't texted you back, he is probably in the delivery room with her, with his phone turned off. And that doesn't mean that there is anything wrong. It just takes a long time sometimes."

Zachary considered this. His eyes were far away. "I don't remember... with my mom... I don't remember it taking that long."

"Some women are faster. And subsequent deliveries are usually faster than a woman's first. You were the third child, right?"

He nodded.

"So you might not remember when Tyrrell was born. And the youngest children, her fifth and sixth, might have come quite quickly. And you probably didn't even know she was in labor for the first few hours. Having had a few, she might just keep working. Or maybe she just laid down for a while. But you wouldn't tell your six-year-old that you were in labor. Probably. Maybe

'Mommy is sick' or 'Mommy needs you to be quiet so she can have a nap.'"

Zachary scratched his chin, thinking about that. "She didn't talk like that," he informed her with a wry smile.

From what Zachary had told Kenzie about his mother, probably more along the lines of "Shut up, you little monster! Get out of the house or I'll tan your behind."

Kenzie sighed. She shifted, pulling the comfy, warm blanket close to her. "Anyway, regardless of how quickly your mother delivered, it's not unusual for a woman's first delivery to take twenty-four hours or longer."

He took a few steps into the kitchen, turned around, and returned to the spot he had been standing in. "So I shouldn't expect to hear anything yet."

"No. Probably not. Gordon not calling you isn't a sign that something went terribly wrong. Just that he had to turn off his phone while he was in the hospital, and she is probably in labor and delivery. And could be for another day."

Zachary let out a long sigh of relief. "Nothing is wrong," he said aloud, attempting to soothe himself and to make his brain believe what she was saying. "There's nothing wrong. She's just having the babies."

"She was getting close to her due date, wasn't she?"

"I don't know her exact due date," Zachary said, but he was nodding his head slightly. Maybe he didn't, but maybe he did. "But she was pretty big. And it's been…" He thought back. "She was in the hospital with morning sickness, back when I was in…"

Kenzie counted the months in her head. It sounded about right. "Twins are often a little premature. There isn't always space for them to grow to full term. They have probably given her steroids to develop their lungs, so that they'll have a better chance of being able to breathe on their own, even if they are a few weeks premature."

"So they'll be okay."

"It's impossible to predict anything with confidence. But we don't have any reason to believe that there is anything wrong with either Bridget or the babies."

"Other than…"

Kenzie nodded. "Other than Huntington's. It doesn't activate until later in life; the babies will have a perfectly normal childhood."

Zachary paced back and forth thinking about that. He didn't say out loud that it wouldn't be a normal life with their mother already suffering Huntington's symptoms, but Kenzie couldn't reassure him in that respect. It was better if she just didn't mention it.

"Does that help? Do you want to sit down and cuddle for a while or watch TV? If you know not to expect anything tonight, can you settle down?"

"I don't know."

He went to the fridge and poured himself a glass of water. At least he wasn't drinking coffee. She didn't understand how he could drink coffee at night and expect to be able to go to sleep. But he said it relaxed him, and she knew that a mild stimulant could help someone with ADHD rein in his restless thoughts.

Zachary drank one glass and poured another, then joined Kenzie on the couch. He bounced around for a bit, trying to calm down and find a comfortable position. Kenzie leaned toward him and tried rubbing his back and shoulders. She closed her eyes and lengthened out her breathing. If his breathing became entrained to the slow rhythm of hers, it might help him to slow down and relax.

"It's all okay," she assured him.

Elbows on his knees, Zachary put his face in his hands and rubbed the muscles around his eyes. He was undoubtedly exhausted. "I'm sorry about going over there again."

"Are you?" Kenzie asked. "I would think that you'd be happy you went over there, since you were able to get her help when she needed it. There was no one else with her and she couldn't exactly call for help herself when she was unconscious."

"Gordon said she had a fall alarm. It had already beeped him and he was trying to call her back to talk to her. So... he would have been calling emergency to help her anyway, even if I hadn't called."

Kenzie nodded and didn't say anything. He couldn't see her, with his hands over his face.

"I was glad I was there," he admitted. "But I'm sorry I... broke your trust."

"If you try your best, that should be good enough," Kenzie said neutrally. She preferred not to tell him how much it hurt that he had to keep going back to Bridget. They had already discussed it in therapy with Dr. B. and Zachary couldn't help that his brain kept going back there.

"It's never been good enough before."

Kenzie rubbed Zachary's back some more. She couldn't tell whether it was helping him at all. But at least he wasn't pulling away from her or telling her to stop.

In the morning, when they had both had some sleep, their emotions would not be so raw. Zachary was bound to be more depressed and Kenzie more annoyed and disappointed when they were tired. Tiredness amplified negative emotions. Her mother had always told her "Wait until morning. Everything always looks better in the morning."

But for her to feel better in the morning, she would have to have some sleep before then.

17

Dr. Wiltshire looked at Kenzie's face in the morning, then down at his large coffee. Maybe regretting the fact that he hadn't bought Kenzie a coffee that morning as well, as he sometimes did when he knew they were going to have a more than usually difficult day.

"Kenzie. Good morning. Are you… feeling all right?"

"If I look bad enough for you to notice, then you can assume I am not."

"Well, it's not that," he lied.

Kenzie shook her head. She had done her best to camouflage the bags under her eyes and the tired lines across her forehead and around her mouth. But there was too much to hide her state. It was still obvious to Dr. Wiltshire, who was not the most observant person she knew.

"Are you sick? You should have stayed home," he reprimanded gently.

"No, just tired. We didn't sleep very well last night." Kenzie grimaced at the *we*, which had slipped out inadvertently. She didn't mean to imply that it was Zachary's fault or suggest that they had been kept up by amorous activities. She felt that he needed an explanation. "We have friends who are expecting twins.

She went into labor last night, and we were both a little too wound up to get much sleep."

"Oh, I see," Dr. Wiltshire gave her a big smile. "Well, congratulations on the imminent arrivals. Is everything going okay?"

"Don't know. That's one of the things that kept us awake. I'm sure that everything is fine, but phones have to be turned off in the hospital, and I wouldn't expect him to be calling us during labor and delivery anyway. But you know how babies make you wait."

"Yes, they do," Dr. Wiltshire agreed. "Well, maybe if we don't have too much land on our desks today, you can sneak out early. Get in a nap and be refreshed for the evening."

"I'll try," Kenzie agreed. It sounded like a great idea. She didn't know whether she'd be able to leave early. But if she were too exhausted to work and made mistakes, that would be worse than cutting her hours short. Mistakes would cause a lot more trouble than being late on a deadline or taking an extra day to release a death certificate or a body.

But Dr. Wiltshire hadn't been there for an hour when he informed Kenzie that they were expecting two bodies in that afternoon. Both were exhumations of Dr. Philemon's former patients. The first two families that he had been able to talk into signing off on an exhumation so it didn't have to be ordered by the state's attorney. It would be a lot easier to keep it quiet and out of the media if they were able to do it privately.

It was fitting that both of them would come in when Kenzie felt like the walking dead herself.

Kenzie glanced at the caller ID and saw that it was Agent Menendez.

"Hi, Josie."

"Kenzie. I just wanted to call and make sure that you got my bodies."

"*Your* bodies?" Kenzie repeated.

"Darling and Scott. The ones that we got exhumation approvals on."

"I know who you mean… but they're not exactly *your* bodies," Kenzie pointed out. In fact, the FBI had no claim to them. They had been released by the families to the Medical Examiner's Office, not to the FBI. Dr. Wiltshire would report any findings to them, but the bodies themselves were the property of the families, on loan to the ME's Office.

"No, they're not mine!" Menendez agreed. "I didn't mean it literally. Just wanted to make sure that they had arrived."

"Yes. They are both here. Dr. Wiltshire and I will be looking them over this afternoon, preparing samples to be tested."

"I don't suppose you can tell anything by looking at them."

"They are well-preserved. We shouldn't have any problem finding poison. If they were poisoned and if the poison doesn't have a short half-life."

"But they'll be like Mr. Michaels. You found the potassium in his system."

"If it is the same poison, we'll find it. But there's no guarantee that the killer, if there is a serial killer, will use the same substance on every victim."

"That's the way it works, though. Serial killers use the same method each time. It's what makes them serial killers."

"No… I've been reading up on Angel of Death killers, and they often vary their methods. It isn't the method that makes them serial killers, it's the fact that they kill repeatedly."

"Those are exceptions. In all the well-known cases, the killer used the same method each time."

"People only recognized it as the work of a serial killer if they used the same method repeatedly. They couldn't identify a serial killer if they varied their methods. But Angel of Death killers sometimes confess to their crimes, and they have often varied their method from one victim to another to avoid detection."

"Hmm." Menendez sounded unconvinced. "All the cases that I've studied, the killer has used the same method."

"What about the Golden State Killer? DNA shows that he operated in various areas around California and used different methods at different times. They couldn't tie them all together until they could match the DNA."

"That's one exception."

"That is just one example. Anyway, if the killer uses potassium chloride in all cases, then we will be able to find it. If he or she used insulin sometimes, we won't find it. That's a popular method. And if they used smothering or an air embolism, we won't find those either. So it depends. We'll do our best to find any foreign substances or anything else that confirms that they didn't die of natural causes or of the illness that they were being treated for, but there's no guarantee. There isn't even a guarantee that any of these other cases *are* murder. If something like this had happened to a patient of mine... I'd be paranoid about any other death that seemed the least bit out of the ordinary or unexpected. Dr. Philemon put together a pretty extensive list. But that doesn't mean that all of them were victims of an Angel of Death killer. He's just looking back and worrying over these previous cases."

There was silence from Menendez for a few minutes. Kenzie was beginning to wonder whether she had insulted the woman or the connection had been broken.

"Josie?"

"We're counting on you and Dr. Wiltshire, Kenzie. We're counting on you to produce the evidence that this is a serial killing."

"To find evidence, you mean," Kenzie said. "If the evidence is there. It isn't like you want us to manufacture evidence."

Again, there was a lengthy silence. Kenzie was getting uncomfortable with the situation.

"You need to follow your professional requirements," Menendez said eventually. "And your conscience. We need to catch this person. We can't let her keep killing. Men and women are at risk. We need to track her down and prove what is happening before it is too late."

"Yes. And we will. If the evidence is there."

"Just think about it," Menendez cautioned. "Think about all of the vulnerable patients under Dr. Philemon's care before you go into autopsy. And then you find what we're looking for."

"I'll let you know the results as soon as we have them," Kenzie promised. She hung up the phone firmly. She sat looking at it, feeling like she needed to wash her hands.

"Was that Agent Menendez?" Dr. Wiltshire asked, coming from the suite of offices into Kenzie's reception area. Kenzie wondered how much he had overheard.

"Yeah. That was her. And I think she just told me to manufacture evidence that each of these patients was killed by the same person and in the same way as Mr. Michaels."

Dr. Wiltshire raised his brows. "Really." He took a deep breath and let it out. "I have been getting a vibe from her. I didn't want to believe that it was true, but..."

"So I'm not just imagining it or being dense, right? She did... want us to prove her theory. Whatever it takes."

"But we're not going to," Wiltshire said firmly. "We will follow the evidence."

Kenzie nodded her agreement. She was glad they were both on the same page. Of course Kenzie wanted to catch the serial killer, if there was one, just as much as Josie Menendez did. But she wasn't willing to go to any lengths to secure an arrest and conviction as Menendez seemed to be suggesting.

18

Kenzie was glad to get out of the autopsy and into the fresh, crisp December air when they were finished examining the bodies of the two potential victims and gathering samples. She drove from garage to garage, so it wasn't as if she were outside for a stroll, but it was still much nicer to be breathing the air in the underground parking and the air that filled her own garage when she raised the door than it was to be breathing the putrefying scents of the two bodies.

Zachary was sitting at the kitchen table. He didn't generally work at the kitchen table, and he certainly didn't eat there unless Kenzie cajoled him into it. His back was to the door. She touched him on the shoulder as she entered.

"Zach? Everything okay?"

Zachary breathed for a minute before answering. He didn't pull away from her, and she could feel the tension in his body as he sat there. Not relaxing and hanging out, that was for sure.

"Pretty rough day," he said finally.

"Yeah?" Kenzie rubbed his shoulder and slid her hand over to the back of his neck to rub it as well. "What's going on? Still worrying about Bridget?"

"She had the babies," Zachary offered. His voice was flat and without emotion. If she didn't know him better, she would assume that it didn't mean anything to him. That it was news he felt he should pass on to her, but not something that he was personally connected to. But Kenzie knew that he only spoke that way when he had pulled back from his feelings. When he was trying very hard to separate himself from the pain and to feel nothing at all.

She sat down at the table and put her purse down beside her. She didn't take off her coat or go to the fridge to get a bite to eat. Nothing that would distract her attention from him.

"You want to tell me about it? Is Bridget okay? The babies?" For once, she didn't feel the stab of jealousy when she talked to him about Bridget. She wasn't worried about whether Zachary was attracted to his ex more than he was to Kenzie. She needed to reach Zachary in the dark corner of himself that he had walled off. There was a real, physical pain in her chest as she gripped Zachary's arm and tried to give him some kind of comfort and relief from his distress.

"She's recovering well. Gordon said she was a champ."

Kenzie nodded and waited. Zachary swallowed. After sitting in stillness and silence for a few minutes, he reached into his pocket to pull out his phone. He thumbed it on and turned the screen to Kenzie so she could see the picture. Two tiny babies in an incubator. Both around four pounds, Kenzie guessed, both with respirator tubes affixed to their faces, wearing impossibly tiny diapers and hats.

"They both survived," Kenzie said, pointing out the good news. Despite all that modern medicine had to offer, people still lost infants in childbirth. Especially twins and preemies. Gordon had the money to get Bridget whatever medical treatment she needed, but he hadn't been able to prevent her falls while she was pregnant, her collapse in the garden—whatever that had been caused by—or the expanded form of the Huntington's disease gene that the twins had inherited. Money couldn't prevent medical problems.

Zachary nodded. He was looking down, his expression difficult for Kenzie to see or to interpret.

"Did he say what the doctor told them? About the babies' condition?"

"They are 'guardedly optimistic.'"

"Well, that's good. They aren't in critical condition. Even though they're on respirators now, that doesn't mean that they won't recover. They may just need support for a day or two until they are able to breathe on their own."

"They're so tiny."

"Yes. It would be better if they were bigger. But they are not micro-preemies. They have a good chance of survival. Maybe with no ill effects."

Kenzie squeezed Zachary's hand, trying to connect with him. To get some feedback that he understood and believed what she was telling him. He didn't squeeze back or look at her.

"They'll be in the hospital for a few days," Kenzie said. "But they will go home. When they are breathing on their own and are up to five pounds or so, Gordon and Bridget will be able to bring them home."

He said nothing.

"Is there another problem with them that you aren't telling me?" Kenzie asked.

He shook his head. "No. That's all I know. It was just a short message from Gordon, and I didn't think I should ask any more." He gave a shuddering sigh. "It's not my business. Not my family."

"No, you're right. You're doing really well, not pushing him for more. That must be hard."

He nodded his agreement. Kenzie could only imagine the struggle that must be going on in his brain. His brain told him that he needed to see her. It produced feel-good neurotransmitters when he did, reinforcing the message. Not engaging with Gordon or going to the hospital was the equivalent of a junkie in withdrawals refusing a fix rather than chasing it.

Zachary licked his lips and breathed in and out, his breath still shuddering and catching.

Kenzie gave his hand another squeeze. "Let me get you a drink of water."

She got up and went to the fridge to take out the water pitcher and pour him a glass. She opened the door of the fridge and reached for the pitcher, then froze in place.

What appeared to be every sharp kitchen knife she owned was piled on one of the refrigerator shelves.

19

Kenzie stood there for a moment, just staring at the glistening blades. Then she did what she had planned, pulling out the pitcher and pouring a tall glass of water for Zachary. She poured one for herself too. She put the pitcher back in the fridge and took both glasses back to the table. She sat down and positioned each of the glasses in easy reach.

Zachary picked his up and drained half of it in a few gulps.

"So… what's with the knives in the fridge?" Kenzie asked.

"It seemed like the safest place to put them."

"Why is that?"

"Because… I'm not hungry. So I wouldn't open the door and see them."

Kenzie looked at the empty butcher's blocks on the counter. Maybe there was something to be said for not displaying an array of knives in full view of a severely depressed person.

"You haven't said that you were having thoughts of self-harm."

He wiped his nose with the back of his hand, sniffling. "I… am."

"Okay. How bad is it?"

"I thought it was okay. Under control."

"But maybe not, now?"

"Maybe not."

"Have you had any sleep?"

"No."

"In how long?"

"I'm not sure. Maybe… three days."

"Maybe up to three, or maybe more than three?" Kenzie's heart was pounding, adrenaline coursing to every part of her body. Her partner was in danger. Yes, it was from himself, but he was still in danger. Just as if someone else were standing over him, threatening him with a knife.

"At least three," Zachary said after some consideration.

"Well, you know you're not supposed to let it go that long. Without sleep, your brain can't operate properly."

He mumbled something she couldn't hear.

"Do you want to take a pill and lie down?"

"It's too early."

"If you haven't slept in more than three days, then what time it is doesn't really matter. You should have said something."

He said nothing in response. Kenzie waited for a while in silence. Her instinct was to rush into things and to try to fix him. She would tell him all the things he was doing wrong if he wanted to maintain good mental health. Order him to sleep. Order him to take all the meds he'd been prescribed. And most of all, to put Bridget and her babies out of his mind. He needed to think of himself and his safety. He needed to think about how his actions affected Kenzie and the other people who loved him.

But she waited, letting all her impulses and criticisms flow through her until her brain was quiet enough to listen.

"What do you want to do?" she asked Zachary.

"Do you want me to call Dr. B?"

"If that's what you think you should do. Sure."

"Do you think she'll tell me to go to the hospital?"

"If you think you should go to the hospital, you don't need her to tell you that."

"Do you think I should?"

"I think that's your decision. If you think that you need to, you should. If you think you are going to harm yourself, then we should take action."

He rubbed a hand over his face. "You think I'll feel better if I can sleep?"

"I think you'll feel much better if you can get a good sleep. I don't know if that will be enough, but you can decide that yourself. Do you want to have a sleep and then see how you feel?"

He nodded.

Kenzie was relieved that he didn't say he needed to go to the hospital immediately. She knew he had checked himself in before, and she hoped that he wasn't to that point again. But if he were, then of course that was what she wanted him to do. A sleep was a good first step.

"Would you get me a pill?"

"Yes, sure. Just one? You're allowed to take two at a time, aren't you?"

"Yes… but I don't know whether I should. What if I don't wake up again when I should?"

"You should sleep as long as you can, not confine yourself to a certain time limit."

"But it could mess up my sleep schedule. My… rhythm thing."

"Circadian rhythm. Don't worry about that. We'll set up a schedule once you've had a nice long sleep. And we'll stick to it so that your sleep cycles are not thrown out of whack. I'll help, okay?"

"Okay."

"So can I get you two sleeping pills?"

"Yeah. I guess."

Kenzie left him at the table and went to the main bathroom to get his pills from the medicine cabinet. But when she opened it, the cabinet was nearly empty. None of his prescription pill bottles were there.

"Zachary?"

"Yeah?"

"Where did you put your pill bottles?" Maybe she should have checked the fridge.

"They're in your bathroom."

Zachary never used the ensuite bathroom attached to Kenzie's master bedroom. Unless he were sick and couldn't make it from the bed to the main bathroom. Kenzie went through her room and opened the door to the smaller bathroom, to find all the pill bottles in the sink.

They followed the practice of only getting small numbers of pills prescribed at a time, refilling them often, so that it would be harder for Zachary to overdose on an impulse. But it was a bit of a shock to see how many bottles there were. She needed to go through them and cull out the ones that Zachary wasn't taking anymore because they were older prescriptions or dosages. Or have Zachary do it when he felt up to it.

She sorted through the bottles for a few minutes before finding the prescribed sleep aids. She took out a couple of pills and then read the label and the warnings carefully. She also found his antidepressant and took one out. She took the three pills out to Zachary in the kitchen.

"I don't take the antidepressant again until nine," Zachary pointed out.

"Not usually, but you're going to be asleep at nine. And once you're asleep, I'm not going to wake you up. You need to get a good long rest to recover. So you're taking it now rather than having to skip a dose."

Zachary nodded. He knew that skipping even one dose of the antidepressant could cause him problems. He'd missed a dose while they were on vacation. It had taken a week to start feeling an improvement again, and she had counted them lucky. The destabilization could have lasted for a month or more, and they couldn't afford that so close to Christmas.

He drank down the three pills, draining his glass. He set it down. "I'd better use the john before falling asleep. Would you… get me another drink?"

"Sure."

She didn't want him opening the fridge and looking at the knives.

When Zachary returned from the bathroom, Kenzie looked him over, wondering if there were anything else she needed to worry about. He'd already moved the two biggest temptations out of sight, which showed that he was thinking and was aware that they might be too much of a temptation if he had to look at them. Was there anything else that she should put away? Anything that he might have on him that could be dangerous if she weren't in the same room with him?

She was glad that he wasn't a hard-boiled PI like those on the old movies. A firearm in the house would be a very bad idea.

"Do you want to cuddle on the bed or sit on the couch?"

"I'll try the bed."

She knew he must be very tired, but he didn't look much worse than usual. She was too used to the dark shadows under his eyes and the sunken cheeks he tried to camouflage with his growth of whiskers. They retired to the bedroom, Zachary taking his glass of water with him to put on the nightstand. He didn't bother undressing for bed. Maybe because he still felt it was too early to be going to sleep. Maybe because he couldn't summon the energy. He lay down on the bed, facing the window, his back to Kenzie's side of the bed. She lay behind him and rubbed his shoulders and back for a few minutes before putting her arms around him and snuggling up against his back.

"Everything is fine now," she told him. "You just need some sleep, and you'll feel better when you've had it. Everything will look better when you wake up again."

He shifted. "Will it?" His voice didn't sound confident or hopeful.

"Yes. Everything seems worse when you're tired, and you are

exhausted. Your brain is too tired to deal with anything. It will seem more manageable after you've caught up on some sleep."

He didn't express his doubt about this, but Kenzie still knew he was thinking it. She snuggled up so that her face was next to his neck and cheek, and concentrated on long, deep breathing. It wasn't long before she was drifting off to sleep.

20

Kenzie knew she had been asleep for a couple of hours when her consciousness finally forced itself to the surface. She moved slowly and carefully, withdrawing from Zachary. She had fallen asleep with her arms around him, and her hand was asleep as a result. She listened to Zachary's even breaths in the dark room. Hopefully, he would sleep all the way through the night, maybe even into the next morning. If he hadn't slept for three or four days, he needed a lot of hours to be functional again.

She left the room quietly. She woke up her phone after returning to the kitchen and glanced through the notifications on the screen. She swiped a text from Gordon. It was brief, but telling.

How is Zachary?

Kenzie texted him back. *Sleeping now. Hope he didn't bother you too much. Any update on the girls?*

There was no answering text or "message read" notation. He was probably back inside the hospital, his phone dutifully turned off while he sat with Bridget or the babies.

She was relieved that the babies had been born. Hopefully, that would ease Zachary's anxiety about Bridget's health and help him to resist the impulse to follow her. If the babies didn't have any setbacks, they would be out of the hospital in a couple of weeks and he could stop worrying about them too. Kenzie wasn't sure why Zachary was so concerned for the babies. It wasn't just because they were Bridget's. Another man, pining after his ex-wife, would be put off by her pregnancy and not interested in her offspring by another man. But Zachary still seemed to be hanging on to the fantasy that he'd had when they were married of raising children with her. Maybe it was partially the being separated from his siblings when he was ten. He and the older girls had helped to care for and raise the younger children, so the loss of his younger siblings was akin to the loss of his own children. And he was still trying to recreate that bond with someone else.

Kenzie rifled through the fridge and pulled out random leftovers. She didn't have the energy to make anything. Even warming up a frozen dinner or ordering in felt like it would take too much energy. She could eat cold pasta and vegetables dipped in salad dressing. That would have to do for her supper. She sent out another text, this one to Dr. B.

Zachary in crisis. May need to be admitted.

The response from Dr. Boyle was swift. *You both know what to do. Don't wait too long.*

Sleeping now. Apparently hasn't slept last 3-4 days.

Good if he can sleep at home. Keep me apprised.

Kenzie texted back a thumbs-up, and considered whether there was anyone else she should call or message. Lorne Peterson, Zachary's old foster father and the closest thing to a loving parent that he had, would want to know of any developments. But he knew it was a bad time of year for Zachary and that he was going through a depressive cycle already. Unless Zachary were admitted to the hospital, there wasn't really anything new to tell him.

Tyrrell? The same applied to him. And Kenzie was a little leery of putting any extra burden on Zachary's younger brother. The Christmas season was difficult for him too. As he was a recovering alcoholic who may or may not have had a recent slip, Kenzie didn't want to push him.

She would let Heather know if Zachary slept through the next day. Since she worked with Zachary, she would expect to hear from him and would need to be informed in case there were deadlines to be met between them.

Kenzie was feeling better after having something to eat. It was several hours past when she normally ate supper, so her body had not been happy with her. Add to that the hours standing in the odoriferous autopsy, and it was no wonder she still had a headache despite her nap. Now she had the rest of the evening to entertain herself, since Zachary would not, she hoped, be getting up again before the next morning.

She had jinxed herself by thinking about having free time to do whatever she wanted to. Her phone rang and, looking down at the screen, Kenzie saw that it was not Gordon or one of Zachary's family members, but Agent Menendez. Who of course wanted to know what they had found in the autopsies.

Kenzie drew in a deep breath and let it back out. She answered the call. "Josie. Hi."

"I was expecting a call from you, Kenzie!"

"Someone will get back to you in due time. We need to wait for the transcription of the autopsy audio and Dr. Wiltshire needs to draft his summary report. We were in autopsy most of the day."

"That doesn't keep you from giving me the unofficial news."

Kenzie sighed. "There isn't much to report. We have sent samples off to the labs for analysis and won't have the results for a few days. There wasn't anything remarkable about either of the bodies."

"That means that you can't tell whether they were poisoned until you get the lab results back."

"That's right."

"You said that sometimes Angel of Death killers use smothering or other methods."

"Yes."

"Did you find any indication of that? Smothering?"

"Smothering, unfortunately, does not leave many signs. I know that on TV, there is always petechial hemorrhaging, bruising around the mouth, and fibers in the throat or lungs. But in real life… you don't always see those signs. You might see nothing at all."

"Then how can you make a determination?"

"Like I said, a lot of times, you can't tie deaths to a serial killer until they confess. If they're careful… it might be impossible to figure that out without their confession."

"Well, considering we don't even have a suspect yet, much less a confession…" Menendez said irritably.

"I know. It's still early days. These things take time."

Menendez muttered. "I understand that. This isn't my first rodeo."

In which case, Kenzie couldn't see why she was so impatient and worked up. She had to understand that a case like that was solved over weeks and months, not days.

"We will let you know when we know something. Maybe there will be something in the lab tests. We just have to wait and see."

"My boss said that Dr. Wiltshire has a very good reputation."

"Yes, he does." Kenzie wasn't sure where Menendez was going with the comment.

"I just wonder whether he's really putting all of his effort into this case."

"Of course he is!" Kenzie was indignant. She couldn't believe the nerve of the FBI agent, suggesting that Dr. Wiltshire might be falling down on the job. He always did his best. They might have a very small office compared to the big cities, but Dr. Wiltshire was very professional and diligent in all his work.

"I would think that he would be able to keep me apprised of developments without me chasing him down. And that when he did an autopsy, he would be able to actually tell me what the person died from." Her voice, though light, was biting.

"Listen," Kenzie said. "It isn't my fault or Dr. Wiltshire's that you have unreasonable expectations. Maybe that is just because of your inexperience. But you need to back off and wait. We will let you know what we find out when we have had the time to do a full investigation. How are you doing on screening the hospital staff and the others in Dr. Philemon's practice?"

"No one with a criminal record or any significant complaints to the Medical Board. But there really isn't a place to report nurses, volunteers, or janitorial staff. I need access to all their personnel files, and there is no centralized place for that. I can look at Dr. Philemon's HR records, but they are sparse. Doctors aren't actually very good at screening and hiring and the administrative stuff. Some of them, we don't even know what their last job was, let alone who to contact about getting their previous records. Even why they were terminated or left."

"So you still have plenty to do," Kenzie pointed out.

"I'm fully aware of my job. I just need you to do yours."

"We are," Kenzie said tightly.

Mendendez's sigh carried over the phone lines. "I'm sorry. I don't mean to be so hard-nosed. But I'm getting a lot of pressure to show some progress on this case."

"It isn't our problem if your superiors have unreasonable expectations."

"I know. And I appreciate that you guys did both autopsies today, as soon as you could, when you probably had other work to do."

"Yeah. We were there late. And we do have families and personal responsibilities. We don't spend twenty-four hours at the office."

"Tell me about it," Menendez agreed with a laugh. "I don't know the last time I actually went out on a date..."

She left space at the end of her words, as if expecting Kenzie to chime in with her personal issues or talk of her social life.

"If that's everything," Kenzie said evenly, "I need some time to relax before bed."

"Dr. Wiltshire said that you were married to a private investigator? What's that like?"

"Not married. And really, I don't want to chat about it right now. Maybe we can share war stories some other time. But not tonight. I need some time and space tonight."

"Things not going well?" Menendez asked sympathetically. "I don't hear any TV in the background, so maybe he's off on surveillance somewhere? Leaves you alone a lot at night, does he?"

Kenzie shook her head in disbelief. "Talk to you later, Agent Menendez. I'll call you Monday if we know something."

She didn't wait for any further inquiries from Menendez, and quickly ended the call.

21

Kenzie considered her course of action. She didn't normally communicate with Dr. Wiltshire during her off time, but she thought the situation warranted it. She first planned to text him, but then decided that text would probably not communicate her tone, and she didn't want him to misunderstand her reasons for calling him. She thought through several scripts, and then called him.

"Dr. Wiltshire, I'm sorry to call you at home…"

"Kenzie. What can I do for you?" He sounded friendly, not irritated with her calling him on his personal time.

"I just wanted to give you a heads-up… Agent Menendez called me tonight and was pushing hard for the results of the autopsies. I told her that we wouldn't have the lab tests back yet for a few days, and that we hadn't found anything obvious on the examinations… she's making a lot of noise about us being unprofessional… I don't know. She's a very… eager investigator. She wants results, and she wants them now, even if that isn't the way that the real world works."

"Ah." She could almost see Dr. Wiltshire's familiar nod of understanding. "She has been a little troublesome. I suspect she is probably getting a lot of pressure from her superiors to make some headway on the case. Show that it is a serial killer or shut it down so they don't have to waste resources on it."

"Yeah, she said her superiors were pressuring her."

"Don't worry about it. Just handle it as you would any inquiry from the public. We will publish our report when we have satisfied ourselves as to the cause of death. Until then, it is in the works."

"Okay. That's basically what I told her, but she's very... persistent."

"I have noticed," he agreed dryly.

Kenzie snickered. "Oh, and... don't share anything about my personal life. She keeps asking about medical appointments, how I spend my time, Zachary, all that. She's not my girl friend and I don't feel like sharing anything personal."

"I haven't said anything."

"She said that you told her I was married to a private investigator."

"Hmm. I'm pretty sure I didn't say married. I might have mentioned Zachary in passing, talking about the Salter case. There are similarities between what happened with Robin Salter and an Angel of Death case. Two different sides of the same coin."

"Well, she's picked up on it. Wants to know what he's doing tonight. If I'm alone. It's kind of creepy, to be honest."

"Do you want me to talk to her superiors? Have them speak with her about maintaining professional distance?"

"Not yet. But if she keeps it up..."

"I'll be more aware of it. Sorry if I caused you any trouble."

"No, it's okay. Normally it wouldn't be an issue. But she seems to... have some problems with boundaries."

"Yes. Changing the subject, if we're done with this one..."

"Yeah, that's everything I wanted to say."

"I'm wondering how Zachary is. You've seemed distracted lately. I know you were worrying about him before Halloween and said that Christmas was a bad time. Is everything okay...?"

Kenzie tried to think of what to say. She did not want her home life to interfere with her job. But she also didn't want to lie to Dr. Wiltshire or to say that everything was fine, only to call him on Monday to say that she needed to take a personal day because Zachary had been admitted to the hospital.

"Confidentially and as a friend," Dr. Wiltshire said. "No notes on your personnel record. Your work is stellar, as always."

"Well…" Kenzie blew out her breath. "A bit of a crisis this week. I told you that we had a sleepless night last night. It turns out that Zachary's had a few more than that, and he was in pretty bad shape tonight. He may need to be admitted to the hospital psych ward. I'm not sure yet. Going to see how he is over the weekend."

"Oh, I'm sorry to hear that. Are you okay?"

"I've had a nap, so I'm good now. He fell asleep and will hopefully get a good number of hours in before he's up. Sometimes when he crashes, it could be ten or twelve hours, or more."

"And… are you safe? Some people can get violent when they are in a crisis."

"Oh, I'm fine. Nothing like that. I've never seen Zachary do anything more violent than to grab someone, and only when I was in danger. He's not a violent person."

"No weapons in the house?"

Kenzie thought about the knives in the fridge and gave a slight chuckle. "No."

"Okay. Sorry to be an old man fussing over it, but when you've seen as many bodies come through the office as I have…"

Kenzie had only been there for a couple of years, but she noticed how many of the deaths were related to domestic violence. She appreciated Dr. Wiltshire for being straightforward enough to ask and make sure she was safe.

"Thanks for caring. No, I'm only concerned about Zachary's safety, not my own. And hopefully… he'll be able to cope better once he has slept."

"Good. You let me know if there is anything I can do to help.

Anything. And just give me a heads-up if you're going to need Monday off or come in late."

"I will."

"And I won't mention it to Agent Menendez!"

"Yeah. Just tell her I'm out in the field. That should get her nice and wound up!"

Dr. Wiltshire laughed. "Take care, Kenzie. Talk later."

Kenzie followed up her cold supper with a helping of ice cream. Maybe hot chocolate would have been more appropriate for a chilly December night, but she liked her ice cream, and there were a few flavors in the freezer to choose from. She really needed to finish one of them off to make room in the freezer for other things. So, putting an old movie on the TV, she curled up under one of the throw blankets on the couch and used Zachary's portable computer desk as a table for her treat.

She was awakened later by the buzzing of her phone. She hadn't even realized that she was still tired enough to drop off again, but she had clearly fallen asleep at some point during the movie. Maybe she should have gone back to bed with Zachary after eating dinner.

Kenzie rubbed a crick in her neck and focused on her phone. She touched the screen to wake it up, unsure whether it had been ringing a moment before or whether it was vibrating from other notifications. She saw a text from Gordon.

Baby 1 holding her own. Baby 2 fluid on lungs. Praying she'll make it through the night.

Kenzie's heart went out to Gordon and Bridget. As much as she disliked Zachary's ex-wife, she wouldn't wish a critically sick newborn on anyone.

So sorry, Kenzie texted back. *Will hope for the best.*

Thank you. Zachary ok?

Still sleeping. Will see what morning brings.

Two different vigils being kept through the night. Kenzie was glad their positions were not reversed. But she did worry about how Zachary would take it if he knew that one of the babies had taken a downturn. Or if they lost her in the night. He had been so concerned with Bridget's unborn children right from the start, behaving as though he were responsible for keeping them safe.

Kenzie didn't really believe in God or religion, but she couldn't help reaching out mentally to the universe, pleading that Baby 2 would pull through.

After checking her mail and making sure she hadn't missed any important calls, Kenzie changed for bed and crawled in beside Zachary. She pulled a light blanket over him, but didn't want to make him too hot, as he didn't normally wear much to bed. She didn't want to wake him up by causing him to overheat.

In the morning, when she awoke, the room was light, testifying to the fact that she had slept late. And Zachary was still there beside her.

She held her breath and listened for a moment to make sure that she could hear him breathing. His respirations were long and slow, a sign that he probably wouldn't wake for a while yet. She whispered a good morning and luxuriated for a while beside him, enjoying their closeness and the fact that she didn't have to hurry out to work or to run any errands. It was rare for her not to have a list of things to do. But for once, the thing that was at the top of her list was to ensure that Zachary slept for as long as possible and that he was okay when he got up.

She eventually got up and had her morning shower. She dusted, then cleaned the bathrooms, but did not run the vacuum cleaner, which she feared would wake Zachary. There were no further texts on her phone, so she didn't know how the two babies had fared through the night. As she cleaned, she thought about the autopsies, about Mr. Michaels, and about how an

Angel of Death killer would think and feel and how they would operate.

If an Angel of Death killer was that hard to catch, then how were they going to catch him? Would it be the killer's signature? Tabulating who was on the floor with every death that they could connect to him? And what if he weren't a nurse, but was someone who wouldn't be tracked through the medical charts? A volunteer, janitor, security guard, or someone she hadn't even thought of? The water boy? A flower delivery person?

Who else could walk in and out of the unit without even being noticed? It was something she could bounce off of Zachary. He was good at hiding in plain sight. Using his homeless appearance so that people looked away in disgust or to avoid being asked for money. No eye contact, keep moving on… and five minutes later, they couldn't even tell you that he had been there, let alone describe him. That wouldn't work in a hospital, where a homeless man wandering around the floor would be obvious, but there had to be other people whose comings and goings were so ubiquitous that no one even saw them.

Kenzie heard movements from the bedroom and left what she was doing to check in on Zachary.

"Hey, sleepyhead. How are you feeling now?"

Zachary made a face. He wiped his eyes and scratched his head. "Like something curled up in my mouth and died there." He saw that his glass of water was still sitting on the side table and picked it up, gulping down the first few swallows, and then swishing it around his mouth to get rid of the taste. He drank down a few more swallows and put the nearly-empty glass down.

"Ugh." He groaned and scrubbed his eyes with his fists before looking for his phone. He pulled the charge cord off and looked at the time. Kenzie saw him look toward the window to see what time of day it was. He cleared his throat and tried his gravelly voice once more. "It's noon?"

"Yeah. I'm thinking about making some lunch. What do you want?"

"Nothing. Need to take my meds."

There were a couple that he was supposed to take on an empty stomach. And then another that he was supposed to take with food once the nausea from the first couple died down enough to force something down.

"Right. Let me get them for you."

Kenzie went back to the ensuite bathroom, where she had lined the bottles up along the wall instead of leaving them all in the sink as Zachary had done. She needed to be able to wash up and brush her teeth, after all. She located the two early-morning pills and took them to him. It was late to be taking them, of course, but it was the lesser of two evils. He had needed the sleep more than to be awakened to take them.

"What day is it?"

"Saturday. You got about sixteen hours."

Zachary shook his head. "I never sleep that much."

"No. You really needed it. Starving your body of sleep is just as bad as starving it of food. Worse. You can't function without it. Why didn't you take a pill sooner?"

"Couldn't last night. The night before," he amended, trying to keep his days straight. "Not when… what if Gordon had called?"

"Why would Gordon call? He doesn't need a private investigator to help deliver his babies. If the babies had been born during the night and he had wanted to let you know—since clearly you had been asking—then he could have sent you a text and you could read it in the morning."

"I was too wound up. I couldn't have slept even if I had taken something that night."

Which was probably true. Someone like Zachary who was really determined to stay awake would, even with a full dose of the sleep aid. It could be overcome by strength of will. Or obsessive thoughts.

"You said it had been at least three days. Maybe four. So you had other opportunities to take a sleeping pill and get caught up.

If you don't sleep at all one night, you *need* to take a sleeping pill the next."

Zachary scratched at the seam on his jeans, saying nothing.

Kenzie had to remember that reason didn't win all arguments. Especially not when dealing with mental illness and disordered thinking. Zachary had probably had a reason for not taking a sleeping pill that first night that had seemed perfectly reasonable to him, even if it didn't make sense to her. Or to him when he was having a better day.

She opened her mouth to ask him how he was feeling, to try to get a general idea of whether he would need to be admitted to the hospital. Then she forced it closed again. The man had just woken up. He wouldn't know how he felt yet. He had just taken his meds and nothing had kicked in yet. He probably felt pretty groggy and like he was hung over. It was not the time to ask, however much she would like to plan her day or the rest of the weekend.

"It's Saturday?" Zachary repeated.

"Yes."

"I think I lost a day. I didn't sleep a whole day, did I?"

"No. About sixteen hours," she told him again.

Zachary looked down at his phone and started scrolling through notifications. "Have you heard anything...?"

"I talked to Gordon last night. One of the babies was having trouble. I haven't heard anything this morning."

Zachary's right hand moved to his chest and clenched into a fist, like he was squeezing his own heart. "You don't know if she's okay?"

"Not yet. Unless he texted you. He hasn't texted or called me. If he stayed up all night with the baby, he might be sleeping now, so I don't want to call. He'll get back to us when he's ready to tell us something." She shook her head. "You're lucky that he's so open to communicating with you about it. Most men would not be talking to their wives' exes."

Zachary nodded. "Gordon's a good guy. But I was probably… over the line asking him."

"Maybe. But at least you were asking instead of going over there. So that's good."

Zachary shrugged.

"Why don't you have a shower, see if that makes you feel a bit better? I'm going to make myself some lunch."

He nodded. Kenzie backed out of the room and gave him some space.

22

Kenzie thought by Sunday morning that Zachary was doing pretty well, and that she would be able to get through the weekend without needing to take any further action. He would settle back into a proper sleep schedule, the worries over Bridget and the babies would fade, and he would immerse himself back into his business.

The house was quiet, and he had slept two nights in a row. Saturday afternoon, Gordon had gotten back to them to advise that both babies were still alive and getting stronger, and that Bridget would soon be allowed to go home.

Kenzie was just lying in bed, checking through her email and social networks and trying to avoid reading anything about politics or thinking of anything to do with work and the Angel of Death killings. She could almost convince herself that there was no Angel of Death, it was just one medical mistake or accident.

There was a crash in the kitchen, and Kenzie was out of bed in an instant, her heart pounding. "Zachary?"

"No!"

She hurried into the kitchen. The knives that he had previously stashed in the fridge—Kenzie hadn't thought of a better place to put them yet—were scattered across the floor. The crash she'd heard had been Zachary sweeping them all out at once. She looked at him in fear, expecting to find him holding one of the knives threateningly to his throat or wrists, or even worse, covered in blood. But he appeared to be unharmed, just standing there looking angry and aggrieved, his skin chalky white.

"Are you okay. Are you hurt?"

"I'm fine!"

"Okay. Do you want to sit down? What's going on? Sit. You look like you're going to pass out."

He looked at the kitchen chairs and shook his head. Kenzie motioned to the living room. "On the couch? Please, tell me what's going on."

"My *stupid* brain!"

"Yeah. Okay. I'm going to pick these up and put them somewhere. You didn't cut yourself?"

He shook his head. Kenzie looked him over once more but could not see any blood or even small cuts.

"Please sit down. You may not be big, but I don't want to move bodies around on my day off. Sit down so I know you're not going to pass out. You can think about if you want to talk to me. Or Dr. B. I think… you need to talk. So you should sort out who you want to talk to and what you want to say."

He stood there for a moment in silence, glaring at her, then finally turned and went into the living room. Kenzie took several deep breaths to calm herself. Her heart was pounding hard and fast. She felt like she had been attacked. But Zachary wasn't angry at her. It was his own recalcitrant brain and emotions that he was frustrated with.

She gathered the knives slowly and laid them out on the counter to make sure that they were all accounted for. The knives from the butcher block. The set of steak knives. A couple of paring knives from the drawer. Then she took them all into the garage and put them into one of the file boxes with her old financial and school papers. She settled the lid and went back into the house.

Zachary was in the living room but had not sat down on the couch.

"Okay," Kenzie said, in as calm a voice as she could muster. "You want to talk?"

"I can't."

"What do you want to do, then?"

He clenched his teeth, making the muscles and tendons in his neck stand out. "Will you drive me to the hospital?"

"Sure. You want to take anything with you?"

"No."

"What about your prescriptions?"

"Dr. B will email the list to the hospital. They wouldn't let me take mine anyway."

Possibly patients tried to smuggle in drugs that they weren't supposed to be taking and pass them off as legitimate prescriptions. Kenzie nodded her acceptance of this.

"I'd drive myself, but then I have to pay for parking," Zachary explained. "Long-term parking at the hospital…" He shook his head.

Kenzie waited for him to joke that it cost an arm and a leg, but Zachary didn't.

"You probably shouldn't be driving right now anyway. If you don't need to bring anything, then let's go."

He followed her to the garage and slid into the driver's seat in the convertible without a word. Kenzie waited for an explanation. What he was thinking or feeling. If there had been a particular trigger. If he thought he needed a med review or evaluation or a longer-term admission.

She had hoped that she'd be able to keep him out of the hospital until Christmas. She'd really thought that she'd be able to do it. That if she were just careful about what Christmas reminders he was exposed to and encouraged open, nonjudgmental communication, things wouldn't get too bad.

It wasn't fair. It just wasn't fair.

She felt like throwing a pile of knives on the floor herself.

Something loud and dramatic to show how frustrated *she* was. But she couldn't indulge herself. She had to be the strong one, giving Zachary whatever support he needed.

She swore under her breath.

Loud enough that Zachary could hear it, but not loud enough that he knew he was *supposed* to hear it and respond in some way.

At the hospital, she stood back as Zachary spoke with one of the triage nurses in emergency, explaining that he needed to be admitted. Kenzie had seen or heard of cases where people were turned away from the emergency room with the explanation that their depression was not bad enough and that they should go home and talk to their regular professionals for evaluation or medication changes. But the triage nurse hooked Zachary up to a monitor and switched her gaze between him and the monitor as they talked, jotting down notes about his appearance, vital signs, and what he told her, and apparently was convinced that he did, in fact, need to talk to someone in psych about possible admission. She gave Zachary a bracelet and instructed him to sit in the waiting room. She watched Zachary walk up to Kenzie, and after meeting Kenzie's eyes, the nurse nodded and called the next person waiting in the triage line.

Emergency room waits were always long and tedious. At least, as a patient or friend accompanying a patient who wasn't bleeding out. For a doctor, emergency medicine moved forward at a frantic pace, with one priority interrupting another, and then dealing with angry parents who brought a child to the ER because he was throwing up and then couldn't understand why everyone else saw the doctor ahead of him.

Zachary, usually busy with his computer or phone, sat in a chair and watched the silent TV hanging on the wall or the other patients waiting to be helped. He didn't even have a book. But then, Zachary had never been one to read for pleasure. His dyslexia and ADHD made that too difficult. He read what he had to for work but never could understand the joy that other people got out of reading fiction or exploring new concepts.

She was going to suggest that he find a game to play on his phone or message Rhys or give Lorne a call. But if he didn't have his phone in his hands, there was probably a good reason for it. She wasn't even sure whether he had brought it with him, or if he had left it behind at the house. She'd never seen him separated from his phone before, but if something on his phone had been causing more depression or distress, then he was undoubtedly right to stay off of it.

They had been there for a couple of hours, not saying more than half a dozen words to each other, when Zachary finally spoke.

"One of the babies had a heart attack. Or whatever you call it when it happens to a baby. A cardiac event."

Kenzie looked at him. "And…?"

"They got it going again. He said they're both on monitors that will ring if… their hearts go too fast or slow or in the wrong rhythm." He looked at her eyes to confirm he got this right.

Kenzie nodded.

"How can they be talking about Bridget going home? Doesn't she need to stay here with them?"

"She'll probably come back during the day to be with them. Express milk to feed them until they're big enough and strong enough to nurse. She's not going to abandon them."

Zachary swallowed. He stared down at his hands, too overcome with emotion to discuss it any further.

"Mackenzie Kirsch!"

Kenzie looked up, startled. Her first thought was that her mother was at the hospital. Few people other than her parents, still called her by her proper name.

A woman in a nursing smock bustled toward her. A middle-aged woman, her hair still blonde rather than gray, substantial, but not really overweight. It was her smile that Kenzie remembered. A broad, toothy, pleasant smile, both friendly and motherly. It took Kenzie a few seconds to place her, her mind going rapidly through her mental database to find where the woman belonged in time and place.

"Nurse…" Kenzie fumbled, unable to remember the woman's name. She had been one of Amanda's nurses. One that they had seen a number of times over the years as Amanda was readmitted to the nephrology unit for various kidney issues. Kenzie stood up to greet her. The woman got close enough for Kenzie to read her name tag. "Nurse Debbie! I can't believe it's you! How many years has it been?" Kenzie gave her a hug and received a firm squeeze in return.

"Oh, I don't think we want to be counting the years!" Nurse Debbie laughed. "How are you? I heard you went into medicine."

Kenzie nodded. "I did. I'm an MD now. I'm with the Medical Examiner's Office."

"Amazing!" Debbie looked Mackenzie over, shaking her head. "Not that I'm surprised, of course. You always were very quick to understand the medical issues and to pick up on nuances. You have a very quick mind."

Kenzie smiled, her face getting warm. "Thank you. Uh, Nurse Debbie, this is Zachary Goldman." Kenzie felt a little awkward introducing them. Zachary was sitting with his face in his hands and was clearly not in a place to be excited about meeting anyone. "Zachary, Debbie was one of my sister Amanda's nurses. Always took very good care of her."

Zachary peeled his hands away from his eyes to look Nurse Debbie in the face, and gave a smile that was more of a grimace.

"That's great," he said, forcing the words out. "It's nice to meet you."

Kenzie gave Debbie an apologetic look. Nurse Debbie might

deserve a more enthusiastic greeting, but she wasn't going to get it when Zachary was feeling so bad.

"Zachary Goldman," Nurse Debbie repeated. She lifted the clipboard that she was carrying and looked at it. "Actually, it is you I'm here to see."

Zachary stared at her, uncomprehending.

"I'm with the psychiatric unit," Debbie explained. "I'm here to talk with you. Do your intake and get you admitted. Okay?"

Zachary looked at Kenzie, frowning. Maybe wondering whether she had somehow engineered things so that her old friend would be the one to do his intake. Kenzie just shrugged. It wasn't any of her doing. The meeting was serendipitous.

"Debbie will take good care of you," she told Zachary. "She's a really good nurse."

He nodded and stood up. Nurse Debbie dutifully checked his bracelet and compared the name or ID number to that on her clipboard. She smiled. "Great, if you'll just come with me, then, we'll get you started."

"Do you want me to come with you?" Kenzie asked, unsure whether Zachary had been counting on her moral support or if the only thing he'd needed her for was to drive him to the hospital.

"I need to interview him alone," Nurse Debbie said. "Lots of privacy laws, you know."

And the fact that he would be asked whether he was in an abusive situation. He had to be alone when they asked him that, even if he consented to Kenzie joining them and hearing his private medical information. She might be able to join him later, but not until they'd had a chance to ask him questions about his circumstances without someone else there to hear his answers.

"Okay. Do you want me to stick around, Zachary?"

He shook his head. "You don't need to. It'll be… I'll be safe once I'm admitted. You don't need to worry about me."

"Of course I'll worry about you." Kenzie looked at the time on her phone. "I'll come back and see you tonight. If that's okay."

Zachary shrugged as if he didn't care.

"Do you want me to bring you anything? Pajamas? Something from home?"

"No."

"Okay." Kenzie leaned in to kiss him on the cheek and gave him a squeeze around the shoulders. "You take care. You're in good hands. I'll see you later."

Zachary nodded. "Thanks for bringing me."

"Of course." She kissed him once more, then nodded to Nurse Debbie. "Take care of him for me."

23

Kenzie was accustomed to spending time alone. Or at least, she had been before Zachary had started staying over. Now he was at her house almost all the time when she was home, only going back to his own apartment when she was gone during the day or running errands. He really didn't have to maintain his own place anymore, but supposed it was good for him to have something to fall back on just in case. Or just if he needed some mental space for a few hours.

But she'd gotten used to his being around the house and it felt empty whenever he wasn't there.

She didn't have to worry this time that he was off on surveillance that could turn bad, or that he might be following Bridget again. She knew where he was, and that the hospital was the safest place for him to be. They would keep a close eye on him and he wouldn't have access to anything he could cut himself with or meds that he could overdose on. She didn't have to be aware of his every move and mood. That meant that she could start on the backlog of chores and other things she always put off because she didn't have the time, either at work or spending time with Zachary most of her waking hours. Or too tired to start anything.

But she didn't. She didn't even look at the task list on her phone.

The first person she called was Lorne. He sighed, but wasn't surprised to hear that Zachary had admitted himself. He'd seen Zachary through a lot of difficult times. "It's not your fault, Kenzie," he comforted her. "I know it feels like a personal failure, but it isn't. Zach knows you're there for him. But he also knows from experience that when things get bad… he needs to be in a safe place, with a team behind him. You can't expect yourself to be his sole support."

"I know. And I'm not. He has you guys, and Dr. B and his other doctors, other friends here and his siblings now too. There are a lot of people who can be there and help out."

"Yes, but you can't keep a watch on him twenty-four hours a day. You can't remove everything that isn't safe from his environment or give him intensive therapy. Or make changes to his prescriptions. They'll take care of him and make sure that he's safe until he gets past the crisis."

"You think he'll be there until Christmas, then."

"More than likely. It won't just be a seventy-two-hour hold. He knows he needs to be there. It's voluntary. And he knows that he's not going to start feeling better until after the anniversary. It's possible that he'll end up with a doctor who tries to push him out before then. It's happened before. But if they try to release him to you before then, tell them you won't take responsibility for him."

"Okay." Kenzie was hesitant. What if Zachary was feeling better and agreed to coming back before Christmas? She couldn't tell him that he couldn't come home. If they managed to get him to a better place, it was possible, wasn't it?

"You can't, Kenzie," Lorne told her. "You remember how bad he was last year on Christmas Eve? He's not going to be ready to come home before Christmas."

"But we got him through it last year. He didn't have to be admitted."

"And if Tyrrell hadn't been there that night, do you think it would have been safe to leave him alone?"

"No. Of course not. But as long as we had someone to stay up with him…"

"Every night? You don't know when he's going to hit the lowest point, and if he seems to be okay and the person up with him falls asleep… it's just safer at the hospital, where they will check on him every fifteen minutes. Where it is more difficult for him to find a way to harm himself."

"I don't know how you have dealt with this for so many years."

"He is pretty good about recognizing when he reaches the point when he needs to go to the hospital. Of course we worry. All the time, but especially in December. But Zachary is a grown man and he's independent. We can't treat him like he's helpless. That would just make it worse."

Kenzie sighed. "I hate this."

"Of course you do. It's emotionally draining and mentally exhausting. You need to build yourself up. Recognize what your needs are right now. He'll be home in a few weeks. Look forward to that. He will be back."

Kenzie called Tyrrell and Heather to give them the news as well. No one was that surprised. They had both heard an abbreviated account of Zachary's life and his many visits to the hospital and other treatment facilities. Heather admitted that she had sensed it coming.

"He hasn't been doing a lot of work. I don't know what he was spending his time on, because I would call and he wouldn't answer, or if he did answer he didn't say where he'd been. I've still been taking the small jobs, but he hadn't taken on much else new."

"He's been a little distracted by Bridget and her health,"

Kenzie kept it deliberately vague, not wanting to give away anything that Zachary or Bridget wouldn't want spread around.

There was a snort from Heather that sounded more like Joss, the oldest and most jaded of the siblings. "A little distracted, yeah."

So Heather had been aware of Zachary's activities or had at least suspected them.

"How is Bridget?" Heather asked.

"She's okay. Had the babies a couple of days ago, but they are struggling. I think that's what pushed Zachary over the edge today. They nearly lost one of them."

"Zachary always did love babies," Heather said, her voice tender. "That boy was hell on wheels, but put a baby in his arms, and he was the most attentive person ever."

Kenzie had seen how, when focused on an important project or protecting someone else, Zachary could hyperfocus. He was kind and compassionate, and she had seen how well he got along with teens and children.

"He's talked a little bit about it. It sounds like your mom might have had some pretty severe postpartum depression. She's lucky she had you older kids to look after the younger ones."

"Yeah, I guess that must have been the problem. I had some postpartum after my births, but... well, it wasn't anything like Mom's. She wouldn't be able to get out of bed. I seriously think she would have just died, if there weren't people feeding her and looking after her. And the babies. Mindy wouldn't have survived if it wasn't for Zachary. I'm sure of that."

"What was wrong with her?" Kenzie asked, fascinated to hear Heather's perspective.

"She was really hard to feed. She wouldn't take the bottle and Mom wouldn't nurse. Zachary would dip his finger in formula to get her sucking on it, and then slip the nipple in... he was the only one who could get her to eat anything. He'd skip school. Stay home with her until the truant officer started showing up, and then skip out of classes to run back home and take care of her. It was a good thing they didn't slap him in some detention center. I'm sure Mindy wouldn't have made it."

"That's amazing. He would only have been… how old, eight?"

"Yeah, that sounds about right. But he was so determined. Nothing was going to keep him from taking care of Mindy."

Kenzie's heart ached when she thought about everything his mother had put him through after a showing like that. How she had told him that he wasn't good for anything and she didn't want him anymore. All the abuse and challenges that he had gone through in foster care and at school because she had abandoned him. A little boy who cared so much about his family.

"I'll have to ask him about it," Kenzie said. "He's probably never even been told what a good job he did. What a difference he made."

"No," Heather agreed after a moment. "He got told off when he did something wrong, but if he was quiet and out of the way… no one would have ever said anything about it."

"Do you think we should let Joss know about him being in the hospital?" Kenzie asked. "I don't know her very well… whether she would want to know, or just not to be bothered."

"Who knows what makes Joss happy," Heather said, with a slight laugh in her voice. "I'll call her and let her know. You don't have to deal with her."

Kenzie thought about saying that Heather didn't really have to do that, Kenzie didn't mind calling Jocelyn. But it wasn't true. She was relieved that Heather had offered, because Kenzie would prefer not to have anything to do with Joss's sharp edges.

"Would you? That would be really great."

"Sure. Thanks for letting me know. I'll try to come in and visit him. If that's allowed."

"I'll give you a call once I know what the visitor situation is. I assume visitors will be restricted to the bare minimum to begin with, until they feel as though he is stable enough."

"Okay. Yeah. Let me know. I need to come in to do some Christmas shopping anyway, so I'll plan around it."

"Just don't plan on talking to him about your Christmas shopping."

There was a pause, Heather not answering right away. Not chuckling about it like Kenzie expected her to.

"Is it that bad?" Heather asked.

Kenzie realized that it had been less than a year since Zachary and Heather had been reunited. It seemed like a lot longer than that, with the two of them working so well together. Zachary had hit it off with both Tyrrell and Heather right away. But Heather hadn't been around the previous year, or for any of the previous Christmases, so she had no way of knowing how bad Zachary's depression was around Christmas, how even a discussion about Christmas or seeing all the Christmas lights or decorations around town could bring him down farther.

"Well… yes, it is. Christmas is a really bad memory for him, and as a kid he was almost always institutionalized around that time. Sometimes as an adult too, like now."

"It was terrible," Heather recalled. "I was really scared that we were going to die. And when the firemen got us out, Zachary was hurt, and I thought he would die. But I was older than him when it happened, and I guess I also have happy memories of Christmases with my own kids. Same with Tyrrell. Zachary was just… I wish he could understand that it's in the past. It was terrible, but… it was a long time ago now."

"He understands that logically," Kenzie said. "But his brain is… damaged in a way. He would like to stop being depressed. He'd like to be able to stop thinking about the fire and just enjoy Christmas. But his brain is convinced that anything to do with Christmas is dangerous. That the fire could happen again this year, just like it did decades ago. He's made some progress on the fire thing. But he didn't even tell his therapist about his problems with Christmas and why until this year, and that was with… a bit of encouragement from me. I was hoping that with better support this year he would do better, but…"

"It's not your fault," Heather pointed out, just as Lorne had.

Kenzie didn't think that she'd been blaming herself. She knew that Zachary had severe depression every year, and that it centered around Christmas Eve and the house fire when he'd been ten. That wasn't her fault. But maybe she was blaming herself a little bit for not being able to stop it. She was a medical professional and his partner, and she thought that with everything she knew about mental illness and how much she was willing to go all-out for Zachary, that she would be able to help him through it. That she would be sitting back at Christmas, satisfied that she'd been able to get him through it without a major depressive episode or the need for hospitalization.

Taking Zachary to the hospital had shattered the egotistical vision she'd had of herself. She wasn't a miracle worker. She didn't love and understand him enough to change his brain chemistry. And it was true, she did blame herself for not having what it took to do that.

How did that make her any better than Bridget, who had assumed when she married Zachary that she would be able to fix him? Bridget thought she could get rid of all the parts of Zachary that she didn't like and train him to be the husband she expected him to be.

Was that any different from Kenzie thinking she had what it took to heal him?

24

K enzie sulked around the house for a while and ate a bowl of ice cream. If she were going to resort to treating any negative emotions with ice cream, she would have to start getting more exercise. She would put on fifty pounds before Christmas.

She tried watching TV. Tried reading. Eventually, she decided to talk to her mother.

Kenzie didn't usually go to her mother with her problems. She considered herself a big girl, an adult who could solve her problems by herself. She had decided what to do for her education and career and had gone out and done what she had to. No one had to coach her through that, and she had a trust fund so she didn't have to take out loans or go to her parents to ask them for money. She prided herself on her independence and in the fact that she didn't *worry* her mother.

Lisa had suffered enough with Amanda, worrying day and night about her daughter's health and what she needed. And Kenzie had vowed to herself that she would never cause her mother any anxiety. So she didn't go to her with problems or discuss the speed bumps in her grown-up life.

But maybe it was time to stop acting like a rebellious teen who didn't need anything from anyone and to give her parents a chance to be a part of her life again. Even if it were only in a small way.

Kenzie tapped her phone to dial through to her mother and listened to the phone ringing. Dread clutched at her guts, but she ignored it. Calling her mother did not mean that anything was wrong. Having a conversation with her was not a dangerous or stressful proposition. Lisa was always there, always happy to help with anything Kenzie asked for.

"Mackenzie," Lisa greeted, her voice a little over-loud. "It's good to hear from you! Is everything okay?"

"Sure. I just wanted to talk," Kenzie assured her breezily. Then she realized what she was doing. Calling her mother for comfort and then pretending that nothing was wrong. How much sense did that make? How was that going to help her. "Actually, Mother…" Kenzie spoke over Lisa to correct herself. "Actually, I'm having a crappy day, and everything is not all right."

"Oh." Lisa stopped short in her pleasantries. "What is it, honey? Did something happen?"

"Yeah. Zachary had to go into the hospital. He'll be okay, that's why he checked himself in, but I'm feeling really down about it and thinking I should have been able to do something for him. So I thought…" She trailed off.

"What is he in the hospital for? Was there an accident?"

"No. He has depression. And some things have been going on that are making it worse, and he had to check himself in because he's suicidal."

"Oh!" Lisa gasped. "Oh, no! I'm so sorry, honey."

"It sounds worse than it is. I mean, I knew that this might happen. And it's good that he recognized he was a danger to himself and asked to be admitted so that he can't self-harm. But it's also… a real disappointment. I feel responsible, even though I know that I'm not."

"Of course. If you're anything like me, you take it all personally. Everything that goes wrong in the family. A mother or wife should be able to manage it all. Even though you know it's not true, that doesn't stop you from feeling betrayed and guilty and responsible for letting something bad happen."

Kenzie's heart throbbed extra-hard. She put her hand over the spot where it pounded away in her chest. It felt full and warm and painful, but a little bit better because Lisa understood what she was talking about.

"Is there anything we can do?" Lisa asked.

"No. There isn't really anything that anyone can do. I mean, he has the doctors at the hospital and his usual medical team, and they help."

"And I'm sure it helps him to have you in his life too; it just doesn't mean you can change things like that."

"I don't feel like that right now, but you're right. At least I try to be understanding and don't usually lose my temper. Which is more than I can say for his ex."

"You were always so good with Amanda, even when she was tired and whiny, and nothing would soothe her."

Kenzie breathed in and out, thinking about Amanda. There had been good times and bad, of course. She preferred to remember the good times, but there were always times when Amanda was sick and nothing any of them did helped her to feel any better.

"Yeah. I guess that's where I developed some patience. I knew that she couldn't help it. Anyone would have been crabby, having to go through dialysis and everything else she had to deal with."

Lisa made a noise of agreement.

"Do you remember one of the nurses Amanda had in the kidney unit? Nurse Debbie?"

"Hmm. I'm not sure. What would I remember about her?"

"She was a big blond woman. Very cheerful. Jolly."

"Ohhh…" Lisa drew the word out, thinking about it, clearly remembering some impressions. "I do recall her… she was there for a long time. One of the regulars that knew Amanda because she'd been there so much."

"Yeah. And she was so good. She wasn't brusque and dismissive like some of them. She was always willing to help out, whether it was turning Amanda over or bringing her some ice chips…"

"Yes. That's right."

"Well, I ran into her at the hospital this morning!"

"You're kidding! How did that happen? Is she still in the same unit? I haven't seen her in years."

Lisa spent a lot of time on kidney causes, so she probably would have known if Nurse Debbie had still been in the nephrology unit. Even though Lisa was no longer required to be at the hospital, as she had been when Amanda was there sick, she still went back a lot, chatting with the administration and raising funds. Making sure they had all the latest equipment and treatments for the young people who, like Amanda, lived out much of their lives there.

"No. Actually, she's in psych. She was there for Zachary's intake."

"Well, isn't it a small world! You be sure to tell her hello for me."

"I will. I'm planning to go back in an hour or two. I haven't heard anything, but I should be able to see him and find out what the plan is for the next little while."

"They won't send him home, will they? When he's feeling so badly?"

"No. I don't think so. They'll have me to deal with if they try a stunt like that. He's there for a reason."

"What does he need? Can we send him a care package? Pajamas? Cookies? I don't know if that unit will allow me to send anything."

"He said he doesn't need anything. I offered to bring him things from home, and he said no. I'll find out more tonight about the rules for visitors and anything brought into the unit. They have to be very careful, in case it is something that could be used… for self-harm."

"Of course. But maybe a potted plant, with some flowers…"

Kenzie smiled. "I don't know how long it would last. Neither one of us has much of a green thumb."

"You let me know."

"I will."

"And what about Christmas? You don't want to be worrying about making Christmas plans while you need to look after him in the hospital. Why don't you plan to come here?"

"I can't plan anything like that."

"He'll be out by then, won't he?"

"No. Christmas is a very bad time for him… the anniversary of a family tragedy." Kenzie tried to put it into words that her mother would understand, without telling her too much of Zachary's story. "Hopefully they can stabilize him, but he won't really feel *better* until after Christmas."

"Oh." Lisa's voice was sympathetic. "You should have told me that before. Christmas can be such a difficult time for people. I understand the suicide rate is very high—" She cut herself off. "I don't need to tell you that. I just mean… I have friends who have a difficult time then too, because of loved ones they have lost. I remember years when Amanda was sick… when we didn't know if she would make it to Christmas. We even had it early one year…"

Kenzie remembered. She thought it was before she had turned eighteen and given Amanda one of her kidneys. The girl had been gravely ill, and the doctors had advised them to say their goodbyes and not wait. So they had opened their Christmas presents and had a little party. Amanda had fallen asleep, exhausted. And they had just sat around her and watched her breathe. Kenzie choked up thinking about it.

In the morning, Amanda had rallied, and they'd joked that she had just wanted to open her gifts early.

"Yeah, that's right. I remember."

Lisa was quiet for a moment.

"So we can't have anything before Christmas," Kenzie said. "He won't be out before then and discussing anything about Christmas will make him worse." She was thinking it through out loud, not having processed it yet previously. "But after Christmas, then it will be better."

When Kenzie arrived in the psych unit, she wasn't surprised to be met with some resistance. A doctor on Zachary's team shook his head adamantly.

"He is under observation right now. We need to get an accurate read on his baseline. Visitors right now would just disrupt that. After we've had a chance to evaluate him, then he will be able to have a limited number of visitors whom he will approve."

"I'm his girlfriend. I'm going to be on the list. And I'm a medical doctor."

"You will still disrupt our observations. So you may not see him today."

Kenzie shrugged. She wasn't going to argue it. She had only given herself a 50/50 chance of being able to get in.

"Has Dr. Boyle or anyone on his medical team been by? Do you have all of his prescription information and anything else you need from them?"

"Yes. They have been very responsive; we have everything, or else it is on the way. I gather this is not his first admission." His lips twisted in a slight sneer. As if Zachary could help being a repeat offender.

"If you've read through his history, then you must know that. This is a bad time of year for him."

"As it is for many. That's not unusual."

"But the amount that he reacts to Christmas stuff is. It isn't just that he gets more depressed because it's cold and dark. He has a history."

"Yes, Dr. Boyle mentioned that."

"Okay. You need to know that. This isn't just seasonal depression. It is a traumatic reaction."

The doctor nodded. "Thank you for your input, Miss Kirsch," he said in a dismissive tone.

"Dr. Kirsch," Kenzie reminded him. He didn't correct himself.

"Oh, are you Kenzie?" A nurse walking by turned toward Kenzie, smiling.

Kenzie raised her brows and tilted her head slightly. "Yes… I'm Kenzie."

"You're Zachary's girlfriend."

"Yes. Have you been in to see him? How is he doing?"

"Don't you worry about our Zachary." The woman patted Kenzie on the arm. "We know how to look after him."

The familiar way she spoke of him made Kenzie inquire further. "Do you… know Zachary? From before this?"

She nodded. "Of course. I've been here for six years." She gave Kenzie a broad smile. "He's had a few visits during that time."

"Oh. I guess so. Well, I'm glad there are people here who know him." Kenzie glanced at the doctor, who definitely didn't know Zachary. It was good there were nurses there who knew him from past admissions and would be looking out for him.

"And I understand that you know Nurse Debbie!"

Kenzie nodded. "Yes. Funny thing. I just ran into her when Zachary was admitted. I had no idea she was in this unit!"

"She's just new here. So *she* doesn't know Zachary, but she was telling us all about you."

Kenzie chuckled uncomfortably. "I don't know how much there is to tell. It's been a lot of years since I've seen her."

"Nurses don't forget as easily as you might think." The nurse gave her a wink. "We remember the patients and families that we have spent a lot of time with. She knew you as soon as she saw you in the waiting room."

"Well, yes, I guess she did." Kenzie didn't offer that she'd had to check Debbie's name tag. She patted the nurse's hand on her arm. "Is there anything Zachary needs? Anything I should bring for him?"

"No, he doesn't need anything. You just take care of yourself, and we'll take care of him. Someone will call you once he's able to have visitors. He'll be happy to see you."

Kenzie nodded. She wished that she could go in and see him and let him know that everything would be okay. When she thought about him being there all by himself overnight, fighting his demons and nightmares, her throat got tight and hot. She blinked rapidly, not wanting to cry in front of the nurse, and especially not in front of the doctor.

"Thanks. I'll be happy to see him too. Thank you… for looking after him."

Sunday night was rough on Kenzie, and she was glad to go to work in the morning to try to get her mind off things. Monday passed in a blur. Kenzie hoped she didn't screw up too many things in her distraction. Agent Menendez called several times to ask about tox results, but they didn't have anything in yet. Kenzie eventually stopped answering, letting the persistent calls go through to voicemail. Agent Menendez needed to learn a little restraint.

Monday night was also rough, but in the morning, she got a call from one of the nurses on the psych unit advising that she had been added to Zachary's visitor list and could see him that evening if she chose. So Kenzie went into work feeling a little more cheerful and relaxed. Instead of being distracted by the fact that she couldn't see Zachary, she was distracted by the fact that she would be able to. She shook her head at the irony of it and tried to focus on each job at hand. There would not be any multitasking, or she would end up putting reports in the fridge and samples in the outgoing mail.

"How are you this morning, Kenzie?" Dr. Wiltshire greeted.

"Better today, thanks. But I still wouldn't trust any calculations I do. Double check any of my work before it goes out. I'm trying to triple-check everything myself, but I could still miss something."

"Zachary doing any better?"

"I don't know if he is any better, but I'll be able to see him tonight. So I'm a lot happier about that. It's been months since I've gone two nights without him home… it's weird. You would think that I would adjust pretty quickly to being alone, since that's what I'm more used to. But… not so much."

"I'm sure it will give him a boost to see you too."

"I hope so. I'm all about making sure he gets whatever boosts I can give him!"

Dr. Wiltshire raised an eyebrow questioningly, making Kenzie laugh. It felt good to laugh. She slit the next envelope in the stack of mail and scanned it to see how to sort it. She dropped the piece of paper like it had burned her.

"What is it?" Dr. Wiltshire drew closer and peered over the edge of Kenzie's reception desk to see what it was.

STAY OUT OF THE HOSPITAL KENZIE KIRSCH. OR ELSE

Kenzie blinked, trying to make sense of the note, written in black Sharpie in large block letters. Stay out of the hospital? Her mind went immediately to Zachary, and whether someone didn't want her to visit him. But that didn't make any sense.

Dr. Wiltshire's forehead was creased with lines. "Stay out of the hospital. You don't suppose this is something to do with the Michaels case, do you?"

"Oh…" It suddenly made more sense. "Yes, I suppose it is. I must have upset someone with my questions in the geriatric unit last week."

He nodded.

"What do you suppose the 'or else' is?" Kenzie asked with a nervous laugh. It was like some melodramatic murder show on TV. Stuff like that didn't happen in real life. People didn't make threats. And they didn't say "or else."

"I don't know. I don't imagine you have anything to worry

about, but you should probably call Agent Menendez and update her on the situation."

"Oh, great. I've been trying to avoid talking to her."

Dr. Wiltshire laughed. "Well, maybe if you have something to tell her, she won't be as annoying."

"Except I don't really have anything that will help the case. I mean, this... This isn't what she wants. She wants positive tox screens on the two exhumations, and I don't think we're going to get anything she can use."

"I have my doubts too," Dr. Wiltshire admitted. "I'm afraid that if those two deaths *are* somehow related to Mr. Michaels's death, the killer has changed his method enough that we cannot detect it months later."

"That's what I told Menendez. But of course... she doesn't want to hear that. She wants something we can trace and prove it's the same person."

"We might have to get more exhumations to find a pattern. And the more we do, the more likely it is that word will leak out. Then either people won't want to give us permission, or everyone will think that their loved one's death is related, and we'll be over-whelmed. And we'll start getting letters from every crackpot in the county." He looked down at the note on Kenzie's desk.

"Do you think this is just some crackpot?"

He shook his head slowly. "This is someone who knew you were asking questions at the hospital. That's not a member of the public, it's a very small group of people."

Kenzie's mind immediately went to Roda with her letter writing supplies. Kenzie hadn't seriously considered the possibility that one of the volunteers was involved. But here was someone who had not chosen to email her or to contact her on one of the social networks, but had written a letter and mailed it to her. Kenzie thought back to Roda in the hospital. Of course she had been holding a pen, not a Sharpie. But did that mean that there wasn't a Sharpie in her bag too? Or that she didn't have one at home that she could grab?

"Where was a volunteer at the hospital writing letters for the patients," she told Dr. Wiltshire.

"Well, that sounds like a possibility. Be sure to pass that on to Agent Menendez." He considered the letter on the desk. "What about the stamp? They could get DNA from it. It would take forever, I suppose, but it's a possibility."

Kenzie shook her head, laughing. "They're all self-stick these days, Doctor. I don't know when the last time was that I licked a stamp."

"Oh. Of course. And the same with the envelope flap, I suppose?"

Kenzie picked up the envelope and examined it. She nodded. "Yes. Not all of them are self-sealing, but this one is."

"Today's inventors just don't understand how valuable saliva is in solving a case," Dr. Wiltshire lamented, his eyes twinkling. "Or they never would have done that."

Kenzie forced a laugh. "Yeah. Investigators constantly need to upgrade their skills and look for answers in different places as they are sabotaged by inventors." She looked at the envelope, wondering if there were any other clues as to where it had come from. There was, of course, no return address. Little of the mail she got had visible postmarks on it anymore.

"I guess I shouldn't be touching this, in case it has fingerprints or other evidence on it."

She handled the envelope and the letter by the edges and slipped them into a page protector. She would, as Dr. Wiltshire said, have to give Agent Josie Menendez a call to pick up the letter and find out whether there were anything the FBI could find out from it. Maybe handwriting analysis or some kind of behavioral analysis based on the language that was used. But it was a pretty short note, not like the Unabomber Manifesto.

"Well..." Dr. Wiltshire took a deep breath and stepped back slightly from Kenzie's desk, giving her space. "Sorry about getting *that.* But I don't imagine you really have to worry about the 'or else.' It isn't like you're the investigator in this case anyway. You were only over there one day to preview the unit and pass your impressions on to Agent Menendez." He sighed. "I am glad to hear that you'll be able to visit Zachary tonight. Give him my best. I hope he's able to get turned back around quickly."

"Thanks."

Dr. Wiltshire nodded and left Kenzie alone, heading to his own office.

***

Most of the day's work was routine, and Kenzie didn't have to worry too much about fouling something up because she was distracted. Her brain knew what to do with the routine stuff and she didn't have to pay that much attention to it.

Midway through the afternoon, a review of her email inbox revealed that they'd received some of the lab results back on the Darling and Scott postmortems. She saved them to file and printed them off, reading from the screen as they printed. She grabbed the sheaf of papers and went to Dr. Wiltshire's office.

"Kenzie. What have you got for me?" Wiltshire asked genially.

"Tox results." Kenzie thrust them at him, eager to discuss the reports.

"I gather from your expression that they were not all negative."

"Nothing on Darling. But Scott..." Kenzie indicated the report that she had put on the top and flipped past the first couple of pages to the results as Dr. Wiltshire looked at it. "They detected the presence of succinylcholine."

"Sux."

Kenzie nodded. "Sucks for him," she agreed wryly.

Dr. Wiltshire rolled his eyes and shook his head. "And there was no reason for Sux to be present."

There were few reasons for a patient to be treated with the paralytic. It had not been used in any procedures that were recorded on Mr. Scott's chart.

"Nope."

"All right. We now have our second confirmed homicide. Give Agent Menendez a call."

"Do you want me to do it here?" Kenzie asked, motioning to Dr. Wiltshire's phone.

"Sure, you may as well. Then I can give my confirmation at the same time."

Kenzie turned the phone to face her and tapped in the number that she knew by heart from Agent Menendez's repeated calls to her.

"Agent Josie Menendez," the agent acknowledged on picking it up.

"Josie. Kenzie Kirsch here, with Dr. Wiltshire."

"I got your message regarding the letter you got," Menendez said, sounding a little annoyed. "I'll pick it up later, when I have the time. Or maybe tomorrow," she amended, probably looking at the clock and realizing that the office would be closed by the time she got around to it. "But I really don't think you're in any immediate danger."

"No, it's not that," Kenzie said. "You can pick that up whenever you want. Or I can have it sent over to you, if you prefer. But we got some of the tox reports in on the two exhumations."

"And you found something? Was it potassium chloride?"

"No. Something called succinylcholine. It's a paralytic. It—"

"I'm familiar with succinylcholine. It paralyzes all the muscles. Including breathing, right?"

Kenzie nodded, surprised that Menendez knew about it. But then, it had been used in a number of TV and thriller plots. And it had been used by Angel of Death killers in the past, which was why it was on Kenzie's list of drugs to test for. Menendez might have run into it in another case that she had reviewed as she investigated Dr. Philemon's list of deceased patients.

"Yes, that's right," Kenzie agreed, realizing that Menendez couldn't see her and was still waiting for her answer.

"So will Dr. Wiltshire change the cause and manner of death?" Menendez inquired. "Did you find it in both?"

"Only in Scott," Dr. Wiltshire advised. "And yes, I will be amending his manner of death to homicide. There was no reason for sux to be in his system based on the medical procedures he had been given. The only reason for it to be there was that someone wanted to kill him. Or to almost kill him and revive him. Sometimes these Angel of Death killers want to be in the spotlight for having saved someone's life."

"I have begun to compile a list of possible suspects," Menendez said. "Maybe tomorrow, we can get together and go through it so I can get your thoughts."

Kenzie pondered the developments on the Michaels case —or more correctly now, Dr. Philemon's serial killer case—as she drove to the hospital. Both to ponder whether there was anything they had missed and what their next steps should or would be, and also to think through her visit with Zachary. He wouldn't want a visit that was focused on his mental health or the Christmas season. It would be better to talk about something that would interest him and distract him from his own troubles and from Bridget and the babies.

The threat in the mail was disconcerting. It confirmed, just as much as the positive tox screen, that they were on the right track, that there was a serial killer on Dr. Philemon's team, and that the Angel of Death was aware of their investigation. Kenzie wished that the killer's attention had been focused on Agent Menendez and the FBI instead of her.

Maybe best not to tell Zachary that the serial killer was aware of her involvement in the case and where she worked. Zachary's own experience in disturbing a serial killer's work had been pretty traumatizing.

It took her a few minutes when she got to the psychiatric unit to get checked in. They had to check her name against the visitor list, which seemed to take much longer than it should, and then to confirm that Zachary was taking visitors, which Kenzie assumed meant both that he wanted to and that he wasn't isolated in an observation room, as he probably had been initially. Then she waited as an orderly was called to escort her to the common room where she would be able to visit with Zachary, even though Kenzie was sure that she could have just found it herself.

The orderly escorted her to a large open room that was mostly filled with chairs and tables that were probably used at mealtimes. Since it was not suppertime, most of them were clear, though there were a few puzzles and games out. No big poker games going on; everyone seemed to be doing their own thing. There was not much conversation. There was a TV and some upholstered furniture near the window at one end of the room, the TV volume turned down low so that anyone who wanted to hear would have to be sitting within a couple of feet of it.

Zachary was sitting at one of the tables waiting for her. Kenzie nodded her thanks to the orderly. "There he is. Thanks."

He nodded back and watched her approach Zachary. Kenzie smiled, forcing herself to look happier than she felt at seeing him there, looking fragile in the light hospital garb.

"Are we allowed to hug?" she inquired.

In response, he stood up and they embraced. Nothing that would embarrass anyone watching or make the staff worry that Kenzie was trying to pass some contraband on, just a quick but heartfelt hug to let him know how much she had missed him and how glad she was to see him again.

"Hi, Kenzie. Thanks for coming," he murmured.

"Of course. I've missed you. It's weird, the house being empty."

They both sat down.

"You're still there. And your stuff," Zachary pointed out

"I know, but it's not the same. Even though I was used to living alone, I don't like the way it feels when you're not around."

He looked down at the top of the table, nodding slightly. She thought she detected a slight reddening of his earlobes, a sign that he was pleased and embarrassed.

"I miss being there too."

"Well, you'll be back once you're feeling better," Kenzie said bracingly. It wasn't the end of the world that he was in the hospital for a bit. At least she knew that he would be feeling better and back home after Christmas. Back when they'd been in a car accident and his spine had been bruised, there had been a few scary days during which she didn't know whether he would recover fully. It had taken time and physiotherapy for him to get back on his feet. Now she couldn't even see the aftereffects.

She didn't know for sure how much to say about his mental health and his treatment plan. But she figured it was best to be up front, and if he didn't want to answer certain questions or told her to back off, then she would know.

"How are you feeling, being here? You feel... safer? Protected?"

Zachary's eyes wandered around the room. "Yeah. I don't have to worry about what I might do... they've got me doing more therapy, but I don't think they really understand... that I've been through all of this before. Talking about it isn't going to make that much difference."

"Well, I guess you have to give them leeway to figure it out. Doctors have a lot to learn. You know how it works for you, but they don't."

He nodded.

"I ran into a nurse who works in this unit. She said she's been here for a few years and that she knew you, because you have been here before. So there must be a few people that know more about your history, even if the doctor doesn't."

"Which nurse? That one that you knew that used to treat Amanda?"

"No, no. Not her. Someone who knew you from before. Oh... she was brunette, taller than me. Older. Said she'd been here for six years maybe?"

"Oh." Zachary nodded, a smile of recognition coming to his face. "Val."

"Val." Kenzie nodded. "So you know her from other admissions?"

"Yeah. She's good. It's nice to come here and see people you know. To have things that are… familiar. It makes it easier."

"That makes sense. It's a pretty drastic transition. Having familiar people and things around you would help."

"Not a lot changes, even if the people here do. And sometimes, I even know some of the patients. Because we've all been here before."

It wasn't a long-term facility. If Zachary had needed to stay there for a few months, or longer, he would have been transferred to one of the other facilities where those with mental health issues were able to stay longer-term. Kenzie was surprised that she knew some of the other patients, but she supposed there was no reason she should be. Mental health issues didn't just go away. The doctor would try to get the patients onto a medication cocktail that would provide long-term support, but you never knew when a medication would suddenly stop working, or the patient would stop taking it, or, like Zachary, there would be some other trigger that would push them past the point where they could handle things alone.

"Are they going to do anything else?" she asked Zachary. "Change around any meds or try some other therapy?"

"No. Don't want them to. Things have been okay… mostly. It's just… with the other stuff going on right now. The season and… you know."

Bridget and the babies. Kenzie wondered whether she should talk to Zachary about them, or whether that would just make things worse. She decided she'd better let him bring it up on his own.

"Everybody sends their love. Lorne and your family. And Dr. Wiltshire says to get better soon."

Zachary rubbed his ear. "Dr. Wiltshire knows…?"

Kenzie nodded. "If you don't want me to tell anyone, let me know. I thought that you wanted to be open about it."

"Yeah, I do," he agreed. "I just didn't think about him knowing. You don't think that will cause you any problems, if he thinks you have trouble at home? Or if I am trying to get copies of documents or a case opened?"

"No," Kenzie shook her head. "Not at all. He's cool with it. He told me to take time off if I need it and said to let him know if there's anything he can do. If you need anything."

"And it won't affect his opinion of you?"

"No. And not of you, either. He's a doctor. He understands that mental illness isn't something that you can control and that it doesn't mean that you're weak or that you're not competent in your work." Kenzie met Zachary's eyes, trying to impress these words on him. "You are a strong person. Coming here isn't taking the easy way out. Acknowledging your problems openly isn't easy, is it?"

"No."

Kenzie nodded firmly and decided it was time to move on. She had resolved not to spend the whole time talking about depression.

"You remember the case I was telling you about? That the FBI is in on?"

Zachary's eyes immediately brightened, interested in hearing more about it. "Yes. How's that going?"

"We had a couple of the doctor's previous patients exhumed. These are patients that he identified as possibly being suspicious, and the families gave permission for us to re-examine them."

"How long ago…? What kind of condition were they in?"

"Not bad, all things considered. Modern embalming procedures are pretty good. But they did still stink. You just can't get that smell out of your nose at the end of the day, it seems like it clings to everything."

Zachary nodded.

"I looked up as many other Angel of Death serial killers as I could to research their methods. Because people generally stick with what has worked before, right?"

"Yeah."

"So when we got the bodies, we did a bunch of tox screens,

based on that research. Not just the usual illegal drug screens, but specialized testing for some of the drugs that we were hoping to find."

"And you found something? Was it more potassium?"

Kenzie held up her finger. "Not potassium."

"What, then?"

"Succinylcholine."

"I've heard of it. Don't know much about it."

"It's a paralytic. They use it in some surgical procedures. But you have to provide respiratory support because it also stops the patient's breathing."

"Ohhh."

"It paralyzes the person, but they stay awake and aware; they know what's going on until the end, when they can't get enough oxygen to stay conscious. Then the heart stops, and they're gone. It looks like a natural death, if you're not looking for it."

"It has to be injected?"

"Yes. But that's easy enough in a hospital setting. The people that an Angel of Death killer is taking out are usually already in bad shape. So they probably already have an IV."

"And even if they don't, they've probably had some kind of injection in the past few days. So another needle mark wouldn't be noticed, or you could go in through an existing location," he suggested.

"Yeah. There are definitely ways around it. And needle marks are easy to miss if they are well-hidden. Between the toes. In areas that are hairy. Spotting injection sites isn't always easy, like you might think."

"Did you find succin— this drug in both of them?"

"No, only in one. No clear cause of death in the other yet. We don't have all the testing back, so we might still be able to find something. But not yet."

"It could be insulin."

"Yes, in which case, we're not going to find anything. But we'll keep looking. And hopefully, we'll get a few more bodies for examination, and we can establish enough of a pattern to find out who was present for all of them."

"Will you be able to? Not everyone who is working in the ward gets on the chart, do they?"

"No. It makes it tricky. Especially if it was someone who was supposed to be off shift, or if it was someone who wasn't a medical professional at all, but who could come and go in the unit without looking suspicious."

"Janitors."

"Yup."

He rubbed his chin, thinking about it. "There must be other maintenance staff too. Plumbers and electrical. Builders. Security guards."

"Volunteers. Chaplains."

"Social workers."

Kenzie hadn't thought of that one. She made a mental note.

"Technicians—people who take blood, deliver test results, bring the food up to the ward."

"Hmm." Zachary closed his eyes, thinking about it. "I like people who bring the food up. Some drugs or poisons could be administered in food. Maybe not that one, but others."

"Yeah. Especially something like antifreeze. Easy to slip into drinks or put into Jell-O or yogurt." Antifreeze wasn't something that Kenzie had included in the tests that they had requested. "Huh. Hadn't thought about that."

Zachary gave a half-smile. "Always happy to help."

Kenzie caught the movement of a nurse walking toward her out the corner of her eye and turned to look. She saw that it was Debbie and stood up to greet her and to give her a friendly hug.

"Hey. Good to see you again."

"And how is my favorite patient?" Debbie asked Zachary cheerfully. "Don't you go telling anyone else I called you that," she added conspiratorially, "The other patients will be jealous!"

Zachary smiled, but Kenzie could see it wasn't genuine. He wasn't in the mood to be teased or treated like someone's eight-year-old nephew. Kenzie had always appreciated Nurse Debbie's good cheer when things had been so grim, but she could understand how it might grate on a person.

"Especially that old grouch, Kennedy," Nurse Debbie told him, leaning in a little. "If he thinks that I have a boyfriend in the ward, he's not going to make my life easy."

Zachary rolled his eyes and looked at Kenzie, hoping she would save him from the ebullient nurse.

"I don't think you're allowed to have even one boyfriend on the ward," Kenzie countered, trying to take Nurse Debbie's attention off of Zachary. "How are you? It's sure nice to have you here in the ward. I'm sure Zachary appreciates having you around, knowing what a professional you are."

"And I love having him here." Debbie gave Zachary a light tap on the shoulder. "He's one of my easiest patients. No whining from this one. Always polite and trying not to make any waves. A real gentleman."

Kenzie nodded. "How long have you been here? In this ward, I mean?"

"I'm pretty new! Just been here for a few weeks. I needed a change of pace. You know, you get tired of the same thing day after day. And there aren't as many diapers to change or vomit to clean up in psych!"

She must have been in pediatrics before.

"I would hope not," Kenzie agreed. "So you're enjoying it?"

"Certainly. What's not to like?" Nurse Debbie laughed, then leaned closer to Kenzie, taking the spotlight off of Zachary. "Well, of course there are challenges in every department. We do get our share of crazies in this ward. And I don't mean the depressives…" She flipped a hand in Zachary's direction. "The schizophrenics and psychotics who go off their meds. Kids with their brains fried by LSD. Transfers from the jail." She blew out her breath, making a noise of disgust. "We get our share of colorful characters, I'll tell you!"

"Yeah, I bet." Kenzie remembered a few characters she had

met on her psych rotation. And not all of them had been patients. "Well, we shouldn't keep you. I'm sure you have a lot to do."

Nurse Debbie nodded her agreement and started to move away. "Yes, that's true. A nurse's work is never done. If it is, it must be time for another shift! Don't you worry." She slapped Zachary on the back. "We'll take care of Zachary while he's here. I can already tell he's a favorite."

Kenzie nodded politely and watched as Nurse Debbie moved away. She sat back down. "Sorry about that."

"She seems very nice," Zachary said, trying to excuse his reaction. "She's just very… intense. It's hard to handle all that extra emotion."

"I could see that. And I'm sorry because I think that because she knows me, she's giving you extra attention, which is uncomfortable for you."

"She's pretty much like that with everyone.; I don't know where she gets all that energy. All of the smiling and joking." Zachary shook his head. "It looks exhausting."

"She was always like that with us too, when Amanda was in hospital. Well… maybe not always, I can remember once or twice seeing her when she wasn't putting on as much of a front. When she didn't know anyone was looking and she seemed tired or upset about a patient or frustrated with a doctor. Like anyone does in unguarded moments."

"So she's actually human?"

"Apparently so. Or she was then, at least. She may have been replaced by an artificial life form since then. It seems just as likely."

"I'm sure it cheers people up. All her jokes and smiles and backslapping. Just… not me."

Kenzie was also starting to fade. Not because she'd done too much physically, but just because it was difficult being around Zachary when he was so depressed, and she had to watch everything she said. He sucked the energy out of her, and she found herself getting down when she didn't really have any reason to be.

"You look tired," Zachary said, reading her face. "You don't have to stay here all night. I'm okay."

"I'm glad to know that you're safe here. But you must be bored. There's not really much to do." Kenzie looked around. There weren't a lot of people just sitting staring off into space. Most were playing with cards or puzzles, visiting, or watching the TV. There were probably more in their rooms. Maybe reading books or writing letters. But there wasn't much excitement.

"I'll watch TV after you go. That's probably what I'd be doing at home anyway."

But he'd be doing work at his computer while he was doing it. Or he might not have been home at all, but off watching Bridget's house or following her around town. TV might not be that exciting of a pursuit, but he was safe, and they would help him until he was well enough to be home again.

"Okay. I guess so. But if you want me to bring anything. Something that I'm allowed to bring, I mean. Just let me know."

"I don't need anything right now."

"I know you're not into reading, but…"

"Yeah. That's okay. I'd rather watch TV."

"Who else is on your visitor list? Your family would like to visit you, but I didn't know what the situation is."

"Lorne is already on there. I'll get them to put Tyrrell and Heather…"

"Joss too. I don't know whether she'll come, but you'd better not include your other siblings and not her."

"Yeah. Okay." Zachary nodded. "I'll add her too. She probably won't want to come." He tapped his fingers on the table. "And Rhys. Would you let him and Vera know?"

Rhys wasn't family, but Zachary had taken the teenager in under his wing. They had both been through various institutionalizations and had to deal with being "broken" by past traumas. Rhys was mostly mute, but he was still able to communicate and had visited Zachary in the hospital before.

"Sure. I'll give Vera a call."

"Thanks."

"Anyone else?"

Zachary shook his head.

"Mario?" Kenzie suggested. Mario Bowman was one of the police officers that Zachary knew. While not all of them were tolerant of a private investigator, some of them had become friends over the years and the various cases that Zachary had investigated. Mario had allowed Zachary to sleep on his couch after he'd lost everything in the apartment fire. For several months. That kind of friend didn't come along very often.

But Zachary shook his head again. "No. I'm not ready for anyone else."

Kenzie nodded her understanding. "Okay. No problem." She blew out her breath, anxious about saying goodbye to him again. "Well, then…"

She stood up. Zachary recognized his cue and stood as well. The hug that Kenzie gave him this time was longer and tighter. She didn't want to overwhelm him with emotion, but she wanted to convey to him all those things that she couldn't say.

"Take care of yourself," she whispered against his neck, and gave him a kiss on the cheek. "Hang in there, okay? I'll be back tomorrow."

Zachary kissed Kenzie gently, then let her go, stepping back slightly to put space between them. He nodded. "See you tomorrow. Thanks for coming."

Kenzie needed a few minutes after she left the psych ward. She found a cluster of furniture in an alcove area, where families or friends might meet in small groups, and she sat down, breathing heavily in and out, trying to relax her body and keep her emotions under control. She kept repeating to herself that Zachary was safe where he was and would be home soon. She wasn't abandoning him by going back home.

She managed to get herself calmed down. She wiped her face and got up and walked down the hall to the elevators. She was planning to go straight back out to her car, but when she got into the elevator, she saw the departments and their floors listed on the back of the elevator and her eyes caught on the Maternity Ward and NICU. She could stop in and see whether she could find anything out about Bridget and Gordon and the twins while she was there. It would be an efficient use of her time.

So she pressed the floor number and got back out of the elevator a couple of floors down instead of going all the way to the parking garage.

NICU was generally off-limits to everyone but the parents, unless they brought someone else in with them, so she didn't attempt to get in and find out about the babies by herself. The nurses wouldn't give her any information, even if she held herself out as a doctor. She wasn't their doctor, so the privacy rules still applied.

She headed instead to the maternity unit, following the signs on the walls until she reached the nursing station for the unit. She ignored the desk and started to walk around the cluster of rooms, peeking in the doorways for Bridget and Gordon.

She knew that they might have gone home. Zachary had been worried about Bridget being released before the babies. With the cost of health care, it wouldn't make much sense for Bridget to stay at the hospital as a patient if she didn't need to.

"Uh, miss...?" She heard a nurse calling after her but ignored the call and kept going. She could probably get most of the way around the unit before anyone actually caught up with her or stopped her to ask her business there.

Kenzie looked in the next doorway and saw a man she thought was Gordon sitting beside the bed. He was blocking Kenzie's view of the woman, so she couldn't be sure, but she stepped in anyway, hoping she didn't make a fool of herself. But would it be so awful to say that she thought they were someone else? She only had a view of the man's back, after all.

"Uh, hi?" Kenzie took a couple of steps into the room for a better view, and both faces turned toward her. It was Gordon and Bridget after all.

Bridget looked at Kenzie for a moment before her face went taut and Kenzie supposed Bridget recognized her from when she had been together with Zachary out in public. Gordon smiled politely.

"I'm Kenzie," she introduced herself. "Sorry, I know you weren't expecting me here. I don't mean to disturb you."

"Kenzie." Gordon gave her a welcoming smile. "You don't need to apologize. What a nice surprise."

Bridget didn't look nearly so welcoming. She looked at the

doorway behind Kenzie, waiting. Kenzie realized she was looking for Zachary, expecting him to come in behind her.

"It's just me. I'm alone."

The nurse who had been calling after Kenzie walked up to the doorway to look in at her and seemed satisfied when she saw that Kenzie was engaged in a discussion with the couple, apparently an expected guest. She turned and walked back away. Kenzie bit her lip and smiled at Bridget, acting as though she'd been greeted with warmth as a friend.

"I was here, and when I realized how close I was to the maternity unit, I thought I would just stop in and see how everyone is."

Gordon stood up to retrieve another visitor chair and slid it beside his. "Come, sit, sit."

Kenzie sat down in the uncomfortable chair and smiled once more at Bridget, the muscles in her face feeling the strain.

Bridget was pale and didn't appear to have put on any weight with her pregnancy; not that showed in her face, anyway. She swept long, blond hair over one ear and looked at Kenzie accusingly.

"Bridget is recovering quite well," Gordon said, as if he didn't notice any of the awkwardness between them. "It was quite an ordeal, but they tell me women have been having babies for thousands of years and I just need to stay out of the way and let her do her job." Gordon smiled affectionately at Bridget. "She really was a trooper. I can't imagine any man I know going through such a thing."

"Then it's a good thing that they don't have to," Bridget said.

Gordon nodded his agreement. "I never have bought into the 'weaker sex' thing. The strongest people I know are all women."

Kenzie nodded politely. "I'm so glad everything went well. I can tell you; we have been quite concerned."

Gordon let out a sigh and nodded. "The girls have had a difficult time. But if they are anything like their mother, they will pull through."

"I heard something about a heart attack?" Kenzie ventured, being careful not to name Zachary or to indicate that this news had come to them from Gordon. She didn't want to say anything that might trigger a tirade from Bridget.

Gordon nodded. "Julia. They managed to revive her, and she's still holding her own. They can't tell us anything about brain damage or any other permanent effects at this point. Just that she's improving. We haven't had another incident, which is what they warned us about. That sometimes, they just aren't strong enough and even though they are revived the first time…" Gordon trailed off. "But it's been a couple of days, and it hasn't happened again, so maybe she's through the danger period."

"I'm sorry, that must have been terrifying." Kenzie made sure that she met both of their eyes, not just speaking to Gordon and ignoring Bridget because she was more difficult to deal with. Bridget was the mother; she should be a full part of the discussion as well.

"Tricia, though, is off the respirator now," Gordon told her, smiling at this. "And that is very good news. She has been breathing on her own for twenty-four hours. The next step is feeding. She has a tube right now, but if we can start getting some milk into her by mouth…"

"That's great. I'm glad to hear that they're improving."

"What are you doing here?" Bridget demanded. "Where is Zachary?"

Kenzie swallowed and looked at her, trying to decide whether Bridget were trying to start something, or if she actually wanted Zachary to be there. She did go through occasional periods when she wanted something from him or started to show concern for him, before her mood started swinging the other direction again and she was haranguing him for something.

"He's not with me," Kenzie said slowly.

"Why wouldn't he come with you?"

Kenzie felt her way through the conversation uncertainly.

"This is a difficult time of year for him, and he's been quite concerned for you and the twins. It's been hard on him."

Bridget wasn't being put off. She stared at Kenzie, waiting for Kenzie to give a proper answer to her question.

"He's been admitted," Kenzie said finally. As she and Zachary had discussed earlier, it was not a secret. Not something that Zachary wanted to hide as though he were ashamed of it. "He's quite depressed right now and felt that it was best if he was here, where it's safe."

"Here?"

"In the psychiatric unit." Not in maternity, obviously. Kenzie waited for the explosion—Bridget demanding to know why Zachary just happened to be in the same hospital as she was at the same time as she was. Was it a coincidence that they had both ended up in the same place? Kenzie waited for the accusations that the only reason that Zachary had admitted himself was because he wanted to be close to Bridget. To spy on her.

But the medication that Bridget was on seemed to have smoothed out some of the paranoid and angry outbursts that she had displayed previously. Or maybe she was just too tired from the births.

"Always at Christmas," Bridget said, nodding. "I thought that it would be different. We both thought that it would be different when we were together. And he did manage to stay out of the hospital those years. But it was not fun. Trying to drag him out to functions that we needed to appear at when he just wanted to curl up on the bed in a darkened room. Getting home from them and fighting half the night. I didn't think he was trying hard enough."

But the first year that Kenzie had known Zachary, Bridget had gone to Zachary's apartment at Christmas to check on him and clear out his meds to make sure that he couldn't overdose, even though they had no longer been together. So at some point, she had realized just how severe Zachary's depression was and that it wasn't something he could control.

"So that's why he's here," Kenzie said. "And why I'm here. He didn't ask me to come see you, but I thought I would check in on you and then I can reassure him that you are all okay when he asks next time."

"Why does he care how I am? Or how the twins are? After everything that we went through, all the troubles, why would he care?"

Kenzie gave a little laugh. "If it was me, I'm pretty sure I would stay away as far as possible," she agreed. "If somebody didn't want me around and we'd had as rocky a relationship as the two of you have, I wouldn't even want to know that you were pregnant."

"No. It's none of his business."

"But you and I don't have to deal with having his brain. With all the trauma and mental illness and everything that goes along with his ADHD and learning disabilities. He doesn't really want to be obsessed with you."

Bridget pondered that, a crease between her eyebrows. Gordon shifted in his seat. "You are looking tired, my dear." He looked at the shiny gold watch on his wrist. "It's late. You know you can't neglect your health."

Bridget closed her eyes and held her hand over her eyes and forehead for a moment. "Yes. I am getting tired."

"Go to sleep." Gordon got up and leaned over her to give her a kiss. Kenzie stood and prepared to leave.

"Let me walk you out," Gordon offered.

Kenzie walked to the door and waited for him to finish his goodbye with Bridget, then he joined her, and they walked out of the unit together.

"Would you like to see them?" Gordon asked.

Kenzie didn't have to ask who. "Yes, of course I would!"

He smiled and walked her past the elevators again, toward the NICU. Kenzie remembered her internship in maternity, and visits to the nursery and NICU, looking at the tiny, miraculous infants.

No matter whether she believed in God and heaven or not, she believed that every baby was a miracle.

As a child, she had been thrilled when Amanda had been born. She had held her hand over Lisa's stomach to feel the baby kick. She had not been present for the birth but had been introduced to baby Amanda soon after that, and she had been enthralled. Despite her youth, she had changed diapers, fed Amanda, and entertained her for hours on end.

But she didn't think she could ever have worked in the NICU. Not knowing that she could lose any of those tiny infants at any moment. It was amazing to walk around and look at them, to see what challenges they had survived, but she hadn't wanted to know the long-term outcomes. Too many of them would die.

Gordon led her to an incubator that held two babies. Kenzie was glad to see that they were being kept together. She had seen videos and news reports on twins who had languished when they were kept apart and had immediately improved when put back together again. They needed each other.

One baby had breathing support.

"Julia," Gordon murmured, indicating her. He reached in through the access port and stroked her little stomach and arm.

Kenzie looked at the baby's vital signs monitor. Her oxygen saturation was good.

"And Tricia," Gordon said, and switched to the access port on the other side to touch her as well. Tricia stirred, turning her head toward him slightly. "Hello, sweetheart," Gordon crooned to her. "This is Daddy. You're getting so strong, aren't you?"

They were both pink and small, but not as tiny as some of the neonates Kenzie had seen. They had good skin color and vitals, and she hoped they would both be able to pull through. For their own sakes, and for Bridget and Gordon. And for Zachary.

"He's been so worried about them," she told Gordon in a whisper, not wanting to disturb the twins or confuse them with another voice. "When he heard about Julia's incident... I don't know if that is what triggered his suicidal thoughts this weekend, but he was very upset by it."

"I probably shouldn't have told him."

"If he asks, then you're being kind to tell him. You don't have to tell him anything, but you've been very compassionate toward him."

"I figure if I don't tell him, he'll be here checking up on them himself," Gordon said with a smile. "The only hope of keeping them separated is to let him know what he asks."

Kenzie chuckled and nodded. "Yes, you're probably right," she agreed. None of them would be able to keep Zachary away from Bridget and the twins if he thought that they were in danger and that Gordon was keeping information from him.

Gordon leaned in toward the incubator, getting his face as close to the little girls as he could. "Did you know that he was there again, when Bridget collapsed?"

"He told me."

"He must have ESP where she is concerned. To be there at that exact time."

"I'm sure that wasn't the only time he was there. We are talking to his medical team, by the way. They are increasing his meds and therapy to try to keep him away from her. Hopefully once everyone is out of the hospital…"

Gordon nodded. "It isn't like he doesn't try. I've seen that."

Kenzie hesitated to say anything further, then decided to bite the bullet. "But you need to stay away from him, too. Quit hiring him. Don't ask him for his opinion on anything. Putting him on surveillance of Bridget…!"

Gordon grimaced. "Not my best idea, maybe. But I knew he would be like a dog with a bone. He wouldn't rest until he knew the truth."

"You sent him back over the edge. I don't think he would have gone back to stalking her, if it weren't for that."

Gordon shrugged. In the end, he had gotten what he had wanted. Zachary had chased down the information Gordon had needed, so it had all worked out in the end. It may have wreaked havoc on Zachary's life, but that wasn't really Gordon's problem.

"I won't hire him again," he conceded.

"Good. If he asks you about Bridget or the twins and you want to answer him, that's fine. But don't reach out to him."

He nodded.

But Kenzie wondered whether he would keep his promise.

It had been a long day and Kenzie was ready to go home. She had done everything she could for Zachary, and she needed to take care of herself so that she could do her job and so that when Zachary eventually got out of the hospital, she would be ready for him, and not worn away to nothing because she had been so focused on taking care of him. He had people there to look after him. The hospital staff would see to his physical needs and do what they could to improve his mood.

She left Gordon in the NICU. He looked as if he would be there for a while. She couldn't imagine that he was staying with the twins overnight. He had a business to look after. Like Kenzie, he would need to leave care of the patients to the hospital staff and to take care of himself.

But she didn't think that taking care of himself had ever been a problem for Gordon. He didn't strike her as someone who was shy about going after what he wanted. Even though it was the first time she had met him face to face, she had known that about him for some time. It was obvious by the way that he treated Zachary.

As she walked toward the elevators, Kenzie was surprised to see another familiar face. She blinked at the young male nurse walking toward her and tried to remember where she had seen him before. Had he just been up at the psych unit? She didn't think that was it.

She smiled and nodded at him, then studied his name tag as he walked toward her, until she could focus on the name.

"Nurse Stevens," she greeted. "I didn't expect to see you here."

And then she remembered where she had seen him before. He had been one of the nurses on duty in the geriatric ward. He had been there the day she had been conducting her investigation into Mr. Michaels's death and who had been on the floor when he had died.

Stevens was looking at her in confusion. He had only seen her once, and probably couldn't place her either. Kenzie lifted her chin slightly, holding his gaze.

"Dr. Kenzie Kirsch," she reminded him. "With the ME's Office."

"Oh, yes. I'm sorry, I recognized your face, but I couldn't remember where we had met." He looked around, checking whether anyone was watching them or within earshot. "So… what brings you here? I didn't think the Medical Examiner made house calls."

"Well, we do attend the scene when there is a suspicious death," she reminded him. "Even at a hospital."

"Well… yes, I suppose so. But there can't be many of those. Especially… in the NICU."

"As it happens, I'm not here on business. I was visiting a patient. And stopped in to see someone else I know."

He nodded, and his eyes darted around. "Sure. Of course."

Kenzie waited for him to say what he was doing away from his unit. It wasn't as if he could claim to have forgotten where the cafeteria was. There wasn't much call for a geriatric nurse to be on a maternity floor.

"I'm just up here to see a friend too," Stevens said eventually.

"Oh? How is she doing?"

"Uh… fine. Really good." He started moving again, passing her in the hallway. "Have a nice day."

Kenzie turned her head and watched him go, wondering what he was really there for. Pretty lame to use the same excuse as she had. It could be true, of course, but then she would have expected more of an explanation of how mother and child were doing, rather than just a generic "fine."

She waited until he had turned the corner and was out of sight, and then tapped his name into her phone.

Agent Menendez was at the Medical Examiner's Office bright and early the next morning. Well, not particularly early, but she was there the next morning. She examined the threat that Kenzie had received and looked down at it without much apparent interest.

"How did you get it?" she asked. "Was it in the mail? Dropped off in person?"

"The envelope is in there too," Kenzie pointed out. "It came in the postal mail."

Menendez studied it through the plastic sleeve. "Stamp hasn't been canceled. You're sure someone didn't throw it into interoffice mail or bring it down and leave it here in person? Are you just assuming it was in the postal mail?"

"No." Kenzie was irritated that Menendez would think she didn't have the intelligence to know whether something had come in through the mail or other channels. "We have a locked mailbox. No one but USPS can put anything in there."

"You don't have a mail room that sorts and delivers your mail?"

"No. I get it out of the box myself. The police have a mail-room up there," Kenzie motioned overhead. "But that isn't shared with the Medical Examiner's Office. Our mail system is completely separate."

"So no interoffice mail, you're totally autonomous."

Kenzie nodded. "Our interoffice mail is me taking stuff down to Dr. Wiltshire's office. But most of the time, I wouldn't even do that. I'd just email him."

Menendez nodded. "Right. Makes sense."

"It came in through the mail. I know that for sure."

She nodded and slid it into her soft-sided briefcase. "Great. I'll take care of it. See whether trace can get anything from it."

"Thanks. I don't usually get threats!"

"I guess that would be a bit of a shock, then. FBI..." Menendez shrugged. "We get them all the time."

Kenzie raised an eyebrow. She wasn't surprised about that. Especially with Agent Menendez, who didn't have quite the social skills Kenzie would have expected from an FBI agent working in the field.

"And you've got my tox reports?" Menendez asked.

"I have *my* tox reports," Kenzie corrected. "Which I've made copies of for the FBI."

Menendez put out her hand, flicking her fingers in an impatient *give-it-to-me* gesture. Kenzie picked up the envelope of reports that she had printed out for Menendez earlier.

Menendez took it with a nod and slid it into her bag as well.

"You said that you were starting to put together a suspect list," Kenzie said, "and that you might want to go over it with us?"

"Is Dr. Wiltshire available?"

"Not at the moment. He's on a conference call, but he should be off soon."

Menendez gave her a look of exasperation, as if Kenzie and Dr. Wiltshire should have known at exactly what time she would come by and have made sure that no one would be occupied with anything else when she arrived.

Kenzie rolled her eyes.

"I guess I'll wait, then," Menendez said.

Kenzie sat back down in her chair and leaned back. "Something kind of funny happened at the hospital yesterday. I wondered what you would think of it..."

"What happened? What were you doing back at the hospital?"

the agent frowned, studying Kenzie "Especially after receiving this note?"

"I was visiting a friend who is sick," Kenzie said evenly.

"A friend who is sick. This friend wouldn't happen to be in the geriatric unit, would they? I would think that you'd know well enough to stay out of the way once our investigation started."

"No, he isn't in the geriatric unit. I wasn't anywhere near there."

"Okay. But still. Why would you go after getting this note?"

"I don't think that note meant anything about me visiting a friend. It just meant not going to investigate anything. Not to keep asking questions about who was around the day that Michaels died."

"It doesn't say that. If someone happened to see you there, they could spread the word to our killer that you are still hanging around. It could cause you trouble."

Kenzie shifted uncomfortably. "I didn't imagine that I would run into anyone who was from the geriatric unit or who knew that I had been there. Usually, professionals stay pretty close to their units. They might go down to the cafeteria for something to eat, but they wouldn't have a reason to go traipsing to other parts of the hospital."

Menendez studied Kenzie for a moment, then gave a wide shrug. "Well then… what happened that was funny?"

Kenzie cleared her throat, not so sure that she wanted to tell Menendez about it now. Not right after she had said that it didn't make sense that someone who worked in another area of the hospital would show up somewhere else.

"I saw one of the nurses who I had seen in the geriatric unit when I was asking questions. I thought it was really strange to find him there."

Menendez glared at her. "Well, as you said, maybe he was just on his way to the cafeteria."

"Well… I know that he wasn't. It wasn't anywhere near the

cafeteria. When I asked him about it, he said that he was there to see a friend."

"Maybe he was. People who work at the hospital can have friends. Friends who might invite them to come over for a visit if they happen to have a free moment."

"Yeah. It's possible. He just didn't sound to me as if he was telling the truth."

"Maybe he was, or maybe he wasn't. No way for us to know. What did you tell him that you were doing there?"

"Visiting a friend."

Menendez grunted her acknowledgment. "So why couldn't he be too? How far away from the geriatric unit were you?"

"I was in the NICU."

Menendez leaned in and didn't say anything.

"Neonatal Intensive Care Unit," Kenzie explained.

Again, there was no response from Menendez. She was not perky and friendly, unlike the other days she had been by. Maybe she'd been told by one of her superiors to shape up and start acting like a grown-up FBI officer.

"It's practically the other side of the hospital and up five floors," Kenzie explained. "It's not close. I had no reason to think that I might run into someone from the geriatric unit there."

"Well, there's no reason that a nurse couldn't go visit a friend in another unit. If you want to give me their name, I'll make sure he's on the list of people to investigate and see whether we can get any details of why he was there and who he was seeing."

"Stevens. A male nurse. I don't remember his first name."

"Stevens." Menendez nodded, appearing to thaw a little. "Yeah, I remember that name. He's already on the list."

"Good."

Menendez leaned on the edge of Kenzie's desk. "And who were you there to see?"

Kenzie could see that things were just going to continue to be more awkward if she tried to preserve her private life. Insisting that Menendez interrogate others about what they had been doing in another part of the hospital, and then refusing to explain her presence would not be taken well.

"I would like a little privacy," Kenzie said. "My life away from this office really isn't anyone else's business."

"You having an affair or something?"

"No." Kenzie's face warmed. She tried to ignore the blush and press forward. "I'm not having an affair. I was visiting Zachary. We live together. It's just that this is very private information. Personal, private medical records," she said firmly.

"Who am I going to run around telling? Your boyfriend, Zachary." She lifted one eyebrow and stared at Kenzie.

"Yes. What?"

"Did Zachary recently have a baby?"

Kenzie had to laugh at the incongruity over her answer and what she had already told Menendez. "No—no, sorry. I was there to see Zachary. He's upstairs, in psychiatric. But a friend of ours —" Kenzie elected not to tell Menendez that she was Zachary's ex, "—just had twins, and they are in the NICU."

"So who were you there to see? Your boyfriend or these friends?"

"I had already been in to see Zachary. I was on my way out. Going home. Then I realized that maternity was right there, so I went in to say hello."

"And ran into this Nurse Stevens."

"Right. I ran into him on my way out of NICU; he was on his way in. And he didn't say who he was there to see or what had happened. Normally, if you go to visit someone with a baby in the NICU, you would talk about what happened—the baby was premature or they had to deliver early because of some medical problem—but he didn't. He just said he was there to visit a friend."

"Which could be perfectly correct."

"Of course," Kenzie agreed. "Absolutely. It was just disconcerting to see him there, especially after getting this threatening note. He didn't 'belong' there in my mind. But that doesn't mean he didn't. It could be completely innocent. The only problem is that he was one of the people who was around the day that Mr. Michaels died. And that doesn't mean he had anything to do with it."

Menendez nodded. "As long as we are agreed."

30

It was a while before Dr. Wiltshire got off his conference call. Kenzie set Menendez up in the boardroom and got her a coffee, so that Kenzie could get back to work. She didn't want to sit around talking to Menendez, who seemed to think that Kenzie wanted to be her best friend and tell her all about her life.

"Kenzie, sorry to keep you waiting." Dr. Wiltshire looked toward the boardroom. "Everything okay?"

"Yes, just fine. She's been out of the way. Mostly."

"Why don't you freshen your coffee, and we'll see what she has to share."

Kenzie thought that sounded like a pretty good idea. She went to the kitchenette to get a refill, then joined Dr. Wiltshire in the boardroom where he was talking casually with Agent Menendez.

"Well, looks like we're finally all here," Menendez observed when Kenzie sat down at the table. "I've been away from the office longer than I should have been, so let's get started here."

Kenzie hadn't seen Menendez take any calls or have to make abject apologies to her bosses. Kenzie got the feeling that she was allowed pretty wide latitude to do whatever she wanted to do, not that she was only let out of the office for limited windows of time. Kenzie couldn't judge by TV shows, of course, but on the ones she had seen, they always spent a lot of time in the field and could pursue leads as they came up. They didn't just sit at their desks all day and make inquiries on their computers or phones.

Just like Zachary didn't do all his investigative work from home. He had to get out on site, talk to people, make contact in the real world.

Kenzie pulled her thoughts away from Zachary yet again as Menendez took a few items out of her briefcase. It was difficult to stay focused on the task at hand and not wonder how Zachary was doing. She just had to keep reminding herself that he was fine where he was. There was nothing to worry about.

Menendez leafed through several pages of notes, some computer generated and some handwritten.

"So, you were talking about Nurse Stevens, and he was one of the nurses that we had down as having been on the floor the day that Mr. Michaels died. He has not been in the unit for a long time, though, so if we are trying to reach all the way back on the list that Dr. Philemon provided, he could not be involved in the earlier ones."

"But we don't know whether any of those cases are actually related," Kenzie said. "It's all just speculation until we can prove that they were homicides."

"Right." Menendez nodded and took a sip of her own travel cup of coffee. "It's difficult to come up with a concrete list when we don't know which deaths were actually homicides and which were not. We don't know which ones we have to correlate schedules with, so it all becomes a little… amorphous."

Kenzie knew this to be true from previous cases. It was hard to correlate when you didn't know which deaths were representative. It all ended up being a hodgepodge of facts.

Menendez read off a few of the names on her list. Some of them, Kenzie recognized, like Nurse Pierce. Even Dr. Philemon had to be considered. Sometimes people wanted to be caught. They wanted to explain to someone how smart they were, show them how much they had gotten away with. Just because he had started the investigation himself, that didn't eliminate the young doctor from the list of suspects.

"And the people who were not medical professionals?" Kenzie asked. "There was a volunteer there, her name was Roda. I don't know who else might have been there the day Mr. Michaels died. There are a lot of administrative and support people who could have been around. Even if they don't normally interface with the patients, like a security guard or a plumber, they could still get around the ward and put something in an IV without being noticed."

"There's no way for us to track all those people. Not unless they have gotten themselves noticed enough for someone that we interview to bring them up. There's no way to know who might have walked in and out. But history says that it is likely to be a doctor or nurse, so that's really what we need to focus on."

Kenzie nodded slowly. It was frightening, when she thought about it, how many people could walk in and out of a place that you thought was secure, like a hospital. How someone who was dangerous could be lurking right under their noses and they wouldn't even know it. Any of the doctors and nurses she had talked to that day. The ones she had seen in the psychiatric unit when she had gone to visit Zachary. The ones she had seen in maternity and NICU. Any of those people could be deeply disturbed to the point that they were murdering patients, and if they were clever, they could kill dozens before they were caught.

Finding the one person who really was dangerous was like searching for a needle in a haystack. Or in a box full of needles.

"Can I see the list? Get a copy?" Kenzie asked.

"I only have one copy. And I shouldn't really let it out of my control."

So she wasn't likely to let Kenzie make a copy of it or write the names down herself. But just looking at the list might trigger something.

"Could I just see it then? Read through it?"

Menendez looked wary. Where was the girl who wanted to be Kenzie's best friend now?

"I can't really be of any help if I can't even see the list," Kenzie pointed out. "I helped you to compile that list. It isn't like it's a secret."

"I really shouldn't..." Menendez trailed off. She looked around her as if one of her bosses might have snuck into the boardroom without her noticing and be listening to see what she said.

She slid the papers across the table to Kenzie.

Kenzie picked them up and started to read through them. She had no doubt that Menendez had them organized in a particular way, but Kenzie couldn't make sense of it. It all seemed to be slapdash, cobbled together. But it wasn't like Kenzie's thoughts on the topic were any clearer than the FBI agent's.

Kenzie stopped as she read through the notes and put her index finger on one of the names. "Nurse Debbie. That's funny, I just met a nurse that I knew a long time ago when my sister was sick, and her name is Nurse Debbie. But she doesn't work in that unit. She's in the psychiatric unit."

Menendez frowned. "Really." She scratched the back of her neck. "That name was specifically suggested by one of the other nurses. She used to be in the geriatric unit, but isn't any longer."

"Well, I'm sure it couldn't be the same Nurse Debbie. It isn't exactly a rare name."

"You don't know her last name?"

Kenzie knew she had seen Nurse Debbie's name badge and tried to remember. She shook her head. "No. I don't remember. We always just called her Nurse Debbie."

Menendez picked up her phone. "Easy to find out." She tapped the screen for a moment, then put it to her ear.

Kenzie couldn't hear who answered it; the volume was low enough that she could only hear Agent Menendez's voice.

"Hi. Agent Josie Menendez here," the woman snapped out. "I just had some follow up questions to our conversation."

She listened for a moment.

"This will only take a few minutes," she said, overruling whatever objection the other party had. She ran through a few casual questions and comments before getting to the one she actually wanted to ask. "You mentioned a Nurse Debbie. You said she wasn't in the geriatric unit anymore. Where did she go? Is she still with the hospital?"

Kenzie held her breath in anticipation.

"In psych," Menendez confirmed, raising an eyebrow at Kenzie. "Thank you very much. I'll let you know if I need anything else." She tapped to close the call and looked at Kenzie. "The same."

"Nurse Debbie?" Kenzie gave a laugh of disbelief and shook her head. "There's no way it's *her*. I know her, Josie. I've known her for years. I've seen her in action, what a good nurse she is. My younger sister was in the hospital a lot. She had kidney failure. She spent a lot of time in the nephrology unit when Nurse Debbie was there, and the woman was a saint. Always cheerful. You know how many of these nurses drag around and complain about anything you ask them to do that makes them raise a finger. She was never like that. Always happy to help with whatever she could. Cheered everyone up. She was just amazing."

"Then why isn't she still doing that?"

"People burn out. If she went from nephrology to geriatrics, then she's probably tired of dealing with people who are slowly dying. So she gets transferred to psychiatric instead, where you aren't usually dealing with patients who are dying."

"Just people who are crazy," Menendez laughed.

"No. Not crazy. Mentally ill. Remember that Zachary is one of those people. He's not crazy, but he's depressed. He needs support. And Nurse Debbie is just the kind of person he needs." Kenzie pushed aside the memory of how uncomfortable Nurse Debbie had made Zachary. Most people in psych needed someone just like Nurse Debbie. Always cheerful and upbeat, trying to include everyone and to make them happy.

"You can't make a judgment based on whether you think she's a good nurse or not," Dr. Wiltshire pointed out. "Nurses who follow this pattern tend to be very competent and well-liked."

"Well, there's more to it than that," Kenzie said. "For one thing, how long has she been out of geriatric? I thought she's been in psych for a few weeks."

"Yes," Menendez agreed. "She did transfer units a little while ago."

"Then she couldn't have been involved in Michaels's death, and that's one of the two that we know was actually a homicide."

"She was still in the hospital. As you were saying this morning, there's nothing to stop nurses from going to visit someone in another unit."

Dr. Wiltshire looked at Kenzie, raising an eyebrow. Kenzie shrugged. "Yes, of course." She stared down at the notices. "But if she was an Angel of Death killer, then she wouldn't transfer to a unit where nobody dies. People might notice if there was a sudden rash of deaths in psych, people dropping dead from apparent heart attacks when there wasn't anything physically wrong with them."

"The body and the mind are intertwined," Dr. Wiltshire said. "People with severe psychiatric disorders are often unhealthy in other ways as well."

"I know. But don't you think it's true? If she wanted to watch people die, then why not go to oncology? Or stay in geriatrics?"

"She couldn't stay in geriatrics," Menendez said.

"Couldn't? Why not?"

"Because there were questions about her patients dying."

31

Kenzie stared at Agent Menendez. "I don't think that's very funny."

"It was one of those situations where no one could prove anything or even back it up with statistics, but your Nurse Debbie was one of those people who often ended up with patients who died."

"If you can't prove it statistically, then she didn't get any more than anyone else," Kenzie said flatly. "It's simple math."

"She's a suspect; she hasn't been arrested. Obviously, we don't have the evidence to back it up, or she wouldn't still be working at the hospital. And the same goes for her superiors. If they could prove that there was anything wrong, they would get rid of her, not let her stay at the hospital."

"Maybe they're the ones who figured it would be safer to put her in psychiatric," Dr. Wiltshire suggested. "Like you said, not many people dying there. So either they put a stop to deaths on her watch, or she decides to quit and go somewhere she can do what she wants to."

"Or they wanted to put her where she belongs," Menendez said. "Into the psych ward. Maybe they couldn't commit her, but they could transfer her there as a nurse."

Kenzie glared at Menendez. "I don't appreciate the psych ward jokes, Josie."

"You're being overly sensitive. Just because you have a boyfriend there. If you didn't, you would think it was funny."

"I'd appreciate it if you would stop."

"You make jokes about your work, don't you?" Menendez challenged. "Don't tell me you've never made inappropriate jokes about dead people."

Kenzie looked at Dr. Wiltshire and grimaced. They tried to keep the Medical Examiner's Office a solemn and respectful place, but they did enjoy their puns and gallows humor, when circumstances called for it. Sometimes the only way to deal with a horrific death was to find the humor in it.

"You see?" Menendez said smugly. "We all joke about things that are inappropriate. All this proper and politically correct stuff is just politics. We joke to relieve stress. If you don't take offense, it doesn't hurt you."

Kenzie tried to explain it in a way that was logical, but couldn't. "Okay, then I'm being oversensitive," she said. "I'm feeling pretty raw about it. You would too if you had to worry about a loved one committing suicide. I don't want to hear jokes making fun of people like Zachary who have serious problems to deal with, and who have no control over the problems they have."

Menendez shrugged. "All right. I'll try to temper it," she agreed. "But if I slip up…"

"I'll try to be more patient."

They both eyed each other, dissatisfied.

Kenzie was thinking about the conversation as she drove to the hospital for another visit with Zachary. Why did she feel like it was okay for her and Dr. Wiltshire to make morbid jokes about their work, but not for Menendez to joke about Nurse Debbie taking a job in the psych ward?

For one thing, Menendez didn't work there herself. Maybe Kenzie would have felt as though it was okay for her to make crazy jokes if she worked there herself. But on the other hand... she didn't think so. Even if it was just a way to relieve stress, it was still disrespectful of people like Zachary who were struggling with mental illness, in a way that Kenzie's jokes were not. They didn't target the dead or treat them disrespectfully, they just made puns, mostly. It was something that she might have to watch, even if it were just so that she could explain to people like Menendez what the difference was.

The nurse at the front desk of the psychiatric unit recognized Kenzie this time, and nodded at her. "Nice to see you again. You're here to see Zachary, right?"

Kenzie smiled at her. "Right. How is he today?"

"I wouldn't want to say. You can't tell what's going on in people's heads. He's seemed pretty calm."

Kenzie took a step toward the common room, but the nurse held her hand up. "He has other visitors right now, and we try to limit numbers, not have too many people in to see one person at the same time."

"Oh. Who is with him?"

The petite nurse pushed a lock of hair away from her eyes and looked at the register or notes that she had in front of her. "Let's see, a Lorne Peterson and—"

"Patrick Parker," Kenzie finished. "We'll be quiet and not get him wound up. Three people isn't too many, is it? We're not going to be playing poker or starting any fights."

The woman smiled and shook her head. "Well... I suppose that will be okay. But we would appreciate it if you could coordinate, so that you don't get too many people here at the same time. Or overwhelm Zachary with too many visitors."

Kenzie nodded. "Sure, of course. We'll talk."

The nurse looked around for an orderly to escort Kenzie, but there was no one around. Kenzie made a motion. "I know where it is. I'll just go in."

"Well… yes, of course. I'm sure that would be okay."

Kenzie slipped past the desk and went to the common room where she had met with Zachary before. He was sitting at one of the tables with Lorne, a former foster father he'd kept in touch with over the years, and Lorne's partner, Pat, who fell somewhere between Lorne and Zachary in age. He and Lorne had been together for more than twenty years, since Zachary had been a teenager.

Zachary saw Kenzie as she arrived and stood up to greet her. Pat and Lorne turned around and were all smiles. Kenzie hugged and kissed Zachary first, then hugged each of the older men. "Nice to see you! I didn't think you'd be around until the weekend."

"We both had some time, so we thought we'd make the trip," Lorne said with a shrug. "See how this troublemaker was doing."

They all sat back down. Kenzie drew her chair close to Zachary's. As usual, he had picked a position that would allow him to see the rest of the room. No one could enter or approach without his seeing. Was it because of his training as a PI? Or learned behavior from being in situations where he had to be wary of abusers or bullies when he was growing up?

"How was the drive?" she asked the two men, keeping the focus from Zachary to begin with. She was sure he didn't want to be asked again how he was doing, to have to come up with an answer that would not upset any of his visitors. No one would expect him to say "fine," under the circumstances, but she didn't want to put him into the position where he had to talk about suicidal thoughts in front of all of them.

"Some ice and snow, but the highways have been cleared, so it wasn't too bad."

"Not like when we got snowed in at the Lodge!" Kenzie offered.

She and Zachary had been trapped for several days by a snowstorm that had blown in. An experience that Kenzie did not want to repeat.

"No. I'm glad we got out before the snow came in," Pat agreed. "I don't know how you guys managed without any electricity or cell coverage. Especially you," he told Zachary in a teasing tone. "The way you're attached to your phone."

"You should have seen Mason," Zachary said with a smile. Mason was Tyrrell's son, Zachary's nephew. "He'd never been without power or internet connectivity before. He kept telling Tyrrell to just call or message someone."

Kenzie laughed. "He was climbing up on the table, trying to get a signal on Tyrrell's phone. Couldn't understand how it was possible that there was no connection."

"How did he survive being snowbound?" Lorne asked. "He was so hyperactive while we were there…"

"It was a challenge," Zachary said.

Kenzie nodded and agreed. "He did get into some scrapes. But there were board games, and he and Alisha played quite a bit. He still got bored, but without any screens to entertain him, he was a little easier to get to bed."

"Maybe they'll get a chance to visit you," Pat suggested to Zachary. "The kids will be getting out of school for Christmas, and didn't Tyrrell say that he had them for the holiday this year?"

Zachary nodded. But he looked around at his surroundings, frowning. "I don't think he'll want to bring the kids here."

Kenzie glanced around. It wasn't the happiest place, but it didn't look any different from the rest of the hospital. No one was raving, threatening, or obviously delusional. Nothing that should be too traumatic to the kids.

"Why not?"

"I just don't think it's a good place for kids. He shouldn't bring them here."

"Do you want me to tell him that? Not to?"

Zachary hesitated. "Well… maybe. Yeah. But he won't be able to come then either. Because someone will have to watch the kids."

"I can look after them for a while. They know me."

"Where, at the house? Mason might make a mess."

"I can manage a little mess."

"Maybe you could take them somewhere else. One of those play places at the mall."

Kenzie rolled her eyes. "And what if Mason takes off and I lose him? I'd rather have him at home where I know he'll be safe."

"Well… yeah, I guess so. Maybe just tell Tyrrell that I can see them when I'm out. I don't want him to have to drag the kids here and then not be able to bring them in."

"It's up to you. You can decide who you want to see and who you don't. I'll just pass the message along."

"It isn't that I don't want to see him. Just that the kids…" Zachary looked around again. "It's not a good place for kids."

"It's not that different from Bonnie Brown, where you spent most of your Christmases as a kid," Lorne pointed out.

"But that was because I belonged there. They don't belong here," Zachary said stubbornly. He rarely talked about his time at Bonnie Brown, but Kenzie knew that the institution was a pretty grim place for kids like Zachary. Kids who were unable to keep a placement with a foster family due to behavioral issues or delinquency.

"Okay," Kenzie agreed. "I'll call Tyrrell and let him know."

"It's quiet right now. But it isn't always." His eyes were restless, moving back and forth at the other patients. "Sometimes patients get agitated. They can be loud and scary for little kids."

"You can get together with them after Christmas, like we had planned."

"Yeah." Zachary tapped the table in front of him, fidgeting.

Kenzie studied him covertly. He didn't look too bad, all things considered. The year before, when he had been able to stay out of the hospital before Christmas, he had looked pretty rough on Christmas Eve. And even the previous week, when he hadn't been sleeping, it had really showed physically. She suspected that the hospital was probably insisting that he take a sleeping pill at bedtime and forcing him to eat, two things that she couldn't do when he was at home. And maybe if they could keep him sleeping and eating properly, he would be able to avoid slipping further into depression.

32

S he's coming over to talk to you again," Zachary said.

Kenzie followed his gaze and saw Nurse Debbie, who was, as Zachary said, heading with deliberation in their direction. Kenzie could feel Zachary tense beside her.

"Sorry," she said. "I know she annoys you."

"It wouldn't be so bad if she would keep her hands to herself."

Lorne raised his brows and turned his head to see who they were talking about.

Kenzie stood up to greet Nurse Debbie. If she could stop the woman's progress a few feet away from Zachary, then she wouldn't be able to pat him on the shoulder or the back as she tried to cheer him up.

"Debbie! Hi, so nice to see you again," Kenzie greeted, giving her a social hug and keeping her body between Nurse Debbie and Zachary. "How are you doing?"

"In the pink," Debbie declared with a big smile. "And how's my favorite patient tonight?" She took a half-step to the side to get around Kenzie, but Kenzie mirrored the movement, smiling and touching Nurse Debbie's arm warmly, as if she wanted to tell her something important.

"He's looking pretty good," Kenzie said. "You guys must be taking good care of him."

"Well, we do our best! And I know that Zachary isn't feeling himself, but at least he doesn't get crabby and grouch at the nurses the way that some of these people do."

Kenzie nodded in agreement. She knew that Zachary tried not to bring her down with his moods, but living with him, she couldn't help but be affected.

"It must be hard working with patients whose moods are all over the place," Kenzie observed. "And when it's chemical, there's not really anything you can do to cheer someone up and make them feel better. You know it's not personal, but it's hard not to take it personally."

"You hit the nail on the head," Nurse Debbie agreed. "I do my best to be in control of my own mood and not to take any of it personally." She shook her head. "But some of them do get under your skin!"

Kenzie dropped her hand from Nurse Debbie's arm. "Well, we should let you get back to work. I'm sure you have a lot to do."

Debbie didn't take the hint and withdraw. She leaned a little closer to Kenzie. "What are these rumors I hear about you," she asked, dropping her voice. "That you're working with the FBI on some serial killer case?"

Kenzie hesitated. She didn't want to make a big deal of it in front of Zachary and the others, who were all likely to get anxious at the idea of her trying to identify a serial killer. But she also wanted to hear what Nurse Debbie had to say about it and couldn't very well deny her own involvement in the case.

"Well..." she drew the word out and kept her voice low. "I can't really say anything about it, of course..."

"Oh, no," Debbie agreed, looking excited about it. "Of course not. And I won't breathe a word of it to anyone else."

"We're still establishing the facts. Of course, I'm not really involved with the FBI, but my services at the Medical Examiner's Office have involved me in it collaterally..."

"And they really think that there's a serial killer in the geriatric unit? Do *you* think so?"

"I can't say what the Medical Examiner is going to put on the death certificates. But…"

Debbie shook her head, grinning. "That's my old unit, did you know that? I worked with those people. I just can't see it. Everyone that I worked with is completely trustworthy. I just can't imagine how you could think that one of the staff would do something like that."

"You used to work there?" Kenzie repeated, feigning surprise.

"Yes! For several years! But it got to be too much for me, you know. People burn out. I needed to try something else. Get away from all the death and despair…"

"It must be very difficult to work there day in and day out," Kenzie agreed. She wondered whether Nurse Debbie were telling the truth that she trusted everyone she had worked with there completely. Did a person ever know their coworkers that well? Kenzie knew she would be looking askance at the people she worked with if there were any suggestion that one of them might be a killer.

"Yes. So… I came up here." Debbie smiled. "And I'm so glad that I did, or I would not have reconnected with you."

Kenzie smiled in return. All of Debbie's exuberance seemed a little too dramatic to be genuine. But she certainly didn't seem like the person they were looking for. Kenzie had seen her in action and knew first-hand how well she took care of her patients and cared for them and did what she could to make their lives easier.

But word was apparently getting around that Kenzie was involved in the serial killer investigation case. If Nurse Debbie had heard it when she wasn't even in that unit anymore, then Kenzie had no doubt that a lot of people must know. And that was going to make it all the harder to work out who had sent her the threatening letter.

After watching Nurse Debbie walk away, Kenzie sat back down beside Zachary again. He blew out his breath.

"Thank you."

Pat looked over his shoulder in the direction that Debbie had gone. "I get that she might be a little overbearing, but I think she's just trying to be friendly."

Zachary didn't answer at first. He rubbed the back of his neck, staring down at the top of the table. "Sometimes, that 'being nice' is a way of bullying people into doing what you want. Nurses are especially good at it, but there are others, too. Salespeople. Teachers and principals. Police, sometimes. It sounds like they're being nice, but they don't stop until they've talked you into doing what they want. And when they won't stop touching you, putting their hands on you to encourage you to do what they say…"

Pat's brow wrinkled as he thought about that. He shook his head slightly. "I've never thought about it that way. I just think… people are being nice and polite like society says they should. Sometimes they might push harder than you're comfortable with, but if you just say 'no'…"

"They don't listen to no. Have you ever listened to any of those training videos for marketing? *No is just another way to get to yes…*"

"Well, if they really won't listen when you say no, then that's wrong."

"Yeah."

Pat still looked as if he were having a hard time with this idea. He looked at Lorne, then back at Zachary, his head cocked slightly. "Do you feel like *I* act that way toward you?"

"You?" Zachary looked up from the table, eyes widening. "No!"

"Because I might be like that. Trying to cheer you up. To make you eat something. You say no to one thing, and I offer something else instead. Giving you… a pat of encouragement…" He shrugged. "If those things bother you…?"

"No, it's not the same," Zachary told him. But Kenzie had to admit, it was hard to see the dividing line between the two.

"No?"

Zachary chewed on his lip. "I know you do those things because you're... family. We have a relationship. You're not some stranger trying to twist my arm. You care, and you're looking for ways to help, not... trying to force me to do what *you* want."

"Yes," Pat agreed thoughtfully.

Lorne put his arm around Pat. "Zachary knows that we love him. No one forces him to come over to the house. And he knows when he comes over that you're going to make him something to eat and do your best to make sure that he's happy and comfortable when he's there."

"Yeah," Zachary agreed, nodding vigorously. "You trying to help me isn't the same as them—" Zachary nodded to indicate the direction Debbie had gone, "trying to make me behave the way they think I should." He paused, blinking and looking up toward the ceiling. "Even if you *said* exactly the same thing, it wouldn't *feel* the same."

"Hmm." There were a few minutes of silence. Then Pat said, "Can I ask you a favor?"

Zachary nodded.

"Since I can't feel what you're feeling, will you tell me if you feel like I'm pushing you or not respecting your boundaries? Tell me 'no' if it's a firm no, instead of 'I don't know' or 'maybe later'?"

Zachary grimaced. "I'll try," he agreed, dropping his eyes again. "It's hard. Dr. Boyle says that I need to be better about saying what I'm feeling to people I love. I'm better at deflecting and telling people what I think they want to hear."

"Well, if you try that, I'll try not to push you into things that you don't want to do."

33

Pat turned to Kenzie. He smiled brightly. "So… you're working on a serial killer case?" he asked in a light tone.

They all laughed. Kenzie glanced around to make sure that they were not disturbing anyone around them. A few glances swung in their direction at the laughter, but then everyone looked away again, going back to their own conversations or activities.

"Well… I'm not really working the case. The FBI is working the case. I am just involved because I was helping out with a few autopsies."

"Is this something I'm going to regret asking about?" Pat checked. "Is it gory or," he glanced at Zachary, "too close to home?"

"No, it isn't like that at all. It's what we tend to call an Angel of Death or Angel of Mercy killer. Usually a doctor or nurse or other medical practitioner who kills patients. On the surface, at least, to put them out of their misery. To send them to a better place, where their suffering is over."

"Oh, well, that's nice of them."

Kenzie smiled at his sarcasm. "Of course, whether that's really why they're doing it, or whether they have a morbid fascination with death and just pick the most vulnerable victims… that's for the psychologists to figure out. Or sometimes, they have a 'hero complex' and want everybody to see them as a wonderful, heroic caregiver. So they *almost* kill patients, and then bring them back from the brink. Or aren't able to, but they at least try. It's like a fireman who lights a fire and then comes back with his brigade to put it out."

"So this one that you're trying to catch, what do you think their motivation is?"

"I don't know. I'm not a psychologist, and we don't have enough data yet. So far, we have only been able to prove two of the cases in the series were homicides. We'll need more to prove that there is a serial killer, and then something distinctive or some connection between them to be able to find the killer." Kenzie shrugged. "This kind of killer can be very difficult to find. They might get away with it for years before they get caught. Some of the most prolific serial killers in history have been Angel of Death killers."

"But they're not dangerous to *you*," Lorne said. "As someone investigating the killings. They're only a danger to the patients they work with."

Kenzie thought about the note she had received. *Or else.*

It was probably best not to mention that detail.

"No. They're not usually dangerous at all to authorities. When they get caught, they usually confess. To everything. And..." Kenzie pointed a finger at him. "*I* am not investigating the killer. The FBI is. Even if, for some reason, they decided to focus on the Medical Examiner's Office, they would threaten the Medical Examiner, not me. I'm just a lowly worker bee. It's Dr. Wiltshire's name that will be on the death certificates."

"That's good," Lorne nodded. "We don't want to run afoul of a serial killer."

Pat looked down at his watch. "We should probably be getting on our way. We want to get home in good time."

"Yes. And we don't want to tire Zachary out."

They stood and began their goodbyes, giving hugs and

murmuring encouraging things to Zachary, promising to come back and see him again.

"Let me walk you out," Kenzie offered.

Lorne shook his head. "He wants you to himself for a bit. We can find our way out."

Kenzie looked back at Zachary and saw his expression. Lorne was right; it did look as though he wanted to discuss something with her. But the wrinkles around his eyes told her that he was tired, so she shouldn't stay too much longer. She said goodbye to the two men, then sat down across the table from Zachary, where Pat had been. She took his hands in the middle of the table.

"Hey," she greeted, smiling.

"Hey."

"You look like you're doing good. Do they have you on anything new?"

"No. And it wouldn't make a difference this quickly if they did."

"You're sleeping better?"

"Yes."

"What's up?"

He looked away, uncomfortable.

"Come on," Kenzie encouraged. "I'm here. What did you want to talk about?"

"Well, it's nothing. Not about my treatment or about *us*."

"Are you worrying about your work? Heather's holding down the fort."

"No. I've been able to handle it before, when I didn't have her working with me. People are impatient, but when you are in the hospital, they just have to wait. If they can't wait, they go to somebody else."

"Okay." Kenzie waited.

"It's just... I never heard anything about the babies. If everything worked out. I don't feel like I should be asking you to talk to Gordon... but..."

"I saw him yesterday."

Zachary blinked, looking surprised. "You did?"

"Yes. After I left here, I saw the sign for maternity and thought I would pop in and say hello. Get caught up in case you wanted to know how everyone is."

Zachary chuckled. "Well… I didn't expect that. You know me too well."

"It's been obvious how concerned you've been about the babies ever since you found out that Bridget was pregnant. I didn't think that would stop just because you were in psych for a while."

"Maybe Dr. B would say that I should stay out of it. Am I just… feeding my obsessive needs if I ask? Will it make them worse?"

"You'd have to ask her. I don't know. You know yourself pretty well, though. What do you think?"

"I think…" Zachary pondered the question. "I think that if I get the information from you or Gordon… then I don't feel as compelled to go see Bridget and find out for myself."

"That's good enough for me. Is it good enough for you?"

"You shouldn't have to put up with this," Zachary said, his face getting pink. "Women don't want to hear all about their partners' exes all the time."

Kenzie remembered one of the men she had dated briefly who had done just that, talking about nothing else, all the way through their date, but the woman he had just broken up with and every single thing about her, until Kenzie thought she probably knew the woman better than she could know herself. What had his name been? Roger? Kenzie hadn't gone on a second date with him.

"No," she agreed. "But you don't talk about her most of the time. If you want to know how the babies are, then I can understand that. As long as that's not the only thing you talk about."

In fact, if he could obsess about the babies instead of Bridget, that was a little easier on Kenzie's ego. She would prefer that he was thinking about a couple of helpless infants than a woman that Kenzie could never be. She would never be able to live up to the image Zachary had built of Bridget in his imagination. *That*

Bridget was not real and did not reflect the flaws of the real person.

Zachary finally nodded, satisfied that it wasn't a relationship-breaker for him to ask about the twins.

"Okay. What did he say?"

"The one who had the heart attack, her name is Julia. We may as well refer to them by name, instead of just 'the babies.' They are real people, not just a concept."

"Julia. And… she's okay? You said her name *is* Julia."

"Yes. They are both still fighting."

It was interesting that they used the verb *fighting* for life. A word that normally had negative connotations, that referred to violence. Yet in this context, it was positive.

"The other baby is Tricia. And she's off the respirator, breathing on her own."

Zachary's eyes brightened. "That's good."

"Yes, it's real progress. They can start feeding her by mouth, and that will help her to gain weight and develop more quickly. She'll get stronger."

"But the other—Julia—is still on the respirator."

"For the time being. And both are on lots of monitors to try to catch any problems before they become serious. Julia has not had any more heart problems. So maybe it was just a one-time thing, caused by a blood clot maybe."

"Thanks for checking on them. I really appreciate it." He pressed his lips together, and Kenzie had an inkling that he was trying to keep himself from asking how Bridget was. And if he didn't ask, she wouldn't bring her up.

"I actually got to see them," she told Zachary. "Julia and Tricia. They're in the same incubator, which is really good. It means they can touch each other and not be totally isolated. It's hard to balance a baby's need for the controlled environment of the incubator with their need for human contact. There are access ports, so that the parents can touch them without taking them out of the environment. And as they get bigger and stronger, they will get more opportunities to touch and hold them."

Zachary looked pleased at this. "That's good. Babies need to be held."

"When I talked to Heather, she told me about how you helped to take care of Mindy when she was born. You never told me about that."

Zachary looked uncertain for a moment, then smiled. "I haven't thought about that in a long time. It was so long ago."

"She said that you were the only one who could get Mindy to eat anything."

"Yeah. You kind of had to fool her into taking the bottle. It was tricky."

"If you hadn't gotten her to eat, she wouldn't have survived."

"Well… I guess they would have taken her to the hospital. And maybe social services would have taken her away if she was starving."

"It's possible, yes. But it can also take hardly any time at all for a baby to get dehydrated and die. Sometimes that happens before you realize there is a serious problem and can get them to the hospital. A parent thinks that they are just off their feed, maybe fighting a flu bug, and then they're dehydrated and it's too late to do anything for them."

"I'm glad that didn't happen to Mindy."

"Me too. You took good care of her."

Zachary smiled his shy, proud smile. He didn't get a lot of praise. Especially for things he had done as a child. His own mother had told him he was worthless and that she didn't want him. And from what she gathered from the little that Lorne and Zachary said about his years after the fire, he had been unmanageable and had probably never been praised for doing his best.

"And now… you look tired. Are you ready for bed?"

His eyes roved to the clock on the wall. It was much earlier than he ever went to bed at home, but the psych ward was probably very strict about his going to sleep, and with no electronics to occupy him, there was nothing to keep him up but his own thoughts.

"I'm not tired."

"You look tired, even if you don't feel it. And once you take a pill, that will help."

He nodded.

"All right. I'm going to leave you alone, then. You take care of yourself." Kenzie leaned forward and kissed him. Not on the cheek this time, but on the lips. "I miss you."

"You too. I'm sorry… that I have to be here."

"I'm sorry too, but I'm glad that you're safe."

34

It was getting easier to sleep without Zachary there, though Kenzie still missed him and wondered how he was doing while he was away from her. It helped to know that he was sleeping better. Not having dark raccoon shadows around his eyes helped her to see his hospital stay as a positive thing, something that was helping him, even if they couldn't reverse the depression brought on by the upcoming anniversary. They were still doing what they could for him.

She woke up the next day feeling well-rested. That, combined with the assurance that he was okay without her, helped her to be able to focus on her own work. It would be nice not to have to do every job twice because she was so afraid of screwing things up due to her preoccupation and lack of restful sleep.

She used to leave her phone messages until later in her morning routine, but after running into trouble once for not picking up an early-morning message from Dr. Wiltshire, checking them was the first thing she did when she got into the office. She was glad that she had, because he had left one for her late at night or early in the morning.

"I have a suicide to attend early, Kenzie. So I won't be in until later, and we will be checking in the remains later today. If you could do some prep for me..."

She could hear him moving around as he dictated his instructions. Maybe dressing, or maybe already doing a scene review, with the police standing back respectfully while he talked into the phone.

Kenzie jotted down notes so that she wouldn't forget anything and got started. She wanted to have everything prepared by the time Dr. Wiltshire got there, whether it was sooner or later. After that was done, she went on with the rest of her routine.

Dr Wiltshire arrived at the office a little later than usual but, of course, she knew that his day had started quite a bit before hers. He stopped at her desk to offer her a Starbuck's coffee and Danish. Kenzie took them without objection.

"Going to be a tough one today?" she asked.

Usually when he brought her treats, it was because consciously or unconsciously, he recognized it was going to be a long or particularly stressful day. And those were often days when he came in with a body in the morning.

"Suicides are never pretty," Dr. Wiltshire sighed. "No matter how much TV movie dramas like to romanticize it, making it look as if the victim just slides peacefully into oblivion, that's not what it looks like. Physician attended end-of-life choice being the exception, of course. Anyone killing himself without assistance... just leaves behind a mess for everyone else to clean up and grieve over."

"What have we got?" Kenzie asked. She hoped it wasn't a young teenager. Those deaths always seemed to hit her the hardest.

"Ken Kennedy, fifty-nine, single and alone. Psych ward patient."

Kenzie tried to suppress her reaction to this news, but she couldn't hide it from Dr. Wiltshire. He nodded gravely.

"Gave me a turn when I heard I had a male suicide in the psych ward to attend. My first thought..."

Kenzie nodded. Of course he had thought of Zachary. Zachary, who had been admitted just a few days earlier for suicidal thoughts. She took a deep breath in and let it out slowly.

Zachary was fine. He had been okay when she had left him the night before, and she knew the name of the deceased that Dr. Wiltshire had brought in. It had not been Zachary.

Ken Kennedy. A man she had never met before. She would see him for the first and last time on the autopsy table. It was not personal. He was no different from any of the other remains she had worked with in the past.

"Will you be okay?" Dr. Wiltshire asked. "Do you want me to take this one myself?"

"No. I'll be fine. I'm pretty much caught up from my vacation —finally—so I can make time to assist. And I know that Mr. Kennedy is not Zachary. I will get through it."

"If you need to bow out at any point during the procedure, just go ahead. I understand completely."

Kenzie nodded. She took a bite of her Danish, girding up her loins.

The autopsy was scheduled for the afternoon. Kenzie looked at the time and decided that she had time to check the postal mail and get it sorted and then to have lunch. Then she would assist with the autopsy of Mr. Kennedy.

She stood at her desk as she slit open envelopes and quickly sorted them into the various piles, baskets, and workflows that she had organized. It usually took her no more than ten minutes, even when scanning hard copies into the system when necessarily. Most of the reports that came in print form, they had already received electronic copies of ahead of time, so they just went into the basket destined for the file cabinet.

She held the sharp letter opener in one hand as she sliced open an envelope, removed the contents, and then sliced open the next. But when she saw the piece of paper she pulled out of one of the envelopes, she accidentally stabbed herself in the hand with the letter opener.

She swore and dropped the letter opener, then grabbed a tissue and pressed it over the cut. It was an unusually sharp letter opener, not one with a safely-rounded tip, which would have been more difficult to get under the letter flaps. She swore again and looked down at the letter.

"Everything all right, Kenzie?" Julie asked.

Kenzie startled, not having realized that she was there. She had called Julie earlier to cover the phone and reception desk for her while she assisted in the autopsy. And Julie had arrived early so that Kenzie could sit down and have a quiet lunch instead of wolfing down a sandwich while she worked at her desk.

Kenzie picked up the corner of the paper, and hesitated about whether she should let Julie see it or not. Reluctantly, she turned it around to show to the younger woman.

Julie gasped and covered her mouth as her eyes scanned the letters block-printed with a marker. The same as the last one. Except the language in this one was quite a bit more explicit.

"Do you get a lot of those?" Julie asked, eyes big.

"No. I don't usually have to deal with threats." Kenzie sat down abruptly. Her legs were shaking like she had just climbed a hundred stairs.

"I'll get you a drink of water," Julie offered, and sped into the office suite to fetch a drink from the kitchenette.

In a few minutes, both Dr. Wiltshire and Julie were at her side, Julie handing her the water and encouraging her to drink and Dr. Wiltshire teasing the letter out from under Kenzie's hand to look at it.

"Another one!" he exclaimed, looking at it.

"There were more?" Julie asked.

"One other." Dr. Wiltshire looked at Kenzie. "I assume there was just one other."

She nodded. "Yeah. I'm not saving them up."

"Are you hurt?"

Kenzie looked at her left hand, at the bloody tissue wadded up over the wound, remembering what had happened. "It was an accident. Stabbed myself with the letter opener."

He prodded the tissue and looked underneath. "I don't think you need stitches. Just a bandage."

"I'll get one," Julie offered, and again headed to the kitchen, where the first aid box was stored.

Kenzie looked at the letter again, shaking her head. "I guess we should call Agent Menendez about this. Not that she seemed too excited to get the last one. I thought that at least they have some evidentiary value…"

"I haven't heard back whether there were any fingerprints on the last one. But yes, we should at least keep her up-to-date on what's going on. This one is… considerably worse than the last."

Kenzie nodded. Both the words used to address her and the threat were much more explicit this time. There could be no doubt that she had seriously disturbed someone with her questions in the geriatric ward. She looked at the envelope for a postmark to see when it had been mailed. It didn't make sense to her that the killer would be getting angrier when she hadn't had anything else to do with the investigation. At least, not on the public end. But it was possible that both letters had been mailed some days ago and were just arriving at her desk now.

This time, the envelope did have a postmark on it. It had only been mailed the previous day.

"Well, it's local," Dr. Wiltshire observed, also looking at the stamp.

"It would have to be. For someone to know that I was involved in the investigation personally, it would have to be someone at the hospital. Someone in the geriatric unit who saw me or talked to me."

"Right. You have a list of the people you talked to that day, right?"

"I already gave it to Agent Menendez."

"Good."

Julie returned with an assortment of bandages. Kenzie looked through them. She only needed one. It wasn't that big of a wound. Just deep. A good thing that, as someone who worked with needles regularly, she was up-to-date on her tetanus shots.

"You should use one of those flat, rectangular letter openers," Julie suggested. She took the bandage that Kenzie had selected from her and peeled off the wrapper and backing to apply it to Kenzie's palm. "They have a razor blade on the inside edge, so that you can't cut yourself on it. You just poke the little end under the flap and slide it along, with the cutter on the inside."

Kenzie nodded. "Yeah, I guess I might need to get something a little safer. I've never done that before. I thought I was better-coordinated."

"Anyone can have an accident," Dr. Wiltshire said, brushing it off. Kenzie was glad he wasn't making a big deal out of it. They both knew it was just a small cut, nothing life-threatening.

Kenzie smoothed down the edges of the bandage Julie had expertly applied. "I guess I'm ready for that autopsy now."

"Are you sure, Kenzie?" Dr. Wiltshire asked. "You don't have to scrub in on this one if you are having second thoughts. After all this, maybe you want to just stay out of it. This letter is reason enough to be upset; you don't need to pile on anything else."

"I'll be just fine." Kenzie glanced at Julie and didn't explain to her why Dr. Wiltshire thought that the autopsy might bother her. She was friendly with Julie, but she hadn't explained about Zachary's issues and Julie didn't know anything about his being in the hospital. "Let me just finish sorting the mail."

"I can do that," Julie offered.

"No. I know whether we have already received stuff through email or not. There's no point in processing reports a second time; they can just go straight to file."

Julie nodded. "Okay. Do you want me to open the envelopes? That would make it go faster."

Kenzie sighed. She didn't need to be babied. But she just nodded. "Fine, yes, go ahead and open them." Julie might as well do something useful and not just stand there watching Kenzie.

"I'll get autopsy prepped," Dr. Wiltshire said. "See you in a few minutes."

35

———

Kenzie was glad not to have Dr. Wiltshire hovering over her while she finished processing the mail with Julie. He seemed to sense that she didn't want a big thing made of either the letter or the autopsy that might make her think about Zachary. She appreciated that he didn't see the need to mother and fuss over her and would instead just go on with the autopsy. The more normal everything was, the easier it would be for her.

After finishing the mail, Kenzie took a quick minute in the restroom to gather herself and do some deep breathing. She would put the threatening letter out of her mind. She would put Zachary out of her mind. She was assisting with the autopsy of Mr. Kennedy. Not someone she knew. She could maintain professional distance and not get wrapped up in it emotionally. Dr. Wiltshire had not given her a heads-up that it was anything more bloody or gory than she was used to. Patients in the psychiatric unit didn't generally have access to guns or knives, so it was far more likely to be an overdose, strangulation, or head trauma. She could manage that.

Kenzie entered the autopsy and suited up. The clean surgical surfaces shone. Everything was neatly laid out in its proper place.

A homicide detective was standing by to observe. Dr. Wiltshire had not yet begun with the body, but appeared to be ready to once Kenzie joined him. As she walked up to the table, he tapped the button on the floor that would start the recording, and announced Mr. Kennedy's name and file number, followed by his height, weight, and appearance. Kenzie concentrated on keeping her breathing regulated and settled into the usual routine of an autopsy.

Kenzie couldn't see any wounds when Dr. Wiltshire folded down the cover to reveal the top portion of the body. No bruising around the neck, so it would appear he had not hanged or strangled himself.

Mr. Kennedy, aged fifty-nine, single, no children. He was white. A little overweight, but not in bad shape. Kenzie suspected that when he wasn't in the psych ward he was in a physically demanding trade. His hands were rough and calloused. He was well-muscled under the layer of fat. Not cut like a bodybuilder, but someone who could hold his own in terms of physical labor.

He had a dark but grizzled beard. His hair was cropped short, but not buzz-cut like Zachary's. Easy care. His temples and body hair were also going gray.

"No obvious wounds or bruising," Dr. Wiltshire observed. "No tattoos or birthmarks. Let's examine Mr. Kennedy for any needle marks or smaller wounds."

The two of them spent some time with the magnifying lenses, checking carefully for needle marks. They didn't find any. Unlike the geriatric patients they had dealt with recently, he had not had an IV.

Kenzie thought fleetingly of her conversation with Nurse Debbie. *At least people don't die in the psych ward.* But of course they did. People died everywhere; there was no predicting where and when the end of the line would be. The psych patients were not dying of cancer or kidney failure, but suicide was a risk. Usually, it could be prevented while they were in the hospital, but if a patient were desperate enough, he could find a way.

Kenzie took a couple of deep breaths, trying to reset. She needed to stay focused on Mr. Kennedy and the examination of his body. Nothing else.

Dr. Wiltshire raised his eyes and checked on her, then looked back down at the remains and continued his examination.

"Indications at the scene were of drug overdose," he told her in a professional, detached tone. "Vomitus present. Indications of cyanosis." He picked up the hand closest to him and indicated the nails. Kenzie looked down at the hand on her side of the table to confirm the dusky blue-gray under the nails. He was slightly blue above the mouth as well. Cyanosis. Something that had kept him from getting enough oxygen. Possibly a medication that had slowed or stopped his heart, since there were no marks to indicate strangulation. There were other possibilities, but Dr. Wiltshire classified it as a potential drug overdose, and he was probably right.

They continued with their careful review of Kennedy's body and found no signs of recent violence. Kenzie noted scarring that showed he had been a cutter at some point, but he didn't have any recent self-inflicted cuts. The marks were all old.

When they had completed a full review of his body, top and bottom, front and back, Dr. Wiltshire indicated it was time to begin with the internal examination.

"Would you like to make the Y-incision, Dr. Kirsch?"

Kenzie was eager to do more than just gross examination, slides, and samples. She nodded and moved over to the instrument tray to begin. Dr. Wiltshire talked her through the process, even though Kenzie had previously practiced on medical school cadavers, and her lines were neat and straight. Dr. Wiltshire nodded his approval.

"It is my suspicion that Mr. Kennedy died of a drug overdose," Dr. Wiltshire said. "So…"

"Stomach contents first?" Kenzie suggested.

Dr. Wiltshire nodded. He didn't move in to take over on the procedure, so Kenzie proceeded carefully herself. Without any nicks or other mishaps, she removed the stomach and emptied the contents into a tray.

Examining and smelling stomach contents was not her favorite part of the job. But a close examination of Mr. Kennedy's stomach contents was not required. It appeared as if he had swallowed the entire contents of a couple of bottles of pills. The yellow tablets and blue tablets were partially dissolved, but still intact enough that there could be no doubt what they were.

"Well..." Kenzie made a gesture toward the pile of mushy, acid-covered pills. "There you go. We can take blood levels, but I think it's pretty obvious what we are going to find."

"Yes," Dr. Wiltshire agreed.

His eyes remained fastened on the stomach contents, and Kenzie wasn't sure why he wasn't moving on.

"How many pills would you say that is?" Dr. Wiltshire asked.

"I don't know. A lot. I was thinking it looked like a full bottle of each. A month's worth, maybe?"

Dr. Wiltshire nodded slowly. Kenzie knew he was looking for something more. For her to follow the question to a conclusion. It took a few seconds for her to get there.

Zachary's doctor wouldn't even give him a prescription for a full month's worth of any of his prescriptions at a time. She considered it too risky. When Zachary was feeling particularly tempted to put an end to his life, he had Kenzie dispense them. And in the psych ward, he would be given his meds on a schedule. He would never be given more than one dose at a time.

"Where did he get that many pills from in the psychiatric unit?"

"That's a good question."

"Maybe he broke into the dispensary?"

"That is a question we should ask. Certainly no one mentioned that early this morning when I attended at the scene."

"They might not have discovered it until it was time to dispense the morning's medications. But they should have called by now if they realized that he had broken in." Kenzie looked at the clock on the wall. They probably dispensed the morning meds at seven or eight o'clock. It was mid-afternoon.

"The other possibility is that he saved them up," Kenzie said. "They should check, but he could be cheeking them or even regurgitating them. He would have to find a place to stash them, somewhere they wouldn't search regularly."

"There should be protocols in place to ensure that patients can't do that. And with patients at higher risk, they should be doing blood tests to ensure that the concentrations are where they should be."

"And you would think that they would notice if he were off his meds for a month."

"You would think," Dr. Wiltshire agreed.

Kenzie caught a movement out of the corner of her eye and turned to see the homicide detective writing in his notepad. Questions to follow up on, areas to investigate based on their discussion. He looked at her. Kenzie nodded awkwardly and looked down at the pile of pills.

"What else should we do? This is pretty conclusively the cause of death."

"I would suggest weighing the pills to get an idea of how many he consumed. It won't be accurate, since some have dissolved and some have soaked up liquid, but it will give us a ballpark. Identify exactly what they are. Markings have worn off, but we can get a pretty good idea by comparing color and shape to an identification chart, then talk to the hospital and run a couple of tests to verify. And we need to check other organs for pathology. See if there was anything else going on. Was he self-medicating for pain? Were they any tumors or brain abnormalities? Examine and weigh the heart and lungs. Slides of the kidney and liver."

Kenzie nodded. Even with a case that was so clearly suicide, they needed to dot all the i's and cross all the t's. Sometimes there were still surprises or additional factors in the death.

She proceeded with the autopsy carefully, following Dr. Wiltshire's instructions step by step. A couple of times, he stopped her to offer advice or to show her a technique. Even though she had watched him do dozens of autopsies, she didn't always notice the finer points or better ways to do things.

After completing the autopsy, Kenzie was rubbing her shoulders and neck, which were definitely feeling the effects of her work. Dr. Wiltshire frowned.

"You're sore?"

"Yes." Kenzie dug her fingers into the muscles and tendons, searching out the sore spots. She would need a heating pad in the evening before bed.

"Show me where."

Kenzie's face warmed as she demonstrated the movements that were painful. Mostly the ones requiring her to lift her hands and arms to chest level or higher. She was worried that Dr. Wiltshire was going to offer to massage the sore muscles and wasn't sure how she felt about that. Dr. Wiltshire had always treated her with respect and had never made any romantic overtures or suggested anything to make her uncomfortable in that way, but she wasn't sure she wanted him rubbing any part of her body.

But he did not. "The table is too high for you," he observed.

"Oh… yes," Kenzie admitted. She always left it adjusted to the level that Dr. Wiltshire used it at, as he was the lead on the autopsies. She hadn't expected to be the one doing most of the physical work this time and had not adjusted the table once she had started. "I didn't think…"

"Next time we'll have to remember to lower it for your work. It's very quick to adjust it to the level most comfortable to you. And it will save you a lot of pain and having to load up on ibuprofen after an autopsy."

Kenzie nodded. "Yeah. I'll do that next time."

He demonstrated how to find the table level that was

ergonomically correct for her, and they raised and lowered it a few times for practice.

"You'll find the most comfortable height for you after a few times. It's different for everybody, just depends on your individual skeletal structure. Once you know the best height, we can always set it to that exact height."

"Great. Thank you."

Dr. Wiltshire nodded. "If you don't take care of your body, you could end up with crippling stress injuries. You don't want to have to retire from a career you enjoy just because you didn't take the time to figure out the right table height and use it."

Kenzie nodded her agreement. She took a sip of her coffee, which had gone cold several hours earlier, and looked over the samples to be processed and sent out for testing.

"You go type up your notes on the autopsy," Dr. Wiltshire advised. "Get your thoughts down while it is still fresh in your mind. I will get these sent out."

"Oh, I can still do it," Kenzie protested. That was part of her job description, not his.

"You are sore enough already. We don't want to inflame those muscles any more. Do your computer work, check the email, and go home. Take ibuprofen and put some heat on those muscles."

Kenzie made one more protest and he again instructed her to go do her computer work while he sent out the samples. Kenzie nodded and obeyed.

Kenzie relieved Julie of her duties and sent her back up to her administrative tasks on one of the upper floors. She sat down at her desk and realized that the threatening letter had been set to the side and not yet taken care of. She slid it into a plastic folder as she had the previous one and shot a text off to Agent Menendez so that she didn't actually have to talk to her.

She created a new document to jot down her notes on the autopsy. They would have the dictated notes back the next day, but thought processes were important too. There were things that might need to be followed up on or investigated further, feelings about their findings, maybe a small observation or two that hadn't seemed important enough to comment on while they were in the midst of the autopsy but started to niggle at her later. Normally, this was Dr. Wiltshire's job, and she would just review his notes to see whether she had anything to add, but since she had been the primary doctor doing the work on the Kennedy autopsy, this time it was her job.

She noted Mr. Kennedy's name, file number, and statistics. She started to write out an introductory note giving the circumstances of the death, and realized with some embarrassment that there was a lump in her throat that would not go away. She swallowed a few times, took a drink of water, and tried to go on. As she wrote about his being a patient in the psychiatric unit, tears started to leak out of the corners of her eyes. She wiped them away a few times, then stopped typing and covered her face with her hands, breathing slowly and trying to center herself and get back her composure.

Kenzie had performed the autopsy without getting emotionally caught up in it. She had properly maintained a professional detachment and demeanor. She didn't understand why she was suddenly fighting waves of sorrow over a man she had never met before.

She stopped and started several times, writing what she could and then dealing with the emotions that consumed her. Not just sorrow, but anger too, unaccountably furious at somebody for Mr. Kennedy's death. It was suicide, and she knew it was no one's fault but his own. His family and friends and the doctors had undoubtedly done their best for him, but sometimes that wasn't enough. Sometimes, no matter what everyone did to head it off, a suicide simply couldn't be prevented.

Kenzie wiped her eyes and blew her nose and looked back at her screen to see where she had left off.

"How's it coming along?" Dr. Wiltshire asked gently.

Kenzie startled slightly at his words, not having realized that he was there, watching her. She sniffled.

"I'll be done before long." She used a tissue to wipe her eyes. She was going through a lot of tissue for one day.

"I understand it's hard."

"You don't do this when you write up your notes," she pointed out.

"Well, I've been at it a lot longer than you have. You can bet that there have been some cases that really hit me hard. Sometimes it is the death of a child, a particularly brutal murder, or someone dying of the same thing that Aunt Jayne died of a month ago. You never know what it's going to be, but some of them will hit you hard. It's just part of the job. Don't beat yourself up over it."

"I was fine for the autopsy."

"You did a great job on the autopsy. But one of the reasons that I had you do the work was to keep you focused on the mechanics, rather than the patient's circumstances."

Kenzie looked at Dr. Wiltshire for a moment before the light went on. "Because of Zachary, you mean? Is that why you think I'm so emotional over it?"

"Isn't it?"

Kenzie felt a huge sense of relief, as if a burden had been taken off her shoulders. Of course it was because of Zachary. Dr. Wiltshire knew very well that the suicide of someone in the same unit that Zachary was in would be difficult for her. She couldn't help but compare the two cases. To think about Zachary and put him in Mr. Kennedy's place. To think, as she had so many times before, about how she would feel if Zachary did harm himself one day, and if it were his body on the autopsy table.

Of course she thought of his bottles of pills and his sweeping all the knives in the fridge onto the floor in frustration. He was fighting his illness the best that he could, but what if one day he was no longer able to resist the impulses or deal with the fact that he would be fighting depression for the rest of his life?

Kenzie dabbed at her eyes as the tears flowed faster and a sob escaped her throat. Grief for Mr. Kennedy, a stranger to her, and for Zachary, fighting his lonely fight, and for herself, worrying that one day she might lose him. There were a lot of emotions to unpack.

"Sorry," she apologized to Dr. Wiltshire. "This is so silly."

"It's not silly at all. You've done a fine job, and you're going through some very difficult stuff in your life right now. There's nothing wrong with letting yourself feel your emotions instead of bottling them up."

"Sure, but not at the workplace."

"You will always be free to cry in my office," he told her sternly. "And if you should ever join a medical examiner's office where you are forbidden to feel emotion over the work that we do… you should find another office. These people deserve our sympathy just as much as anyone else in our lives."

Kenzie nodded and blew her nose. "Okay." The tears were starting to slow a little, as if acknowledging and allowing them took away their power over her.

"Never let the job take your humanity."

Kenzie managed a weak smile. She looked at the document on her screen, determined. She only needed another five or ten minutes to finish it, and then she could go home and relax for a while before visiting Zachary at the hospital.

"All right. I can do this."

"I never doubted it."

Dr. Wiltshire nodded and headed down the hallway toward his own office.

The long day and the emotion over Kennedy's suicide had taken a lot of energy. She was tired after eating supper and didn't really want to go out again, but she knew it was what she had to do.

She couldn't avoid seeing Zachary just because of the day she had been through. He still needed her support just as much as any other day. Maybe more. He would know that there had been a suicide in the ward and it was bound to be weighing on his mind. It wouldn't be easy to avoid his own suicidal thoughts when that's what everyone around him was talking about. Or being careful not to talk about.

Kenzie allowed herself one small scoop of ice cream to soothe her battered soul, and then forced herself to get up and get ready to go. It would be nice to go out in her baby, her cherry red convertible. It was too cold to put the top down, of course, but she always enjoyed going for a spin.

Then she would be able to see Zachary, and then she could relax for the night. All good things.

The nurse at the check-in desk for the ward handed Kenzie a printed notice.

"We want to make sure that our visitors know before going in that we had… an unfortunate incident last night. It is important that we acknowledge what has happened and not pretend that it didn't. Your loved one may need to talk about it."

Kenzie glanced down at the notice, outlining the bare facts of the discovery of Kennedy's death.

"Thanks. I appreciate that, and I'm sure your patients do too."

"There is extra counseling available for everyone, and that includes family members, not just the patients. Something like this can hit close to home for everyone, and we encourage open discussion and getting the help and counseling we need."

Kenzie nodded. She didn't bother to advise the nurse that she already knew far more about the case than anyone else in the ward, including the doctors. They would not get the Medical Examiner's report for a few more days.

She was escorted by a sympathetic-looking nurse to the common room. Kenzie could feel a shift in the energy and activity from the last couple of times that she had visited. It had been fairly calm and relaxed on her previous visits. There might be minor disruptions by individual patients, but overall, the ward was kept quiet and peaceful.

Without being able to put her finger on exactly what the difference was, Kenzie sensed the patients' agitation and restlessness. The air was charged with emotion. As she approached the table where Zachary sat, Kenzie folded the printed notice into quarters and then eighths, and pushed it into her coat pocket. She greeted Zachary as usual and sat down.

"How are you?" she asked, her lifted eyebrow and eye contact indicating that it was an important question and that she knew the answer was not "fine."

Zachary looked around. His eyes returned to hers, lines of stress radiating outward from them. "It's been pretty rough," he admitted. "They told you what happened?"

"I could tell them more than they could tell me."

Zachary frowned, then nodded. "I guess he would be taken to the ME's office."

Kenzie nodded. "I performed the autopsy."

His eyes got wider. "Yourself?"

"Not alone, but I was the lead."

"It seems... cruel to make that the first autopsy you were in charge of."

"Actually, it helped to keep my focus on the work. It was a good call by Dr. Wiltshire."

Zachary looked doubtful. He shook his head slightly but didn't argue the point.

"So..." he seemed uncomfortable with his question before posing it. "It really was suicide, wasn't it?"

"Yes. Definitely. He swallowed a lot of pills." She remembered the discussion with Dr. Wiltshire. "Do you know, did he break into the dispensary?"

"They're not telling us anything like that. Nothing about the 'how.' Which is probably good." He shrugged one shoulder. "Telling us how to get away with it would not be the smartest idea."

Kenzie chuckled uncomfortably. "No, probably not," she agreed. "That's okay, we'll be asking questions through the proper channels."

"You don't think it's the hospital's fault, do you?"

"There is always the chance that they are partially liable if they are negligent in the way that they store medications, dispense them, or supervise patients. But that's not for us to determine. We do our best to determine exactly what happened, and then let the police and courts take over from there."

Zachary's eyes roamed around the room, moving from one person or group to another, evaluating them all, aware of all the movements and dynamics around him. Years spent in institutions had taught him to watch everything.

37

S omething doesn't feel right," Zachary said.

Kenzie considered the comment. "What does that mean? Are you talking about your symptoms?"

"No. About... here. Something is not right here."

"Okay. Can you describe what?"

Kenzie was prepared for it to be anything, from an actual administrative problem to a delusion caused by the increase Dr. B had made in his antidepressants. Zachary looked at her, weighing his words.

"I'm not really sure. That's why I asked whether you thought it was the hospital's fault. I get the feeling that... they're worried about something. Not trying to cover it up, exactly, but maybe to *spin*..."

"Well, Kennedy should not have been able to get his hands on that many pills, so I imagine they have reason to be worried about the optics, even if they didn't do anything wrong or negligent."

"So you don't think I'm imagining it?"

"No."

Zachary looked relieved at that. "I worry sometimes about paranoia. Whether I'm being suspicious of something when I shouldn't be."

"Well, I think usually you're pretty close to the mark. Times when I've wondered if you're just imagining things, you've turned out to be right. So I think you can trust your instincts on most things."

Zachary scratched at a mark on the table.

"Has someone said something?" Kenzie asked. "One thing in particular that made you suspicious?"

"No, I don't think so... I've been places other times where there have been attempted suicides or deaths. And they mostly say the same things. They're better now about offering therapy rather than just telling you not to talk about it, like they did when I was a kid. They're saying all the usual things. It's just... I don't know. Body language? Nonverbal signals?"

"Sure. That makes sense. People who are worried act a certain way, give off a vibe." Kenzie looked around. The medical staff she could see seemed watchful and stressed, but not guilty. How would she expect them to look after they had been unable to prevent a suicide? How would she have felt? She didn't see anything that seemed out of place.

As she looked around, a movement that didn't fit attracted her attention. She focused in on a young black man and older black woman being escorted in. The boy was moving jerkily, as if angry and agitated. The orderly was trying to hold him by the arm, and the boy was pulling away.

When he saw Zachary at the table, he broke away from the orderly and charged toward them. It all happened within a second or two, and in that time, Kenzie recognized Zachary's teenage friend, Rhys Salter, and his grandmother Vera.

The orderly followed close behind, determined to quash whatever disruption Rhys was going to cause. Kenzie shook her head and motioned him back. The orderly stopped and watched, scowling.

Rhys made his way to Zachary. He flapped a white piece of paper in his hand, the notice of Kennedy's suicide. His expression was upset and worried.

Vera lagged several steps behind Rhys, unable to keep up with his long legs and energetic movements.

Zachary stood up. "It's okay," he told Rhys. He reached out his arms to engulf Rhys in a hug. "It's okay. It's okay."

Rhys clasped him tightly and pounded him on the back. Zachary pulled back after a minute so that they could look each other in the face.

Rhys pointed at the notice and then at Zachary, his movements still jerky and agitated.

"You thought this was me?" Zachary asked.

Rhys nodded.

With his own set of traumatic childhood events, Rhys was mostly mute, speaking only a word or two at a time now and then. He communicated mostly with gestures, supplemented by graphics and a few typed words on his phone. Despite all the therapy that Kenzie assumed he had been through, he did not use any standardized communication set. While he could read and write, it was only a few words at a time, and long sentences and paragraphs defeated him.

Clearly, he had been able to grasp just enough of what was written on the paper that was handed to him to understand that a patient had committed suicide, and he had thought they were telling him about Zachary.

Zachary motioned to the table. "Sit?"

Rhys slid into one of the unoccupied chairs. Zachary shook Vera's hand and received a wrinkled cheek pressed against his in return. He pulled out a chair for Vera, and she sat down.

Zachary sat down. He reached across the table and grasped Rhys's hand. He squeezed it tightly.

"I'm sorry they scared you. I'm okay, you can see that."

Rhys nodded. He crumpled the notice into a ball and threw it away from him angrily.

"Rhys!" Vera said, exasperated. "You go pick that up and throw it in a garbage can."

Rhys folded his arms over his chest and shook his head.

Kenzie got up and disposed of the paper. She could understand both of their positions. Vera's that he needed to behave properly in public and not throw garbage around no matter how frustrated he was, and Rhys's that they had just scared the crap out of him making him think that his friend was dead. They were both right, and it was easiest to just pick it up herself and not let them have an argument over it.

Vera made a face that told Kenzie she should not have interfered. Kenzie ignored it. As Dr. Wiltshire had said earlier, people needed to be allowed to show their feelings and not to be forced to stuff them down just because their emotions made others feel uncomfortable.

"How is school?" Zachary asked Rhys, choosing to focus on something other than who had committed suicide and how.

Rhys rolled his eyes dramatically and looked at Vera. He mimed writing and writing and then shaking his hand out in pain.

"Yes, he had had lots of work to do," Vera acknowledged. "There are a lot more demands as they try to get kids ready for college."

Rhys pointed at himself and shook his head firmly. *Not me.*

"Well, college isn't for everyone," Zachary said.

Rhys pointed at him, raising his brows. *You?*

Zachary shook his head. "No, I never got a college degree. But I have done other training. On private investigation, photographic techniques, that kind of stuff. As I could afford to."

Rhys nodded. He looked at Vera and jerked his thumb toward Zachary.

"I know not everyone goes to college," his grandmother said. "But try asking Kenzie the same thing."

Rhys tilted his head to the side slightly. He knew the answer to that question without asking. He put a couple of fingers over the pulse point on his wrist and shrugged. Doctors of course had to do lots of post-secondary schooling. But Rhys didn't have any plans to become a doctor.

"I did a little bit of general studies at university after I graduated," Kenzie said. "I didn't really know what I wanted to do, and I figured that was enough. I wasn't until a few years later that I decided to go into medicine. So then I was one of the oldest students in my classes."

Rhys scratched his chin, nodding.

"Sometimes it takes a while to decide what you want to do," Kenzie said.

"I really couldn't get a degree," Zachary offered. "I didn't have anyone to help support me once I turned eighteen. I would have needed a full scholarship or to join the armed forces. I never got good marks at school and didn't really want to do night school. I didn't want a degree just for the sake of having a degree. Too much work for a piece of paper."

Rhys pointed at him and made a pulling-the-trigger motion. *You got it.*

38

The visit with Rhys and Vera was brief. Conversations with Rhys were taxing on both sides and, after the first few questions, Rhys didn't want to discuss school or any of the other topics Kenzie or Vera tried to raise. He watched Zachary carefully, and Vera carried the conversation for a while, then decided it was time to go.

"I'm sorry to cut it so short," she said. "I'm an old woman and I go to bed early. And Rhys has school tomorrow. I'm sure he probably still has homework to do."

She looked at Rhys. He shook his head and moved his hands together as if brushing dust from them. *All done.*

Vera looked as if she doubted it was the truth, but she didn't pursue it. Maybe she would in the car or after they were home. There was no need to have an argument about it in front of Kenzie and Zachary.

Zachary and Kenzie said goodbye and watched the two of them head out. Kenzie turned back to Zachary. "I should be going too. But I wanted to make sure that you're okay today. This suicide… I'm sure it doesn't help your state of mind."

Zachary shook his head. "No. But I'm okay. I haven't been saving up pills, and you can bet that security here just got a whole lot tighter. They'll be watching all of us like hawks for the next little while."

"I suppose they will. And the nurse at the front desk said that if anyone needs extra therapy to deal with it, that's available. So if it's bothering you and you need to talk to someone…"

"Yeah. I could get in to see someone."

"Okay." Kenzie gave him a kiss goodbye. "Try not to think about it too much. I know it's hard not to obsess over it, but… it wasn't you. Mr. Kennedy had his own problems. Just because he failed, that doesn't mean that you can't succeed."

He stared past her; eyes unfocused. "But this will never be over. It's not something that they're suddenly going to cure."

"No. Not like that. But you'll get through your time here, and after Christmas, you'll feel better and be able to carry on with your life. I know that fighting depression and everything else sucks, but… you've got a good life." She raised her brows, encouraging him to think about it and count his blessings.

"Sure," Zachary agreed, too fast. He didn't want to hurt her feelings, of course, or to argue about it. But that didn't mean that he agreed. He was too far down the hole to see things clearly. "I just mean… it's discouraging. Knowing that there's only one way this will ever end."

Kenzie squeezed him tightly. "You're wrong," she whispered in his ear. "It will end after a long, happy, satisfying life. You're going to feel better. I promise."

He gave her a gentle hug and didn't argue the point. He was an avoider, not an arguer. He'd rather just coast past any hint of conflict. Kenzie kissed him again and got herself out of there.

There wasn't any way to argue him out of his depression.

Kenzie was relieved to get out of the ward. It would have been great to have a long, satisfying visit with Zachary in a pleasant environment, but the psychiatric unit was even more dark and oppressive than usual. Zachary was right about it feeling *off*. It was probably just the shock waves of Kennedy's death, and it would go back to normal after a few days.

She saw a small cluster of people stopped to talk in the corridor, and it wasn't until she was nearly upon them that she realized it was Rhys and Vera, stopped to talk to a second set of visitors, Zachary's sister Jocelyn and Luke, the teen that she was helping to look after. Zachary had been instrumental in rescuing Luke from his life on the streets, an addict controlled by human traffickers in his role of bringing new, younger girls and boys into the sex trade. Joss had some experience in the trade herself and had agreed to take Luke under her wing to help him rehabilitate.

The boy was not supposed to be back in Roxboro where he might be recognized by someone from his past life. As far as the cartel knew, he was dead. Showing up again could cause some real problems.

Not only that, but Rhys had developed something of a crush on Luke and none of them thought it was a particularly good idea for the two of them to get together. If Luke slipped back into the life, Rhys would be a good asset to bring back to the traffickers.

The two boys had their heads together, Rhys with his phone out to facilitate communication. Vera stood to the side watching them uncertainly. Joss did not engage with her, as the two parents of younger children who were friends might have done.

Joss was a thin, angular woman, all sharp edges in Kenzie's mind. Her tone was frequently biting and sarcastic. Zachary said that she had softened a lot upon taking Luke in, but Kenzie was not encouraged by her expression as she stood there watching the two boys.

"Joss!" Kenzie called out.

Joss turned her head and saw Kenzie. She didn't look excited to see her. She moved about two inches in Kenzie's direction, but made no other move to greet her.

"Hi," Kenzie greeted, trying to keep her voice warm and welcoming. "I didn't know you were coming tonight."

"We had some time, so I thought it would be a good idea to pop in," Joss said, her tone defensive. "Since he *is* my little brother."

"Of course. I'm sure he'll be happy to see you."

Joss snorted, as if she doubted the fact. Why would she come to visit him, if she thought that he wouldn't even be happy to see her? Because it was expected? Kenzie didn't get the feeling that Joss did anything just because it was the socially expected thing. She'd been through too much in her life to give a care what anyone else thought of her.

"He might be tired, though," Kenzie warned. "Since he's already had visitors." She indicated Rhys and Vera. "And he's feeling pretty low tonight. You should know… they had a suicide last night. So it's a difficult time. Hard for him to get away from his own suicidal thoughts under the circumstances."

"They had a suicide?" Joss repeated. "Well, that gives me confidence in the people looking after my brother. How did that happen?"

"It's under investigation. I'm not sure how he got his hands on so many pills. But Zachary said that he is okay, and they're taking stronger security measures in the wake of this incident…"

"I would certainly hope so. If they don't want anyone suing their butts off. Isn't there any kind of oversight? Guidelines to make sure that kind of thing doesn't happen? Inspections by some higher authority?"

"There are guidelines, and I'm not sure what happened. The man may have broken into a locked facility to get the pills he took. It's unclear right now. And it is the case that… someone who is really intent on committing suicide… it is impossible to prevent every possible thing they could do."

Joss stared at her, a deep crease between her eyebrows.

"Then what is the point in Zachary being here?"

"He's safer here than he is at home. I can't keep him under twenty-four-hour supervision. He knew he needed more intense therapy and a safer environment. So he checked himself in."

Joss grunted, dissatisfied. She looked over at the two boys with their heads together.

"Luke, I'm going in. Are you coming?"

Luke looked at Rhys.

Rhys shrugged. He slid his phone into his pocket and looked at Vera, nodding that he was ready to go. Luke slapped him on the shoulder in a friendly goodbye and followed Joss. Joss broke away from her conversation with Kenzie.

"Thanks for the warning."

"Okay. Take care. Have a nice visit."

Kenzie looked at Luke once more, wishing that Joss hadn't brought him along. Joss had undoubtedly made the choice that she thought the best. Maybe leaving Luke alone would have been a bad idea. But they could have made other arrangements. Kenzie could have brought a tablet with her and let Zachary visit with his sister over a video call instead of their coming into town where Luke might be seen.

39

Kenzie awoke with a start, and sat bolt upright in bed, breathing hard. She was soaked with sweat. She looked around the room for Zachary, feeling in the bed beside her and wondering whether he were asleep on the couch before remembering that he was in the hospital.

She turned on the lamp on the side table, knowing that it wasn't going to wake anyone up. She was the only one there.

It helped to see the familiar surroundings. Her racing heart started to slow.

It had been a weird dream, but one clearly born of the stressful events in recent days. In it, Agent Menendez was at the hospital with Zachary, trying to get him to agree with her injecting something into his arm, telling him that he would feel better and be able to rest if she did. Kenzie shuddered.

She picked up her phone and browsed her mail and social networks, waiting for the adrenaline to subside and her brain to remember that it was time to sleep. She was getting caught up on her sleep; she didn't want to take a step back with only a few hours under her belt.

There was an email back from Agent Menendez, who hadn't picked up the new threatening letter before the end of Kenzie's workday, but had promised to pick it up the next morning. There was nothing in her email to indicate that she thought it would be any help. Kenzie felt sort of like Menendez thought she was just being dramatic and that the note was inconsequential.

And maybe it was. Kenzie had heard that people who wrote poison pen letters didn't generally resort to actual violence. Like peeping toms, they were thought to be annoying, but safe.

Though Kenzie had heard a few stories on TV of serial killers who had started out as peepers. So maybe that theory didn't hold water.

There was nothing interesting going on in her social networks. Some Christmas memes and events. Things that Kenzie wouldn't be able to get to now that most of her evenings would be spent going to the hospital to visit with Zachary.

Maybe she should talk to friends about going to one or two weekend events, just so she didn't miss out on everything. While she wasn't a huge Christmas person, she did enjoy the holiday and didn't want to let it pass by without some kind of recognition. Just because Zachary couldn't celebrate the season, that didn't mean Kenzie had to isolate herself from it. He would understand if she explained that she wanted to do some Christmas stuff without him. Not that she needed to explain anything.

Kenzie blinked and rubbed her eyes, then decided maybe she was ready to go back to sleep again. She plugged her phone in, turned the lamp back off, closed her eyes, and waited for sleep.

The morning was quiet. Kenzie hadn't anticipated how much she would miss spending breakfast with Zachary. How had her eating a slice or two of toast with marmalade and his trying to force down a granola bar become such an important part of her life? It seemed completely out of proportion. A few minutes lingering over a few crumbs of breakfast should not be that big of a deal.

But she missed him. Kenzie was counting the days to Christmas. To the day when he would start to feel better and be able to return home safely to become a part of her routine again.

Agent Menendez was waiting for Kenzie when she arrived at the Medical Examiner's Office in the morning. Kenzie looked at her and shook her head.

"You're here early."

"I have a busy day," Menendez said pointedly. As if Kenzie were already keeping her from important meetings by not arriving at the office in time and taking the moment to say hello and exchange pleasantries.

"Well then..." Kenzie unlocked the double doors across the hallway and pushed them open. She went to her desk and unlocked her desk drawer to retrieve the latest letter. "Here it is."

Menendez received the letter and envelope in the plastic sheet protector and glanced over the message. "Well... she escalated, didn't she?"

"She?"

Menendez shrugged. "My best guess. I don't like to say 'they' like it is more than one person, or he/she. Chances are, it's a nurse, and most of the nurses are women." She looked down at the letter. "You wouldn't think that one woman would talk this way to another, though, would you?"

In Kenzie's experience, it was mostly men who called women sexually explicit names. But there were women who did it too; she couldn't rule out the possibility.

"It's the threats that bother me more than the language."

Menendez studied it. "Well... if it's any consolation, these Angel of Death killers don't usually attack people who are well and strong. They stick to those who are helpless and dying."

"As far as we know."

"Historically..."

"I know. But historically we only know who they have killed because they confess it. If there is someone who falls outside their pattern and they don't confess to it..."

"I really don't think you need to worry about that."

Kenzie did not feel reassured. From what she had seen, she was more familiar with the kind of killer they were looking for than Menendez was. Shouldn't an FBI agent be better trained in abnormal psychology and the profiles of serial killers than a medical examiner's assistant?

And even if it wasn't in her normal wheelhouse, then shouldn't she do the research to figure it out?

"So… how is the investigation coming along? Any progress on ruling out any of your suspects? Or figuring out which patients to focus on?"

"Not a lot of movement there," Menendez admitted. "We need more autopsies to identify which patients were even homicides. We are asking families for permission, but most are dead set against it."

Kenzie nodded.

"*Dead* set against it," Menendez repeated, with a chuckle.

Kenzie rolled her eyes. "You can understand how they would be," she said, without acknowledging the pun. "They've buried the person, mourned, put it behind them. They don't want to go back emotionally, and think it is morbid or disgusting to have to exhume the person and do an autopsy."

"They're more interested in putting it behind them than in finding out the truth," the agent said with disgust. "I would think that the truth would be more important than the inconvenience of an autopsy. It isn't like they even need to be there at the exhumation or autopsy. They can pretend it isn't even happening. If it was my grandma, I would want to know if someone had killed her!"

"For some people, that's important. Others, I think, they know grandma was going to die anyway, and even if they don't like the fact that a law was broken and grandma was hurried along, it doesn't bother them that much that she lost a few days or weeks of life."

"It would bother me; I'll tell you that."

Kenzie shrugged and didn't argue, but she wondered if it were true. Situations were often different when she was on the inside instead of outside looking in. What a person felt and did when they were battered by a spouse, when a family member committed a crime, or when they witnessed a robbery were often completely different from what they would have predicted before it happened. The primitive brain or emotional attachment took over the logical brain.

"I still like your Nurse Debbie for it," Menendez offered.

"She's not *my* Nurse Debbie. And I still think you're wrong. She wasn't even there for one of the two deaths that we know were murder. It doesn't make sense to me. Maybe she comes across as not being genuine and makes people uncomfortable with her cheery attitude, but that doesn't make her a murderer. I've seen her work and she is very good at what she does. She is not a killer. She's a healer."

"Just be glad she's not changing your grandma's bedpan," Menendez advised.

Kenzie didn't point out that Nurse Debbie was in Zachary's unit, and she wasn't worried about that. It was obviously going to take more than a few days to unwind the case and find out the identity of the murderer. In real life, things didn't come together magically at the forty-five-minute mark.

Kenzie looked at the digital clock on her desk phone. "I need to get to work here so everything is ready when Dr. Wiltshire gets in."

"Fine." Menendez nodded. "Let me know if you get any more correspondence. I'll turn this over to trace to see what they can find, if anything."

"And I guess I'll hear if you manage to talk anyone else into allowing an autopsy."

Menendez nodded. "I'll let you know."

After she had gone, Kenzie got to work with her usual routine, checking on any evidence that had been logged in during the night, making sure that all remains were properly labeled and documented, that Dr. Wiltshire's desk had been left clean, and all the other little things that she did to smooth the way for the rest of the day to unfold successfully.

Back at her desk to process her email inbox, Kenzie let her mind wander back to Agent Menendez. It had been exciting at first to be involved in an FBI case. But it had turned out to be very different from what Kenzie had imagined or the way it might have been portrayed on TV. Things moved very slowly, and Josie Menendez was no Samantha Spade. She had not even wanted to go to the hospital to do the initial inquiries, preferring to lay it on Kenzie instead.

Kenzie typed and printed and forwarded email reports, thinking it over.

What if there was a reason Menendez did not want to go to the geriatric unit? Not that she wanted an actual doctor to ask the questions, but for some other reason?

Was it possible that there was something Menendez did not want anyone to find out?

40

When Kenzie went to visit Zachary at the hospital that night, the nurse at the desk stopped her, looking apologetic.

"I'm sorry, I have to check ID's for anyone who visits," she advised.

Kenzie stopped and fished through her purse for her wallet. "I haven't had to show ID before."

"I know. We should probably have been checking before too. It seems a little silly when we recognize you and know who you're here to visit and everything, but that's the policy."

Kenzie pulled out her driver's license and handed it to the nurse, who looked at it briefly, then up at Kenzie's face. She nodded.

"Just give me one more second."

Kenzie watched as the nurse wrote down her name and driver's license number in a log.

"Why the increased security?"

"I guess there have been some issues of people going places where they are not authorized and getting into mischief. I don't know the details." She gave a little laugh. "It all sounds a little funny to me. We shouldn't have to card everyone who goes past this point."

At Kenzie's raised eyebrows, she nodded.

"Everyone. Nurses, doctors, janitorial, security, plumbers, IT, *everyone*. Picture me having to ask the security guard for *his* identification!"

It was sort of a funny image. But all things considered… maybe if they'd had such a policy in place before Mr. Michaels had been killed, they would be a lot further ahead on the investigation. As it was, they couldn't account for who had or had not been on the unit when he had died. And the same applied to Mr. Scott and any of the other deaths that they managed to connect to the potential serial killer. If they had proper logs of everyone who had been through the door before the death, it would be a lot easier to pin down the culprit.

"Well, sorry that you have to go through all the extra trouble," Kenzie said, tucking her driver's license into her wallet and pushing the wallet into her purse. "But it probably is a good idea. Especially in a unit like this."

"We really haven't had any security problems, though," the nurse said in a confidential tone. "We never have. It isn't as if people are walking in and out of here if they don't have to be here. Not like, say, the nursery, where people want to get a peek at the cute babies. Friends, family, even strangers and kidnappers." She rolled her eyes. "It isn't like anyone is trying to kidnap any of *our* patients."

"No," Kenzie agreed with a laugh. The image of someone trying to make their way off with Zachary or one of the other men or women she was used to seeing in the unit was pretty ridiculous. It wasn't going to happen. "But there are other things to be concerned about. Drugs or weapons being taken into the unit. Maybe a spouse or family member that is bad for the patient. You don't want someone coming in who you know will start a fistfight!"

The young nurse nodded her agreement. "Yeah. But we generally know who the troublemakers are. And we do leave notes for each other if there's someone who is likely to cause a disturbance, or who always disrupts a patient. I just don't see the need to card you and every other visitor and doctor who comes through here. We can use our eyes. We know who belongs and who doesn't."

"I guess you do what the bosses tell you to."

"Exactly. Well, have a good visit."

Kenzie walked by the desk and went to find Zachary. She was surprised not to find him sitting at the usual table in the common room, and she stood there for a moment, unsure what to do with herself.

"Can I help you?" asked an orderly standing nearby.

"Uh… maybe. I was just looking for Zachary Goldman. He's usually waiting for me here. Maybe he's gone to the restroom…"

"I'll check his room. You wait here."

Kenzie nodded. He walked away, and Kenzie looked around awkwardly. She didn't want to make anyone uncomfortable staring at them, but also didn't want to look like she was avoiding looking at anyone and felt as awkward as she did. It was important for her to be aware of what was going on around her. Not that the psych ward was a particularly dangerous place, but there were certainly people there who could act unpredictably.

Why wasn't Zachary there waiting for her?

In a few minutes, the orderly returned, Zachary walking beside him. Kenzie analyzed Zachary's gait and studied his face. He wasn't shuffling and seemed to be alert, not like they'd given him a sedative. He nodded a greeting at Kenzie and looked away. Maybe embarrassed that he had not been there waiting for her as she had expected. He might have fallen asleep in his room.

"Hey, Kenzie."

Kenzie leaned in to give him a brief hug. "Hi. Do you want to sit down to visit? If you were sleeping…"

"No. We can sit down."

Kenzie nodded her thanks to the orderly and headed toward

their usual table. Zachary followed her, but did not sit down when she did. Kenzie looked up at him.

"Something up?" she asked.

"No."

She looked at his usual chair. Zachary looked at it, but still didn't sit down. He scratched his head and ran his fingers through his hair.

"Actually… do you think we could walk?"

"As long as it's okay with the staff."

He walked away from the table. Kenzie got up to follow him. She caught up and walked beside him in silence at first, following his lead and walking around the loop that took them all the way around the ward.

"This is nice," Kenzie commented. "Get some exercise."

"Don't feel like sitting right now."

"That's fine. I don't mind."

She was interested in seeing the layout of the psychiatric unit. She noted where everything was. The patient rooms. The common room. The dispensary. A shower room that was wheelchair accessible and contained a lift for maneuvering patients. Administrative offices. Interview or therapy rooms, some of them bare and plain and some of them with soft furniture, TV's, and toys or games. A couple of isolation rooms for patients who were out of control or needed to be monitored.

"That was his room," Zachary said, pointing to one of the patient rooms they passed.

Kenzie looked at him. "What? Whose room?"

But then she knew before he answered and kicked herself for asking.

"Kennedy's. That's where they found him."

"Oh. I'm sorry. Where is your room? Are you close?"

Zachary indicated a room three doors down. "There. I didn't hear anything. Not until early morning, when they called Dr. Wiltshire."

"Did they wake you up?"

"I don't know. With these sleep meds… I don't always know if I have been asleep or just in a sort of… twilight. I guess I was asleep. I was by myself and there is no clock, so it's hard to judge… it's disorienting."

"Makes sense."

"I saw Dr. Wiltshire come in. So… I knew what had happened before other patients did. I knew he was dead."

"Did Dr. Wiltshire see you? He didn't mention it."

"I don't know. I was there. But he had a job to do. He was probably focused on that."

Or he hadn't mentioned it to Kenzie because protecting the confidentiality of a patient was required by law. Even though he already knew that Zachary was there, and that Kenzie knew he was there, and that Kenzie knew Dr. Wiltshire knew he was there… Dr. Wiltshire would still obey the letter of the law, which said that he couldn't divulge it to Kenzie.

"What's going on?" Zachary inquired. "Did Dr. Wiltshire issue his certificate? Saying that it was suicide?"

"Yes. There are still some questions to be answered by the hospital, but I expect the police are following up on those. As far as cause of death goes, though, we know it was suicide. There wasn't anything else that showed up in the autopsy or lab tests."

"He seemed okay."

"Did you talk?"

Zachary nodded. "He'd been here before. Not last year… maybe the year before? I don't remember."

"What was he like?" Kenzie assumed that since Zachary had brought it up, he wanted to talk about Kennedy and what had happened.

"He was… kind of gruff. Irritable. He didn't get along very well with the staff."

Kenzie remembered how Nurse Val had gone on about how polite and well-behaved Zachary was, and that they appreciated him as a patient. That was the way Zachary was. He didn't want to offend people. He didn't want to bring them down and didn't whine or complain about his life or the troubles he had. He'd been brought up to be cooperative and compliant, and generally tried to follow the rules, though he didn't always succeed in that.

"I don't imagine the staff is always easy to get along with either," she said to Zachary, laughing slightly. He tried to get along, but people like Nurse Debbie with her enthusiastic *bonhomie* could be a bit much.

"Well… no," Zachary admitted, half his mouth turning upward in a smile for just a second. Then it was gone again.

Kenzie had a sudden rush of memory. Talking to Nurse Debbie that first day she had been allowed to visit Zachary. Nurse Debbie saying what a good patient Zachary was, and how grouchy another patient was in comparison.

Was that Kennedy?

Kenzie was almost sure it had been Kennedy that Nurse Debbie had mentioned. *That old grouch Kennedy.*

enzie stopped walking. Zachary looked back at her, hesitating. "Kenz?"

"Sorry." Kenzie stepped forward and fell into place beside him once more. "Sorry. Just had a thought."

He didn't ask her what it was.

"At least he's in a better place now," Zachary said in a flat tone.

Kenzie glanced sideways at him. She'd never heard him speak of any belief in an afterlife before. They'd discussed it once or twice, whether it was possible that there was anything after the mortality they knew, but both of them were of the opinion that there probably was not. When life ended on that plane, that was the end.

"In a better place?" Kenzie asked. "My morgue?" she teased.

Zachary tugged on his ear. "I mean... he's not in pain anymore. That's all gone now."

"Yes," Kenzie agreed. "For him. Not for his family, any loved ones he has left behind. For them... he's caused a lot more pain."

Maybe it was cruel of her to point this out, to remind Zachary that if he were to leave her behind, she would suffer for it. She wouldn't be happy to have him out of her life. She wouldn't be happy that he was no longer suffering. She would grieve and miss him terribly. The guilt would probably cling to her forever. Guilt that she hadn't been able to stop him. That she hadn't been enough to keep him. That she went on living when he felt there was nothing else left for him.

But she wanted to remind him how much she cared and how much it would hurt her if he did harm himself.

Zachary nodded slowly, acknowledging Kenzie's comment. Pain glistened in his eyes, and she did feel guilty for a moment for causing it. But if it brought him down to earth and reminded him that there were people who loved and cared for him who would be hurt if he were gone, it was worth the momentary stab of guilt.

"I'm sorry," Zachary said.

"Sorry for what?"

He didn't answer at first. "For everything," he said finally.

"You haven't done anything you need to be sorry for." Kenzie turned to him and met his eyes, making him stop walking and meet her gaze for a minute. His pupils seemed normal, not dilated or pin-point. She didn't think he'd taken anything. She really hoped that the apology was just guilt over making her life harder because she cared for him and he was in the hospital instead of at home. Not for having made the choice to end his own life.

Zachary dropped his gaze. They continued walking slowly along. Past the common room again. Past the dispensary. Dr. Wiltshire had said that there had been bottles of pills missing from the dispensary, but there was no sign that it had been broken into. Kenzie couldn't imagine how Kennedy had managed to walk into it or grab a bottle of pills that had been left within his reach without anyone catching him. Maybe he could pick a lock. A lot of people, including Zachary, had that ability.

"I don't want you getting sucked down because of what Kennedy did," Kenzie said. "Because you're thinking about it all the time. If you need to talk to someone about it, to work it through in therapy or whatever, you talk to someone. Okay? It doesn't have to be me. You choose who. But don't let it get you down."

Of course she knew he couldn't help it if it got him down. If his obsessive brain decided to cling to the thought of Kennedy's suicide and not let it go. No amount of therapy could *make* him stop thinking about it or letting it affect his mood.

"Who else do you talk to here?" Kenzie asked, deciding that a switch to a more cheerful topic was in order. "Is there anyone else that you already know?"

"The nurse, Val. The one you talked to."

"Right. I remember. She seems really sweet. Anyone else? Any of the patients?"

"One of the doctors. He's been here a few years. I've seen him on other stays."

Kenzie nodded. Zachary considered.

"One of the other patients. Freddy."

"Freddy. What's he like?"

"She."

"Oh, she. I just assumed. What is Freddy like?"

"She's okay. She's schizophrenic. Ends up here a lot in the winter."

Kenzie was puzzled. "Why in the winter?"

"Because it's somewhere warm and safe. Three meals a day."

"Oh. Is she homeless?"

He nodded. "Mostly, I think. So she intentionally goes off her meds, or acts like she's off, and gets herself admitted."

"Clever girl."

"She is really smart, actually. Like *rocket scientist* smart. But because of her schizophrenia..."

"She can't keep a job?"

"I know there are schizophrenics who do. Ones who manage really well. Who respond to medication and can have pretty normal lives as long as they follow the protocol. But Freddy..." He shook his head. "She's not one of those. She really goes off. Ranting, conspiracy theories, paranoia, seeing hallucinations."

"Kind of hard to get along in the outside world when you're dealing with that, isn't it?"

"Yeah. Most of the time, she lives on the street, and she's okay, people look out for her, and she manages. But when it gets too cold, she comes here."

"At least she's figured that out. She has a safe place to go."

"Yeah. I guess that's the best thing for her."

He was staring off into the distance, not seeing anything around him. Kenzie put her hand on his arm as they walked. "I'm glad you have a safe place to go, too. That they take care of you here."

"Uh-huh."

"Zachary."

He continued to stare at nothingness in front of him.

"I'm worried about you."

"Everything will be for the best," he assured her.

"Have they changed your meds?"

"No."

"You're acting different. Kind of spacey."

"No." He brought his hand up to his face and rubbed it tiredly. "No. Nothing different. Just feeling really…" He trailed off, and the silence drew out for so long that Kenzie didn't think he was going to finish his sentence. "Heavy," Zachary finished finally. "I'm just feeling… very heavy."

"You should tell your doctor that." She didn't like the change in him. She didn't know whether it was caused by Kennedy's death, or the advancing season, or something else. But it worried her.

"Same as usual," Zachary said. "Nothing has changed."

"Are you tired? Do you want me to go?"

She thought that he would immediately object, but he didn't. He turned toward the room that she now knew was his. "Maybe I'll just lie down."

Kenzie watched him walk away from her and return to his room without even a goodbye or peck on the cheek.

When Kenzie looked for someone she could talk to, she found that Nurse Debbie was on duty.

"Mackenzie!" Debbie greeted cheerfully. "How are you doing?"

"I'm good. But I'm a little worried about Zachary."

"Oh, he'll be okay," Nurse Debbie assured her. "He's coming along."

"Well, I know his history, and I know he's unlikely to get better before Christmas. Chances are, he'll continue to get worse until then. But tonight he seemed very different. He said that nothing in his med cocktail has been changed…?"

"No, not that I'm aware of." Nurse Debbie went to the computer at the nursing station and clicked the mouse a few times to bring up Zachary's chart. "No, he hasn't had any changes prescribed." She shrugged. "He could just be tired. A lot of the patients have been feeling extra stress today. After *you know.*"

"Yeah. It's been pretty tough on them, I know. It must be really difficult fighting your own suicidal ideation knowing that someone else here has just committed suicide."

Nurse Debbie nodded. "We're doing the best we can to keep things normal and upbeat. And to make sure that everyone is seeing their doctors and doing extra therapy as necessary. But sometimes, you just have to give people time. You can't rush mental health."

Kenzie nodded. She lingered there, thinking about everything that had happened. "So your Mr. Kennedy… I guess you don't know what happened?"

Nurse Debbie raised her brows. "What do you mean? Of course I know what happened."

"I mean… how he managed to get so many pills. I haven't heard word back from the hospital on where he obtained them. You know, whether he was stashing his own prescription, and if not, how they came into his possession."

"Oh, that. I don't know. They are investigating, I guess. There were pills missing from the dispensary, but how he managed to get his hands on them is a mystery."

"Aren't there surveillance cameras? I would think that the dispensary is a place you would want to position a couple of cameras, so that you can keep your eye on it even when it isn't in use. If someone picks a lock or breaks in…"

"I'm not in charge of security," Nurse Debbie laughed. "They're not going to be taking any advice from me. You'd best talk to hospital administration about that."

"But there isn't a camera there already?"

"There probably is. Umm…" Debbie looked at the computer, pursing her lips. She used the mouse to click a few times. Kenzie moved around the desk so that she could see the monitor. It wasn't a big screen and wasn't at the right angle for her to view, but she could see enough to tell that Nurse Debbie had brought up the security menu and was clicking through cameras, looking for one that pointed to the dispensary. "No… I don't see one pointing there. We do have a couple that are out," she clicked back and brought up a couple of black screens. "You see?"

"Who would know that those cameras were out? Did Mr. Kennedy know, or was he just lucky?"

"Who knows? He wasn't confiding anything in me. Why would he tell me about any security holes if he was going to steal meds?"

"He wouldn't, of course."

"He's better off where he is," the nurse said briskly, clearing the camera feeds from the monitor. "He isn't suffering anymore."

Kenzie shifted uncomfortably. "No, he's not suffering," she agreed. Kennedy was in a refrigerated drawer in the Medical Examiner's Office. Nowhere else. And that was where he would stay until his next of kin made arrangements to pick up his remains and have them interred.

"Does he have family?"

"No. Single guy, all alone. No one to look after him."

"I thought maybe parents or siblings…?"

"He didn't get any visitors. If there was any family around, then shame on them for not caring about him enough to come in now and then."

Kenzie thought about what it would be like for someone like Zachary, barely managing to hang on, to be all alone at home or in the psych ward. No one to tell his feelings to. No one who came by, even just briefly, to tell him that they hoped he would feel better soon. Zachary had seen Kennedy there before. The man would have known, like Zachary, that he likely had a lifetime of admittances in front of him. That he would never be able to completely shake the disease that plagued him. And he had chosen to cut that lifetime of pain short.

"Well… thank you for your help. Will you check in on Zachary in a bit? Make sure he's okay?"

"Of course, Mackenzie. I would check for you, even if I wasn't required to by my job! You know that he's being monitored while he's here. We are here to keep him safe."

Kenzie nodded a polite thank you and didn't bother to point out that they had failed to keep Mr. Kennedy safe. Where had they been when he was swallowing two full bottles of pills?

42

K enzie grabbed a sandwich from the vending machine in the hall. She didn't know why she hadn't made herself lunch to bring in. She had known it would be a busy day and that she wouldn't have time to go to a grocery store or nearby restaurant over lunch. But she had not had the energy or motivation to make herself a sandwich to take in with her, even though she knew the only other option would be buying something from the vending machine, which she hated.

She had sabotaged her own lunch and she didn't know why.

She heard the elevator ding and heard footsteps in the hallway leading to her desk, so she pushed the sandwich to the side and looked attentive, watching to see who came around the corner. It was Joshua Campbell, a police sergeant that Zachary knew and who Kenzie had dealt with on various cases.

"Dr. Kirsch," Campbell greeted, a smile on his face. "It's good to see you. How is everything?"

"Well… coming along." Kenzie didn't jump right in to give him details about her life or Zachary's admission to the hospital. It was just a social inquiry, as far as she could tell, no heartfelt response required. "What can I do for you today?"

"Is Dr. Wiltshire in?"

"No. He had a lunch meeting to attend to, and as soon as he gets back here, he's performing an autopsy. We've got an exhumation in, and he'll want to take care of it right away."

"An exhumation." Campbell made a face. "Nasty business. Best to get them *before* they go into the ground."

Kenzie nodded her agreement. "That would be preferable."

"I was hoping to have some time to talk to him. Maybe ten, fifteen minutes to go over the Kennedy case. The suicide."

Kenzie hadn't known that Campbell was on the Kennedy case. He hadn't been the detective who had attended at the autopsy, but she supposed he had sent a junior to sit in on an autopsy that was expected to be ruled a suicide.

"Okay. If it's just a few minutes, then we could probably squeeze you in. But you'll have to be available as soon as I call."

"I'm going to be heading out myself." Campbell looked at his watch, thinking about it. "I would like to ask some questions at the hospital before shift changes. And then catch the next shift as well."

Kenzie glanced at the time. Between driving to the hospital and asking questions of two or three people, it would be tight for him to get there in enough time to do what he wanted to as it was.

"You really don't have enough time, then. Do you want to leave a message for Dr. Wiltshire instead?" Kenzie poised her fingers over the computer keys. "I can take down a very detailed message, if you would like."

Campbell hesitated. "Well… that may be the best option right now. I should probably just leave him a voicemail. No need to make you take it all down."

"If it is an important message, he will have me transcribe it for the file anyway."

"Oh. Then I guess that doesn't save you any trouble. Okay." Joshua paused, gathering his thoughts. "The police have… some concerns about Kennedy's death. As Dr. Wiltshire noted, he swallowed a very large number of pills."

Kenzie nodded, typing the header for the message, including

Campbell's name, and Kennedy's name and identification number. She jotted down a sentence and waited.

"Having reviewed the security videos for that day, we are concerned that there may have been someone else involved in Kennedy's death."

Kenzie took this down, but she frowned, trying to understand what Campbell was saying.

"Why is that?"

"Kennedy is never seen near the dispensary that the meds came from, except to get his own pills at the appropriate times. He's never hanging around there casing it out. No sign of tampering with the lock."

"I thought that camera was broken."

Campbell raised his brows at her. "How did you hear that?"

"I was talking to one of the nurses yesterday. She looked at the camera feeds and said that one was broken."

"There were a couple of cameras that were not operational. The one that would show the door to the dispensary in particular. But we can see the room around it. Enough to tell that Kennedy only went to get his regular meds and wasn't there when he shouldn't be."

"Then…?"

"Then it appears that someone else was complicit in getting him the pills."

Kenzie's heart sank. Someone had helped Kennedy to get the pills to commit suicide? It couldn't have been someone who thought that it would be good for him. It wasn't like they were trying to give him something that would make him feel better. They had to know that it would kill him. That if Kennedy had those pills in his possession, he would inevitably give in to the temptation to kill himself.

"Oh, no."

Campbell nodded. "It's unfathomable, I know. You wouldn't think that anyone could do such a thing… but we've seen cases where people talk others into suicide. And with Mr. Kennedy, that clearly would not have been difficult."

"No. I would guess not."

"Are you familiar with the autopsy in this particular case?"

"Yes. I actually was the lead."

"Well, that's helpful. I just wanted to be sure… there was no reason for a medically assisted suicide, was there? What I mean is… it couldn't have been someone who thought that it was the best thing, that he was dealing with so much pain he was justified in… choosing to end his life?"

"No. We checked for tumors or anything else like that. Any organic reason that he might have had to kill himself. As far as we can tell, it was just the depression. No other influences." She paused. "Except now, this."

"You can pass that information on to Dr. Wiltshire for me," Campbell said, motioning to the computer. Kenzie had stopped typing as she had understood what Campbell was saying. She typed a flurry of words to summarize their discussion, and nodded.

"I'll let him know."

"I'll be at the hospital to make inquiries, so I'll be out of contact for a while. They always want you to turn your phone off, even if you're not in a unit with sensitive electronic equipment."

Kenzie nodded. Even though there were signs saying to turn off phones in the psych unit, Kenzie didn't bother. As Campbell had said, there were not heart monitors and other sensitive equipment in the ward. She wasn't worried about her phone interfering with anything. But Campbell chose to follow the rule, even though he knew it was nonsense. Or maybe he liked having to turn his phone off now and then. Sometimes being distraction-free was worth it.

"Uh…" Kenzie held her hand up to ask Campbell to wait for a moment. "I don't know whether you know, but I should probably tell you…"

He waited politely for the information.

"Zachary is there."

"At the hospital? Is he investigating something?"

Campbell had, Kenzie knew, run into Zachary at the hospital during the Salter investigation, so it was natural that his mind should jump immediately to that possibility.

"No. He's in the psych unit. Like Kennedy."

She could see that he was still confused, still trying to make the details fit with his case. Maybe he thought that Zachary was undercover there, pretending to be depressed like Kennedy, to see whether he could shake anything out.

"He's a patient," Kenzie told him slowly. "He's depressed and needs to be under a doctor's care."

"Oh! Oh, of course." Campbell shook his head. "I had heard that he suffered from that. Didn't realize that it was so bad."

"This time of year in particular."

"Yes. Christmas is a bad time for people who get depressed," he agreed. "High rate of—" He cut himself off. "Lots of depression this time of year when the days get shorter and there isn't as much sunlight. Or people seeing how happy everyone else seems to be."

"Yes," Kenzie agreed, deciding that Campbell didn't need to know any of the details around Zachary's traumatic memories. "Anyway… I thought you should know, in case you see him or his name…"

"I appreciate it. Do you think… would he mind if I looked in to say hello? Or would that embarrass him?"

"I think it would be fine. He tries to be open about it."

"All right. I'll check in if I get the chance."

He again turned his head to go. Kenzie licked her lips, trying to think of what else she should do. She stood up.

"Do you… have any suspects?"

"I don't have anyone specific yet. I have the list of staff who were on duty that evening. I'll need to get the list of those who were there earlier, too, maybe the last few days, as we don't know exactly when the pills walked off. I didn't see anyone but medical personnel walking away from the dispensary in the recordings that we have, so that would suggest that it was a doctor or nurse who stole them."

Campbell stood there, looking at Kenzie, waiting to see whether she had something else to say about it. He tilted his head slightly, analyzing her.

"You've been there visiting Zachary, I assume? Anyone who jumps out to you as being suspicious?"

43

Kenzie scratched the back of her head, thinking through everything she knew. If someone had given Kennedy the pills intentionally, then that was tantamount to murder. She was already investigating a series of murders. And one of the main suspects in that string of killings had transferred to the psychiatric unit.

She didn't believe that Nurse Debbie could have done anything. She had seen Nurse Debbie at work, knew how well she had gotten along with the patients, how much she had cared for them. A nurse like that did *not* turn to killing patients. And Debbie had left the geriatric unit before Michaels's death. That put her in the clear.

Someone from outside the unit might have visited and given the pills to Kennedy. Maybe even someone from outside the hospital. They were checking ID after that, closing the barn door after the horse was long since gone. The nurse who had been checking ID had said that there was a problem with people walking in that had not belonged there. Did they know that, or was it a guess? It could have been anyone.

Anyone with a key or the ability to pick a lock. Unless it was an electronic keypad, and then they needed to know the combination. She remembered how, on past cases, Zachary had been able to see and remember a phone number he had seen someone dial. If he could do that, then there were people who could have picked up on a four- or six-digit password after seeing it input once or twice.

It could have been another patient.

Anybody.

"Dr. Kirsch?" Campbell prompted.

"I don't know whether you're aware… that the FBI has been investigating a possible serial killer in the geriatric unit. It isn't yet proven that it is a serial killer. The body that's waiting for Dr. Wiltshire, the exhumation, that's another possible killing in that case."

"I'd heard about the FBI being called in."

Then there was Agent Menendez. She didn't seem to have gotten anywhere on the case. It was stalled and she couldn't push it forward. Kenzie had yet to hear anything that they had discovered about the threatening letters. If they couldn't even pull a fingerprint from a letter, how was she going to solve the case of an Angel of Death killer? How many bodies would have to pile up before Josie Menendez could get somewhere on the case?

Did she even want to solve it? Or was there something else going on behind the scenes that Kenzie was unaware of?

"Well…" Kenzie forced herself to go on. If there was a problem with Menendez's investigation, then her superiors would figure it out sooner or later. They wouldn't accept a report that she simply couldn't find any indication that there was a serial killer, let alone who it was.

Would they?

"There is one nurse in that case. A suspect, according to FBI Agent Menendez. And she… has recently transferred to the psychiatric unit. I don't *know* that there's any connection," Kenzie hurried to add. "I haven't seen anything suspicious, and I know her from before, from when my sister was sick. She's a good nurse. I don't see how it could be her. Not when she wasn't even around geriatrics anymore during the time we're looking at."

"But there must be a reason she is a suspect."

"I guess. You would have to talk to Agent Menendez, get her take on the case. Maybe she's moved on to other suspects. But... I just I talked to her last night. The nurse. And I wasn't comfortable with the way she was talking about Kennedy." Kenzie ran her fingers through her curls, as if that might help her to get her thoughts in order. "I don't know. She didn't say anything wrong; it just worried me. Especially with Zachary being in the unit."

"What's her name?" Campbell asked, not asking for any other explanation of what the nurse had said.

"Debbie. Nurse Debbie. I don't remember her last name. I have it written down somewhere, but..."

"I don't imagine there are multiple Nurse Debbies on the unit." Campbell pulled out his phone and started tapping it. Had he received a new message or was he typing a note to himself to follow up on Nurse Debbie?

"I see her on the staff list," Campbell said after a moment. "She was on the floor the night that Mr. Kennedy committed suicide."

"But you don't even know whether that's when the medications were stolen."

"I'm going to assume, until someone manages to prove otherwise, that they were stolen that day. Otherwise, someone should have noticed them missing. These drugs are supposed to be very carefully managed."

Kenzie nodded. "Yeah."

"I will follow up with her," Campbell assured Kenzie. "And I would have been talking to her anyway. You don't need to worry that I will mention your name. I would never say something like that."

"Thanks. I'm sure it's nothing. Like I said, I'm sure it's not her. I mean, one of the patients the FBI is investigating was killed *after* she had left the unit."

"But not killing that patient doesn't mean she didn't kill Kennedy."

"No. I guess not. And there's another nurse that I saw from the geriatric unit *near* the psychiatric unit. But I didn't see him in there; he wouldn't have had access to the drugs in the dispensary."

Campbell's eyebrows went up. He shook his head. "I should obviously have consulted you on this case before putting a bunch of time into it. Who is this other nurse?"

"A male nurse, Stevens is his name. I saw him… going into the NICU unit. But I know that he doesn't work in the NICU. He said he was going there to visit a friend."

"There was no indication that he was going up to psych?"

"No. None at all. It's just that he was close, and that he didn't belong there."

"And a medical professional jumping from one unit to another might not be noticed, if all the conditions were right."

"Yeah. I suppose."

Campbell tapped more information into his phone. Then he nodded. "Just the two of them, then?" he asked, tone ironic. "No one else?"

"No. Sorry. I've been busy with Zachary."

He smiled warmly and nodded. "I'll talk to you later, then. Let you know if either of these names seems to be connected. Enjoy your autopsy, if you're participating in the one this afternoon."

"Yes. Probably. Thanks."

Kenzie told Dr. Wiltshire about Campbell's visit as they suited up for the autopsy. Dr. Wiltshire shook his head, bemused.

"You think this is related to Dr. Philemon's deaths? Why would someone suddenly stop killing geriatrics and start killing people in psych?"

"I don't know. I can't figure it out either. I mean… I understand transferring if she thought that the FBI was getting too close. That makes sense. But… I would think she would move to another state, start over with a different name. No history. Just start over again. That's what usually happens, isn't it?"

Dr. Wiltshire pulled the drape back from the remains on the table, folding it down halfway. "People are not always logical. And despite what they tell you about serial killers in crime fiction on TV, they are not brilliant. They often have low to average intelligence. They're just lucky. They don't get caught because they are brazen and take the opportunities that present themselves. And people don't believe what they see with their own eyes, or don't want to get involved."

The detective Dr. Wiltshire was waiting for arrived. He sketched a wave and apologized for being late, then made his way to the observation area. Kenzie wondered what he'd done to be assigned an exhumation autopsy.

Dr. Wiltshire looked down at the body they were to autopsy and began recording. "The deceased is a Miss Adeline Burger. Age ninety-three. Five feet tall, reportedly ninety pounds at her death. Miss Burger was suffering from pancreatic cancer and died under the care of her physician, Dr. Philemon. Dr. Philemon requested that Miss Burger be exhumed to allow a postmortem to be performed in light of other recent deaths. Miss Burger's next of kin had consented to the procedure. The remains have been embalmed and were buried five months ago. We will begin with a gross examination of the body."

Kenzie was glad that Dr. Wiltshire took the lead on Miss Burger. While she had attended the other two exhumations, Kenzie was not yet accustomed to autopsying remains in a more advanced stage of decomposition. There were many things to be aware of. Dr. Wiltshire walked her through each step, asking questions and pointing out things she should notice. By half an hour in, she was accustomed enough to the sight and smell of the remains that she was no longer distracted by them, fully engaged in the process of the autopsy.

They didn't find anything that indicated obvious foul play in the examination, but knew that they might discover something when samples were tested for toxicity at the lab. There was a lot of bruising in her back, but Dr. Wiltshire said that it appeared to be livor mortis, the blood settling and pooling at the lowest points of gravity after death, rather than any indication of violence.

Like Mr. Michaels, Miss Burger had been on an IV at the time of her death, so there was a puncture wound in one arm, but they were unable to find any other antemortem punctures. Of course, there would be no reason for anyone to inject her somewhere else when a killer already had access to the IV tube draining into her arm.

They took various slides and samples, both for testing and so that Dr. Wiltshire could show Kenzie the effects of decomposition on the various tissues.

Kenzie looked at the clock on the wall, but she didn't need to get back home to have dinner with Zachary. She could grab something quick to eat at the hospital before she visited him.

"It is getting late," Dr. Wiltshire observed, noticing Kenzie's glance at the clock. "We will be done shortly."

"It's fine. I don't have to be anywhere."

"Perhaps not, but I don't want to wear you out too much. It's the weekend; you should be able to relax for a couple of days without being completely wiped out because I kept you too late on top of your other responsibilities."

"I'm fine. A little tired, but I've been sleeping okay most of the time. I can sleep in tomorrow."

She wouldn't be waking up early because Zachary was up. She could stay in bed as long as she liked. Pretend that she was back to her carefree young adult days before she had gone back to school. It seemed like a very long time ago.

"How are things?" Dr. Wiltshire asked. "Any improvements?"

Although he didn't say so explicitly, she knew that he was asking about Zachary.

"No. Not yet. But I don't really expect there to be before Christmas. I was… I'm a little worried about how he was yesterday. The way that he was talking, sleeping or spending more time in his room alone. I don't know. It's scary, not knowing what is going on in someone else's head."

"It might be scarier if you experienced it. I think it's best that we stay in our own heads."

"Yes. I think that his brain is a pretty dark place right now. Especially with the suicide. I thought maybe they had changed his meds, but the nurse said no."

Nurse Debbie.

She wouldn't have any reason to lie about it. If Zachary were reacting badly to a change in his protocol, she would want to know about it so that they could straighten him out again before things got too bad.

Zachary had said that he didn't want anything else changed before Christmas. Dr. B had already raised some of his dosages in hopes that she could get him stabilized. Adding a new medication or taking anything away would be tempting fate. Who knew how badly it could affect him?

"Hang in there," Dr. Wiltshire said.

He didn't tell her that he was sure it would get better or that Zachary would be all right. He had probably seen way too many deaths over the years to be able to spout platitudes to anyone. He knew how unpredictable life and death could be.

"Thanks. I'll do my best."

"That's all anyone can expect." Dr. Wiltshire looked at the tubs of samples on the counter. "Why don't you start getting those into the fridge? We'll send them out Monday when everything is open. I will close up here and put Miss Burger back where she can rest until the funeral home returns for her."

enzie cleared her desk, took another glance at her emails, and started to pack up to leave. She was getting hungry. She should probably have had something else to eat before going into the autopsy. But she didn't like to start an autopsy on a full stomach, just in case. Especially not an exhumation.

The light on her phone was blinking, and Kenzie considered whether to check her messages or just leave it and pick them up the next time she was in. If there were any emergencies, Dr. Wiltshire would have been informed, and he would let her know even if she didn't pick up her voicemail.

But it was the weekend, and she would not be back until Monday, so she should probably just make sure it wasn't anything important. Or something she could do in two minutes so that she didn't need to worry about it over the weekend.

Sighing, Kenzie tapped the message button and waited for it to cue up. It was set up to "verbose" mode, giving the exact date and time and all the other message envelope details before playing the recording. They had to keep accurate records of messages related to patient files.

Kenzie recognized Campbell's pleasant baritone. "Dr. Kirsch. I have left a message for Dr. Wiltshire as well, but I wanted to give you an update to make sure that you are up to speed. I have conducted interviews at the hospital with the last two shifts of medical personnel, as I had hoped to. Your Nurse Debbie was not on for either of those shifts. I have grabbed her shift schedule and personal information and will set up a time to meet with her, whether it is at the hospital or at her home."

There was a pause as Campbell hesitated or planned the rest of his message.

"I don't think there is anything suspicious about her not being here. As far as I can tell, there were not any recent changes made to the nursing schedule. I have also spoken with Nurse Stevens in the geriatric unit. I was lucky enough to find him there after finishing up in psych. I agree that his explanation is a bit fishy, and I will be following up with his alibi witness for the time of the Michaels homicide to see whether we can rule him out. He admits that he did not have a friend in the NICU. He just likes to go and look at the babies."

Campbell gave a grunt of disbelief, and then went on.

"But my main reason for wanting to touch base with you was Zachary."

Kenzie paused in straightening things out in her purse to look at the phone, as if that might help her to understand Campbell better or would hurry him along in his explanation.

"After my interviews were complete, I thought I would stop in to say hello. You said you thought it would be okay, and I thought maybe it would give him a boost to know that someone else was thinking about him. But he wasn't there."

Kenzie dropped her compact. It hit the floor with a smash, but she didn't look at it. She continued to stare at the phone, not believing her ears.

Zachary wasn't at the hospital?

It made no sense. He had known that he needed to be admitted. He recognized his own depression and suicidal thoughts and impulses and knew that he could not be responsible for his own actions. He needed to get help.

Then why would he leave?

She searched for a logical explanation. Campbell had been looking under the wrong name. There was a glitch in the patient records. The nurse helping him had typed in the wrong search string. But wouldn't Campbell have just walked around the unit until he spotted Zachary? It wasn't that big of a place. It wouldn't be hard to find Zachary.

Kenzie waited for Campbell's recording to resume. He had apparently been unsure what to tell her after that point. Zachary wasn't there. So…?

"I'm sorry. I don't mean that to sound dramatic or worried. There is nothing to indicate that there is anything wrong."

Except, of course, for the fact that Zachary had disappeared.

"He checked himself out today. The nurse said that he was a voluntary admission, so he is allowed to check himself out. Of course, if they had concerns about his safety, they could try to keep him here on a Title 18 hold. But he hasn't been making any threats to harm himself or anyone else, so they exercised their judgment and… let him go."

Kenzie didn't stop to pick up the broken compact. She zipped her purse shut and walked away from her desk at a quick clip as Campbell said a pleasant goodbye and wished her luck in a slightly strained voice.

She didn't think about the fact that she hadn't said goodbye to Dr. Wiltshire or locked up her desk. She just moved as quickly as she could. To get to the parking garage and her car and to find out what had happened to Zachary.

There had to be a reason he had left. But with the way he had been talking the previous evening, she was worried what the reason might be. He knew he had to stay there to protect himself.

She wasn't aware of any other time that he had checked himself out early.

She said a brisk hello and goodbye to the guard in the parking garage. She would apologize the next time she saw him. He would be wondering what she was in such a hurry about or if he had done something to warrant being treated so brusquely.

Kenzie turned her key in the ignition and it roared to life. She gave it a bit too much gas as she backed out and narrowly missed bumping into a pillar.

She waited until she was under clear skies and then hit the Bluetooth button and said Zachary's name.

After a few moments of considering her request, the phone dialed out, and then the sound of the ringing phone was played over the speakers. Kenzie bit her lip and stopped for a red light. She was impatient to get to the hospital. It didn't make any sense. And she would hit every traffic light red on the way there, for sure. That was always the way it worked when she was in a hurry.

The phone continued to ring until it went to voicemail.

"Zachary, it's Kenzie. Give me a call back."

She hung up and redialed. Sometimes it took longer to get through to him. Maybe Bridget had been discharged and he felt an irresistible impulse to go see her again. He could be sitting across the street from her house now, watching the lights coming on in the dusk and straining for the sight of Bridget crossing in front of a window.

That actually made sense, and it made her feel better. That was one of the few things that she could imagine Zachary leaving his safe place at the hospital for.

The phone again rang through to voicemail. Kenzie stopped at another traffic light and had to make a decision. Continue to the hospital knowing that Zachary was not there? Go home to see whether he had returned? Or check to see if he had gone to Bridget's house?

Of course, he could be at his own apartment too. She wasn't sure why he would go there, but he still maintained his rent so that he had somewhere to retreat to on the odd occasion when he needed more space or wanted to pick something up that was stored there. He didn't have more than half a closet and a couple of drawers to keep things in at Kenzie's. Maybe she should convert the guest room to an office for him so that he didn't have to sit on the couch and would have room for his client files, photographs, and whatever else he needed to store. She had wanted to keep the guest room free in case her mother needed to stay over or a friend came to visit sometime. But maybe that was silly. And she did have her own home office as well, which she hardly ever used. She could make it into a combined office for the two of them.

There were horns blaring behind Kenzie. The light had changed and she was still sitting there trying to decide where to go. Kenzie blew out her breath. Bridget's house was probably the best bet. But she should check her own house and make sure he hadn't just gone home, expecting her to be there. Maybe he wanted to spend the weekend together and planned to go back to the hospital on Monday. Maybe he felt as though he could manage for a day or two if she were at home.

Kenzie finally took the turn for her house, but she tapped the Bluetooth button again.

"Gordon Drake, mobile."

The hands-free system dialed once more. Gordon answered after only two rings. "Kenzie?"

"Hi, Gordon. I'm sorry to bother you…"

"No, not at all. How can I help you?"

"Well, a couple of things. First, I was wondering how everyone is. Whether Bridget was able to go home…?"

"Yes. She is here. She has someone with her twenty-four hours a day until she is fully recovered. She wanted to get back to familiar surroundings."

"Of course. I'm glad that she's doing well enough to leave."

"The girls, of course, are not yet strong enough to leave the hospital. They are both off of respirators, though. Both breathing on their own."

"Oh, that's fantastic news. I'm glad to hear it. Julia will be catching up to Tricia in no time."

"I certainly hope so. And what else could I help you with?"

"Well, I seem to have misplaced Zachary," Kenzie said, aiming for humor. "He has also checked himself out of the hospital and he's not answering his phone. I'm going to check at home to see whether he is there. He probably is. But I wondered whether he had shown up over there. Maybe he heard that Bridget had gone home and wanted to make sure she was all right."

"I have not seen him," Gordon said slowly, "but the only time I was outside was when we got home this morning." There was a pause as he apparently checked out the window. "He isn't out in front, but of course he doesn't usually park where he is so visible. Perhaps I'll go for a walk."

"Thanks. I hate to bother you. And I will head over there if he isn't at home. But if you can have a look around… it would ease my stress levels a little if I knew that he was okay."

"I will see if I can see him. I'll call or message you back."

"Thanks, Gordon."

Kenzie terminated the call and drove as fast as she dared to her house.

45

There were no lights on other than the ones Kenzie knew were on timer switches. She already had a knot in her stomach as she drove into the garage. He wasn't there. She had told herself that he would be. But of course he wasn't. He had left the hospital for a reason, and it wasn't to come home and spend the weekend with her. If that had been the case, then he would have called her. He would have had her pick him up from the hospital and maybe they would go out to dinner somewhere. At a restaurant that didn't have Christmas decorations up. There were still a few that didn't go overboard on the holiday decor.

Kenzie got out of the car and hurried through the door into the house.

"Zachary? Are you here?"

There was no answer. The house was quiet and still.

The burglar alarm started beeping a warning and Kenzie punched her code into the panel to disarm it.

Of course, if the burglar alarm was still armed, then there was no one in the house. But it was always possible that Zachary had been home for a while and then left, re-arming the alarm again. So Kenzie took a quick walk through the house, looking for anything out of place. He hadn't taken anything with him to the hospital,

278

so she couldn't judge by luggage or clothing dumped by the washing machine.

In the living room, his computer and equipment didn't appear to have been touched. His phone was still sitting attached to the charger, where he had left it. There wasn't any point in continuing to call him if he didn't even have his phone with him. Which also meant that she couldn't use it to track him. Maybe that was why he had left it there and not returned for it when he had signed himself out of the hospital.

She checked the bedroom just for good measure, and just to be sure of herself, checked the row of pill bottles lined up in his bathroom. All appeared to be untouched. Kenzie went back through the house to the garage, pausing to set the alarm again as she left. She checked the bin in the garage where she had left the knives. Zachary didn't know where she had put them, but he was smart enough to figure it out and go looking through the boxes for them if that were what he really wanted. But the knives all appeared to be present and accounted for.

Kenzie checked her phone in case she had missed a message from Gordon, but there was no text from him confirming that Zachary was at the house.

Kenzie was sure that was where he had to be. She shut her mind to all other possibilities. Particularly to the possibility that Kennedy's death had just been too much for him to handle and he had signed himself out in order to be alone to do what he felt compelled to do. He had checked himself into the hospital for just that reason. So that he would not be able to harm himself. She was sure that he wouldn't leave the psych ward to follow through on his suicidal ideations.

She had told him once how she feared being the one to find him one day if he did commit suicide. She had hoped that knowledge, the vision of her walking into his apartment to find his body, would help deter him from taking such action. He was a kind, compassionate person. He didn't want his actions to hurt others.

Kenzie drove to Bridget's house. It was, she knew, Gordon's house rather than Bridget's, but Zachary had always identified it as Bridget's. She was the person who mattered to him. His world revolved around her, not Gordon. And unfortunately, not around Kenzie.

She closed her mind to all other thoughts and focused on reaching the house. Zachary would be there. Watching from some corner or alley. Getting his fix, the positive boost his brain gave him when he watched his former lover.

Kenzie couldn't help marveling at the size and majesty of the home when she arrived. It really was stunning. Comparable to anything Kenzie's parents owned.

She tore her eyes from the building to look around. Where was he? She scanned the road for his car, but didn't see it.

Kenzie drove slowly down the streets, performing a circuit of the house. She looked for the car, watched for Zachary's figure loitering across the street or under a tree, anywhere within sight of the house. He would want to see it. Being close by wouldn't be enough. After three circuits of the house, Kenzie finally had to admit that he wasn't there. She thumbed a quick message to Gordon that she had been unable to find Zachary at either house.

What is he driving? Gordon texted back. *Same car as before?*

Kenzie sat there, staring at the phone screen. She hadn't even stopped to think about how he would get around. She had driven straight to her garage, not even driving past the front of the house to see whether Zachary's car was still parked at the curb.

Not sure, she texted back, *will try to find out.*

She drove back to the house, slower this time, not wanting to risk getting pulled over by the police for speeding. She had been sure that he would be at Bridget's house. Now she wasn't going anywhere in a hurry. She had to figure out where else he would go.

She drove down the street in front of her house and saw the little white car still parked there. So Zachary didn't have a vehicle. He hadn't returned to the house to pick it up.

He was, of course, perfectly capable of calling a cab or Uber, renting a car, walking, or getting around town on the bus. Those were all possibilities. But she couldn't see him traveling around town without picking up his phone and his car.

Zachary's apartment was the only other place she could think of where he might have gone. His own man cave. If he needed to think by himself, needed space to just be himself or to get some quiet and have a nap, then maybe he would go to his apartment. Or maybe there was something there that he wanted to pick up. She couldn't imagine what it would be, but tried to assure herself that there was good reason for him to go back there. He did have a life separate from hers. His own identity.

She looked around the parking lot when she got there. Since Zachary's car was at her house, she didn't feel guilty about using the resident parking instead of looking for one of the rare visitor spaces. She pulled her car in and hurried into the building and up the elevator to Zachary's floor. There were decorated Christmas trees in the lobby. She remembered how much of a problem that had been for him the year before. He snuck in and out the back door to avoid having to see them.

She walked down the hall to Zachary's apartment and found a couple of flyers protruding from under his door. They should probably get someone on his floor to pick those up whenever they were delivered, so that it wasn't so obvious that he was not at home.

Hoping that Zachary had just left them there when he went in, she tried the door and found it locked. There was no TV blaring away inside. No sound of Zachary talking on the phone with a client. Which of course he wouldn't be, since his phone was still back at the house. Kenzie fit her key into the lock and let herself in. She stooped to pick up the flyers that had been shoved under the door, as well as a couple of letters addressed to him, and put them down on the kitchen counter as she entered.

"Zachary, are you home? It's Kenzie."

As if he wouldn't recognize her voice.

"Zach?"

Kenzie knew that he wasn't there without looking any farther. But she knew she had to look. She had to confirm to herself that he had not gone back there to harm himself.

The living room was empty. She walked down the short hall to the bedroom and pushed the door open. No one lying in the bed or strung up to the light fixture. Kenzie let out a long breath that she hadn't realized she'd been holding. How long had it been since she'd been able to breathe properly?

She glanced into the closet and looked for any other signs that Zachary had been there. There was a fine layer of dust over all the horizontal surfaces. He hadn't been there.

Kenzie withdrew from the bedroom and checked the bathroom. Again, no sign that anyone had been there in quite some time. Kenzie looked through the medicine cabinet. There were still a few bottles of pills there, prescriptions that Zachary no longer used or had since refilled and had at her house. Kenzie threw them into the bag in the bathroom garbage can and took it with her. There was no need for them to be left at the apartment. Zachary usually kept a dose or two of his meds on him, just in case something happened and he couldn't return home. That had happened enough times that he'd learned to be prepared for the unexpected.

She took one final glance around the living room and kitchen and left, locking the door behind her. She took the bag of prescriptions down to the dumpster and threw them away.

fter returning to her car, Kenzie sat there for a few minutes, trying to decide what to do. She couldn't go home and wait. That was out of the question. She needed to find Zachary. He was out there somewhere and he didn't have his phone on him. She wasn't going to wait until he turned up in the river.

How long had it been since he had left the hospital? Had it been in the morning? Not until the afternoon when Campbell had been there questioning suspects? Campbell might have missed him by minutes. He hadn't given Kenzie any of those details.

She could call the psychiatric unit, but she figured it would probably take just as long to get ahold of someone who would help her on the phone as it would to drive over there and see them face-to-face. And a face-to-face meeting was a lot harder to ignore. It wasn't as easy to turn someone away when they were standing right in front of you. When they had gone to the effort of coming to you.

So she revved her engine and drove to the hospital.

One of the nurses sat at the reception desk as usual. Kenzie took her wallet and identification out as she was walking down the hall so she would have it ready when she got there.

"I'm looking for Zachary Goldman. Is he here?"

"Oh, Zachary." The nurse smiled and nodded and looked at her computer screen.

"I was told that he had checked out," Kenzie advised.

"Oh, really?" The young woman tapped a search string into her computer and sat looking at the screen. "Oh yes, I guess he did. That's funny, I thought he would be here longer term. Usually…"

"I know. I didn't expect him to check out either. What time did he go, can you tell me?"

"Oh, I don't know, I'm sorry."

"Doesn't it say on your records? There must be some kind of time code attached to that checkout record."

"Hmm…" The woman studied the screen, then eventually nodded. "This morning. Eleven o'clock." She looked at her watch as if she didn't know what time it was. "I actually probably shouldn't have told you that. We're supposed to be very careful of privacy."

"I'm his partner. It's okay to tell me. You can see my name on the visitor list."

"But that doesn't mean I can give you any information, I'm sorry."

"I'd like to talk to someone who saw him this morning. Are any of the nursing staff who were on then still on now?"

"No. I don't think so."

Kenzie stared at her, then nodded at the computer. "Maybe you could check?"

"I don't know whether I can access that." She started clicking around the screen, looking for the information. "Well, it looks like Nurse Val is doing a double shift…"

"Great. I'd like to talk to her."

"We really can't talk to people about private patient issues."

"I'd like to see her anyway. Please." Kenzie motioned to the hall behind the nurse. "I can go find her on my own. Or do you want her to come out here?"

"I…"

"I'll just go in, then," Kenzie said briskly, and took a step toward the unit.

"No, let me call her and see what she wants to do. I'm not sure of this…"

Kenzie waited while she had Nurse Val paged, and then a few more minutes for her to show up. Kenzie shifted and looked around anxiously. She didn't want to just hover over the nurse at the reception desk, but there wasn't really anything for her to do while she waited.

Turning partway around, she saw a man coming toward her and, for a split-second, thought that Zachary had returned.

But of course, it wasn't him. It was Tyrrell, his younger brother. They were similar in coloring and features, Tyrrell had Zachary's dark eyes and hair. But his hair was longer and shaggier, he was taller than Zachary and was a healthy weight, not struggling to keep on the pounds like Zachary.

"Kenzie." Tyrrell smiled and gave her a little wave. "Hey, how are you doing? I tried calling earlier, but…"

Kenzie tried to remember if she had seen Tyrrell's number on her recent call list. He might have called while she was doing the autopsy, but if he had, he hadn't bothered to leave a message.

"How are you doing?" Kenzie gave him a perfunctory hug and looked him over. Something seemed a little "off." She wasn't sure what it was. Maybe he was out of sorts or worried about Zachary. Of course they were all worried about Zachary. Kenzie more than ever, with his disappearance.

"Good, good. I'm just fine."

"Did Zachary know you were coming?"

"Well… no. I thought I would talk to you, but then I didn't get to. So I figured I'd just come by."

He looked at Kenzie, and at the nurse at the reception desk. "Why? Is there something wrong? You said that he was going to put me on his visitor list."

Kenzie looked over her shoulder. Nurse Val had not yet shown up. "Well... the problem is... he checked out sometime earlier today. I don't know where he is."

Tyrrell blinked. "What?"

"Yeah. I'm sorry. I just found out. I haven't had a chance to tell everybody yet. And I don't know what I'm going to say. That I lost him? I can't believe that he did this."

"Well... he must have gone home. Isn't he at home?"

"No. Not at my place and not at his apartment. I've checked everywhere I can think of, but I can't find him."

"Can you call him on his phone?"

"No. His phone is at my house. He didn't bring it with him to the hospital. Same with his car," Kenzie said as Tyrrell took a breath, anticipating his question. "It's parked in front of my house."

Tyrrell shook his head. His dark eyes reminded her so much of Zachary's it was disconcerting. "That doesn't make any sense. Where would he go?"

"I don't know. I'm waiting to talk to a nurse who was on earlier when he checked himself out. We'll see whether there is anything she can tell us about what he might have said or planned."

Tyrrell's expression was concerned. Of course he would be just as worried as Kenzie about what Zachary might have done or be planning to do. He hadn't admitted himself to the hospital for no reason. He had known that he was a danger to himself and he needed to be under a doctor's supervision.

There were footsteps in the hallway and Kenzie looked up to see the familiar nurse walking toward her. She seemed to do a double-take when she saw Tyrrell standing there.

"Uh... hi. Is there something I can help you with?"

"Tyrrell, this is Nurse Val. Val, this is Tyrrell, Zachary's young brother."

"Oh. Well, I'm very glad to meet you," Val said politely, offering a hand. She and Tyrrell shook briefly. Val was clearly still wondering what was going on.

"Val, you were on this morning, right?"

"Yes. Long day today. I've been here the whole time."

"So you were around when Zachary decided to check himself out."

She shrugged.

"We're both really worried about Zachary. Did he tell you where he was planning to go?"

"No. He didn't say anything to me."

"It's really important. I'm not sure I understand why he was allowed to check himself out when he was having suicidal thoughts."

"He was voluntary. He checked himself in. He's allowed to check himself out. I understand your concern, of course, but… there wasn't really anything we could do about it. He said that he was feeling better, that he wouldn't do anything to harm himself, and… he had to go. So he went."

"You know his history. You know he's not going to be better before Christmas."

"Well…" She shrugged. "He said he was. I don't know what else to tell you."

"We need to find him. He isn't at home. He doesn't have a phone or a vehicle. He didn't tell anyone in the family that he was going to check himself out or what else he was going to do."

"He was depressed and suicidal," Tyrrell reiterated, his voice stronger than Kenzie's. And maybe it would carry more weight with the nurse. "Someone like that can just walk out of here?"

"Yes. I'm sorry. He has a history of admitting himself when he needs to, getting the treatment he needs, and then checking himself out. If he says that he is feeling better… I can't just decide that he's wrong. He hasn't had an involuntary admission in years. I don't know whether he ever has."

Kenzie looked at Tyrrell. He shook his head, at a loss.

"What we really need to do is to find him," Kenzie said. "Let's back up a bit…" She swallowed, took a couple of deep breaths, and tried to approach it logically. "I was here to see Zachary yesterday. He was still pretty upset about Mr. Kennedy." Kenzie looked at Tyrrell and filled him in. "Another patient in the ward who committed suicide this week."

Tyrrell nodded, his eyes big.

"He was talking... in a way I haven't heard him talk before. I was worried about him. I asked Nurse Debbie if any changes had been made to his medications because I thought he might be reacting to something. She said that nothing had been changed. So I hoped that he was just working things through, and maybe after a good night's sleep, he'd be feeling better. I was hoping that he would be doing better today."

Nurse Val nodded.

"He's really been having trouble with it," Kenzie reiterated.

"I know. A lot of them are. Things have been very stressful since... the incident. We are trying to give everyone the attention they need. Offering extra therapy. Some group sessions. The nurses are circulating and checking in on everybody, whether they are on watch or not, just to make sure that no one slips through the cracks. Everyone was very concerned, not just about Zachary, but about all the patients in the ward."

"Did you talk to him?" Kenzie asked.

"A little. Mostly just asking him how he was. Making casual observations. That kind of thing. He spent more time with Nurse Debbie."

Kenzie frowned. Zachary didn't like Nurse Debbie, so why would he be spending more time with her? "Are you sure? With Nurse Debbie?"

Val nodded. "Of course I'm sure."

"Did he... seek her out? Or was she checking in on him?"

"Well, that's hard to say. It isn't as if I was watching both of them all the time." Val considered, staring off into space and thinking it through. "It might have been more Debbie than Zachary. She was being proactive. She probably saw, as you did, that he was bothered by the events. Wanted to make sure that he was okay. Maybe because you said something to her."

Kenzie nodded. Her stomach was one giant, hard, heavy knot, but she tried to remain casual, to keep the conversation from becoming adversarial.

"But I thought that Nurse Debbie wasn't in today. Didn't I hear that?"

"No, you're right. She hasn't been in today. She's been on almost constantly since she transferred in. I'm sure she's in need of some major rest and relaxation. Especially after a suicide."

"I wonder… Nurse Debbie is kind of a friend of the family. Did you know that she treated my little sister years ago? In the nephrology unit in Burlington?"

"Did she?" Val smiled. "Debbie always has stories about all the patients she has treated over the years, all the families she has been friends with. She's such a bighearted person. Someone who really puts herself out there, her whole self."

Kenzie smiled and nodded. "My mom was hoping to be able to talk to her. Do you think I could get her phone number? After all these years, it would really mean a lot."

Kenzie could see the hesitation in Val's face. Of course they were not supposed to give out private phone numbers to their patients or the public. They were supposed to be able to keep their personal lives separate from their work, private, to avoid calls from cranks and disgruntled patients and family.

"Do you know who my mother is?" Kenzie asked. "Do you know Lisa Cole Kirsch? She does a lot of fundraising for kidney research and for the hospital."

Of course, the fundraising that Lisa did was more often for the big Burlington hospital than the Roxboro one, but Val didn't need to know that. Val nodded her head, familiar with the name.

"That's your mother? I never knew that. I never put the names together. Of course, I only know you through Zachary, so I didn't even know your last name."

"Yes. I'm sorry. I should be better at introducing myself." Kenzie pulled a business card holder out of her purse and passed a card to Val. She gave one to the nurse receptionist as well. "I'm Dr. Kenzie Kirsch. With the Medical Examiner's Office."

Val's eyes widened when Kenzie revealed that she was not only a doctor, but one with the Medical Examiner's Office.

"Oh, well. Of course… I'm sure it's all right for us to give Nurse Debbie's number to the Medical Examiner's Office," Val said, looking at the other nurse. "That's different."

The other nurse looked wide-eyed and uncertain about this, but when Val nodded at her, she tapped some more information into the computer and wrote a phone number on a little slip of paper. Like the papers they kept by the computers at the library.

"This is Nurse Debbie's number. Now, I really have other things that I should be doing. If you don't mind."

Kenzie looked down at the piece of paper. She was happy to have gotten something. The information was hard-won. But she wasn't sure it would lead anywhere.

"Let's go sit down over here," she said to Tyrrell, motioning to a couch off to the side, a place for people to rest while they were waiting to get into psych or for family members to visit.

Kenzie and Tyrrell sat down so that they wouldn't be hovering over the nurse at the reception desk. Nurse Val spoke with the other woman in a low voice for a minute, several looks were cast in Kenzie's direction, and then she returned to the unit.

Kenzie looked at the phone number.

"Where do you think he is?" Tyrrell asked worriedly.

"I wish I knew. I can't think of where else he would go. I've checked everywhere I can think of."

"What about... his ex-wife? He's always talking about her. How he's doing so much better now, not stalking her. Maybe... he fell off the wagon." He shrugged, ducking his head. "Sorry..."

"Don't apologize. It's the truth. I already know about Bridget and his issues there. There isn't any point in pretending they don't exist, is there?"

Tyrrell shook his head. "No. When you cover things up... they just get worse."

"That's right," Kenzie agreed. "I'm not pretending that behavior didn't happen. But I already checked, and he isn't around there. He doesn't even have his car. There's no sign of him."

Tyrrell nodded. "Well, sorry to bring it up."

Kenzie didn't tell him again that he didn't need to apologize for it. She took out her phone and started to tap the number into it. She hadn't realized how reluctant she was to call Nurse Debbie. She might be able to find something out about what was going on with Zachary. Maybe he had confided in her, and she could provide the key to finding him.

She knew that Zachary wouldn't have confided in Nurse Debbie. She drove him crazy with her ebullience and how physical she was.

But it was the only clue that she had. So she pressed the last button and placed the call on speaker so that Tyrrell would be able to hear it too. There were a few rings, and Kenzie wondered whether Nurse Debbie would answer it. A lot of people didn't bother to answer if they didn't recognize the number. Nurse Debbie would have no idea that it was Kenzie.

"Hello?"

"Oh, I'm glad I reached you. Nurse Debbie. It's Kenzie Kirsch."

"Well, isn't it a delight to hear from you! What can I do for you?"

"I was hoping that I could talk to you about Zachary. I'm in a bit of a bind. I know you're not on right now, but I really wanted to speak with you."

"What about Zachary?"

"I know I told you yesterday... but his behavior really concerns me. He's taken a turn, and I'm afraid it's for the worse. We need to keep an eye on any changes in behavior. We don't want to lose him. Like... Mr. Kennedy."

"I don't think you need to worry that much about Zachary. Why? What did he say?"

"He's been talking a lot about Kennedy. About how he is in a better place now."

Tyrrell was frowning at Kenzie. He mouthed *ask her where he is.*

Kenzie shook her head.

"Well, he *is* in a better place now," Nurse Debbie said. "I agree with that. While he was here, Mr. Kennedy was a tortured soul. He was miserable and made everyone around him miserable. I understand that losing him might have been a shock to the ward, but it really is for the better. Things are much more peaceful without him around. And where he is… he's not in pain anymore."

Kenzie looked at Tyrrell. He bit his lip. His face was very pale. Kenzie returned her gaze to her phone.

"I'm glad that you think Mr. Kennedy is at rest now. But I'm still worried about Zachary. I wouldn't want him copying Kennedy's actions."

"That's always a danger in a situation like this," Nurse Debbie acknowledged. "Copycats. Other miserable people."

"I don't want Zachary ending up like that."

"I'm sure you don't. You want him to be with you. But if he really was happier moving on… you have to consider that too."

Kenzie wrapped her arms around her stomach. She felt like she was going to throw up. She breathed shallowly, trying to keep herself together. If Nurse Debbie thought that Kenzie was upset with her viewpoint, she would stop talking, and Kenzie might need what she had to say.

"He wouldn't be happier. He would just be gone."

"I choose to believe that they go to a better place," Debbie said placidly. "You may not. But I think you are missing the big picture. When your sister died, weren't you relieved that she wasn't suffering anymore? Wasn't it better that she wasn't still sick? Hardly able to breathe? She was in so much pain. You didn't want to force her to stay, did you? Going through all of that?"

"That isn't the same," Kenzie said evenly. "Amanda was in a lot of pain. She was really sick. And I wasn't happy or relieved when she died. We were all devastated. We would have done anything for her, to keep her alive and well."

"But you couldn't, and if she had lived, she would have been in ongoing pain for months or years. You wouldn't have wanted that."

What Kenzie had wanted was for Amanda to get better. For her to be able to get another transplant, and again live a normal life, like she had after getting Kenzie's kidney. It had been miraculous, seeing her get off the machines and living a normal, vigorous life again. Kenzie had never seen anything like it. She had not wanted things to end the way that they had. No one would have wanted to see their loved one go through that ghastly process, eventually drowning in her own fluids.

"Zachary isn't going through what Amanda did," Kenzie said firmly. She didn't want to shout, but she needed to speak up against the nurse. "He is going through a depressive episode. And if you know his history at all, you know that when he gets past Christmas, he'll start to feel better. He isn't dying. He's just going through a dark patch and needs everyone's support."

"Would you want to keep going through that every year, over and over again?" Nurse Debbie challenged.

"Yes. His life is good. He's happy. He has a family again. He is in a relationship. He has his own business and is doing well enough to support himself. He has a good life, and he doesn't want to lose that because of cyclical depression. That's why he goes to the hospital. Because he wants to live!"

There was no response from Nurse Debbie. Kenzie stared down at the phone, blood pounding in her ears. She was furious with Nurse Debbie for insinuating that Zachary would be better off dead. Was that the way that she had been talking to Zachary when Val had seen them together? Not a nurse trying to cheer up her sick patient, but a poisonous serpent whispering in his ear, driving him closer to suicide just like a cyberbully had done the year before?

What was wrong with people?

"Did you talk to Zachary today?" Kenzie asked.

"I haven't been on shift today."

"I know that. But he could have called you on the phone. Said that he needed to ask you something or that you had told him it would be okay to call when you weren't there."

"Now, I haven't talked to him today."

"Did the two of you talk last night? After I left?"

"I checked in on him. That's my duty, and you said that you were concerned about him. So of course I went in to see how he was doing. Of course I talked to him to gauge how he was feeling."

"And…?"

"I think you have reason to be worried. He is very depressed. But that was last night. You've visited with him today. You know his state of mind better than I would."

"I haven't visited with him today."

"Didn't you go to the hospital? I thought you went every day."

"I went to the hospital to see him, but he wasn't there."

"He wasn't there?" Nurse Debbie echoed, sounding stunned.

"He checked himself out."

"But… why?"

"We're still trying to understand it. He checked himself out and he didn't go home. We don't know where he is."

"Oh goodness. I had no idea, Mackenzie. You must be so upset. Do you want me to call someone for you? Or to come visit you? I'm so sorry this has happened."

"No. I don't need you to come visit me. I'm still trying to figure out what to do. Where to look. I haven't given up on him."

"No, of course not. Here I am, going on about how he could be at peace, and you don't even know where he is. You should have told me earlier. I didn't mean to be so insensitive."

She sounded so sincere. But Kenzie was changing her mind about Nurse Debbie. She was starting to see that maybe she wasn't the woman she pretended to be. What if Agent Menendez's suspicions were true? What if Nurse Debbie had been killing patients in geriatrics? What if she had been doing it for years before that? And what if transferring out of the geriatric unit wasn't just a way to escape suspicion, but looking for new excitement? People who were not old, sick, and dying, but people in good physical health but suffering mental pain?

Someone had taken pills out of the dispensary. Someone who had legitimate access to the dispensary. And those pills had killed someone. Maybe Nurse Debbie had not forced the pills down his throat, but if she had talked Kennedy into killing himself, encouraged him to do it, and given him the pills, then she was just as guilty as if she had done it herself.

"Did Zachary talk about going anywhere? Did he say anything about going home or to someone else's house or some other place where he would be happier?" Kenzie asked, hoping to get something more from the woman.

If Nurse Debbie thought that Zachary had checked himself out to harm himself, then she might be as eager to find out where he had gone as Kenzie was.

But for very different reasons.

"No, I can't think of anywhere," the nurse said slowly. "I'm sorry."

"Did he talk about… Lorne and Pat? Going back to a place he'd known in childhood? Searching for the rest of his family…?" Kenzie dug desperately for clues as to where he might have gone. They needed to find him.

"He didn't have much to say to me," Nurse Debbie said. "I'm sorry. About the only thing I ever heard him talk about was those babies."

"Babies?" Tyrrell echoed.

"Who is that?" Nurse Debbie asked.

"Zachary's brother. He's helping me."

"Oh. Yes. The babies. The twins. He kept talking about Bridget and the twins. Who is she? A sister? He was always worrying about them."

"Something like that," Kenzie agreed. She thought about it. She had checked in with Gordon, done the circuit around Bridget's house several times. But she had not checked on the babies.

"I have to go now," she told Nurse Debbie. "I'll call you back if I find something."

Kenzie hit the red button to end the call. She looked at Tyrrell.

"What?" Tyrrell asked.

"The babies are just a couple of floors down. in the NICU."

"Then…"

"We should go see them."

Tyrrell cocked his head slightly, not understanding. "Okaaay…"

"Don't you remember about Zachary and Mindy?"

"What does Mindy have to do with it?"

"Zachary helped to take care of you younger kids when you were born. And Mindy didn't eat and needed lots of attention. And Zachary was the one who made sure she got enough to eat."

Tyrrell tilted his head, thinking about it. "I didn't know that. I was still pretty young when Mindy was born."

"He's been worried about Bridget's babies from the time she got pregnant. Worried that Bridget won't be able to take care of them. She's been released from the hospital and went home. Where do you think Zachary would go?"

Tyrrell looked relieved. "He would want to see the babies."

Kenzie led Tyrrell down to the NICU, her heart beating fast. Of course that was where Zachary would be. She should have thought of it right from the start. Of course he didn't need his car or his phone. He'd never left the hospital.

The only thing that could have persuaded him to leave the psychiatric unit where he was safe was to take care of someone else.

They walked at a brisk pace. A nurse tried to stop them as they entered. "Excuse me, can I help you?"

She followed them when they didn't stop. Kenzie led Tyrrell directly to the incubator she had previously visited with Gordon. Zachary sat in a chair next to the incubator, watching the infants with his dark, sunken eyes. He looked at Kenzie and Tyrrell as they entered, sat up straighter, surprised, and looked around at his surroundings.

"Zachary!" Kenzie kept her voice to a low whisper. She hurried to his side and bent down to give him a hug and a kiss. "We've been so worried! You should have let me know what was going on. Where you were going."

He looked uncertain. "What time is it?"

"It's almost nine. I've been looking everywhere for you."

"Oh." He looked around again. "There's no clock or window in here. I didn't realize."

Tears started falling down Kenzie's cheeks, she was so relieved to find him safe. She tried to wipe them away. "You need to let me know what you're doing!"

His eyes dropped back to the babies. "I didn't think you'd want to know that I was here. I planned to go back up to psych after a few hours, once I was sure they were safe. I didn't mean to be here so late."

"Have you had anything to eat? You've been here all day."

"No. I've just been sitting here."

The nurse was at Kenzie's shoulder, angry at being ignored. "There are too many people in here. We only want one person here at a time. And no conversation. These little ones need to sleep undisturbed."

Kenzie didn't give up her place. She put her hand on Zachary's shoulder. She wasn't leaving him alone.

"If you haven't had anything to eat, then we should go to the cafeteria," Tyrrell suggested. "I don't suppose there will still be staff there, but there are vending machines, at least. You're not going to get anything if you go back to your ward now. They'll have already had their meals."

"It's okay. I'm not hungry. I'll just stay here."

"You can't stay here all night," Kenzie told him firmly.

"They don't have visiting hours," Zachary said. "Parents can sit with their babies all night."

"There is one obvious flaw in that plan," Kenzie said, but didn't say in front of the nurse that Zachary was not a parent. "But besides that, you are exhausted. You need to eat and sleep. If you don't, you are going to feel worse. You remember what happened when you stayed up for three days. You need to take care of yourself."

Zachary gazed in at the sleeping babies. "They need someone here to look after them. Bridget went home."

"I know. And I'm sure she'll be back to visit them tomorrow and to make sure they have everything they need. They'll be okay for a few hours. They'll just sleep. And if there are any problems, they are still hooked up to monitors and the staff will know what to do."

Zachary shook his head. "I don't trust her."

It was the first time that Kenzie had heard Zachary say he didn't trust his ex-wife. He had couched his concerns in much more careful terms before. That he was worried about Bridget. Worried that she didn't have the resources. *What if* she couldn't take care of them because of her health?

"Bridget is still recovering from the birth. You know she has been somewhat frail since the cancer and this pregnancy was not easy on her. She'll sleep better in her own bed tonight, and tomorrow she will be back by to look after them."

Zachary looked sideways at Kenzie. "What?"

"Bridget. She will come back. And Gordon will make sure she has all the help she needs. He said she has someone to help her twenty-four hours a day right now."

"Bridget. I wasn't talking about her."

It was Kenzie's turn to look askance. "What?"

"Not her. I know she'll do her best. And Gordon. But they aren't here twenty-four hours a day. And someone needs to guard the twins."

Kenzie was flummoxed. She felt her way through the conversation, trying to make quick judgments and to figure out what was wrong with Zachary and how she could help him, when she felt as if she only knew half of the information she needed to.

"Maybe Tyrrell could guard the twins while I take you for something to eat," she suggested. "You'll be able to think more clearly if you've had something to eat. And you need your night meds soon too."

Kenzie looked at Tyrrell, hoping that he would understand and agree to sit with the twins while she got Zachary back on track. His brows were drawn down in a worried, confused frown. Kenzie imagined her own face looked much the same.

"Come on." She tugged on Zachary's arm. "You need food."

Zachary got rustily to his feet. He'd probably been sitting there all day, unmoving, and his muscles had all seized up. Zachary looked at Tyrrell.

"You're going to stay with them? The whole time? Make sure nothing happens to them?"

Tyrrell nodded. "Of course."

Kenzie was glad that he didn't challenge Zachary on what the infants needed to be protected from. She would be able to figure that out as they had something to eat together. He would unwind the story for her so she could understand his thought process, and then she would be able to make a judgment about how logical his concerns were. There wasn't really anything that Zachary or Tyrrell could do if Julia went into cardiac arrest again. They would just be in the way.

Zachary looked at the nurse who was still standing by, waiting for them to sort things out so that there was only one person visiting the NICU. Zachary put his arm around his brother's neck and led him off to the side, speaking earnestly in his ear. Kenzie couldn't hear what Zachary was saying. He looked back at the nurse several times. At first, Tyrrell was shaking his head, objecting to whatever it was Zachary was telling him, but eventually he stopped shaking and was still, listening. He gave a couple of nods, and Zachary finally let go of him and let him return to the incubator and take the spot that Zachary had occupied.

Tyrrell shot Kenzie a look, one that she interpreted as meaning that he thought Zachary was delusional.

Kenzie's heart sank. It was not a good sign if he were having additional symptoms on top of the depression. They might have to completely overhaul his cocktail. Again. And it could be weeks or months before he was stable again.

"Okay. Let's get something into you," she told Zachary firmly. "You'll feel a lot better once you've had some nourishment."

Zachary looked at Tyrrell, who nodded cooperatively, indicating that he would stay there with the babies and protect them from whatever evil influence Zachary had been warning him about.

The nurse looked at each of them. "Are any of you actually parents to these children?"

"Bridget asked me to look after them," Zachary explained. "You can call her and check. Though I wouldn't want to wake her up. She needs sleep to recover. I can't stay with them..." He looked like he wanted to go sit back down by the incubator, but Kenzie kept a firm grip on his arm and he didn't pull away from her. "I need to go eat, but Tyrrell will watch them until I get back."

The nurse looked uncertain about this. She looked at Zachary's face, frowning. "Did you show someone your ID when you got here?"

Obviously, she hadn't been on shift that many hours ago. Zachary began to pat his pockets.

"Zachary Goldman. The nurse who was on then took it all down. Talked to everyone to clear me."

He found his wallet and extracted his driver's license. While she looked at it and compared it to his thinner, more cadaverous face, he pulled out a business card and handed that to her as well. Her eyes went over the words on the card.

"And Kenzie is a doctor," Zachary said, pointing to her. "Do you want to show her your ID too?" he suggested.

The nurse shook her head, getting too much information at once. She handed Zachary's driver's license back to him and tried to give him the business card, but he wouldn't take the business card back. "Hang on to that. And Tyrrell—"

"No, no," the nurse waved off any further ID's. "Fine. You go get something to eat. You look like you should be in the eating disorder clinic. I'll let the other one sit here," she made an off-handed motion to Tyrrell, "until you get back."

Kenzie pulled Zachary toward the exit. "Let's go, then, and you can tell me everything."

It was like Zachary's feet were stuck to the floor, but eventually he managed to pry them loose and walk with her out of the unit and to the elevator.

They didn't say anything on their way down the elevator to the cafeteria.

The lights were turned out and all the food serving stations closed. It was a dim, echoing, spooky sort of place to be so late. But the vending machines were still brightly lit and Kenzie made several purchases. They carried the food over to one of the tables and sat down to eat in the dimly-lit room.

"So… what's going on?" Kenzie asked. "Why do you think you need to guard the babies if Bridget and Gordon aren't here? The nurses are there to take care of them. They are on monitors if they start to have some kind of medical problem. There isn't anything you could do even if they did. So…?"

Zachary poked at the sandwich she had bought him, as if it were something alien. It was in the refrigerated vending machine, and it looked better than the ones they stocked down the hall from the Medical Examiner's Office. If he hadn't eaten all day, then he should be getting hungry. His morning medications would have worn off, so that he shouldn't be nauseated anymore.

"Zachary?"

"I saw the way you and Tyrrell were looking at each other. I'm not crazy. And I'm not blind."

"No one said you were. But you were behaving strangely. I don't know what you said to Tyrrell; I couldn't hear it. So bring me up to speed."

"I wasn't trying to keep it from you, just from the nurse."

Kenzie nodded and waited.

Zachary looked around the room, but it was completely empty. The only other person there was Kenzie, which hopefully helped to ease his anxiety. He would see if anyone else showed up. Anything he said would be just between the two of them.

"I don't trust the nurses."

"Why not?"

Zachary picked at the edge of the plastic wrap of his sandwich, trying to unwrap it.

"Some of them… aren't who they say they are. And that friend of yours… I don't want to say anything against a friend, but…"

"Do you think… she had something to do with Mr. Kennedy's death?"

Zachary raised his eyebrows in surprise. He had obviously not expected her to make that connection.

"Maybe. Is that what you think?"

"The surveillance video shows that Kennedy was never hanging around the dispensary. He didn't steal the pills himself."

Zachary finally caught the edge of the plastic wrap and drew it back slowly, as if any tears or stretches would be unacceptable.

"Somebody else must have stolen them, then."

Kenzie nodded. "Yes. When I was talking to Nurse Debbie today… she said some things that worried me. I don't want to think that she could have anything to do with any deaths, but she's already being looked at for the deaths in geriatric. And if she also had something to do with Mr. Kennedy's death… if she was the one who provided him with the means, and possibly encouraged him to do it…" Kenzie felt sick at the thought.

"She was here?" Zachary asked immediately, looking alarmed. He glanced around as if she might be hiding in the shadows of the room. "She wasn't supposed to be on shift today!"

"No." Kenzie wondered how he happened to know that. Because she had told him that she would be off? Or had he managed to look at one of the computers the nursing staff used? "She wasn't at the hospital. I talked to her on the phone."

Zachary blew out his breath noisily and nodded. He took a bite of his sandwich and chewed it slowly as if it were some new food he'd never tried before, like eel or blood pudding.

"She's different when you're not there. When she's alone with a patient."

"How is she different?"

"It's hard to explain. She still talks the same way, all bubbly and smiles, and touches you like she's your best friend. But there's... an undertone. Something menacing."

"You said before that you thought the way she was so cheerful was bullying."

He nodded. Kenzie thought about the way that Nurse Debbie had acted each time she'd stopped to talk to Kenzie. Overbearing. Treating Zachary like he was a child. Acting so cheerful even after Kennedy's death. She did kind of demand that everybody else around her should behave a certain way, to put on a smile and act like there was nothing wrong. Like the bully who roasted someone and expected them to laugh about it.

"How does this all relate back to the babies?"

"Oh. Yeah. She's been... pushing me. Talking about how Kennedy is in a better place now. That it was painless, and now he isn't suffering. Asking questions about my depression and ideation... what I think about... how I feel."

"Isn't that what you would expect the nurses to do? They need to be aware of your frame of mind and relay any concerns back to the doctor. Especially after a death like this. Are you sure you're not just... looking for things to blame her for?"

"No. They might ask you for specifics in therapy, but not the nurses. And they don't want to know whether... you prefer cutting or pills."

Kenzie shuddered at the ghoulish question. She took a quick

drink of water, trying to keep down the acid rising from her stomach. "She didn't!"

Zachary nodded. "Stuff like that… it's weird. I don't think it's right. I've had lots of therapy over the years, lots of different approaches, new ideas… but not asking me exactly what I think about, or whether I have anything to live for."

"Oh, Zachary…" Kenzie breathed his name. She was lucky to have found him unharmed. She couldn't imagine that Nurse Debbie would have been ignorant about questions and comments that might push Zachary over the edge. Had she done the same thing to Kennedy? Finding out that his preferred method of suicide was by pills? Asking him if he really had anything to live for, as a single, childless man in a dead-end job. Leaving the pills in his room for him and watching to see what would happen?

Zachary nodded. He took a couple more bites of the sandwich, chewing more vigorously now, finding it to his taste. Maybe surprised to find out that he could enjoy anything anymore.

"You do have something to live for," Kenzie pointed out. "So much. You have a good life. Your business, our relationship, your family. You've gone through some tough times, but things have been good lately. Some minor inconveniences… viruses and poisoners… but overall, you've got a good life, don't you think?"

Zachary nodded. "It's hard to see through the depression. Like looking through muddy windows. At night. But I know what's on the other side. I'm doing everything I can to hold it together, to get through this. Because I know what's on the other side, if I can just keep pushing through. I try to listen to you and Lorne when you tell me that it will get better after Christmas. That it always does. Sometimes I think that's just a myth I made up myself to trick myself into holding on when there is no hope."

"It's not. You'll feel better again. In just a little while… Christmas Eve will be past, and you'll wake up, and you will feel better."

"I'm so scared, Kenzie." He reached across the table for a moment and squeezed her hand. Kenzie squeezed back, trying to impart to him the depth of her feeling. How much she wanted and needed him, and how sure she was that things would get better again, if he just hung on.

"I know. It must be so hard."

"I'm scared for the babies."

50

Kenzie shook her head. They had circled around to it again, but she still had no better idea now than she'd had before about what Bridget's twins had to do with anything. Why was he so worried about the babies? What did that mean to him?

"Tell me why. Because of your mom? Because she couldn't take care of her newborns, so you think that Bridget won't be able to deal with hers?"

"No." Zachary sniffled and wiped his nose with the back of his hand. He took a couple of long gulps of his cola.

While Kenzie had to watch her calorie intake and stuck to water, she had aimed to give him the most calorie-dense foods she could, including a sugary drink.

"When I was talking to Nurse Debbie, and she asked what I had to live for… I told her about the babies."

Kenzie frowned, still unable to connect this up with anything else he'd said. And irritated over the fact that someone else's babies were his main reason for wanting to live.

"I told her how… precious they are. And how they were fighting for life. About Julia's cardiac event and Tricia being off the respirator." Zachary paused and looked at her. "They're both off of the respirator now."

"Yes, Gordon told me."

"She said that a hundred years ago, they wouldn't have survived. That maybe we were playing God by using all these artificial means to sustain them. They would grow up disabled, and it would be our fault, for allowing the doctors to do something they shouldn't. They would be brain-damaged. Have trouble in school. Be made fun of."

Something that Zachary could relate to, considering the number of learning disabilities and other issues he had battled throughout school. He wouldn't want to think of Bridget's precious babies going through the same thing.

Zachary swallowed. "She wondered how I would feel if one or both of them died. Why I was keeping my hopes up because of two tiny babies like that."

It was starting to dawn on Kenzie. She was starting to get what Zachary had seen during his conversation with Nurse Debbie. Her twisted sense of who should survive and who should not. It wasn't just old people in the geriatric unit who needed help leaving the mortal coil, but also the patients in the psychiatric unit, who could be nudged into committing suicide. And babies who shouldn't be receiving dramatic life-saving measures and using up precious resources. Babies who would never have survived without the modern equipment and knowledge.

"And you were worried that she would go down to the NICU. That you needed to watch over the twins, to make sure she couldn't get anywhere near them."

Zachary nodded.

"Why didn't you go to the authorities? Tell the doctor? Call the police? Why just go down there to sit with them yourself? You didn't even call me."

"They wouldn't let me near the phone. She told them that I was causing trouble and couldn't be allowed to use it. That I was making crank calls. Swatting. That I was delusional."

"But they let you check yourself out?"

"I waited until today, when she wasn't there. So it wouldn't be the same medical staff. I don't think she put anything on my chart saying about having delusions, but I was very calm and polite, and they couldn't see any reason to block me and insist on a psychiatric hold."

Zachary had eaten half of his sandwich and had lowered the level on his bottle of cola. His fingers danced over a cookie that Kenzie had bought, looking at her face to see whether she had bought it for herself or for the two of them to share.

"It's yours," Kenzie said.

He hesitated for a few more seconds, maybe waiting for her to act like a parent and tell him that he couldn't have the cookie until he had finished his sandwich. But she would be delighted if he ate the cookie.

"I should have called you this morning when they might have let me," Zachary admitted. "But I was so worried about the twins. I just wanted to get down to see them as soon as I could. I wanted to make sure that she couldn't get in there to do anything to them."

Kenzie nodded. She could understand that. It had probably been torture for him to be calm and polite to the medical staff to convince them to let him check himself out. The checkout procedure could take an hour or more, especially if they had concerns about his well-being. He must have been on pins and needles the whole time.

"I'm glad you looked after them. But we should probably call the police now and talk to them about it. Joshua Campbell was here today to talk to the medical staff about Kennedy's death. He knows that Kennedy didn't get the pills himself."

"I can't prove that it was Nurse Debbie."

"Well, you can tell him what you know. He can investigate it, and you can't."

Zachary opened his mouth to argue about this. He was a private investigator. Of course he could investigate it, he didn't need Campbell's permission. He always passed on any information that the police should have and had given Campbell leads more than once.

"I have to go back to psych," he said, sounding defeated.

"Probably. How are you feeling?"

"I can't leave the twins unguarded, though. Someone needs to watch them."

"We can talk to the police. The nursing staff. Security. It doesn't have to all fall to you."

Zachary shook his head. "I have to be sure. No one else is going to be as careful as I would be…"

"That's the same reason as Gordon gave for having you follow Bridget to see if she was having an affair. How did that work out?"

He looked down at the table and picked at a piece of dried food that the cleaners had missed. "He was right."

"But he should never have gotten you involved. And you should never have accepted."

"But this is different. They're babies. They are helpless."

"We'll work something out. Are you finished eating?" Kenzie nodded toward the half-sandwich he had not eaten. Zachary picked it up, sniffed it, and put it back down again.

"Yeah."

"Let's go upstairs, then, and we'll see."

They threw the rest of the food and wrappers into the garbage and went back up to the NICU.

51

As they got closer, Kenzie could hear Tyrrell's raised voice. She glanced at Zachary, and the two of them started running.

"Where's your ID?" Kenzie heard Tyrrell demand. "If you work here, then show me your ID."

"I showed you my security badge," a female voice responded. "Now move aside so I can check on the patients."

"No."

"Sir, you need to calm down and let the staff do their work," another voice interrupted.

Kenzie and Zachary turned the last corner to see the incubator and the people gathered around it, voices raised despite the "quiet please" signs on the walls. Tyrrell. The nurse who had earlier asked them to leave.

And Nurse Debbie.

Kenzie moved in quickly.

"Nurse Debbie does not work here," she said sharply.

The NICU nurse looked at Kenzie, frowning. She shook her head. "I know *you* don't work here. Nurse Carrie, on the other hand," she looked at Nurse Debbie, "has the correct hospital ID badge and has been volunteering here on her own time to hold infants when their parents are not here."

Kenzie shook her head. "That's not her name!" She looked at Nurse Debbie's ID badge, which indeed said Nurse Carrie. "These are fake credentials."

Nurse Debbie looked at Kenzie as if she had never seen her before in her life. "I don't know what you're talking about. You must be mistaking me for someone else." She shrugged at the NICU nurse. "I've been here before. You know me."

"There was a hospital-wide warning about people using fake badges to get into secure areas," Kenzie shot back hotly. "You must have received that. Did you check her driver's license?"

Nurse Debbie's lips compressed, making them long and thin. "I don't drive."

"You are still required to have photo ID. Where's your legal identification?"

Nurse Debbie looked back and forth at the people gathered around her intent on keeping her from accessing the twins.

"I'm volunteering," she insisted. "I'm doing a service. What's wrong with you people?"

"Like the service you did to Mr. Michaels by putting him out of his misery in geriatric?" Kenzie accused. "Or giving Mr. Kennedy the pills he needed to commit suicide? Or the wonderful advice you've been giving Zachary on how *he* has nothing left to live for?"

Nurse Debbie swore. She shoved Kenzie away from her violently, calling her an undeserved name and then making a break for it. Kenzie hit the hard, tiled floor with a crash.

"No you don't!" Tyrrell shouted and launched himself at Nurse Debbie. Zachary too tried to get a hand on her to prevent her from running away. If Nurse Debbie got away, she might flee to another state to start over, and they would never be able to prove what she had done in Vermont.

But the NICU nurse was faster and in better shape than either of them, and it was she who tripped Nurse Debbie up and got a hand twisted into her hair to force her down and hold her still.

"Where is security?" she shouted. "There should be a guard on the floor. You go get him!" She pointed at Tyrrell.

Tyrrell looked behind him as if to check to see whether she were pointing at someone else, and when it was clear that she was talking about him, he turned and hurried out of the unit and down the hallway to find a security guard.

52

It took some time for everything to get settled down. Security detained Nurse Debbie and the police were called, with patrol units getting there before Campbell. He spoke with the NICU nurse and to Zachary, Kenzie, and Tyrrell, shaking his head over how bold Nurse Debbie had been in using a false ID card and simply walking into other units.

"She would come to hold the babies or give them stimulation," the NICU nurse said. "I don't understand. Why would someone use a false ID for that? She had hospital ID, I relied on that."

"A NICU baby could be very vulnerable," Kenzie said, looking into the incubator where Bridget's twins lay, oblivious to the worry they had caused. "Did you ever have a baby go into distress while she was holding it?"

"Well… yes. But these are very fragile patients. We are careful not to move them around too much, but human touch and interaction is powerful medicine. They languish without any human touch, and improve when you can stroke them, talk to them, and hold them. So it's a balancing act, trying to judge which babies are strong enough to be held and how long we can keep them out of the incubator."

"And you didn't watch her the whole time she was holding these babies," Campbell suggested.

"No, of course not. She was a nurse. She was here to give us a break, to help us out on her own time. We wouldn't sit here and watch her any more than we would a parent. The parents we always watch to begin with, until they get used to handling their child. But once they are confident and know what they are doing… we have work to do."

Kenzie called Agent Menendez as well, since Nurse Debbie was a suspect in the Michaels death.

Kenzie had been so sure that she couldn't have had anything to do with it. But now, realizing that Nurse Debbie had gone to other units using false ID and might be implicated in other deaths, she was forced to reconsider.

Nurse Debbie had seemed like the perfect, attentive nurse. She had seemed to really care about her patients and had always been happy to help the family out. And maybe that had not been faked. But there was more to her than that. She had another side. Was she really driven by her compassion, as she had suggested to Zachary, that she just wanted to keep people from suffering? Or was that just an excuse for what she did and she got a kick out of watching her specially selected patients die?

"Did you ask the geriatric staff if Nurse Debbie ever went back there after she transferred?" Kenzie asked Agent Menendez after they all explained their pieces of the puzzle. "To volunteer or clear out her locker? To see a favorite patient?"

"We asked, but people don't necessarily remember everyone they have seen in a day. And as time passes, they are less and less confident of who was there on what day. We have the logs of who was on shift the day that Michaels died, and on the dates of other deaths on Dr. Philemon's list. But we can't be sure that she didn't just walk in, saying hello to the nurses that knew her, to pick up something she had forgotten, or her final paycheck, or on some other excuse."

"I suppose so." But the fact that they didn't have any eyewitnesses to testify to the fact that Nurse Debbie had been around at the appropriate times meant that they wouldn't be able to prosecute her for Michaels's death. Not unless she confessed. Of all the deaths that they thought she could be responsible for, the one they probably had the best chance of prosecuting was Kennedy's death. They could prove that she had been on shift in the psychiatric unit. That she had access to the dispensary. Zachary could testify about the conversations she'd had with him, both about Kennedy's death and about whether he had any reason to live himself.

"Do you think she is the one who was sending you the threatening notes?" Menendez asked.

"Yes, probably. I couldn't figure out why they were directed at me instead of at Dr. Wiltshire. I figured it was because I visited the geriatric unit and was asking questions there. But if it was Nurse Debbie, then she had reason to target me. She knew me. And she knew that I was still asking questions, getting closer to her. Someone in geriatric wouldn't have known that."

Kenzie caught Zachary's eyes on her, and she grimaced, knowing what was coming.

"Threatening notes?" he demanded.

"Yes. Just a couple. I got them at work, in the mail. I didn't think that there was anything to worry about. Some poison pen… they weren't likely to turn to real violence against me."

"Why didn't you tell me?"

"Like I said… I wasn't that worried about them."

His eyes didn't move from her. Kenzie sighed.

"Yes, I suppose it was because you had enough on your mind already. You were going through a tough time, and it didn't seem like it would be productive to add my own worries to the mix. I'm sorry."

"I still want you to tell me things."

"I know. But I have to judge whether it is the right time to tell you, or whether it is something that might trigger worse anxiety or depression."

He thought about that and clearly didn't like it. But Kenzie didn't know how she was going to get around it. She would always have to consider whether he had to know something, or if it was better to keep it from him until he was at least feeling better. Once the cat was out of the bag, she wasn't going to be able to cram it back in.

It was getting late, and Kenzie didn't know what Gordon's usual hours were, but she texted him anyway, letting him know that she had found Zachary and he was well and safe.

She got a text back from him almost immediately.

Good news. Where was he?

Kenzie hit the button to voice call him instead of responding by text. He was obviously still up, and it would be faster to explain the details than to try to explain over text.

"Kenzie," he answered cheerfully. "Glad to hear that you managed to track that rascal down. He's okay?"

"He was in the NICU," Kenzie explained. "With the twins."

There was a definite pause in the conversation as Gordon processed this. His voice, when he spoke again, was definitely cooler.

"What was he doing there?"

"He believed that the twins were in danger. That someone needed to be watching them. So he was there all day, at their sides."

"I don't want him near the twins."

Kenzie was taken aback by this. She had always thought it strange that Gordon didn't object to talking to Zachary or Kenzie, that he was willing to give Zachary updates on how Bridget was doing and didn't stop Bridget from reaching out to Zachary on the rare occasions when there was something she wanted from him. Zachary was more likely to stay at a distance if he had the answers he needed and he didn't have to see for himself that Bridget was okay.

And maybe that was why Gordon had been willing to talk to them about the twins, too. He had thought that it would keep Zachary away from them.

"I'm sorry. I didn't know he was there, or I would have handled it earlier. But… you should know that he was right. There has been a nurse here at the hospital who has been implicated in a number of deaths. Sort of mercy killings, what we call an Angel of Death killer."

"What?" Gordon's voice was sharp.

"We've been trying to figure out who it was, to catch her. And… it turns out she has been doing some volunteer work in the NICU. I don't know whether she has been involved in any deaths there, but she was trying to get to your twins today."

"You've caught this woman? How could something like this happen?"

"The ME's Office has been working with the FBI and with the local police. And the hospital, of course. No one was ignoring it, I promise you that. But there was nothing to indicate that the same killer might have been in the NICU. We didn't even realize there was a connection between the deaths in geriatric and the suicide in psych this week. Until… today."

"And the twins…?"

"They're fine," Kenzie assured him. "Zachary made sure of that."

"I guess I owe him my thanks. Again. I can't get over there tonight. Bridget needs me here. But we'll be there in the morning. I'll come see Zachary then."

Kenzie hesitated. She cleared her throat. Gordon had been blunt about not wanting Zachary to be near his children. She could be just as blunt.

"I don't want you talking to Zachary. And I especially don't want Bridget talking to him. He doesn't need any more setbacks."

Gordon breathed out in a huff. "Well… fair enough. I won't come talk to him. And if Bridget wants to see him… I'll tell her that he's unavailable."

"I'd appreciate that. Thanks."

"He needs to stay away from the twins. I will make sure that they are taken care of. And you have this woman in custody. So nothing will happen to them."

"I'll tell him. I can't promise anything, but I'll do my best to help him stay on track. He'll be in psych until Christmas. Then after that... hopefully he'll start to get evened out again. Stop worrying that Bridget can't take care of the twins."

"Why wouldn't Bridget be able to take care of the twins?" Gordon demanded, his tone still sharp.

"Of course she can. And I know you'll make sure she has whatever help she needs. I'm talking about Zachary's worries. They aren't necessarily logical. His own mother couldn't take care of her babies, so he's transferred those feelings to Bridget."

"I would appreciate it if he would stay out of the way. I'll give you updates, if that will keep him away. But I won't have him harassing my children."

Kenzie had a vision of Zachary lurking outside a playground, watching a pair of little girls laughing and playing on the play equipment. She could understand why Gordon didn't want him hanging around. Zachary was too obsessive. And while he'd never done anything to harm Bridget, if he thought that she couldn't take care of the children and that he could... things could go very badly for Zachary.

"No. I'll talk to his therapist about it too."

"Good." Gordon sighed. "Good night, Kenzie. Thank you for letting me know that everyone is safe."

After hanging up the phone with Gordon, Kenzie walked down the hall into the psychiatric unit to see if Zachary was settled. There was a quiet murmur of voices from the medical staff. Kenzie followed the noise to the nursing station and gave the nurses there, two women and a man, a nod.

"I'll just check in with Zachary, then I'll be on my way," she announced.

They appeared to be too startled by her assertion to find an objection before she walked by them and into the room she knew was Zachary's. He sat on the edge of the bed, hunched over, rubbing the muscles around his eyes.

"Hey," Kenzie said softly. "How are you doing? All settled?"

He nodded.

"Got your night meds?"

"Yeah. Will be a little bit before they start to kick in."

Kenzie nodded. "I talked to Gordon. Let him know that the twins were okay and you were back where you're supposed to be."

He rubbed his forehead, hiding his eyes from her.

"He says thank you for looking after the twins. But now that Nurse Debbie is in custody…"

"He doesn't want me to go down there again."

"No. He wants you to stay away from them. And I'm sure Bridget would say the same."

Zachary sighed. "Yeah."

"They'll be okay. They have a lot of people looking out for them."

"Okay. I'll… try."

Kenzie bent down to kiss him. "And one other thing. If you're going to check out… please let me know. You don't know how much of a panic I was in when I couldn't find you."

"Sorry." He caught her hand and squeezed it. "I didn't think I'd be there all day. Just… a few hours until Gordon or Bridget got there."

"Just don't do that again."

"Okay."

53

It was too early in the morning on a Saturday for Kenzie's phone to be ringing. She pulled herself out of sleep to look at the screen, sure it would be her mother. Who else but Lisa would call her on a Saturday morning and expect her to be sitting around sipping coffee rather than either sleeping in or going in to work?

It wasn't her mother's picture on the screen, though, it was Dr. Wiltshire. Kenzie fumbled, swiping several times before she managed to answer the call. But at least she managed to get it before it went to voicemail.

"Doctor."

"Kenzie? I'm sorry to disturb you. I know that you have today off."

"Did something happen?" Kenzie rubbed her eyes, trying to force herself to wake up and be alert faster.

"I have a few messages on my phone this morning. No new bodies, you don't need to come in, but I thought I would give you a call and fill you in before items start showing up in the news. After you've worked a case, you don't want to find out the developments in the news."

"Oh." Kenzie suddenly realized what he was talking about. "I should probably have called you last night. Or sent you a message."

Dr. Wiltshire chuckled. "Does that mean you already know everything? I suppose Agent Menendez reached out to you."

"Actually, no. I called her."

"You called her." Wiltshire's voice registered surprise. "How were you involved in this?"

"It was Zachary, mostly. He was in psych, and Nurse Debbie was in psych. He had his suspicions about her after Kennedy's death. He disappeared on me, and when I tracked him down… well, he was—I told you that our friends had twins? Zachary was with the twins, because he was afraid that Nurse Debbie was going to go after them next."

"I see." Dr. Wiltshire sounded baffled, not as if he understood Kenzie's explanation. "And Nurse Debbie is who Menendez has arrested."

"She was already a suspect on Agent Menendez's list. I didn't think that it could be her. I knew her, and she had left the geriatric unit before Michaels died."

"Then it seems a bit of a stretch that she could be involved in his case."

"She was still in the hospital. She could have gone back down and said that she had forgotten something or wanted to check in on one of her old patients. No one would have thought anything of it. Or necessarily have remembered when we started trying to put together a list of everyone who had been there. We were focused on their records, who we could prove had been there. Anyone else who happened to walk through the unit—that's a lot harder."

"But if witnesses don't remember her, the FBI will not be able to put her in that room. And unless there is something else to tie her to Michaels's murder, there is no way to convict her."

"Unless she confesses. Many of these killers do, because they feel that they've done the right thing. A kind, humanitarian thing."

"It should never be up to the doctor or nurse to decide to take a life."

"No," Kenzie agreed soberly. "But I think there's a good chance that they can get her for Kennedy's murder. She had access to the dispensary. And the way she was talking about him, how his life was worthless, and the way she was encouraging Zachary to do the same."

Dr. Wiltshire didn't say anything at first. Eventually, he spoke. "I can't call Kennedy's death anything but suicide, Kenzie. Not unless there is evidence that this nurse force-fed him those pills. I don't know if there is anything the police can charge him with in Vermont in connection with inciting suicide."

"Then we'll get her for the others," Kenzie resolved. "We'll keep going through Dr. Philemon's list of suspicious deaths, and tie as many as we can to her. Once a jury sees how many deaths she was connected to…"

"Don't get your hopes up. The FBI will continue to work on it and to see whether they can tie more deaths to her, but there are a lot of challenges in getting enough proof in cases like this."

54

The last couple of weeks until Christmas passed quickly.

Kenzie woke up early. She hadn't been so excited about Christmas morning since she had been a kid. She could remember that feeling of anticipation. Trying to go to sleep with the knowledge that in the morning, it would be Christmas Day, and she would be getting presents and spending a wonderful day with her family. Everyone together, happy, enjoying each other's company. The house would be festooned with decorations and tiny white lights, transforming it into a Christmas fairyland. There would be food so good she would stuff her stomach until it hurt, and then lie around for hours afterward complaining about it. And then they would eat again.

This time, it was different. She wasn't a kid anymore, eagerly anticipating presents. But she knew that they had finally passed Christmas Eve, and Zachary's anxiety over the season would begin to fade. Even though he knew that it wouldn't happen again, he was always anxious about the fire that had destroyed his home. That somehow, something would happen again on the anniversary and he would lose everything he loved. Now that the anniversary of the fire was past, he could take a deep breath and begin to recover again.

Kenzie called Lisa first. There was no point in rushing to the hospital and getting there before visiting hours. So she lay in bed and listened to the ringing phone and waited to hear her mother's voice.

"Mackenzie?" Lisa's voice was faint and far away, slurred with sleep.

Kenzie laughed about waking up before her mother. Just like on all those Christmases gone past. Lisa knew that she didn't get up early in the morning, but this time Kenzie had turned the tables and was the excited kid once more.

"Hello, Mother. Merry Christmas!"

"Merry Christmas to you too, dear. What are you doing up so early?"

"It's Christmas!"

"Yes, it is," Lisa agreed dryly. "Have you already opened all your presents from Santa?"

"Not yet. I'm still in bed. But I wanted to say Merry Christmas to you first."

"Not to Zachary?"

"He is still in the hospital," Kenzie reminded her. "I'll see him later."

"Oh, I thought you said that he would be doing better now."

"Today, yes. But we'll need to wait until he's stabilized for sure before bringing him home. He should be feeling a lot better today, but that doesn't mean everything is okay. They'll need to see how he is feeling and if he is stable on these meds. Then… when he starts gaining weight and showing an improvement, he'll be released or sign himself out."

"Good. Well, do tell him Merry Christmas for me."

"I will. And you have a good one today. Do you have plans?"

"Your father may come by later. I'll just have a quiet day at home. It's… not like it was when you were little. It's just another holiday. Christmas is for children."

"Tell Dad Merry Christmas for me. I'll probably call him later."

Kenzie took a long shower and lingered over her breakfast of toast and a Christmas orange, but it still wasn't time to go to the hospital. She admired the Christmas magnets on the fridge and twinkle lights she could see glowing softly in the living room. The minutes seemed to be crawling by excruciatingly slowly. She thought about calling Zachary's brother and sisters to wish them a Merry Christmas, but it would be better if she could call them while she was with Zachary. He was the one that they would want to talk to.

Her phone vibrated, and Kenzie pulled it out to look at it. She thought it might be a text from her father. Like Kenzie, he wasn't an early riser, but she expected he would be up by now.

But it was, weirdly enough, a text from Josie Menendez. Kenzie's phone was set not to display text messages on the lock screen, so she had to unlock it to see what the message was. Hopefully, Agent Menendez had not decided that now that they were no longer working the Michaels case together—there didn't seem to be any more exhumations on the horizon—that she and Kenzie could be friends. Or whatever other relationship Menendez wanted. She had always seemed just a bit too up-close-and-personal for Kenzie's comfort.

I have a special Christmas present for you

Kenzie's worst fears were being realized. She decided that ignorance was her best defense against any advances by Menendez.

Really? What is it?

There was no answer. Kenzie put her dish in the dishwasher and looked at the phone again, in case an answer had come in without it vibrating. Sometimes that happened if she already had the text app in the foreground. Still nothing. Kenzie shifted uncomfortably. "Come on, Agent Menendez," she said aloud, frustrated.

Almost ten minutes passed, and Kenzie had decided that it was either supposed to be a joke, or Menendez had been interrupted and had forgotten that she'd even been texting with Kenzie.

She could probably start getting ready to go to the hospital. If she didn't get ready or drive too fast, she should be there right before visiting hours opened up, and she could get in right away.

The phone vibrated again. Kenzie picked it up. Agent Menendez again.

Nurse Debbie confessed

Kenzie blew out her breath in relief. She browsed through gifs, looking for an appropriate one, and selected a Christmas picture to send to Menendez.

Hallelujah!

Kenzie was not the first person to arrive at the psych ward. In fact, the hallway was buzzing with visitors, eager to get in to see their loved ones. Many of them were faces that Kenzie recognized from visiting with Zachary, but others were new, maybe people who had traveled longer distances to visit their friend or family member on the special day.

"Kenzie!"

Kenzie turned, looking for the source of the voice. Lorne and Pat walked toward her. "Hi! Merry Christmas!" Kenzie gave them each a hug and a kiss. "You must have left early."

"We didn't have to get up too early. But we wanted to be here to see Zach. And we have Pat's family later in the day."

Kenzie nodded. "Say hi and Merry Christmas to Gretta and Suzanne for me. I'm glad you're getting the chance to see them."

"If you don't have anywhere to go later, you'd be welcome to join us," Pat invited, smiling warmly.

"No, I'm good, thanks. Maybe sometime in the next few weeks, when Zachary is feeling better, we can get together."

"Absolutely."

The big double doors were opened, and everyone who was in

line shifted and prepared to enter. Kenzie knew that it wouldn't be a race. Everyone would need their ID checked and their names checked against the patient visitor list before being escorted in. With the number of people in front of them, it would be a while.

———

Talking with Lorne and Pat made the wait go quickly and, eventually, they reached the front of the line and showed their driver's licenses and waited while the nurse compared them against the computer. She already knew Kenzie from her previous visits there, but dutifully checked her ID and the computer record anyway.

"Okay, you're all good to go. If you'll wait for someone to escort you in…"

"I know the way," Kenzie offered. "We don't really need directions."

The nurse looked at the next people in line. "Well, I suppose. These folks will need to be shown in."

She nodded, and Kenzie didn't wait for any further instructions. She, Lorne, and Pat walked in without an escort.

The common room was already buzzing with excitement. A lot more people than Kenzie usually saw when she visited. Hopefully, it wouldn't hamper their discussion too much. They found Zachary in his usual seat and sat down. Kenzie kissed him and studied his face. Less lined and weary today. Still hollow-cheeked and pale, but she would take that, if he was on the mend mentally.

"How are you?" She didn't usually ask, letting him pick his own time to discuss his mental well-being.

"Good. It's…" He grasped for words. "It's like my life starts over. It has been so hard, and so dark, and then… it's a new day. One that hasn't been written yet. Anything could happen."

They all smiled. Although Kenzie knew that he *should* start feeling better on Christmas Day as he usually did, she had been afraid that it would be different this year.

"Glad to hear it, Zachary," Lorne approved. "A couple of weeks ago, you weren't doing so well."

Zachary nodded. Even the night before he had been in rough shape. Knowing his history, the doctor had prescribed a strong sedative that would knock him out so that he wouldn't sit up all night, waiting for disaster to strike.

"I think before..." Zachary pursed his lips. "You remember asking whether they had changed any of my meds?" he asked Kenzie.

Kenzie nodded. "Sure. And I even had them check your chart to see. You had changed a lot in just a couple of days. I know it was probably just your reaction to Kennedy's death, and maybe Nurse Debbie's *inspiring* comments, but... you did have me worried."

"I think that she might have been slipping me something extra."

Kenzie raised her brows. "You're pretty knowledgeable about what you take. I think you would have noticed if she gave you anything different."

"Yeah, I know. But... I still think she was. I was foggier than usual. Even with my night meds, they don't make me so... slow."

"Yeah. It worried me."

"You would have noticed if she gave you the wrong pills," Pat said. "But what if she gave you an injection while you were sleeping?"

Zachary shook his head slowly. "No... I think I would have noticed a needle mark."

"Did you take them with something? Water or juice?"

"Usually water," Zachary said. "But she insisted on juice. Said that the doctor wanted me to get more calories." He shrugged. "The doctors *always* want me to get more calories."

"Maybe she put something into the juice, then," Kenzie said, picking up on Pat's suggestion. "And she was hiding the taste with juice, because you might have been able to detect it with water."

"Yeah. Maybe she did. All I know is… I felt a lot better after she was gone."

"Well, I think the two of you have had enough contact with serial killers," Lorne said firmly. "How about you stay away from them after this?"

Kenzie laughed. "That sounds like a good idea."

55

K enzie had enjoyed the visit with Zachary, but it was obvious after a while that he was getting tired and the movement and conversation of the people around him was wearing on him. For someone who was as hypervigilant as he was, it had to be exhausting to feel as if he had to watch and monitor everyone in the room while he visited with Kenzie, Lorne, and Pat. Once they were gone, he would be able to retire to his room and not have to spend so much energy watching everyone else.

"He does seem like he's doing better," Pat remarked.

"It's amazing how much of a difference a day can make. I wish he could be desensitized to the calendar as much as he was to fire. But..."

"But having a 'Groundhog's Day' where every day was Christmas Eve would just be cruel?" Lorne filled in.

Kenzie smiled and nodded. "That would be horrible. I don't think *I* could manage that."

As they got off the elevator, Kenzie saw two more familiar faces. Gordon and Bridget.

Lorne and Pat didn't know Gordon, but they certainly knew Bridget, and she knew them. She looked anxiously at Gordon, holding tightly to his arm, as if she were afraid that the men would attack her.

Nothing could be further from the truth. Kenzie didn't know two kinder men. Though even they spoke of Bridget in clipped tones when they had to mention her.

"Kenzie," Gordon greeted with a smile, not noticing Bridget's reaction to the two men. "Merry Christmas. Have you been to see Zachary?"

"Yes. He's doing a lot better today."

"Good to hear," he approved. He looked at Bridget, as if expecting a "Merry Christmas" from her, but she said nothing to Kenzie.

"Gordon, I assume you haven't met Lorne Peterson and Pat Parker before?" Kenzie said politely. "Zachary's foster father and… stepfather."

"Oh." Gordon nodded. "I've heard so much about you. It's wonderful to meet you."

He extended a hand. Both Lorne and Pat leaned forward to shake briefly. Lorne nodded to Bridget.

"Bridget. Congratulations on your new arrivals. They are doing well, I hope?"

Bridget nodded jerkily.

"We're here to pick them up," Gordon said, smiling broadly. "They go home on Christmas Day. What better present could we ask for?"

Kenzie said her goodbyes to Pat and Lorne and got into her car. It was cold, and she sat for a few minutes waiting for it to warm up so that the windows wouldn't fog once she started to drive. The phone rang. More Merry Christmas wishers, of course.

Kenzie clicked the button to answer the call on Bluetooth without looking to see who it was.

"Merry Christmas."

"Merry Christmas, Kenzie!" Kenzie recognized Heather's voice.

"I hope you're having a good day today."

"Well, yes," Heather agreed. "It's been a nice morning, and we've talked to the children. We are planning a visit to Zachary this afternoon, the three of us siblings."

"He'll enjoy that." Kenzie was glad that he would have a good break between the Christmas visitors so that he wouldn't be too overwhelmed.

"The thing is… I can't seem to get ahold of Tyrrell to coordinate with him."

"Oh. That's odd."

"I know. He's not usually hard to get. He always has his phone with him. He answers. Unless he doesn't have a signal for some reason."

"Right."

"I was just wondering… whether you had talked to him today or seen him at the hospital. Maybe we got our wires crossed and he decided to go visit Zachary on his own or with the kids."

"No, I haven't heard from him. We had talked about me looking after the kids for an hour or two when he went to visit today, but I haven't heard from him. I thought maybe Tyrrell's plans had changed and he ended up working or didn't end up getting the children."

"He's been pretty quiet the last couple of weeks. I haven't heard much from him."

Kenzie remembered how Tyrrell had looked the last time she had seen him at the hospital, the day that he had helped to guard the twins while Kenzie asked Zachary what was going on. He had looked rough that day. Not terrible, but enough that it had crossed Kenzie's mind that he might be drinking again. He had denied it previously, when they'd been at the Lodge, but he wasn't likely to tell her if he'd fallen off the wagon.

"Maybe you should call his ex."

"I already did," Heather sighed. "He didn't show up to pick up the kids."

Kenzie's heart sank as she thought about how disappointed Mason and Alisha would be. Like Zachary, Mason had some behavioral challenges. Maybe just ADHD, maybe more. Kenzie didn't know if he had any official diagnoses.

"Oh, dear. I hope everything is okay."

"Me too," Heather agreed quietly. "Well… have a Merry Christmas. Joss and I will be over later to see Zachary, even if we can't catch up with Tyrrell."

"You too. Merry Christmas."

The call ended, and Kenzie put the car into gear.

She was going to surprise Lisa by going home to spend some of Christmas Day with her.

She didn't voluntarily spend much time with her mother, so she knew Lisa would be happy to see her. Christmas might not be like it was in the old days, but they could still have a pleasant afternoon together.

She was sure Lisa wouldn't mind.

**Did you enjoy this book? Reviews and recommendations are
vital to making a book successful.**

**Please leave a review at your favorite book store or review site
and share it with your friends.**

Don't miss the following bonus material:
Sign up for mailing list to get a free ebook
Read a sneak preview chapter
Other books by P.D. Workman
Learn more about the author

Sign up for my mailing list at pdworkman.com and get
Gluten-Free Murder for free!

PREVIEW OF SHE WORE MOURNING

The next volume in the Kenzie Kirsch Medical Thrillers series not not yet ready to go!

Have you read the Zachary Goldman Mysteries series? If not, read how Kenzie and Zachary met in She Wore Mourning. A preview follows.

Zachary Goldman stared down the telephoto lens at the subjects before him. It was one of those days that left tourists gaping over the gorgeous scenery. Dark trees against crisp white snow, with the mountains as a backdrop. Like the picture on a Christmas card.

The thought made Zachary feel sick.

But he wasn't looking at the scenery. He was looking at the man and the woman in a passionate embrace. The pretty young woman's cheeks were flushed pink, more likely with her excitement than the cold, since she had barely stepped out of her car to greet the man. He had a swarthier complexion and a thin black beard, and was currently turned away from Zachary's camera.

Zachary wasn't much to look at himself. Average height, black hair cut too short, his own three-day growth of beard not hiding how pinched and pale his face was. He'd never considered himself a good catch.

He waited patiently for them to move, to look around at their surroundings so that he could get a good picture of their faces.

They thought they were alone; that no one could see them without being seen. They hadn't counted on the fact that Zachary had been surveilling them for a couple of weeks and had known where they would go. They gave him lots of warning so that he could park his car out of sight, camouflage himself in the trees, and settle in to wait for their appearance. He was no amateur; he'd been a private investigator since she had been choosing wedding dresses for her Barbie dolls.

He held down the shutter button to take a series of shots as they came up for air and looked around at the magnificent surroundings, smiling at each other, eyes shining.

All the while, he was trying to keep the negative thoughts at bay. Why had he fallen into private detection? It was one of the few ways he could make a living using his skill with a camera. He could have chosen another profession. He didn't need to spend his whole life following other people, taking pictures of their most private moments. What was the real point of his job? He destroyed lives, something he'd had his fill of long ago. When was the last time he'd brought a smile to a client's face? A real, genuine smile? He had wanted to make a difference in people's lives; to exonerate the innocent.

Zachary's phone started to buzz in his pocket. He lowered the camera and turned around, walking farther into the grove of trees. He had the pictures he needed. Anything else would be overkill.

He pulled out his phone and looked at it. Not recognizing the number, he swiped the screen to answer the call.

"Goldman Investigations."

"Uh… yes… Is this Mr. Goldman?" a voice inquired. Older, female, with a tentative quaver.

"Yes, this is Zachary," he confirmed, subtly nudging her away from the 'mister.'

"Mr. Goldman, my name is Molly Hildebrandt."

He hoped she wasn't calling her about her sixty-something-year-old husband and his renewed interest in sex. If it was another infidelity case, he was going to have to turn it down for his own sanity. He would even take a lost dog or wedding ring. As long as the ring wasn't on someone else's finger now.

"Mrs. Hildebrandt. How can Goldman Investigations help you?"

Of course, she had probably already guessed that Goldman Investigations consisted of only one employee. Most people seemed to sense that from the size of his advertisements. From the fact that he listed a post office box number instead of a business suite downtown or in one of the newer commercial areas. It wasn't really a secret.

"I don't know whether you have been following the news at all about Declan Bond, the little boy who drowned…?"

Zachary frowned. He trudged back toward his car.

"I'm familiar with the basics," he hedged. A four- or five-year-old boy whose round face and feathery dark hair had been pasted all over the news after a search for a missing child had ended tragically.

"They announced a few weeks ago that it was determined to be an accident."

Zachary ground his teeth. "Yes…?"

"Mr. Goldman, I was Declan's grandma." Her voice cracked. Zachary waited, listening to her sniffles and sobs as she tried to get herself under control. "I'm sorry. This has been very difficult for me. For everyone."

"Yes."

"Mr. Goldman, I don't believe that it was an accident. I'm looking for someone who would investigate the matter privately."

Zachary breathed out. A homicide investigation? Of a child? He'd told himself that he would take anything that wasn't infidelity, but if there was one thing that was more depressing than couples cheating on each other, it was the death of a child.

"I'm sure there are private investigators that would be more qualified for a homicide case than I am, Mrs. Hildebrandt. My schedule is pretty full right now."

Which, of course, was a lie. He had the usual infidelities, insurance investigations, liabilities, and odd requests. The dregs of the private investigation business. Nothing substantial like a homicide. It was a high-profile case. A lot of volunteers had shown up to help, expecting to find a child who had wandered out of his own yard, expecting to find him dirty and crying, not floating face down in a pond. A lot of people had mourned the death of a child they hadn't even known existed before his disappearance.

"I need your help, Mr. Goldman. Zachary. I can't afford a big name, but you've got good references. You've investigated deaths before. Can't you help me?"

He wondered who she had talked to. It wasn't like there were a lot of people who would give him a bad reference. He was competent and usually got the job done, but he wasn't a big name.

"I could meet with you," he finally conceded. "The first consultation is free. We'll see what kind of a case you have and whether I want to take it. I'm not making any promises at this point. Like I said, my schedule is pretty full already."

She gave a little half-sob. "Thank you. When are you able to come?"

After he had hung up, Zachary climbed into his car, putting his camera down on the floor in front of the passenger seat where it couldn't fall, and started the car. For a while, he sat there, staring out the front windshield at the magical, sparkling, Christmas-card scene. Every year, he told himself it would be better. He would get over it and be able to move on and to enjoy the holiday season like everyone else. Who cared about his crappy childhood experiences? People moved on.

And when he had married Bridget, he had thought he was going to achieve it. They would have a fairy-tale Christmas. They would have hot chocolate after skating at the public rink. They would wander down Main Street looking at the lights and the crèche in front of the church. They would open special, meaningful presents from each other.

But they'd fought over Christmas. Maybe it was Zachary's

fault. Maybe he had sabotaged it with his gloom. The season brought with it so much baggage. There had been no skating rink. No hot chocolate, only hot tempers. No walks looking at the lights or the nativity. They had practically thrown their gifts at each other, flouncing off to their respective corners to lick their wounds and pout away the holiday.

He'd still cherished the thought that perhaps the next year there would be a baby. What could be more perfect than Christmas with a baby? It would unite them. Make them a real family. Just like Zachary had longed for since he'd lost his own family. He and Bridget and a baby. Maybe even twins. Their own little family in their own little happy bubble.

But despite a positive pregnancy test, things had gone horribly wrong.

Zachary stared at the bright white scenery and blinked hard, trying to shake off the shadows of the past. The past was past. Over and done. This year he was back to baching it for Christmas. Just him and a beer and *It's a Wonderful Life* on TV.

He put the car in reverse and didn't look into the rear-view mirror as he backed up, even knowing about the precipice behind him. He'd deliberately parked where he'd have to back up toward the cliff when he was done. There was a guardrail, but if he backed up too quickly, the car would go right through it, and who could say whether it had been accidental or deliberate? He had been cold-stone sober and had been out on a job. Mrs. Hildebrandt could testify that he had been calm and sober during their call. It would be ruled an accident.

But his bumper didn't even touch the guardrail before he shifted into drive and pulled forward onto the road.

He'd meet with the grandmother. Then, assuming he did not take the case, there would always be another opportunity.

Life was full of opportunities.

Molly Hildebrandt was much as Zachary expected her to be. A woman in her sixties who looked ten or twenty years older with the stress of the high-profile death of her grandchild. Gray, curling hair. Pale, wrinkled skin. She wasn't hunched over, though. She sat up straight and tall as if she'd gone to a finishing school where she'd been forced to walk and sit with an encyclopedia on her head. Did they still do that? Had they ever done it?

"Mr. Goldman, thank you for seeing me so quickly," she greeted formally, holding her hand out for him to shake when he arrived at her door.

"Please, call me Zachary, ma'am. I'm not really comfortable with Mr. Goldman."

Telling her that he wasn't comfortable with it meant that she would be a bad hostess if she continued to address him that way, instead of her seeing it as a way of showing him respect. He hadn't done anything to deserve respect and was much happier if she would talk to him like the gardener or her next-door neighbor.

Not that there was any gardener. Molly lived in a small apartment in an old, dark brick building that was sturdy enough, but had been around longer than Zachary had been alive. The interior, when she invited him in, was bright and cozy. She had made coffee, and he breathed in the aroma in the air appreciatively. It wasn't hot chocolate after skating, but he could use a cup or two of coffee to warm him up after his surveillance. Standing around in the snow for a couple of hours had chilled him, even though he'd dressed for the weather.

Molly escorted him to the tiny living room.

"And you must call me Molly," she insisted.

She eyed the big camera case as he put it down. Zachary gave a grimace.

"Sorry. I didn't come to take your picture; I just don't like to leave expensive equipment in the car."

"Oh," she nodded politely. She didn't ask him who he had been taking pictures of. That wouldn't be gracious. She would have to imagine instead, and she would probably be correct in her guess.

They fussed for a few minutes with their coffees. Zachary wrapped his fingers around his mug, waiting for the coffee to cool and his fingers to warm. It felt good. Comforting. He waited for Molly to begin her story.

"You probably think that I'm just being a fussy old lady," she said. "Imagining something sinister when it was just an accident."

"Not at all. Why don't you tell me why you don't think it was an accident?"

"I'm not *sure* at all," she clarified. "Maybe they're right. Maybe it was an accident. It isn't that I doubt their findings…" she trailed off. "Not really. I know they had to do an autopsy and all that. We waited for months for them to come back with the manner of death. I thought that once they ruled, everyone would feel better."

"But you still have doubts?"

"I'm worried for my daughter."

Zachary blinked at her and waited for more.

"She's not well. I had hoped that once they released the body… and after the memorial… and after the manner of death was announced… each milestone, I thought, it would get better. It would be easier for her, but…" Molly shook her head. "She's getting worse and worse. Time isn't helping."

"Your daughter was Declan's mother."

"Yes. Of course."

"What's her name?"

"Isabella Hildebrandt," Molly said, her brows drawn down like he should have known that. "You know. *The Happy Artist*."

Zachary had heard of *The Happy Artist*. She was on TV and was popular among the locals. Zachary didn't know whether she was syndicated nationally or just on one of the local stations. She had a painting instruction show every Sunday morning, and people awaited her next show like a popular soap. Most of the people Zachary knew who watched the show didn't paint and never intended to take it up. She was an institution.

"Oh, yes," Zachary agreed. "Of course, I know *The Happy Artist*. I didn't put the names together."

"When it was in the news, they said who she was. They said it was *The Happy Artist's* child."

"Sure. Of course," Zachary agreed. He rubbed the dark stubble along his jaw. He should have gone home to shave and clean up before meeting with Molly. He looked like he'd been on a three-day stakeout. He *had* been on a three-day stakeout. "I'm sorry. I didn't follow the story very closely. That's good for you; it means I don't have a lot of preconceived ideas about the case."

She looked at him for a minute, frowning. Reconsidering whether she really wanted to hire him? That wouldn't hurt his feelings.

"You were going to tell me about your daughter?" Zachary prompted. "I can understand how devastated she must be by her son's death."

"No. I don't think you can," Molly said flatly.

Zachary was taken aback. He shrugged and nodded, and waited for her to go on.

"Isabella has a history of… mental health issues. She was the one supervising Declan when he disappeared, and the guilt has been overwhelming for her."

That made perfect sense. Zachary sipped at his coffee, which had cooled enough not to scald him.

Molly went on. "I think… as horrible as it may sound… that it would be a relief for her if it turned out that Declan was taken from the yard, instead of just having wandered away."

"That may be, but how likely is that? Surely the police must have considered the possibility, and I can't manufacture evidence for your daughter, even if it would ease her mind."

"No… I realize that. I'm not expecting you to do anything dishonest. Just to investigate it. Read over the police reports. Interview witnesses again. Just see… if there's any possibility that there was… foul play. A third-party interfering, even if it was nothing malicious."

"I assume you know most of the details surrounding the case."

"Yes, of course."

"How likely do you think it is that the police missed something? Did they seem sloppy or like they didn't care? Did you think there were signs of foul play that they brushed off?"

"No." Molly gave a little shrug. "They seemed perfectly competent."

Zachary was silent. It wouldn't be difficult to read over the police reports and talk to the family. Was there any point?

"The only thing is…" Molly trailed off.

As impatient as Zachary was to get out of there, he knew it was no good pushing Molly to give it up any faster. She already knew she sounded crazy for asking him to reinvestigate a case where he wasn't going to be able to turn up anything new. For no reason, other than that it might help her daughter to come to terms with the child's death. He looked around the room. There were no pictures of Molly's husband, even old ones. There was no sign she had raised Isabella or any other children there. There were several pictures of a couple with a little child. Declan and Isabella and whatever the father's name was. There was one picture of

Declan himself, occupying its own space, a little memorial to her lost grandson. There were no pictures of anyone else, so Zachary could only assume Isabella was an only child and Declan the only grandchild.

"Declan was afraid of water."

Zachary turned his eyes back to her. He considered. It wasn't totally inconceivable that a child afraid of the water would drown. He wouldn't know how to swim. If he fell in, he would panic, flail, and swallow water, rather than staying calm enough to float. Molly wiped at a tear.

"How afraid of the water was he?" Zachary asked.

"He wouldn't go near the water. He was terrified. He wouldn't have gone to the pond by himself."

"How tall was he?"

Molly gave a little shrug. "He was almost five years old. Three feet?"

"How steep were the banks of the pond and what was the terrain and foliage like?" He knew he would have to look at it for himself.

"I don't know what you want to know... there wasn't any shore to speak of. Just the pond. There were bulrushes. Cattails. Some trees. The ground is... uneven, but not hilly."

Zachary tried to visualize it. A child wouldn't be able to see the pond as far away as an adult would because of his short stature. If his view were further screened by the plant life, the banks steep and crumbly, he might not be able to see it until he was right on top of it. Or in it.

"It's not a lot to go on," he said. "The fact that he was afraid of water."

"I know." Molly used both hands to wipe her eyes. "I know that." She looked around the apartment, swallowing hard to get control of her emotions. "I just want the best for my baby. A parent always wants what's best. Growing up... I wasn't able to give her that. She didn't have an easy life. I wonder if..." She didn't have to finish the sentence this time. Zachary already knew what she was going to say. She wondered if that rough upbringing had caused Isabella's mental fragility. Whether things would have turned out differently if she'd been able to provide a stable environment. Molly sniffled. "Do you have children, Mr.—Zachary?"

Zachary felt that familiar pain in his chest. Like she'd plunged a knife into it. He cleared his throat and shook his head. "No. My marriage just recently ended. We didn't have any children."

"Oh." Her eyes searched his for the truth. Zachary looked away. "I'm sorry. I guess we all have our losses."

Although hers, the death of her grandson, was clearly more permanent than any relationship issues Zachary might have.

In the end, he agreed to do the preliminaries. Get the police reports. Walk the area around the house and pond. Talk to the parents. He gave her his lowest hourly fee. She clearly couldn't afford more. He wasn't even sure she'd be able to pay on receipt of his invoice. He might have to allow her a payment plan, something he normally didn't do, but something about the frail woman had gotten to him.

He put in an appearance at the police station, requesting a copy of the information available to the public, and handing over Molly Hildebrandt's request that he be provided as much information as possible for an independent evaluation.

"You got a new case?" Bowman grunted as he tapped through a few computer screens, getting a feel for how many files there were on the Declan Bond accident investigation file and how much of it he would be able to provide to Zachary.

"Yes," Zachary agreed. Obviously. He didn't encourage small talk; he really didn't want Bowman to start asking personal questions. They weren't friends, but they were friendly. Bowman had helped Zachary track down missing documents before. He knew the right people to ask for permission and the best way to ask.

Bowman dug into his pocket and pulled out a pack of gum.

He unwrapped a piece and popped it into his mouth, then offered one to Zachary as an afterthought.

"No, I'm good."

Bowman chewed vigorously as he studied each screen. He was a middle-aged man, with a middle-age spread, his belly sagging over his belt. His hairline had started receding, and occasionally he put on a pair of glasses for a moment and then took them off again, jamming them into his breast pocket.

"How's Bridget?" he asked.

Zachary swallowed. He took a deep breath and steeled himself for the conversation. Bowman looked away from his screen and at Zachary's face, eyebrows up.

"She's good. In remission."

"Good to hear." Bowman looked back at his computer again. "Good to hear. It's been a tough time for the two of you." His eyes flicked back to Zachary, and he backtracked. "I mean it's been tough for her. And for you."

"Yeah," Zachary agreed. He waved away any further fumbling explanation from Bowman. "So, what have we got? On the Bond case?"

"Right!" Bowman looked back at his screen. "I've got press releases and public statements for you. medical examiner's report. The cop in charge of the file was Eugene. He likes red."

Zachary blinked at Bowman, more baffled than usual by his abbreviated language. "What?"

"Eugene Taft. I know, it's a preposterous name, but he's never had a nickname that stuck. Eugene Taft."

"And he likes red."

"Wine," Bowman said as if Zachary was dense. "He likes red wine. You know, if you want to help things along, have a better chance of getting a look at the rest of that file, the officers' notes and all the background and interviews. If you have to apply some leverage."

"And for Eugene Taft, it's red wine."

"Has to be red," Bowman confirmed.

"Okay." Zachary looked at his watch. "Can you start that stuff printing for me? Is there anyone downstairs?" He knew he would have to run down to the basement to order a copy of the medical examiner's report. Just one of those bureaucratic things.

"Sure. Kenzie should be down there still."

Zachary paused. "Kenzie. Not Bradley?"

"Kenzie," Bowman confirmed. "She's new."

"How new?"

"I don't know." Bowman gave a heavy shrug. "How long since you were down there last? Less than that."

Zachary snorted and went down the hall to the elevator.

As he waited for it, Joshua Campbell, an officer he'd worked with on an insurance fraud case several months previous, approached and hit the up button. He did a double-take, looking at Zachary.

"Zach Goldman! How are you, man? Haven't seen you around here lately."

"Good." Zachary shook hands with him. Joshua's hands were hard and rough like he'd grown up working on a farm instead of in the city. Zachary wondered what he did in his spare time that left them so rough and scarred. He wasn't boxing after work; Zachary would have been able to tell that by his knuckles. "Hey, how's Bridget doing? Did everything turn out okay…?" He trailed off and shifted uncomfortably.

"Yeah, great. She's in remission."

"Oh, good. That's great, Zach. Good to hear."

Zachary nodded politely. His elevator arrived with a ding and a flashing down indicator. Zachary sketched a quick goodbye to Joshua and jumped on. He was starting to regret agreeing to look into the Bond case.

The girl at the desk had dark, curly hair, red-lipsticked lips, and a tight, slim form. She was working through some forms, those red lips pursed in concentration, and she didn't look up at him.

"Hang on," she said. "Just let me finish this part up, before I lose my train of thought."

Zachary stood there as patiently as possible, which wasn't too hard with a pretty girl to look at. She finally filled in the last space and looked up at him. She raised an eyebrow.

"You must be Kenzie," Zachary said.

"I don't know if I must be, but I am. Kenzie Kirsch. And you are?"

"Zachary Goldman. From Goldman Investigations."

"A private investigator?"

"Yes."

He didn't usually introduce himself that way because it gave people funny ideas about the kind of life he lived and how he spent his time. Most people did not think about mounds of paperwork or painstaking accident scene reconstructions when they thought about private investigation. They thought about Dick Tracy and Phillip Marlowe and all the old hardboiled detectives. When really most of a private investigator's life was mind-numbingly boring, and he didn't need to carry a gun.

"And what can I do for you today, Mr. Private Investigator?"

"Zachary."

"Zachary," she repeated, losing the teasing tone and giving him a warm smile. "What can I do for you?"

"I need to order a copy of a medical examiner's report. Declan Bond."

"Bond. That's the boy? The drowning victim?"

"That's the one."

She looked at him, shaking her head slightly. "Why do you need that one? It's closed. A determination was made that it was an accident."

"I know. The family would like someone else to look at it. Just to set their minds at ease."

"You're not going to find anything. It's an open-and-shut case."

"That's fine. They just want someone to take a look. It's not a reflection on the medical examiner. You know how families are. They need to be able to move on. They're not quite ready to let it go yet. One last attempt to understand..."

Kenzie gave a little shrug. "Okay, then... there's a form..." She bent over and searched through a drawer full of files to find the right one. Zachary had filled them out before. Usually, he could manage to do an end-run and Bradley would just pull the file for him. Officially, he was supposed to fill one out. He didn't want to end up in hot water with the new administrator, so he leaned on the counter and filled the form out carefully.

She went on with her own forms and filing, not trying to fill the silence with small talk. Which Zachary thought was nice. When he was finished, he put the pen back in its holder and handed the form to Kenzie. To the side of the work she was doing. Not right in front of her face. She again ignored him while she finished the section she was on, then picked it up to look it over.

"You have nice printing," she observed, her voice going up slightly. She laughed at herself. "No reason why you shouldn't," she said quickly. "It's just that the majority of the forms that get submitted here are... well, to say they were chicken scratch would be insulting to chickens."

Zachary chuckled. "That's the difference between a cop and a private investigator."

"Neat handwriting?"

"Yeah. Cops have to fill out so many forms, they don't care. You can just call them if you need something clarified. Me... I know if I don't fill it out right, it's just going to go in the circular file." He nodded in the direction of the garbage can.

"I wouldn't throw it out," she protested.

"If you couldn't read it? What else would you do?"

"I would at least try to call you."

Zachary indicated the form. "That's why I printed my phone number so neatly."

Kenzie smiled and nodded. "It's very clear," she approved.

"You'll call me?"

"I'll let you know when it's ready to be picked up."

Zachary hovered there for an extra few seconds. He was enjoying the give-and-take of his conversation with her but didn't want her to accuse him of being creepy. He wasn't the type who asked a girl out the first time he saw her.

He gave her another smile and walked away from the desk. Maybe next time.

———————

She Wore Mourning, Book #1 of the *Zachary Goldman Mysteries* series by P.D. Workman can be purchased at pdworkman.com

ABOUT THE AUTHOR

Award-winning and USA Today bestselling author P.D. (Pamela) Workman writes riveting mystery/suspense and young adult books dealing with mental illness, addiction, abuse, and other real-life issues. For as long as she can remember, the blank page has held an incredible allure and from a very young age she was trying to write her own books.

Workman wrote her first complete novel at the age of twelve and continued to write as a hobby for many years. She started publishing in 2013. She has won several literary awards from Library Services for Youth in Custody for her young adult fiction. She currently has over 70 published titles and can be found at pdworkman.com.

Born and raised in Alberta, Workman has been married for over 25 years and has one son.

———

Please visit P.D. Workman at pdworkman.com to see what else she is working on, to join her mailing list, and to link to her social networks.

If you enjoyed this book, please take the time to recommend it to other purchasers with a review or star rating and share it with your friends!

facebook.com/pdworkmanauthor

twitter.com/pdworkmanauthor

instagram.com/pdworkmanauthor

amazon.com/author/pdworkman

bookbub.com/authors/p-d-workman

goodreads.com/pdworkman

linkedin.com/in/pdworkman

pinterest.com/pdworkmanauthor

youtube.com/pdworkman